NET
FORCE
MOVING
TARGET

NET FORCE

MOVING TARGET

A NOVEL

SERIES CREATED BY
TOM CLANCY and
STEVE PIECZENIK
WRITTEN BY
JEROME PREISLER

HANOVER
SQUARE
PRESS

HANOVER
SQUARE
PRESS™

Recycling programs
for this product may
not exist in your area.

ISBN-13: 978-1-335-77766-9

Net Force: Moving Target

Hanover Square Press
22 Adelaide St. West, 41st Floor
Toronto, Ontario M5H 4E3, Canada
HanoverSqPress.com
BookClubbish.com

Printed in U.S.A.

Here is no water but only rock
Rock and no water and the sandy road

—T. S. Eliot, "The Waste Land"

PART ONE

A GAME OF CHESS

1

April 25, 2024
Paris, France/The Crimean Peninsula

Franz Scholl spotted the man on a park bench above the curve where the landmark Michel-Tagrine stairs rose steeply from Rue Georges Lardennois. Large and broad-shouldered, a patch over one eye, wearing a flat cap and corduroy jacket, he sat alone in the dusk facing the weave of streets below Butte Bergeyre, the hillside village in the heart of the great French metropolis.

In April the Parisian nights were cold, and they felt colder still here on the plateau, where the stiff breezes cut over the bare, brown ivy vines on the left side of the stairs. And while the wisteria draping the opposite wall was already green and lush, Scholl was no admirer. It was an aggressively invasive plant, even a ruinous one when allowed to grow unchecked. A restorer of forgotten technol-

ogy, of junked fantasies and old software codes,
he abhorred disorder and loose ends as much as he
valued clean, tidy precision.

His hands in his pockets, Scholl had climbed the
steps two and three at a time, the breath puffing
from his lips. On a previous visit, he'd numbered
them at a hundred and seventy-seven from the street
to the crown of the hill.

Counting the stairs at notable locations was for
him a compulsion disguised as an unusual hobby.

At the upper landing Scholl had turned right and
taken a path into the public garden. In summer it
always reminded him of Renoir's painting *Bal du
Moulin de la Galette*, with its bustling revelers in
the open air. But as he entered tonight it had been
quiet and deserted. Except for the man on the bench.

He sat some yards from a garden path, staring
northwest toward ornate Sacré-Cœur—the Basilica
of the Sacred Heart—on the crest of Montmartre,
the highest of the city's natural rises. Crowding the
streets, lanes and plazas nearby were the stately old
homes of the Nineteenth arrondissement, with their
elegant facades and stone balustrades.

Scholl had followed the path toward the bench,
then stepped off and passed several yards behind it
on the early-season grass. If the man with the eyepatch had glanced around, he would have seen someone about sixty years old with a long white ponytail,
wearing eyeglasses, a short fleece-lined worker's
coat and jeans. Though Scholl gave the impression
of an aging folk singer, a grassroots left-wing activ-
ist, his politics leaned neither left nor right. For him

the simple ideal was liberty, and his goal was to take the truest course toward its realization.

Now the roar of a motorbike tailed up from below, and the man on the bench bent slightly forward, looking down toward the source of the noise. The mark Scholl saw on the back of his neck made him rigid with tension. It was the blood-red lightning of *Krovavaya Molniya*, the elite Russian strike force said to be augmented with neural implants.

Scholl had feared exactly that when coming to the BB, after the city's data-gathering application tipped him off to the man's presence. Paris's traditionalist soul assured that it was not yet among the ranks of wired European cities, but its urban planners had dipped their toes in the water with passive beacons that tracked and logged the usage of public benches. If a visitor had Bluetooth on his phone, it collected and transmitted all sorts of information about them. Ostensibly it was to help determine whether a given location was busy or unused, so they could add or remove benches, or perhaps improve the area to draw more visitors.

Scholl had siphoned the government data onto his own phone for a different reason, monitoring the hill from his hotel room some blocks away. When he noticed the man sitting for over an hour in the forty-five-degree chill, not budging an inch, he had thought it conspicuous. Bowing to his intuition, he'd decided to step out for a closer look ahead of Kali's arrival.

And thankfully so, he thought.

"Engel," he said in hushed German. His words picked up by the sensitive cranial microphone in

the stem of his smart glasses. "The house is under surveillance."

"As we expected."

"Worse. The man wears the Blood Lightning tattoo. See for yourself." Franz blinked to relay the camera image. "We don't know who sent them. Not Moscow, surely. I hear they've broken free of their shackles."

"I've heard the same," she said. "It makes no difference. I'm going in."

"*Engel*, listen to me—"

The hollow silence of a terminated connection. Scholl frowned.

Ich kann sie nicht aufhalten. I can't stop her.

He suddenly flashed on a memory. Kali in the dojo at age nine with a bamboo training sword in her hand, having left her sensei sprawled on his backside. She was like her grandmother in a great many ways. He would not deny it…just as he would never deny having loved Norma with all his heart, despite her hardheaded, uncompromising nature. And perhaps in part because of it.

He opened his mouth and inhaled. The cold wind sliced into his throat.

"May God watch over you," he said under his breath and kept walking across the quiet lawn.

Kali dismounted from her motorcycle, engaged the steering lock, removed her helmet with a shake of her raven-black hair and locked it to the bike's frame. A Ducati Diavel 1260 S Black and Steel with custom red suspension bars and flourishes, it was parked between two cars just south of the Michel-Tagrine stairs.

Tall, straight and athletically lean, Kali was dressed entirely in black, from her riding jacket and fingerless gloves to her leggings and waterproof duck boots. On her wrist was an antique silver compass on a watchband, on her back a scuffed leather satchel, and around her waist a Victorian explorer's belt with a three-sectioned *manriki*—a Japanese chain whip—folded tightly into a drawstring pouch.

She stood alongside the bike a moment, her dark eyes sweeping the street behind a pair of AI/mixed-reality smart glasses. The invisible Bluetooth earpiece through which Franz had spoken to her was synced to the glasses.

Alone on the sidewalk, she walked a short distance north toward the corner of Rue Edgar-Poe, the Glock under her jacket a foreign weight against her ribs…and the handful of extra bullets in her jacket pocket a light but equally unfamiliar cargo. She had carried a firearm only once before, in Romania, while hunting her former lover for his crimes. The choice Mike Carmody had given her that night in the snow was simple and clear. She could take it and stay at his side, or he would go on without her.

I don't want it, she had told him.

Take it anyway…you trained with one of these for a reason.

Kali could still hear his voice in her mind. She had reluctantly accepted the weapon but never used it. With Carmody beside her, there was never any need. Tonight, she knew, things might be very different.

Lucien Navarro's residence was on her left, a

three-story town house with a pink limestone facade, a high arched double door, elaborate railed balconies, and high shuttered windows with metal gratings. Two large planters stood out front on the cobbles, and there was a seven-foot wrought iron gate behind the shrubs. No lights burned behind the wooden shutters.

Kali stopped outside the gate. It had a keyless lock.

"Cas," she said in an undertone. "Clone the system."

Cas. A diminutive for Castor. Her guiding star. She had named her proprietary artificial intelligence after it.

"Cloning initiated." The AI's male, vaguely British voice sounded altogether human in her ear. "Your window?"

"Five minutes. Then wipe everything."

"Affirmative."

Kali waved her palm over the lock's biometric scanner and then tapped in the passcode. The latch opened with a low click. That encouraged and relieved her. Navarro's unexplained disappearance had weighed upon her for weeks, bringing her thousands of miles from the Hawaiian Islands. She had been concerned she would find herself locked out.

But this was no time to relax. She had every reason to suspect the security system was compromised. Cas would give her the five minutes before deleting all of it, including any biometrics and backdoor access codes hackers might have inserted to gain entry. But Kali also knew she could have triggered an alert. A software alarm. And someone might already be waiting for her inside the house.

She would go in anyway. For Lucien's sake, she had to take the chance.

She went through the gate, pushed it shut behind her and strode across the front courtyard to the entrance. There was a second bio-lock on the double doors. Her palm to the scanner, several key taps, and they opened.

The foyer was dark. Kali felt on the wall for a light switch and flipped it. A soft amber radiance filled the room.

She stepped deeper inside, her foot settling on a thick Persian rug. The hall was exactly as she remembered. The domed ceiling and marble fireplace, the round mahagony table in the center. On it was a lamp made from a blue-and-white Ming vase. She inhaled the scent of rich, seasoned wood.

Beyond the foyer was a small parlor. It was still in darkness, but she could see Navarro's piano in the glow of the repurposed Ming. An electric grand, he'd gotten it customized to fit his wheelchair.

She suddenly flashed on a recollection: Lucien phoning her, ecstatic, to declare he'd found a device that gave the full, indistinguishable effects of the foot pedals on an acoustic piano—the sustain, the una corda, the sostenuto—its action controlled by imperceptible nods of his head. *Vive la technologie!* he'd enthused. He was seventeen then, an orphan, his parents killed in the car crash that had taken the use of his legs and left an arm partially paralyzed.

The memory passed. She glanced to her left, where a curved staircase rose to the second story. A computer-controlled wheelchair lift sat to one side of the bottom step. She was tempted to go straight upstairs but wanted to be thorough. She entered the parlor, turned into a room opening directly off it, then went into the kitchen, dining room and living room with its damask sofa, Veraseta curtains and antique sculptures. Everything seemed in place. The valuables had not been removed.

Before leaving the room, Kali paused in front of a gilt wood mirror and saw her features reflected on its polished surface. They were sober and uneasy.

She took the stairs up. Navarro's large master bedroom was unruffled. The same went for the smaller guest rooms. She went down the long carpeted hall into the library and turned on the lights.

Brightness poured evenly from rows of bronze pendant ceiling fixtures. The walls were paneled in red oak and lined with floor-to-ceiling bookshelves. A reading desk in the middle was cluttered with books, sheet music, magazines and newspaper clippings. There was an ornate balcony, where Lucien kept his most prized editions.

Kali stood listening to the silence. Nothing disturbed it. Like the main staircase, the balcony stairs were equipped with a wheelchair lift. She crossed the room and knelt for a look at the platform. It was coated with a nearly invisible film of dust.

Lucien, what's happened to you?

She raced up to the balcony. In a glass case were several precious rarities. A cloth *A Tale of Two Cities*, bound from the monthly serial installments. A two-volume first printing of *The Hunchback of Notre Dame*, signed by Hugo. A first of Voltaire's *Candide, ou l'Optimisme*. Others in the priceless collection. Nothing seemed disturbed. Nothing was missing. If intruders had been inside the house, theft was not their objective.

"Outlier."

Kali's chin tiled slightly upward. It was Cas in the earpiece, using her dark-web handle.

"Yes?"

"I can't complete the system erase."

"Why not?"

"Data migration is forbidden. I'm locked out of all known sectors."

"Can you dialogue with the AI?"

"I've attempted it and failed."

"Is there an error message?"

"Yes. *Access denied for an unknown reason.*"

"That's all?"

"Yes."

Kali remembered Franz's warning. *He isn't alone.* She hadn't disagreed and thought it likely someone had penetrated the alarm system. A few lines of malicious code would create a web shell— an interface that gave an easy backdoor in. There was no point in trying to confirm it. No losing a second. She had to move quickly.

She hurried across the balcony to its wall of books. They were arranged by subject, with their authors in careful alphabetical order.

The political philosophy section occupied the third shelf up from the floor. Kali leaned down and found Montesquieu's *De l'esprit des loix. The Spirit of the Laws.* Once censured by the French and banned by the Catholic church, it had been the ideological basis of the French Revolution and influenced the American Founding Fathers. Montesquieu had published the work anonymously in French, arranging for its rapid translation into English and German, wanting to ensure his ideas could not be suppressed.

What had Lucien said of him? *Ah, how our baron could have thrown royal noses out of whack if he'd had the internet. Though, of course,* they *had the guillotine.*

Kali moved her eyes along the neatly aligned rows of books. The one she was searching for was to the right of the Montesquieu and a collection of Rousseau's major treatises. Deliberately out of order.

She pulled it from the shelf. The binding was heavy buckram, its title printed in plain black letters. She noted its nonstandarized American English spelling: *The Key of Libberty: Shewing the Causes Why A Free Government Has Always Failed, and a Remidy Against It, Written in the Year 1798, by William Manning of Billerica Massachusetts, a Laborer.*

"*Engel.* Can you hear me?"

Franz again.

"Yes," she replied.

"The man from the Butte Bergeyre is approaching your location. He's been joined by another."

"Where are they?"

"Avenue Simon Bolivar."

"And you?"

"Midway down the Rue Manin. I made a circle of the garden and headed down," Scholl said. "The second man came from the direction of Buttes-Chaumont Park."

Kali sprang out of her crouch. Time was short.

She raced downstairs, stepped quickly onto the

oval rug and waited, holding the Manning book face-up to the ceiling. She could almost feel the camera taking its picture, feel the recognition scanners on her cheekbones—but that was all her imagination.

The voice that spoke after a moment belonged to neither Franz nor Cas and came vaguely from overhead. It was Lucien's. Or Lucien's AI, imprinted with his speech patterns and tonalities.

"What is a free government?" it asked.

Kali knew the question–answer code by heart. "One in which all the laws are made, judged and executed according to the will and interest of a majority of the people."

"What is the key to a free government?"

"The key is knowledge."

"What knowledge is necessary for a free man?"

"A knowledge of mankind. Of the different interests that influence all orders of men."

"What is the key to liberty?"

"The key is democratic opposition."

"Finally...of all the books you've nicked from me, which do you love best? Title, subtitle, author and where and when published."

She could not help but smile a little. Lucien had infused the AI with more than just his vocal characteristics.

"*Modern Magic. A Practical Treatise in the Art of Conjuring.* By Professor Hoffman. London, 1876."

"Kali. Welcome home, dearest friend and passable magician. You have full access."

A thin section of wall paneling slid aside. She went

across the library to the opening. Beyond it in near darkness was a stone landing and descending stairs.

"Tinkerer," she said, using Franz's web handle. "Do you see this?"

"*Ja. Ich mag das nicht.* You'll be alone. Out of contact."

"I expect to find others below."

"Fools and jesters. Street hustlers. Oarsman's crowd in the underground."

"Don't sell our allies short."

Kali pushed the book into her backpack, then slid through the gap in the wall onto the landing. The stairway looked almost vertical as it plunged into the gloom. "Wait back at the hotel," she said. "You'll hear from me."

And then she was silent. Time was running out.

Kali stepped off the landing and started down the stairs. Behind her, the wall panel moved seamlessly back into place.

Descending from the Butte Bergeyre, the one-eyed man in the flat cap cast a hasty look at the Ducati parked near the stairs. Then he turned left in his target's footsteps.

He was called Matyas.

At the corner of Rue Edgar-Poe another man silently fell in alongside him. Tall, bald and about a decade younger at twenty-eight, he wore a brown leather car coat and also had the lightning on his neck.

His name was Stefan.

They were *pervaya chast'*. The designated First Unit.

Outside Lucien Navarro's town house, Matyas

showed his palm to the biometric scanner on the gatepost. The gate opened, and the pair walked up to the double front doors. Another scan, and the doors unlocked.

Urgency in their strides, they went straight to the curving stairs, then climbed to the library. They knew their way around.

Neither paused to inspect the shelves in the reading room or balcony. They were not the type of men to care about books or notice *The Key of Libberty* missing from among the thousands in Navarro's collection. All they needed to know was that the woman's last bio-reading had come from this room. They had her where they wanted her.

Matyas stepped onto the rug in the center of the room. His single eye fluttered. After a moment, a voice seemed to issue from all four walls at once.

"What is a free government?" it said.

"Let us in, you fucking shitbag," he said.

A panel in the wall retracted.

The voice said, "Kali. Welcome home, dearest friend. You have full access."

Matyas traded a glance with his companion. He would take a compromised AI over a human mole any day. The machine intelligence was easier to fool. It would have no reservations about its actions. No guilt or pangs of conscience over its betrayals. And its access was often more extensive and far-reaching.

He jabbed his chin at the entry and hurried through the landing on the other side, followed closely by Stefan. The wall panel shut behind them before their feet touched the steps.

* * *

Franz Scholl had watched the one-eyed man and his companion turn the corner, observing them from an elevated vantage on the Michel-Tagrine stairs. After a brief, cautious wait, he went down the remaining steps to Rue Georges Lardennois and strode northeast, initially following the identical path they—and Kali, minutes earlier—had taken to Navarro's town house. Passing the corner of Rue Edgar-Poe, he glanced up the street in time to see them stop outside the front gate.

Scholl mouthed a silent prayer and continued on without missing a step. He had promised Kali he would wait at the hotel. And he meant to keep his word.

The solid gray BMW iX Flow SUV had been about ten yards down the street when Scholl came off the stairs. It followed him unnoticed.

A few minutes after leaving the stairs, Scholl reached the cross street at Avenue Mathurin-Moreau and hooked right toward Avenue Simon Bolivar, with its rows of dated walk-up apartment buildings. The Flow now creeping along behind him was black with a single thin white racing stripe on each side. A big-ticket luxury SUV, it might have seemed conspicuous in this working-class neighborhood, but the trendy bars and nightclubs of its ongoing gentrification attracted Parisians of all social and financial brackets.

Ten minutes after leaving the stairs, Scholl reached the cross street with Avenue Simon Bolivar. He had nearly arrived at the Hotel Ares, where he'd booked a tiny no-frills room for the next several nights.

He went into the hotel through the corner entrance on Avenue Secrétan. The Flow that passed the hotel on Secrétan was white, with two wide black stripes on its hood from nose to windshield.

It was eleven o'clock when it pulled into an empty spot, early enough for the street to be somewhat busy with cars and pedestrians. The man behind the wheel sat waiting patiently for it to clear.

Two men and a woman left the railway station at Strasbourg-Saint-Denis and turned up Boulevard Saint-Martin toward the Place de la République, with its illuminated monument, strollers, joggers, dog walkers, marijuana smokers and neighborhood derelicts on the benches at the square's periphery. All three had athletic physiques, though of different types. The man on the woman's right was built like a competitive swimmer, his long arms, broad back and narrow waist giving him an almost stretched-out appearance. The one on her left was bulkier, with a weightlifter's barrel chest. Both men were tall, blond-haired and in their late twenties.

The woman had a swan's neck and the firm, sinuous body of an Olympic gymnast. In fact, she'd earned a gold medal at the 2016 games in Rio de Janeiro, the same year she was recruited as a foreign intelligence operative by the SVR, and a decade before she gained the high rank of *polkovnik*, or colonel, in the service. Called Reva, she had spiky teal hair and wore a close-fitting crocodile jacket trimmed out with copious zippers and studs. At thirty-four, she was the senior and highest-ranking member of *votoraya chast'*, the Second Unit.

Reva walked with her arm linked through the bulky man's. Named Zoltan, he wore a leather blazer and black enamel earplugs and had the lightning prominently displayed on the back of his neck. An eight-pointed reform-school tattoo from his delinquent youth was on his right wrist.

The leaner man, Dominik, had turned the collar of his bomber jacket up against the chill night wind. That it covered his lightning was incidental. Even back home, few grasped the mark's significance. Moscow's ban on civilian transhumanism was strictly enforced, and the existence of *Krovavaya Molniya* remained a top government secret.

A five-minute walk on the boulevard brought the group to the Métro's Saint-Martin *fantôme*, as Parisians called their abandoned subway stations. Unused since the beginning of World War II, its locked-up entrance was recessed below the sidewalk outside the columned old Théâtre du Petit Saint-Martin. A few bicycles were chained to the rail around the sunken stairs. Two iron doors set into a graffiti-splashed tile wall blocked access to the mezzanine and platform. Crumpled food wrappers littered the steps, and a stew of rank, mingled odors rose from their bottom.

Dominik sniffed and made a disgusted face. "Only the finest of places for us," he said.

Reva slid her arm free of Zoltan's. Stepping ahead, she led the way down to the sealed entrance. Cyclists and determinedly hip-looking café goers moved past on the street, ignoring the group. If there was a Paris state of mind, it was to mind one's own affairs.

The stench of urine outside the doors was overwhelming. It felt sticky underfoot. Reva stepped gingerly up to the entrance, her intraocular implants allowing her to see in the shadows with the clarity of a nocturnal predator.

She thought the graffiti on the wall not art but an angry bombing. The layers of spray paint probably went back years, covering the doors and the hardened biometric reader beside them. Reva recognized at a glance that the reader was an older model. *A portal.*

"Get ready," she said.

She stood in front of it a moment, her eyes fluttering slightly back in her head. The nearness of a brainport interface to the labyrinth of the ear produced brief, involuntary eye movements whenever her optic nerve was stimulated, a common side effect for about forty percent of neurotech-implant recipients. They weren't as pronounced as they had been after the procedure, and the doctors were optimistic they would diminish with time. But for now she accepted them as a price worth paying for the enhancements.

Reva waited as the panel display flashed on. A tiny green readout lit up underneath it, and she heard the lock click open. An instant later Zoltan stepped up, gripped one of the door handles and hauled. The door gritted rustily to one side.

"Follow me," Reva said and stepped through into the darkness.

They followed her.

The Crimean Peninsula, Ukraine

The villa perched on a ledge high above the Black Sea inlet, backing onto an escarpment that soared hundreds of feet in the air. Five centuries old, it was stone with a terra-cotta roof and a single barrel-shaped turret with windows all around, a sight ring overlooking the landscape for miles in three directions. To the east the view was blocked by the high, sheer wall of the escarpment, which tapered upward to a point like a castle spire. On the south side, a door opened onto a promenade where Drajan sometimes came to think, occasionally taking the long stairs leading down from its balustrade for solitary walks on the mountain.

Tonight, as on most nights, the dim blue glow of a computer screen reflected off the turret's windows. Inside its curved walls, Drajan Petrovik sat at his laptop, his fingers pattering softly over its keyboard. Alone for the first time in weeks, he felt almost as he had as a young man, before he became the Wolf to the *technologie vampiri*; before Quintessa Leonides and his Russian sponsors; even before Kali Alcazar, with her almost-black eyes like chips of gleaming onyx.

Eyes that still haunted his sleep, when he could sleep.

He had spent those years in a backcountry town waiting for something to happen. Anything. Cyberspace had been a portal to a world beyond his physical reach, and early on he'd learned to twist, tug and shake it randomly, manipulating it to see how the pieces fell. Chaos magic, at his fingertips. Eventually it brought money and power, but in the beginning he'd only wanted freedom. In hindsight Drajan supposed it was a curse to imagine that was even possible, and he had since outgrown such thoughts.

He straightened in his chair, his features narrow and spectral in the washed-out glow of the computer screen. He'd been alerted that Kali had entered Lucien Navarro's house on Rue Edgar-Poe, followed by the two *Krovavaya molniya*. The map of Paris in front of him showed the rest of the Blood Lightning contractors as icons entering the underground from their designated quadrants. He had baited his trap for Kali, and for her old allies and new friends, especially the one who'd held a gun to his head in Bucharest, the giant who'd nearly killed him in that bloody hallway above the nightclub. He would shake them all good and hard before turning toward America and other unfinished business.

Now he turned from the computer and gazed out his tower window to where the sea met the sand, out toward the massive Russian city in the mountain.

In a sense he'd come full circle. He again felt like a captive, and Crimea and this cushioned tower were only its physical manifestations. But while he no longer held any illusions about freedom, escape from his restraints was a different thing.

For that chaos magic was still his ticket out. One could say he was pulling out an old trick—or spinning up a new one. The result would be the same either way. When he unveiled it, the eyes of the world would open wide.

2

April 25, 2024
Janus Base, Romania

"Dassault oscar three india six, you are cleared to enter airspace FOB Baneasa. Maintain altitude three thousand feet..."

The Falcon 8X trijet winged above the ground at a smooth three-degree glide slope, its approach guided by a pair of radio beacons on the lit runway up ahead. In the pilot's seat, Nick DeBattista listened to the operator give her instructions over his headset and assured himself the absence of a physical air-traffic control tower was really no big deal, leaving aside that he'd never in his ten years as a professional pilot set down on a field that didn't have one.

Not that the base technically lacked a tower. There was a *virtual* one a hundred thirty miles west at Mihail Kogălniceanu Airport, where the sexy-voiced operator was in a windowless room lined with rows of augmented-reality video screens, their remote imagery fed by all kinds of fancy sensors on the ground. Still, it made DeBattista a little antsy.

Which was typical of what happened when you got mixed up with Carmody, he thought. Nothing connected to him was ever routine.

He glanced over at the man in the copilot's seat. Scott Dixon was one of Carmody's guys. The corn-fed Midwestern-farmboy type that military recruiters loved to snag right out of high school. Brown-haired, thick-featured, built like a cement truck, he wore a black short-sleeved T-shirt with a Navy SEALs trident medallion hanging over its collar on a gold chain. On his left arm was a tattoo of a 1960s General Electric television, complete with peacock color bands on the screen. The name *Else* was written across them in big letters. DeBattista figured it was either his favorite classic sitcom or his best girl but hadn't yet asked about it.

"A few more minutes and you're home," he said.

Dixon shot him a look. "No way."

"No way what?"

"No way's this place home," Dixon said.

DeBattista snorted. "Home *away* from home?"

"Never in a jillion years."

"So satisfy my curiosity. Where you from?"

"Indiana."

DeBattista smiled inwardly. He'd had him pegged. "Farm-raised?"

Dixon shook his head. "My dad ran an air-delivery outfit."

"You're shitting me."

"Nope. Whistle Stop Air Transport. That's how I learned to fly."

DeBattista fell silent, his hands on the yoke. So he and Dixon had something in common. Maybe they would bond over it, and he could quiz him about Else. He had a hunch it would be a juicy story.

"Dassault oscar three india six, you are cleared for runway 1. That's runway 1. Descend to fifteen hundred feet, heading two six zero. Please be aware there is a slight ground fog in the landing area."

It was the ATCO again. DeBattista was thinking he liked her attitude even more than her voice. She was feminine but confident. A take-charge woman.

He decided to try and get her name. Being it would be maybe two weeks before Carmody's next escapade got underway and he'd need to find ways to keep from dying of boredom in the meantime.

"Roger, trimming," he said. "Is this Sandy?"

"No."

"Kaitlin?"

"No."

"Leah."

"No, my name is not Leah."

"Tonia, then. With an *o*. I bet you're Tonia from Romania. That kind of rhymes."

"No again."

"To Romania? Or Tonia?"

"Tonia."

"Ah, well, okay. Where in Romania you from?"

"Bucharest."

"Say I met a beautiful woman from Bucharest over the air band. How would I politely ask her name?"

"You wouldn't," she said. *"Wind three hundred, at zero two gust zero six."*

Definitely hot, DeBattista thought. And a slight Eastern European accent that he also found very appealing.

"Thanks. You sure you don't want to share your name with me, Bucharest? I'm DeBattista. Did I mention it?"

"Your frequency is fading, sorry. Good night, DeBattista. And welcome. We are here for you if you need us."

He smiled. *Woo-hoo!* Was she flirting back at him? He'd have to figure out a way to chat her up later. Right now the runway lights beckoned.

"All right, everybody," he said over the cabin speakers. "We'll be landing in a minute."

He lowered his flaps and brought the plane in.

The Falcon's wheels touched down on the ground with a jarring bump. DeBattista applied the brakes and rolled on the taxiway.

In the passenger section, Carmody had stared silently out his window since takeoff in New York. Now he shrugged out of his straps and rose. A moment later, Schultz and Natasha Mori made their way up from the rear, walking alongside each other in the luxury jet's spacious aisle.

"Back again," Schultz said. "Land of cyber vampires, sadistic torturers' castles, psycho robots and Colonel John Howard. Not sure which I hate the most or have missed the least."

In front of him, Carmody barely turned his head. "Leave Howard to me," he said.

Which really hadn't been Schultz's reason for saying what he did. He traded looks with Mori. Tall and bony, white hair, translucent white skin, she just shrugged and nodded toward the door.

The passengers exited first, Dixon and DeBattista following them down the stairs.

Brightness suddenly punctuated the night around them. It came from the runway's edge lights. It came from the headlamps glaring from a pair of joint light tactical vehicles parked on a nearby access lane. It smeared, splashed and swiped across the fine, hovering ground mist and threw the dark forms gathered around the tarmac into stark silhouette.

Dixon saw them and froze in confusion.

"What is this?" he said.

"What the *fuck*?" DeBattista said.

Both men looked around. Dixon thought they were dogs. Huge and lean and long-legged. He counted a dozen or more of them out there.

They stood near the stairs, Carmody, Schultz and Mori loosely grouped together a few paces away. The dogs—if that was what they were—remained motionless in the scattered light and shifting mist.

Carmody slid a hand under his bomber jacket. He was carrying his Sig P225 in a shoulder harness. He unholstered the gun and held it against his leg.

"This is nuts," Schultz said. "Where do you think they came from?"

Carmody stared. The dogs had sleek heads and long muzzles and high triangular ears that rose to tapered points. They stood very erect on the front pads of their feet, like Dobermans. The two JLTVs were several yards behind them, parked abreast, their grilles turned toward the aircraft. Their headlights were off. Their interior lights were off. He couldn't tell if anyone was inside them.

He stood there thinking a little longer. The high LED floodlights around the field were on, but they seemed dimmer than they should have been. The dog pack stood out in the shadows, facing the aircraft and its discharged passengers.

"That's all, Fernandez," Carmody said. His voice loud but flat. "Enough."

The floods suddenly flared and lit up the tarmac. There was a thunderous crash—a drum and cymbals—that shook the group outside the plane to their bones. Then a simultaneous fuzz guitar chord, another crash, the beat pounding and building and thumping, a bass guitar joining the power chords, and then a shrieky "Oooaaayeah..."

Natasha peered out across the runway as the vocals blasted earsplittingly across it.

"Oh, gross. AC/DC, 'Give the *Freaking* Dog a Bone,'" she said. "Please, somebody, end my misery and kill me right now."

She raised a hand above her eyes to shield them from the glare. Then she dropped her jaw in amazement.

The dogs crowding the tarmac had started to dance in the brightened lights. Watching with the others outside the Falcon, Natasha took a long moment to realize they weren't dogs at all, not living ones, but quadrupedal robots. Their bodies metallic and gleaming, their multisegmented legs sprung at the joints, they moved in rhythmic sync, their feet tapping out a percussive beat on the blacktop.

It was an elaborate, tightly choreographed spectacle. They crouched forward and bent backward and spun to the music in acrobatic circles. They formed up into double rows like chorus-line dancers, one behind the other, then switched places, then formed up into an *X*, kicking out with their hind legs and swinging their forelegs from side to side. Three of them backflipped in unison. Three more somersaulted in counterpoint. Another three dropped to the ground, rolled over on their backs, then swung their legs around a hundred eighty degrees to right themselves and dance upside down without falling a tick out of step.

After about two minutes they formed back into a line and stopped. All together. Abruptly, precisely. The music cutting out at the same instant.

An amplified announcement blared from one of the JLTVs.

"Welcome to Janus Base, home of the Net Force Rapid Response, US Army!"

Carmody put away his Sig as he recognized Julio Fernandez exiting the vehicle on the right. He was five foot nine and strongly built, with a broad, square face and wide chin. His hair was thick on top and bristle-short at the sides. There was a sergeant major's patch on his arm, two stars bracketing the coat of arms.

He saw Carmody notice it, cracked a huge smile and extended his arm. "Great to see you, brother. Got me a promotion while you were in New York!"

Carmody said nothing. He didn't take his hand. Fernandez kept it out.

"Hope you liked the entertainment." He chin-nodded at the robots. "They're our new-and-improved patrol bots. Courtesy of Adrian Soto. Dancing watchdogs for us Cyber Dogs. *Ha!*"

Carmody just looked at him.

"We flew a long way. We're tired. So how about you show us our bunks?"

Fernandez dropped his arm to his side. He looked disappointed.

"Sure," he said. "We'll drive you right over to them."

Carmody nodded and walked past him, ignoring the once-again motionless robotic hounds. Fernandez watched him get into one of the JLTVs, the rest of the arrivals following a moment later.

Natasha caught his puzzled expression and lagged a step. Their eyes brushed.

"Misogynous sounds aside, I kinda got a kick out of watching those creepy canines shake their metal butts," she said. "My name's Natasha, and I have an actual sense of humor."

Fernandez gave her a faded version of his earlier smile. Then he nodded toward the vehicle Carmody had entered.

"What's gotten into him?" he asked.

She stepped closer.

"Kali," she said quietly and hurried to catch up with the others.

3

Kali stood at the bottom of the library stairs, peering through the gloom. She had produced a high-lumen spelunker's headlamp from her satchel and hastily worked the band down over her hair.

The steps had brought her down about a hundred feet, well below the basement level of Lucien's town house. She could see a narrow passageway leading off to her right at a sharp angle, and only a solid stone wall to the left. Franz's man with the eyepatch and the Blood Lightning tattoo had almost certainly followed her into the house—the breach of its security system, and his watchful presence on the Butte Bergeyre made it clear her arrival had been expected. It was also safe to assume he wasn't alone.

She couldn't lag.

Kali took a deep breath and hurried into the

passage. It was a perfect rectangle burrowed into the ground, the walls and ceiling flat and even, its floor at a mild downgrade and covered with a fine, chalklike grit. What had Lucien once told her? The quarries of north Paris were its oldest, their gypsum ground to a powder used in ancient Roman plaster. It made her nostrils feel dry.

She reached a bend, then another. Another. Right and left and right and right and left. After a few turns the tunnel's dimensions tightened up, its walls drawing in close, the ceiling pressing lower above her. Soon she needed to bend her head as she scrambled along, her satchel scraping against the top of the passage, tiny bits of rock shifting and crackling underfoot. The stale, stagnant air only added to her feeling of claustrophobia.

Kali went on like that for several minutes. Then the throw of her lamp hit a wall in front of her, and she stopped cold.

About ten yards up ahead the tunnel came to a sudden end. Her light had fallen on a round metal sign bolted to the bare rock wall, its trefoil symbol black against a luminous yellow field. Painted below it was a single word followed by a number:

Plutonium 241

It was several seconds before the surprise on Kali's face gave way to an amused little smile.

She'd been caught off guard, but the sign was pure Lucien, his wit dry as the stone around her. He would have relished making an intruder fear that he or she had stumbled onto a radioactive stockpile. But she was sure the trefoil was one of his hoodwinks. He wasn't referring to the isotope.

Plutonium, she thought. Latin for Pluto's Gate. The ancient Roman name for the portal to the underworld.

She lowered her gaze from the wall. The headlamp had revealed something else…a rimmed, circular metal cap in the floor just before the dead end. It stuck up six inches from the ground and was about five feet in diameter, with what looked like a large cast-iron hinge on one side.

Kali nodded to herself and dashed over to the cap. Knelt, slid her fingers under its rim, and pulled it upward. There was a low hiss as it lifted smoothly on a gas or pneumatic spring. Beneath it, a circular opening and a second set of stairs. A spiral staircase this time, metal, running down between tubular handrails. The vertical shaft around it was cut from the same raw chalky stone as the passage's walls and floor.

She grabbed the rail, dropped onto the top step, went two more. Then she reached a hand up to the open cap and pushed gently on its underside to activate the spring mechanism. It lowered quietly as darkness swamped her.

The staircase wound down and down into the shaft. She counted each step as her foot settled onto it, thinking Franz might be pleased at his influence. *Fifteen, twenty-five, thirty. Forty, fifty, sixty, seventy.*

Ninety. A hundred...

Her descent was dizzying and seemingly endless. But she could feel mild updrafts coming from below. There was air to breathe down at the bottom. She held the rail and rounded the turns and counted, unable to see more than four or five steps below her, the soles of her boots making dull, percussive sounds against the risers.

A hundred twenty....a hundred seventy-five... two hundred...

At the two hundred and sixteenth step Kali paused and looked down at the floor of the shaft. It was four steps below her, a total of two twenty from the metal cap. That surprised her at first. She'd expected it would be two forty-one. But then it struck her that Lucien would not make things quite so simple.

She went the rest of the way down the stairs After a moment she found herself in an oval space about twenty feet across the middle, its floor covered with the same powdery grit as the upper passage. There were three low archways spaced around the edge of the oval—one to her left, another her right, another almost exactly between them in front of her. All were about four feet high, like they were dug by tunneling dwarves. Kali felt cool, dry air wafting softly through them and remembered the updraft from before.

She sat on a lower step, pulled the water bottle off her belt and took two quick sips. She couldn't stay there long. For an unauthorized person to open Lucien's hidden library panel would require a near-total compromise of his AI, a profoundly deeper level of penetration than it took to crack and hijack the security system. Lucien wouldn't have made that easy. But it had happened at Janus Base five months ago and left it in rubble and flames. She had to assume the worst. And she needed to hurry.

She pulled the Manning book from her bag and set it flat on her lap. Then she took a small Swiss Army knife out of her jacket and opened its cover to the front pastedown and endpaper. They were marbled leaves, a heavy, old-fashioned stock. Thumbing out the smallest of the utility knife's blades, she slowly ran its point across the upper edge of the pastedown. She did the same with its outer edge, cutting from top to bottom in a straight line. When the two sides of the pastedown were separated from the cover board, she pocketed the knife, carefully peeled the leaf up with one hand, and slid two fingers underneath it.

When she slid them out, they were scissoring a sheet of extremely thin paper between them. Waxy and translucent, like tracing paper, it was folded carefully in half, the outline of a rose bloom stamped onto the back in black ink.

Kali nodded to herself and unfolded the paper. On its front was a hand drawn antiquarian map of Paris. But she had known it would be much more than that. The surface of the city was sketched out in light overlay, with all its multileveled detail reserved for the complex labyrinth of tunnels, chambers, catacombs, canals and aqueducts below. The system of tunnels south of the river Seine—on its Left Bank—was labeled Le Grand Réseau Sud, or

Great Southern Network. Above the river on its Right Bank was Le Réseau Nord, the Northern Network, a much smaller area that was actually two separate and distinct subterranean tunnel systems. One stretched west to the border of the Eighteenth and Seventeenth arrondissements, encompassing Lucien's district. The other was below the hilltop neighborhood of Montmartre, three miles to the east. Between the systems was a zigzagging, mile-long passage that Kali knew was the one she'd taken coming off the library stairs. The large red hand-drawn X at the end of the passage showed the location of the shaft cap...and the circular space below it her present whereabouts deeper underground, a kind of hub with three linear paths running off it.

One of those paths was highlighted in red, the other in blue. The red path ran east to the Montmartre system of tunnels, then took a short series of turns under the hill, ending in a drawing of a rose. The blue path was far, far longer. It also ran east for a bit, but then curved due south under Butte Chaumont Park. That path had a great many offshoots as it plunged sharply down toward the river Seine.

La Route de Sable, she read. The Sandy Road. It was the underground highway that connected the two halves of the Northern Network to the Great Southern Network. She estimated it extended for over six miles from top to bottom, crossing the Seine blow the Place de la Bastille, in the Fifth arrondissement, then looping back to the north and west when it reached the lower arrondissements, forming a kind of U or horseshoe. Kali ran her forefinger along its rough course, reading off the names of its waypoints, silently translating them from the French. All were written in Lucien's neat hand. Rats' Alley (Where the Dead Men Lost Their Bones), Hall of the Barbarous King, The Throne. Moorgate...

Her fingertip stopped at a location called The Empty Chapel between the two points of the U... much closer to the eastern than the western one. It appeared to be a large, rectangular chamber. Inside was a notation penned in blue:

The Lean Solicitor ;-)

Kali smiled wanly. The emoticon was so typical of Lucien. The place names too, of course. He loved his T.S. Eliot. But his cryptic wit was *not* the important thing right now.

She scanned the map a second longer, then glanced up at the three arches. If she was reading it correctly, the arch on her left led north of Paris into the suburbs of Levallois-Perret. The middle arch opened to the path Lucien had highlighted in red, and she was sure that would take her to him most directly. *If* he was down here and safe. But...

But that's what Eyepatch and his friends expect. What they want. Don't you see they're playing a little game? And they waited till you showed up before making their move.

The thought arrived in Carmody's voice. So distinctly, Kali almost blinked in surprise. It was almost as if he'd spoken over her shoulder.

She took a breath, looked at the arch to her right, then returned her eyes to the map.

After a moment she refolded it and slipped it into her jacket pocket. She took the satchel off her back, returned *The Key of Libberty* to it and wrapped one of its straps around her hand. Then she rose from the metal stair, ran over to the arch and dropped down onto her stomach.

It would not have been easy for Lucien, a paraplegic, to squeeze through one of these openings. Even with assistance. She herself would barely manage, and she weighed a hundred fifteen pounds.

She pushed her satchel through and crawled in behind it. The archway was low and tight but gave into a wider chamber on the other side. Kali sprang upright, looked around in the light of her spelo headlamp. *Much wider...and higher.* The ceiling was easily thirty feet above her head, the walls nearly the same number of feet apart.

She shouldered the bag again and trotted forward. After a few hundred yards she reached the intersection and turned into it.

The new path swung south exactly as shown on the map. Kali raced along, the ground soft and white as talc underfoot.

The Sandy Road. Instead of heading east, where she hoped to find Lucien, she was moving away from him, going down toward the Great Southern Network, playing a little game.

The *Ligne de Petite Ceinture*—or Little Belt Line—consisted of the remnants of a two-century-old steam railway that had once run a full loop around Paris, shuttling passengers and freight between almost thirty outdoor stations. Like the ghost stations of the Métro, the line's platforms and rails had been shut down decades ago, leaving the outdoor track beds presently overrun with vegetation and fenced off for the public's safety. A few sections had been rehabilitated and converted to pleasant green spaces, but extended stretches of track remained abandoned and neglected.

Tonight outside the Twelfth arrondissement's southern Bel-Air district, two men walked the tracks through a carpet of brittle brown weeds and brambles. They had found an opening clipped into the guard fence, shuffled through on their haunches and dropped down onto the gravel bed.

They were *Tret'ya chast'*. Third Unit.

The pair walked between the railway cuttings at a steady pace. One, Luka, was a dark complected Siberian of Tatar ancestry, with the wiry, diminutive build of a racehorse jockey. He wore a blue watch cap with a headlamp set into its cuff over his close-cropped, tightly coiled black hair. His companion, Oleg, was a pale, ruddy-cheeked Belarusian with the massive, towering stature of a lumberjack, and shoulder-length blond hair blowing loosely from under an orange *US Grand Prix* racing cap. His headlamp was banded around its crown.

The overgrown weeds along the rail scraped and hissed around their legs, rising slightly above Luka's knees and bending just below Oleg's calves. Both had donned warm quilted vests, heavy denim jeans and high square-toed work boots for tonight's mission. Like the other teams in Paris, they were former GRU. Unlike the others, neither had the lightning tattoo peeking out from under his collar.

This was no coincidence. Rather it was because they belonged to an elite within elites: the *Svjash-chennaja Druzhina*, or Black Hundred, a secret fraternity of assassins that had originated in Czar Alexander II's reign and remained embedded in the Russian special forces nearly two centuries later… though their number had dwindled to thirty in modern times.

There was no equivalent to their pedigree. Membership in the Black Hundred was a birthright. Their fathers had been assassins. Their grandfathers, great-grandfathers and great-great-grandfathers. The training began when they were children.

With the brotherhood's leadership having asserted a strong antimod stance, Oleg and Luka had been exempt from recruitment by the Kremlin's Blood Lightning program. But that did nothing to diminish their worth to the Directorate. Or to the contractor CHVK Wagner, which eagerly hired them on completion of their military service. A private organization in name only, the paramilitary group was wholly and secretly funded by the Federation's Ministry of Defense—in effect making it Russia's phantom army.

It was Wagner that feathered their caps yet again by assigning them to its special Task Force Rusich. Rusich handled the dirtiest jobs, the ones no one else would touch—the poisonings, gassing operations and mass exterminations that would constitute war crimes to the majority of the international community. As instruments of Putin's outreach in Syria and the Ukraine, Oleg and Luka had carried out their assignments with a one-hundred-percent success rate.

But the praise they received for those successes was no substitute for hard cash. After hearing what Braithwaite Global was paying one-time Rusich operatives, they had decided to leave Russia in violation of their contract with Wagner, slipping overland across the border into Ukraine, and then through Poland into northern Germany. Once there, they had contacted the Australian, who immediately offered them an exclusive, highly lucrative deal.

Their brotherhood's policy on neural modifications notwithstanding, Luka and Oleg each wore a single smart contact lens packed with a micro-LED display, thermal sensors, a broadband radio and an augmented-reality display the size of a grain of sand. The puck-shaped computers at the front of their black leather neck chokers contained processors, GPUs and wireless receiver/transmitters for relaying data to the contact lenses at a refresh rate of a thousand bits per second. The result approximated many of the tactical benefits provided by cyber modification, but without the irreversible surgery and, in their minds, potential side effects.

Now they followed the track for about three hundred yards, turned a curve and saw a large arched tunnel entrance up ahead. A few feet inside the tunnel, their guide stood holding a flickery old-fashioned copper carbide lamp that cast him into wavering silhouette.

"*Bonsoir*, gentlemen," he said. "Did you have any problems?"

Oleg looked at him. "We found you easily enough, if that's what you mean."

The guide nodded. Called Anton—at least that

was the name he'd given them—he was about thirty, five foot eight and slightly built at a hundred forty pounds. He wore an oilskin bucket hat with the brim mashed down over his forehead, work pants and knee waders. There was a large duffel strapped over his shoulders and a fanny pack around his waist.

Luka gestured at the lamp. "Do you really intend to use that relic?"

Anton smiled. "It can burn for twelve hours. I like to keep things simple."

"So what's next?"

The guide reached inside his jacket and produced an oversize sheet of paper. It was folded in quarters.

"Here. Have a look. I'll need it right back from you."

Luka took the paper, unfolded it and moved closer to his companion.

It was a map, coded with place names and cartographic symbols. All were in a cursive, stylized font designed to appear handwritten.

"This is based on Guillemot's IGC inspection charts. From the 1770s. But take a peek at the back," Anton said.

Luka turned it over. The brightness of his headlamp showed the image of a rose bloom stamped onto it.

"That seal makes it one of the rare handful of maps that show the Northern Network in accurate detail. Most only show the lower tunnels."

"And where did you say you got hold of this?"

"I did not say. But I'm fortunate to possess it."

Luka exchanged glances with Oleg and returned

the map. The guide neatly folded it up again and slipped it into his front vest pocket.

"Okay, stay close. And watch your steps to the left." The guide held his carbide lamp over a narrow trench running alongside the tunnel wall. Excavated into the bare ground, it was six or seven feet deep, and three wide. "The conduit's meant to prevent flooding from storms," he explained. "As you'll see, though, it has more than a single use."

He turned and led them deeper into the tunnel, staying carefully between the track and the wall. Some fifty yards in, he halted and once again held his lamp out over the conduit.

"See where the rock projects from the tunnel wall in a kind of lip? The *chatière* is directly below it."

The men peered down in the orange throw of the lamp. The opening was on the left side of the trench. Concealed by the projection of stone, it would go unseen if one wasn't specifically looking for it.

"We can be grateful for the break we've had in the damned rain," Oleg said. "I've seen this conduit filled thigh-high with overflow. But everything's nice and dry."

The long-haired Russian grunted. "It's going to be a tight squeeze."

Anton squatted at the edge of the trench. "Everything is relative. Did you know the average casket is barely over two feet wide? By that measure you'll have room to spare."

Oleg looked at him.

"I suppose that's one way to think about it," he said. "You're a clever fellow, Anton."

The guide laughed. "A morbid sense of humor is a requirement here. As you'll see." He handed the lamp to the bearded man and lowered himself to the bottom. "Pass this down to me? Thanks."

Luka returned the lamp to him and followed, his companion climbing down last. There was, in fact, adequate room for the three of them to maneuver.

The *chatière,* or cat flap, was similarly a bit larger than it appeared from above. Anton pointed to it with his chin. "We go in legs first. The good thing is that the railway track is already sixty feet below street level, which puts us even with the chamber on the other side. The drop is barely a foot."

They did not comment. He once again led the way, slipping his legs into the opening, then shimmying through on his back. The two men followed without difficulty. A moment later they were all through.

The Russians looked around, the combined radiance of their LEDs and Anton's carbide lamp throwing a wide bubble of light around them. They were in a large chamber, with rough stone walls at its shadowy margins.

"We're in a five-hundred-year-old storeroom, where the miners kept their equipment," Anton said. "These days it's only frequented by cataphiles like myself and our valued clients."

"And the city's rats, I imagine," said Luka.

Anton shook his head. "In fifteen years as a guide, I've never seen one in the catacombs."

"Oh?"

"Never. I suppose there isn't enough for the furry little bastards to eat."

Luka looked at him. "Does this place hold no mystery at all for you?"

Anton grinned, his face orange in the firelight. "The catacombs are always ready with the unexpected," he said. "Speaking of which, I'm told there's a private rave in one of the halls tonight. An NFT gallery's showing off some new works by Ali Saldera. She's the artist who does those skeletons—you've probably heard of her. Talented. Sexy as can be, too." He paused, noticing their blank looks. Apparently, they lived in a paper bag. "Anyway, it's supposed to be hush-hush so the ERIC don't break it up."

"The ERIC?"

"Fucking cave cops. They're assigned to stomp out cataphilia or some bullshit. All they do is hassle people and hand out summonses. But we won't have to worry about them."

"How do you know?"

"The bouncer at the rave, Jean Paul, is a friend of mine. He has connections in *La PP*, the prefecture of police, and greased some wheels," Anton said, rubbing two fingers over his thumb. "You can be sure you'll get your five hundred euros' worth. I'll steer you around the party, take you down byways no one else knows. And as someone once said, it's in the byways that the secrets and wonders lie."

Luka gave Oleg a quick glance. Then he fixed his eyes back on Anton.

"Thank you," he said. "But you've already served your purpose."

Anton was puzzled. What had he meant by that remark? And the look he gave his friend with the long hair? He had a second to realize how uncomfortable it made him before the other man moved off slightly to his right, reaching a hand under his jacket. In the next second, it came out with a gun. It was thick and black. An automatic pistol.

Anton fixed his eyes on the weapon's barrel. It seemed immense.

"What is this about?" he said. "I don't understand."

The man extended his arm and fired twice into the guide's head, the double tap of the professional killer. Blood and bone fragments jetted from his temple to splash the chamber wall. He was dead before he hit the ground.

Oleg put another two bullets in the chest for good measure and returned his gun to its holster.

"Those rats don't know what they're missing," he said. "He'd make a fine meal."

Luka crouched, groped inside Anton's jacket for the map and pulled it out.

"How sad for them," he said after a minute.

Etienne Tousaint and Candace Amzalag were on their way to the rave.

The Porte d'Orléans quarter of the city, about four miles west of Bel-Air, had been likewise served by the *Petite Ceinture* for almost seventy years before the passenger line ceased operations in 1934. After hopping down to the tracks near the old Montrouge station, they had walked to a tunnel where a cat flap as round as a doughnut was concealed behind a lightweight foam rubber rock. Bright splashes of graffiti marked it for those in the know, and Candace had used it many times before.

"This way," she said, leading Etienne over to the fake rock.

Tall and thin, with dark Moroccan features and a wild tumble of black hair done up in corn-rows, Candace would be bartending the rave down below tonight and had worn cool iridescent gun-metal eye paint for the occasion. The rest of her ensemble was in her large orange zipper tote. She planned to change into it from her denim jacket, ratty jeans and sweater once they were through the tighter spaces.

She crouched and lifted the fake rock away from the jackhammered hole in the ground.

Etienne knelt beside her. He'd brought his party clothes in a backpack. "I can hardly wait to see the underground," he said.

She smiled. He noticed and smiled back. Her smile widened.

"What is it?" he asked.

"I think it's cute that you're so excited."

"Does it show?"

"The dimples on your cheeks give you away."

He shrugged. "You *do* know I'm a total virgin at this."

"And at other things?"

"All I'll say is I'm an average, full-blooded Parisian male."

Her eyes glinted with amusement within the heavy makeup. A freelance web designer, Etienne had given Candace an enthusiastic swipe right on his dating app a week ago. After a long online chat, she had invited him to the subterranean affair—an exclusive party for an NFT gallery's latest art drop.

"All right." She took a couple of LED strip head-lamps out of her bag and handed him one. "Here, put this on. You'll need it. We go in feet first."

Etienne looked at her. "Wow," he said. "You came prepared."

Candace winked.

"All I'll say is you're with an above-average, ex-perienced Parisian female," she said and slid her legs down into the opening.

The Saint-Martin ghost station was at the bottom of a long and sharply angled flight of stairs leading down through a dark tubular passage. Reva's second unit walked up the platform three abreast, using the map projected on their retinal displays, having no need for lamps to light their way. Their enhance-ments let them see clearly in the granular dimness.

Built in the art nouveau style of its day, the sta-tion's elaborate wall trims and molded columns were now sooty and gray and splashed with graf-fiti. At the far end of the platform, a sign read *Sortie de secours*, emergency exit, the words formed with grime-covered lettered tiles. Below the sign a short metal ladder descended to the track bed. A wall running its entire length had once divided the eastbound and westbound lines, though arched ap-ertures every few yards had given rail workers the ability to pass between them.

The group climbed down the ladder and crossed the track to the dividing wall, stepping carefully over the uncovered third rail. The contact rails lacked wooden guards, and it was a quirk of the French capital that even the disused tracks of its *stations fantômes* would have occasional surges of high voltage.

A few feet along the wall, they turned into one of the arches, again crossed the track, and walked along the base of the opposite platform toward the unlit tunnel beyond. Just inside its mouth, a short length of track split off into a kind of alcove. They followed the spur and looked around.

The darkness here would have seemed complete to most human eyes. But their vision went well beyond the normal. As with most things, it was all in the numbers.

An ordinary retina had ten million photoreceptor cells per square centimeter. For Blood Lightning transhumans, that total jumped astronomically. Their artificial retinas were lined with microscopic sensors made of perovskite, a crystalline substance used in ultrathin solar panels. These nanosensors served the same function as their natural photoreceptors but totaled *four hundred and sixty million* per square centimeter, making them fifty times more sensitive to light.

That was the first set of numbers. The second was found in the bundles of synthetic nerve fibers that had replaced the original ganglia running to their optic nerves. The liquid metal fibers had been developed by Chinese scientists in 2008 and used to replace severed and degenerative nerve tissues as early as 2014. By late 2023, they had become essential to all neural modifications, beginning with the implants that came into illicit vogue at Romanian stim clubs.

There was a huge difference between the wavelengths that natural and synthetic nerves could transmit to the brain. An average eye had ganglia sensitive to light in the three-hundred- to seven-hundred-nanometer wavelengths, setting the limits of human vision squarely within the red spectrum. The lab-grown replacement fibers, however, pushed that capacity upwards of eight hundred nanometers, which was the threshold of the near-infrared to infrared range.

That gave Blood Lightning units eyesight that went well beyond normal human limits. Beyond the optical capacity of nearly all warm-blooded creatures, in fact. Among mammals, only the vampire bat could detect images in the near-infrared spectrum.

Hence, Reva and her companions possessed a form of predatory superhuman vision. They could see things in the dark that no ordinary human could see—and see them from much farther away.

Right now they were looking into a tight, shallow space filled with the rotting hulks of obsolete Métro cars. The cars were uncoupled and shouldered lopsidedly together, perpendicular to the main track. They had broken lights and windows and thick brown patches of rust scabbing their exteriors. Their wheels and axles were detached or missing. Some of the hobbled cars stood on the rail, some in the dirt next to it.

The Russians filed into a narrow gap between two of the cars. Low in the tunnel wall behind them, an iron grating covered a large square accessway. It was badly corroded and had nothing to visibly saddle it in place. The rivets were gone, the concrete around it deteriorated and cracked.

Dominik and Zoltan knelt, hooked their fingers through its crossbars and pulled to work it loose. Cement crumbled and spilled to the ground as the grating separated from the wall with minimal resistance.

Reva moved up in front of them, crouched and peered into the opening. Then she glanced over her shoulder at the two men.

"We've found our cat flap," she said.

"Next, we will find her," Dominik offered.

"And she'll lead us to *him*," added Zoltan.

There is a manhole cover in the sidewalk on Rue Daunou, a five-minute walk from the Place de la Bastille and just steps from the entrance to Pâtisserie Jacques Ermine, where the cakes and pastries reputedly contain the most splendid chocolate fillings in all France. On this Sunday night, two narrow orange-and-white-striped safety cones bracketed its rim on the pavement.

The shops were closed now at eleven o'clock, their windows dark and their gates lowered. No pedestrians were out to see the man in the utility vest and waders approaching from the nearby corner, though he was not a particularly conspicuous presence on the street. Embroidered on the front of his coveralls was the logo of SAUR, the public wastewater management company that maintained the city's sewer system. Its employees were known to work at all hours, even at the tail end of the weekend.

For the past decade and a half, the man had gone by the name Julien Babin. Thirty and single, he lived in the quiet middle-class suburb of Saclay, a short commute from the city. But Babin the utility worker was a chimera, a fabrication, a second skin he used to disguise his true identity. Born Fedora Glaskov, he was in fact a sleeper agent with the GRU's Unit 21955, an elite group of operatives whose tradecraft was *irregular assassinations*—a euphemism for killing Russia's enemies on foreign soil.

The eldest son of a naval officer, Glaskov had spent his childhood and adolescence in Kronstadt on the outskirts of Saint Petersburg, where he'd inherited his father's love of the sea and learned to scuba dive in the cold waters off the Gulf of Finland. While still in his teens, his natural diving skills earned him the nickname Dolphin among friends.

A year ago Glaskov had requested an extended leave of absence from SAUR claiming he needed to care for a critically ill family member. The story was as much a lie as his Babin alias. In reality he'd taken a trip to the motherland, where he underwent a long-planned neural implant procedure that qualified him for the *Krovavaya Molniya*. He now wore the lightning on the left side of his chest above the heart, where it was generally hidden under his clothes.

Braithwaite Global hadn't entered the picture until recently. Glaskov had heard the contractor was paying specialists who'd undergone the cyber-modification process two thousand dollars a day plus a bounty for their services, outbidding the Russian-owned Wagner Group. Several *Krovavaya Molniya* operatives had simply left Russia on the heels of their modding and accepted the offer—including Matyar and Reva and the rest of the senior echelon. Though the GRU had balked, it was powerless to pull in the leash. In fact, there was no leash to speak of. Blood Lightning operatives were cherry-picked for their physical and psychological unassailability. They were required to be unmarried and childless so their families could not be threatened. What prison could hold them? Who could kill them? How could they be compelled to do anything they didn't choose to do? They were beyond coercion and would not bend to threats of retribution and punishment. In profiling candidates for their super-elite unit, the GRU had made a major miscalculation. They had failed to realize the profile for the perfect assassin also fit the perfect renegade.

Glaskov's unique sleeper status had afforded him a different option. Imbeds like himself were rarely activated. In fifteen years, he had not once been called into service by his handlers. He'd therefore seen no reason to tender his resignation or sever his ties to Russia. He could remain a foreign-service agent in good standing while accepting lucrative assignments for Braithwaite. His government didn't need to know what it didn't need to know. It was the best of both worlds.

Tonight Glaskov had walked to the manhole after leaving his utility truck on the nearby Rue de la Paix, where it would be unnoticed until morning. On his back was a tubular waterproof knapsack. Besides all the equipment he would need for his assignment below, it contained a long steel rod with a hook at one end.

When he reached the manhole, Glaskov set the bag down on the pavement, pulled out the rod and inserted the hook into a notch at the edge of the cover, working it around until it caught.

The cover loosened easily. He peered into the maintenance shaft underneath, saw a metal rung ladder on one side and put away the rod. Then he hefted his knapsack onto his shoulders and lowered himself into the darkness.

Glaskov had descended for about twenty yards before his probing foot found a wide stone ledge. He dropped down onto it and turned to look around.

He was at the edge of an underground canal. Four or five feet below him, the calf-deep groundwater flowed smooth and clear and glistening in the light of his helmet lamp. He could hear the sound of it lapping against the canal's stone banks.

He again shrugged off the pack, set it onto the ledge and opened it. From inside he pulled two tenliter diving cylinders and their harness. Next he produced his regulator, hoses, pressure gauge, fins, face mask, saturation bags and a lightweight plastic bump helmet. He had packed his neoprene wetsuit and booties first, so they came out last. He'd also brought three dive lights—a pair of 2000-lumen rail lamps for the helmet and another for his wrist.

Propping the gear against the wall, he stripped down to his briefs and placed his hard hat, clothing and waders neatly inside the knapsack. Shivering in the cold, he suited up, zipped his bare feet into the booties, then shouldered the twin oxygen tanks and sat bags and methodically went through his safety checklist, reading the pressure gauge and inspecting his valves and hoses. Finally he put on his submersible holster belt, fastening the straps of its cargo pouches around each thigh. Its left pouch contained eight transmitter/receivers in waterproof cases. The right, his pistol. He would carry the fins on a bungee cord until needed and leave the knapsack behind on the ledge to be recovered later.

His preparations complete, Glaskov switched on his headlamps and hopped down into the canal with a soft splash, wading out until the water reached his chest. Then he slipped beneath its surface, a map of the underground tunnels overlaying his vision as he swam west and then north to leave his trail of electronic breadcrumbs.

4

Baneasa, Romania

Janus's visitor-housing compound was located in what was once an unmanaged field of ragged crabgrass and brittle brown weeds at the northernmost sector of the base. Before last November, nothing had stood there but some ramshackle wooden domiciles used by CIA personnel back when Janus was a war-on-terror black site. But they were gone now, burned and flattened to the ground in the attack, and the field had been subsequently leveled and blacktopped to create an expansive parking area for a new state-of-the-art troop barracks.

Carmody gazed out the JLTV's front passenger window, picturing the field as he remembered it, searching for the spindly row of trees that had for years formed its outer edge. He couldn't see them in the darkness and wondered if they were gone too—the trees and the pair of mated ravens that had defended them as their exclusive roost.

He turned to look straight ahead. All but one of the structures going up at the west end of the lot were unfinished, and some were hardly more than bare, skeletal columns and crossbeams. Carmody saw a small fleet of yellow bulldozers, loaders and forklifts standing amid piles of dirt and dump rocks in the bright lights illuminating the construction site.

His driver pulled in front of the completed unit and stopped. It looked like a modern condominium. In New York or Los Angeles the units would sell for a fortune. But this wasn't either of those places, and somehow they made Carmody feel bleak and depleted.

"I'll bring your bags inside," the driver said when they exited the vehicle. He was a young private named Graham.

Carmody held up a hand and nodded toward the building. "I've got them," he said. "Where are my quarters?"

"Second floor, sir." The driver nodded toward the barracks. "Hook a left past the entrance, you'll see a row of doors. Your name will be on one of them."

"Thanks."

Carmody exited and went around to the rear passenger door. He saw headlights gliding over the blacktop and saw the separate vehicle with Natasha, Schultz and Dixon inside coming toward him. Then he opened the door and reached inside. He'd brought a single overnight bag and a heavy spinner but didn't bother using the wheels. As the other JLTV drew close he hefted it and carried both pieces of luggage through the entrance.

The building's interior smelled new and fresh and looked bland and functional. There was tan commercial carpeting along a cream-colored hallway. The heat was too low. Carmody saw no adornments, no pictures on the wall. He turned left past a flight of stairs and found his room three doors down. It was unlocked.

The lights were on when he stepped inside. It wasn't too large or small and seemed comfortable enough. Like a halfway decent roadside motel. There was a wide platform bed, a nightstand, a dresser and a full-wall closet with sliding doors. A kitchenette with a coffee maker, microwave and dining nook. The bathroom had a white tub, white sink, white soap bars and plenty of bright white towels. Everything looked clean and unused.

Carmody hung his bomber jacket over the back of a chair, unzipped his spinner on the bed and took out a folded pair of sweatpants and a T-shirt. He felt tired and flat, and his body hurt. He had flown eleven hours and five thousand miles. There had been the deadly business with Grigor Malkira in Hawaii. And before that in New York City. The bullet wound in his arm was barely closed. His neck was sore from his scuffle on the tuft cone.

And Kali was gone.

He inhaled, then exhaled. He didn't want to think about her. He wanted to take a shower and climb into bed and get some sleep. He'd had enough of thinking about Kali Alcazar.

He started toward the bathroom, heard someone knocking at his door and stopped.

He looked around at the door. Waited.

Two more hard insistent raps.

Carmody had a hunch who it was. He went over and opened it partway.

Colonel John Howard stood in the hallway with a wooden tobacco pipe in his mouth. Smoke was puffing up from the bowl. It had a sweet, fruity, mildly resinous fragrance.

"Surprised to see me?"

"Not much."

"And you opened the door anyway?"

Carmody gave no answer. Howard didn't look like he'd expected one. He was a tall, dark-skinned Black man in his early fifties with a sinewy physique, a shaved head and high, jutting cheekbones.

"Happens I was out on my walk when you landed," he said. "It's so quiet around here, I heard the plane from across the base. Figured I'd stroll over and welcome you."

"Fernandez already did that."

Howard's eyes went to his. "Julio isn't the base commander," he said. "I am."

Carmody shrugged. "I was about to take a shower and hit the sheets."

"This won't take long. And it's damn cold out in the hall."

Carmody held the door handle and said nothing.

"Besides," Howard said, "Janus is my house. Which makes you my guest."

"If it makes you feel important, I suppose."

Howard grinned. Carmody looked at him another moment, then pulled the door the rest of the way open. The colonel took two or three steps into the room.

"We should discuss a few things ahead of tomorrow's meeting," he said.

"Okay."

Howard cradled the bowl of his pipe and smoked.

"I'm giving you the men you requested. Sparrow and Begai and the rest. But I need Julio here with me."

"I need him more."

"We have a kid who can handle the job. An AI specialist. He's been working under Fernandez and Adrian Soto. Almost since Soto got here."

"Is that meant to impress me?"

"Yeah."

"Does this kid have a name?"

"Mario Perez."

Carmody grunted. "We'll see," he said. "What else?"

"The training range is ready. Built to your specs. You'll see it first thing in the morning."

"Sounds good," Carmody said and waited.

Howard looked at him over the pipe. "We need to move on from our differences," he said. "Both of us."

"Common cause?"

"You put it that way, I won't nitpick," Howard said. "The Wolf's one of the most dangerous human beings on earth. A cyberterrorist and a mass killer. I'm convinced your operation has the best chance of neutralizing him. And I'm giving you everything you need to do it."

Carmody nodded. "My guess is that isn't all you wanted to say."

Howard puffed smoke from the corners of his mouth. The tobacco in his pipe sizzled softly and flared bright orange.

"I just want everything out in the open," he said. "I agreed to let you bring the Alcazar woman from the States. I would have permitted her to accompany you without any restrictions. But Morse informed me about her skipping out, and I'm not surprised. In fact, I'm convinced our asses are better off for it."

Carmody looked at him. "Okay," he said. "Got you."

"Maybe...but maybe not altogether." Howard held up a hand, crossed his middle and index fingers. "She and the Wolf were like this, once upon a time. We know he used her Hekate superbug to single-handedly take out New York City. And that he almost took POTUS with it." He paused. "She had her chance and fled custody. But we'll find her. And when we do, she's going to answer some questions."

"I thought you wanted to move on."

"Not from Alcazar I don't," Howard said. "Not till I know what falls on her and what doesn't."

Carmody shrugged his shoulders. "Suppose I tell you she isn't my problem. That you can leave me out of anything to do with her."

"Then, we've got no bones left to pick with each other." Howard studied him through a thin veil of smoke. "You better turn in, hoss. See you in the morning."

Carmody watched as the colonel let himself out,

then turned toward the bathroom. He wanted to take his shower, unpack his travel bags and go to bed.

Erected on the site of the former C4ISR—Command, Control, Communications, Computers, Intelligence, Surveillance and Reconnaissance center—or simply *Headquarters* to Colonel John Howard and his base personnel—the new Cyber-Threat Readiness Center (CTRC) standing south of the barracks complex was streamlined in both name and acronym, but far more broad-ranging than the original in terms of its appearance and operations. Nothing at all remained of the low, narrow, windowless, trailerlike concrete structure that had been left in flaming ruin amid November's strike. The first HQ was all cramped Eastern European functionality, its replacement expansive Western planning and design, a sixty-thousand-square-foot building set at a standoff distance from the facility's roads and parking areas, and constructed mainly of prestressed concrete and rigidized high-tech metals. In addition to its spacious command and control room, the CTRC contained administrative offices, an assembly hall, weapons and equipment vaults, vehicle storage and maintenance bays, a hardened and secure medical center, and large temperature-controlled break rooms with east-facing windows to bathe them in sunlight. The halls were similarly open and bright, and rooftop solar arrays provided the vast amount of electricity powering its systems.

Colonel John Howard walked at a clip that was neither fast nor slow as he crossed the parking lot toward the rear of the CTRC. He had left the barracks unsatisfied, his concerns about Carmody heightened rather than relieved. Howard supposed he'd wanted to get a read on his state of mind, his willingness to put the past to rest and, most of all, his feelings about Kali Alcazar. But thinking about his words to Carmody, and Carmody's words to him, Howard could not say he liked what he had picked up. Not the slightest bit.

He turned right behind a row of parked military vehicles, then turned left in front of some others, then stepped up onto a cement sidewalk. The building was just ahead of him. Seven stories tall, with ten squarish sections linked by ten main corridors, its architects had intentionally given it the look of a giant integrated circuit layout. The whole thing was slick and impressive and a massive improvement over what had stood there before.

Howard walked toward the building. A little farther up the sidewalk, he heard the whoosh of jet engines in the sky, paused and looked up into the darkness. Two sets of running lights were passing the east end of base. Fernandez had gone ahead with his little demo though his intended audience was a no-show.

Howard admittedly didn't like the noise in the sky. It reminded him too much of the drones on the night of the attack. The psychologists at Baneasa had assessed him with post-traumatic stress disorder, and maybe they weren't wrong. He still sometimes woke up from a dead sleep thinking he heard the sirens, the crack of the hedgehogs' rockets, and the rattle of their machine guns. Forty-seven men and women had been slaughtered by Janus's own security robots on his watch. The bulldozers and earthmovers could haul off the rubble and strip away the layers of scorched ground. But the scars in his memory weren't so easily erased.

Howard followed the sidewalk as it curved behind the CTRC. The building's fifty-foot clear zone was marked off with a skirt of luminous orange-and-white-painted stripes. Beyond them were high-tensile steel barriers that would rise out of the ground within three seconds if an unauthorized vehicle came speeding up. Beyond them a low perimeter fence, and to his left a manned entry point with a lowered metal security arm, also glowing orange and white in the night. Anyone wanting admittance to the building—driving or on foot— had to pass through the entry point's scanners and visual inspections. Which included him.

He was approaching it on the sidewalk when he noticed the robot hounds. Two of them on patrol in the clear zone, roughly between him and the lowered metal arm. They moved slowly in his direction, their large wedge-shaped heads upraised, their stance erect, their gait smooth and gliding and soundless. He could see the antennas spiking up from their shoulders. The camera and day/night sensor arrays they used in place of eyes. Their partly open mouths showing jawfuls of long titanium fangs.

And the weapons pods on their torsos. The precision rifles inside them fired 6.5 Creedmoor rounds and could spit out accurate kill shots at a mile's distance.

Howard paused with his hand cupping the bowl of his pipe. The hounds came closer. A little closer. Then they stopped about four feet away. He'd heard all of Adrian Soto's reassurances. He had been schooled in their quantum network AI and told it was the most secure on the planet. He still didn't trust them. Not any more than he had ever trusted the hedgehogs. Less, really. Because he had learned an unforgettable lesson from those mechanized sentries. They had shown him what they could do when they turned against you.

He stood there facing them for what seemed like a while but could not have been more than three or four seconds. He supposed they were processing his biometrics, assessing him as a possible threat.

"Not me," he said. "You want to piss motor oil on something, find yourselves a hydrant."

The hounds studied him another second in their coldly analytical way. Then they simply turned and walked off, their evaluation complete.

Howard lowered his pipe, watching them go about their rounds. A minute later they were out of sight, and he resumed walking toward the entry point, calculating that the time in New York would be 1700 hours. Late in the day there, but maybe not too late, he thought.

He wanted to hurry up and make a call to Carol Morse, Net Force's director of operations.

The Terminal (Net Force Headquarters),
Hell's Kitchen, New York City

"Morse," Howard said ten minutes later. He was in his office and had his desk phone on Speaker. "I caught you."

"You're in luck."

"I was born lucky," he said. "Your line secure?"

"Yes," she said. "What's up?"

"I want to confirm your team landed about an hour ago."

"I know," she said.

"'Course you do."

"What else?"

"I already talked to Carmody."

"Any broken bones?"

"Mine or his?"

"I prefer to have you both intact."

Howard snorted laughter and reclined in his chair. His small but strategically located office was just down the hall from the building's command center.

"Neither of us needs a body cast," he said and paused a beat. "We're meeting about the operation first thing tomorrow. I told Fernandez and Soto to be there."

"Good," she said. "Before we continue…remember, Defiant Fly's identity isn't to be divulged."

"He won't like that."

"A bargain's a bargain. We have to honor it. Right now he doesn't need to know."

"Okay I tell him you said that?"

"Not a problem," she said and checked her watch. "So, Colonel, why the call?"

Howard hesitated. He had tapped the ashes out of his pipe and was toying with it on the top of his desk.

"Outlier," he said.

"Did he bring her up?"

"I did."

"Shit, were you *looking* to start a fight?"

"I wanted it out of the way."

There was another tick of silence.

"Okay," Morse said. "Give me the nutshell version, please. I was just leaving for an appointment."

"I told him my thoughts about her. Let him know she has to answer for some things."

"And what did he say?"

"That she wasn't his problem anymore."

"Meaning he feels she is."

"You know your boy," Howard said.

"All right. What else?"

"I can't tell whether he knows something about her we don't. But if he does, I don't believe he'd share it."

She expelled a breath. "Kali Alcazar is an international fugitive. She hightailed it out of the United States for points unknown."

"Uh-huh."

"Carmody, on the other hand, is a sworn officer of our agency. If he learned of her whereabouts and didn't report it to us, *he* would be in violation of his oath to uphold the law. And defend our national security against all enemies." She paused. "Where exactly are you going with this conversation?"

Howard was silent, considering how to answer. Her protectiveness of Carmody had come up like a wall. But the two of them went back to when she was his CIA handler. In those relationships the trust had to run both ways. For her a mission's success or failure could have hung on it. For him it was life or death. That was a mighty powerful bond.

"I need to hear that we're all keen on chasing

down Alcazar," he said at last. "Hear it from your lips. So I know for sure it's really our focus."

"Do you honestly think I'd waste our organizational resources on some pretend hunt? That Al Michaels would go along with it?"

"Isn't what I said."

"It's what you implied."

"Then, pardon me. But it took us three years to hook her the first time."

"Three years of evidence collection and analysis. Of following leads. One quality that helped me immensely at the Agency was patience, Colonel. If you're looking for an instant payoff, it'll only lead to frustration." Morse inhaled. "Listen, I get it. We aren't back to square one with her, if that's what worries you. Before, she was a ghost. An online handle. We had no idea about Outlier's real identity. We didn't know what she looked like. We didn't know how she moved around. Now we have all that and more. For God's sake, she's been right here in my office. And we've got her last known location."

"Yeah, well, you can bet she isn't still catching the Oahu sunshine."

"No. But Hawaii would be her point of departure. And unless she swam across the Pacific to her next destination, we can track her. We just need some time. I remind you it's been less than a week since she gave us the slip."

Gave Carmody the slip, Howard thought but did not say.

He put down his pipe, meshed his hands and stretched his arms out in front of him. His chest hurt on the side where the explosion that killed

Abrams had broken his ribs. The pain wasn't as sharp as before but had dulled to more of a tight, pulling sensation.

Scar tissue.

"Okay," he said. "Appreciate you taking my call."

"Right."

"You need to go where you're going."

"Right again."

"Have fun."

"I'll be in touch."

Across the Atlantic Ocean, Morse disconnected and swiveled around to face her window. It was raining outside, the splattered droplets of water on the glass smearing and blurring her view of the High Line and the river beyond. *Fun* was hardly how she would describe a session with her marriage therapist.

She checked her watch. Five thirty. It would be eleven thirty at night in Lyon, France, and Chief Cybercrime Intelligence Officer Chaput was probably long gone from his office at Interpol. But right before Howard called, she'd meant to leave him a voice mail about their shared problem, Kali Alcazar.

She got that out of the way, grabbed her umbrella and headed out the door.

Sgt. Julio Fernandez pulled his JLTV to a halt near an aluminum flight hangar, got out and glanced up at the night sky. He was in the Special Projects Testing Grounds, a deliberately fuzzy name that added to the secrecy of the classified and black-budgeted projects being trialed here in Janus's extreme western sector.

The three objects above were flying straight and level no more than three feet apart. He'd considered having them do some fancy stunts, but with the low-altitude mist, that had seemed like too much of a risk. Which was okay, since he was the only one around. This wasn't turning out to be a good night for staging spectacles or pushing boundaries.

Fernandez raised his night-vision goggles from his chest. Instantly the objects took shape in his vision. He guessed they were over a mile up, at six thousand feet. About a third their maximum altitude. But in practice they would probably stay well below that ceiling.

He saw their silhouettes come in horizontally above him through the haze, their arms extended behind them like hummingbird wings. They hovered a moment and then reoriented themselves into vertical positions. The turbojets whined and breathed in air, their centrifugal compressors forcing it into powerful combustion chambers and then out the engine nozzles at a hundred pounds of thrust her second.

Fernandez watched the two figures descend through his goggles. He was in awe. For all his years of working with advanced technology, he couldn't stop being in awe.

They were almost directly overhead now. Coming down and down. Both jet suiters had two micro gas turbines on each arm and a larger engine on their backs. When they were within about three hundred feet in altitude, Fernandez lowered his goggles. He could make them out well enough with his unaided eyes.

Though he had plenty of safety clearance, he still reflexively backed away from the circular glow-in-the-dark ground markings to avoid their superheated engine exhaust. Faye Luna and Doug Wheeler had come a long way since they first suited up and thrashed around on their tethers like wounded ducks. They had undertaken weeks of practice and persisted through a nasty mixed bag of bumps, knocks, bruises and near disasters to get as good as they were. And Fernandez knew they'd done it for Carmody. Which was why he also knew his failure to show up would be a major disappointment to them.

They made perfect touchdowns, landing on their feet inside the zeros. Fernandez strode over to them as they lifted off their helmets.

Luna was looking around. "Where's the big guy?"

"He decided to skip the entertainment," Fernandez said.

"Are you *serious*?"

"Yeah."

"Well, that sucks," she said. "Any particular reason?"

Fernandez decided on the spot to keep what Natasha had told him to himself. "Dunno," he said, and shrugged. "He seemed tired."

"Tired, shit," Wheeler said. "I wanted to see the look on his face when he saw how we turned into superheroes."

Fernandez looked over their suits. "You know what Einstein said about time?"

Wheeler gave Luna a frown. She in turn relayed the frown to Fernandez.

"No, Sergeant," she replied. "What did Einstein say about time?"

"The only reason for it is so everything doesn't happen at once."

Luna just stood there a minute.

"Thanks for nothing," she said sourly.

5

The Paris Catacombs

Kali had gone about a mile south, hurrying along the Sandy Road, when she felt a sudden vibration underfoot. It quickly grew stronger and louder and was joined by a deep, low-pitched rumble from close up ahead. There was no mistaking what it was.

She stopped and pulled out Lucien's map. It placed her under Rue de Montalent and just east of the Métro's Place de la République. The station at République in particular was a large, busy transit hub where trains came and went constantly, which would account for the noise and trembling vibrations.

Kali stood in the gloom, the map bathed in the

radiance of her headlamp. She was checking the secret entrances to the upper and lower subterranean networks—*chatières*, or cat flaps, as they were called in the legend on the lower right. These were marked with bold black forward slashes, and she saw one on Boulevard Saint-Martin practically across the street from République. A slender transverse ran from the cat flap to the Sandy Road, giving access to the entire underground network of tunnels.

She flashed on a recollection from long ago. On one of her many childhood visits to Paris, her grandmother had brought her to the plaza to view the famed statue of Marianne, Guardian of Liberty. Kali was no more than ten or eleven years old, but she remembered the day clearly. Lucien was with them, two years her senior, his parents having left him in Oma's care for some reason or another. Like all boys obsessed with mysterious urban legends—in his case a boy goaded along by insatiable curiosity and an encyclopedic memory—Lucien was far less interested in the statue than a nearby ghost station...the old Saint-Martin Métro. Located outside a landmark playhouse on the boulevard, it had been abandoned in the 1930s upon completion of the larger République terminal, the subway system's planners having decided it had become superfluous. The transverse was probably an unfinished track spur, meant to connect the stations if both had stayed in operation.

The ghost station was in the same spot on the map as the *chatière* symbol.

Kali thought furiously. She was convinced the

men who'd followed her into Lucien's town house weren't alone. There would be others in Paris coordinating with them. Others with copies of the map. Though only Lucien's would show the path to his hiding place, all copies would reveal the Sandy Road's existence. It was likely that some could enter the tunnels unwitnessed through the cat flap in Saint-Martin station.

But would they really do that? Lucien was a paraplegic and in chronically poor health. His mobility was limited even aboveground. Down here it would be even more restricted. Wouldn't they assume he was closer to home and therefore enter the tunnels farther north?

Back up. These people are professionals. And they hacked into a security system you helped design. Who and what does that remind you of?

Kali drew a long breath. The thoughts were hers, the voice Carmody's. And of course the answer had already been lurking in her mind. She had once loved Drajan Petrovik, and he had rewarded her for it by using her Hekate code to take down New York City. Months later, she believed, a variant of the code was used to hijack the robotic sentries at Janus Base. She had been excluded from the forensic analysis and had no concrete proof of that. But the attack had occurred when the base was short on personnel, its key defenders having accompanied Carmody on his raid of Drajan's hideaway.

She did not think the timing coincidental. Drajan had clearly known about the raid in advance and fled the country. With his hacking skills, he could have learned of the plan by penetrating the base's computer systems. The Hekate variant would have allowed him to corrupt and subvert the hedgehogs and launch a counterstrike. Kali knew of no other software capable of it. And even if he had developed something as effective on his own, she knew why he would have used it.

To set you up. To get at you. To hit you where it hurts for walking away from him. The same reason he'd go after Navarro. Or one of the reasons.

Or one of them, yes, she thought. She'd never known Drajan's motivations to be simple or straightforward. They were nearly always layered constructs, his actions driven by more than a single goal. He knew Lucien was her oldest and dearest friend. If he targeted him, revenge would be part of it. But not all.

Kali returned the map to her pocket as another train rumbled through the nearby station. Lucien had vanished, and it was vital that she find him. But the men Franz had spotted from the Butte Bergeyre were searching for him as well and had seemingly waited for her to arrive so she could lead them to him.

Instead, she had gone in the opposite direction to lure them away. It was a tack that made sense. But it wouldn't fool them for long. She was not the Pied Piper, nor they mindless rats lining up to blindly follow her into the river. *These people are professionals.* And more. Much more. They were Blood Lightning. They would have anticipated her move and planned to counter it.

She needed to prepare.

* * *

"There. Up ahead." Reva motioned with her chin. "I see the exit."

She paused on her belly, the crawlway's rough rock sides shuddering around her—probably, she thought, a train pulling in or out of the nearby Place de la République station. Dominik and Zoltan had been clawing through the passage behind her. They craned their necks to look around for themselves.

That was redundant. Their onboards interfaced to provide full situational awareness. They could see what she saw. She could see what they saw. If they hadn't been separated from the other Blood Lightning units by thick rock walls, all three teams could have linked up to the same visual data stream, essentially sharing each other's eyes and ears.

Nevertheless, Zoltan and Dominik had the impulse to see the exit for themselves, like creatures that had evolved beyond needing tails but felt their lingering absence. Nature hardwired the brain for individual perception, not sensory fusion. Old reflexes died hard.

So they looked. And saw a circular opening like the one they had squeezed through at the derelict Saint-Martin track spur. If anything, it was even smaller. The crawlway itself had tightened around them as they went on, grading downward for many long yards, snaking one way and another, then leading at a fairly steep, straight incline. At several different points they had gone past the entrances to branching passages. At others they had crept by what appeared to be drainage culverts on either side, each of them shaped like an inverted U and low to the ground, none on any of the maps or references in their databases. It was as if they had entered a wormhole. An underground burrow. One small section of a vast maze of passages, some wide, some narrow, some straight, some curving, all close and cramped and dug out of the bare, ragged earth. The overlay map on their retinal screens indicated the crawlway intersected with a short cross passage on the other side of the exit and that it would then connect with the Sandy Road.

So they moved toward it on their knees and elbows and bellies. Like ants, Zoltan thought. Like moles, Dominik thought. They felt stifled and claustrophobic and eager to put this cramped twisting tunnel behind them.

"Come on, don't slow down. We're almost out," Reva said as if reading their minds.

Otherwise she said nothing. And thought nothing. She kept her mind free of thought except when necessary, an ability she had honed through years of rigorous mental discipline. She saw the opening ahead. Her unit needed to reach it. Right now that was her goal and her focus. Thought would be largely superfluous, so she did not think beyond the minimum.

She scrambled up the passage, leading the way.

Kali trotted along until she came to a juncture she thought was the one on Lucien's map. A check of the distance she had covered so far confirmed it. The recess in the wall was on her left side, and she could see the cross passage up ahead on the right. Ahead of her the passage sloped noticeably downward.

She stopped outside the recess. It was a ten-foot square and appeared to have been roughly hacked out of the passage wall with hammers, pickaxes and shovels. In the southeast corner of the wall below the ceiling, she saw what was instantly recognizable as a fixed pulley, its grooved iron blocks and fastenings clearly blacksmithed long ago. At one end of the cable was a large counterweight on a kind of rock shelf. The other end ran up to a hatch in the ceiling about the size of a loft door, then back down through the system of blocks to a lever projecting from the wall about two feet below the ceiling.

She took a couple of steps into the recess, thumbed her headlamp to its brightest setting and craned her head for a better look at the hatch. It was seeping water. There was moisture around its edges and dribbling down on the ground underneath. Made of thick slabs of wood and metal bands, it probably had been fashioned by a carpenter about the same time the pulley mechanisms were forged. But it looked surprisingly well maintained. There was no rust on the hardware, no corrosion, no mineralization. And the cable was unmistakably new, or least newer, than the rest of the setup. A modern stainless-steel wire rope about the thickness of a clothesline.

Kali reached for her map and opened it. The Canal Saint-Martin was about three miles long, feeding off the Bassin de la Villette and Canal de l'Ourcq in the northern suburbs, and running downstream toward the Seine to the south. It was calm and sluggish, with bored, tired tour guides ferrying sightseers in gondolas and trip boats out on the water. Her eye went to a particular spot on the map, a place where the canal slid underground at the intersection of Rue de la Grange-aux-Belles and Quai de Jemmapes. She had been there with Lucien many times in her visits to the city and could picture the gray stone tunnel entrance, the lock in front of it and the iron footbridge just below that.

Many times, during their long walks together. Lucien the scholarly, bespectacled introvert who would only thrust his head out of his shell in her presence. Lucien with his bowl-shaped chapeau, wild, tangled hair and heavy brown beard, a young student of history and literature who had spent countless nights pulling deep secrets from academic archives. *That* Lucien, before the car crash that had left him orphaned, his spine part of its irreparable wreckage.

One day, she recalled, when the shade trees lining the banks of the canal were in their high-autumn colors—their thick, broad crowns studded with red and orange and yellow—he had noticed a candy wrapper floating on its surface and given her a cross frown.

"Parisians are filthy! It's in their blood! Every quarter century, workers drain the canal to find all sorts of rubbish and debris. Chairs, trash cans, Vélib rental bikes—dozens of them, classic green and electric. The bohemians come for their romantic spins and café poetry readings and then flip them into the canal. I salvaged a boom box larger than a suitcase and repaired it. Did I tell you?"

"More than once, Lucien. I relayed the story to Franz."

"And was he impressed?"

"Very. And proud."

"*Ah, bon*, Kali. When I think about what's dumped in this canal, it's easy to see what inspired Napoleon's wicked jest."

She had waited for him to explain, which he'd only done after a dramatic pause.

"In his later life they called him Le Général Entrepreneur, the champion of public works. But you must appreciate the pun. It was indeed Napoleon who ordered the canals built and the catacombs opened. But he was, above all, a *military* general and tactician. And a bit of a madman, which isn't the worst thing."

"Oh?"

"We should look for a little madness in our leaders! It goes hand in hand with inspiration. The underground passages were a ready way to move his troops about the city unimpeded. And a hidden escape route from his enemies in case of a wartime invasion..."

That lesson in obscure urban history—Lucien's favorite category—had been given long ago. Now Kali looked up at the ceiling again, remembering. The tunnel that channeled the canal underground extended for over a mile from north to south, and she estimated she was forty or fifty feet below it. If she was correct about her bearings, the water would be flowing directly overhead.

She stood with her gaze fixed above her, and her thoughts again turning back toward that day on the bridge. Lucien had wrapped himself in silence, seeing she was intrigued. He enjoyed the theatrics, and she had played willingly into it, letting him build the suspense.

"And Napoleon's jest?" she'd asked him.

He had cocked his head toward the tunnel entrance. "Like you, he appreciated a good trick," he said. "His charming public toilet can flush!"

A sparkle in his eyes, mischief in his voice, so long ago.

Kali remained very still, her attention narrowed on the hatch. She studied it for several more seconds, then moved her eyes across the ceiling to the pulley mechanism.

Which was precisely when she heard someone approaching from down the passage.

Reva leaned through the narrow mouth of the crawlway, glanced left and right and saw she was several feet above the floor of the cross passage. She slid out headfirst, her hands extended to buffer the drop. Dominik followed, with Zoltan exiting last. His bulk made it difficult, and he had to twist and turn his shoulders and upper body in the opening to maneuver through, landing heavily and awkwardly in the sand below.

Reva and Dominik had already gotten out their gas masks and were putting them on. Zoltan slapped grit off his clothes and took his mask out of his pack and did the same, pulling it up over his chin, fastening and adjusting its elastic straps.

They spent a moment getting accustomed to the masks, Spetsnaz-issue PMKs, their voice amplifiers and cheek-mounted filters giving them a typical insectile appearance. The large faceplates offered a wider field of view than the older masks and just mildly reduced peripheral vision.

Reva tilted her head toward the crawlway. "Seal it," she said to Dominik. "I don't want her using it to escape us."

He nodded. The grenade he extracted from his carryall was about the size and shape of a plumb, resembling the spherical Russian Federation grenade it was based upon. Its shell consisted of two aluminum hemispheres divided by a thin, single-layered partition, each hemisphere containing a separate liquid polymer. On detonation the partition would disintegrate, the polymers chemically interacting to create a rapidly expanding and hardening foam.

Dominik thumbed out the pin to release the lever and tossed the grenade into the crawlway. It landed about two feet inside the neck of the cavity, rolled a few more feet downhill and blew with a loud crack. Smoke coughed from the exit as within seconds a foamy white material swelled and spread and consolidated and solidified inside to plug it like a cork stopper.

Reva gave the sealed-off opening a quick look and then silently glanced to her right. The passage was high enough so they could stand up straight, but still too narrow for all three to walk comfortably abreast. A few yards to her left it came to a dead end. On the right it ran at a steep incline for about fifty yards and then took another right-hand

turn. Its bottom was covered with coarse, granular
sand in both directions.

She turned right, Dominik beside her, Zoltan
again falling in slightly behind. The passage continued climbing sharply until it reached the bend,
where it leveled off somewhat but remained at a
steady incline. As they turned the corner, they
could see its exit another thirty or forty yards
straight ahead. A man-made arch carved out of
the raw limestone, it had been reinforced with large
blocks of masonry, as was the facing wall of the
tunnel into which it opened.

Reva reached under her jacket. In a hard-shell
strut holster tucked low in her waistband was a
lightweight South Korean Crich projectile launcher
about the size and shape of a .38 handgun.

She pulled a CS/smoke canister from her waist
belt, broke open the barrel and fed it in. Meanwhile
Dominik and Zoltan were assembling their tranquilizer pistols, attaching sights to the rails and
screwing on the CO_2 cartridges, then pushing the
etorphine darts into the ports.

After a minute Reva nodded toward the arch, her
right hand wrapped around the pistol grip.

"That's it over there," she said. "The main passage is on the other side."

They strode toward it, sand and pebbles crunch-
ing underfoot and pushing into the treads of their
boots. Reva stepped through into the passage
and glanced down at the grit covering its floor in
both directions. She saw no footprints. No distur-
bances. Their quarry could have tried to obscure

her tracks—there were ways—but she doubted she would miss seeing any signs at all.

No, she thought. Alcazar had not yet been here. Which meant they could overtake her from the rear if she had gone toward the Northern Network after leaving the town house. If she had, on the other hand, gone south toward *Le Grand Réseau Sud*, they would be able cut her off before she reached this juncture. In any case she would be trapped, wedged between her second unit and the others closing in from all four quadrants of the underground.

"Let's go," she said through the voice amplifier.

She turned quickly to the right, heading north on the Sandy Road.

Five seconds had passed since Kali noticed the sound. She stood inside the recess, waiting to hear if it returned. It was nearly inaudible. A fraction as loud as the trains. But loud enough to seize her attention.

She listened. Nothing. Just the rumble of the trains pulling into or out of the station.

Another few seconds went by.

She listened.

Then she heard it again.

Close. Much closer than the train. A scuffling, scraping noise. Footsteps coming toward her.

Multiple sets of footsteps. Careful. Deliberate. Quiet. But not altogether soundless. She wasn't Mike Carmody. She had never been a soldier. A hunter of human beings. But she knew quiet was easier on grass. On soft, pliant earth. The tunnel floor wasn't either one of those things. It was sand and pebbles and gravel on top of solid rock. People put pressure on the ground when they walked. The hard, dry bits of silicate shifted under their weight. They clung to their shoe bottoms and spilled off as they rose and fell. Avalanches in microcosm. The sound could be softened and mitigated but not altogether eliminated.

Kali listened to the footsteps. To their rise and fall. To the scrape and slide of the tiny particles of displaced sand. She couldn't judge their distance. The walls of the passage dulled and swallowed up sound. But they were getting closer and closer.

She reached a hand down to her hip bag and turned left, hurrying south on the Sandy Road.

Janus Base

Fifteen hundred miles across Europe, Carmody reached over to the bedside table for his sat phone and saw that it was one in the morning. He hadn't been able to sleep.

He put the phone back down and lay in the dark a while longer with his eyes wide open. Then he tossed off his blankets, put on his clothes, grabbed his cigarettes and went to the door. He needed some fresh air.

The night was cold and dank and felt like it had rain in store. But the ground mist had lifted, and he could see out across the new construction, bulldozers and dump rocks to where the trees once stood in a row at the edge of the north field. What they had called Janus Heights in the old days.

Carmody lit up and stared into the darkness. He remembered watching the birds with Kali, a pair of them, the large black shadows of their wings defined by the area lights. They had flapped over-head and gone racing out across the tall, dry grass to the trees.

"Stone the crows," he'd said to her.

"Ravens. There is a difference."

They had stood in silence, watching the birds settle on a branch. Carmody hadn't been sure he knew the exact right words for what he wanted to tell her and had finally given up on trying to find them.

"Coprox," he'd said. *"Ever hear of it?"*

"The sleep drug."

"When I was with Special Tactics, we just called it the Candy. You're on 'round-the-clock alert, time-zone hopping, amped up for missions, flying in choppers...you need your shut-eye. The dose for insomnia is five milligrams. We'd get on a long flight and pop twenty mils like it was nothing. I kept using it after I got out of the service."

She had asked about him joining the CIA, and he said something to brush past the subject. It wasn't his favorite, and he'd found it hard enough getting out what he had wanted to tell her.

They had continued watching the ravens as they leaped from branch to branch.

"You use the Candy long enough, in heavy doses, it can make you confused. It messes with short-term memory. You look around for your phone and real-ize it's in your hand. Then you can't remember the code to unlock it. And that code's your mother's birthday."

Carmody told her some more things, looking straight out at the ravens. Their cries loud in the air, they had bobbed and pranced and stretched their wings in what seemed like some kind of elaborate rite.

And then Kali had explained it to him.

It wasn't a ritual, she had said, but a special kind of dance. Between a pair mated for life...

Carmody finished his cigarette and ground out the stub on the blacktop. Then he bent down and picked it up and returned to the barracks. He didn't like leaving messes for other people to clean.

Back inside, he flipped the stub into the trash, turned to the dresser, opened the top drawer and lifted out a small, neatly folded stack of T-shirts. He had put the brown prescription-pill bottle underneath them.

"Coprox. Ever hear of it?"

"The sleep drug."

Carmody lifted the bottle from the dresser drawer, opened it and shook a pill out into his palm. He stood there a few seconds, shook out a second and capped the bottle, dropping the folded shirts back down on top of it.

His duffel bag was sitting on a corner chair. He went over and opened a side pocket. Inside was a hip flask he'd picked up in New York. It was pewter with black enamel on the outside.

He opened it, popped the pills and took a long, deep swig of whiskey. It was a good Irish single malt.

Carmody took another pull on the flask to make sure he had properly washed down the Coprox. Then he returned it to the duffel and went to sit on the edge of his mattress. He sat there, fully dressed, thinking about things for a while, and then not thinking about anything. Finally he got drowsy, leaned back across the bed, shut his eyes and fell asleep.

Paris, Nineteenth arrondissement

Cybercrime Intelligence Officer Renault Chaput watched Scholl enter the hotel from inside the parked Flow electric, reached for his sling bag and checked its contents. He'd raised and prepared the single delicate item inside with exceeding care.

Satisfied it had made the trip from Lyon undamaged, Chaput flipped the bag shut, shouldered it, and tapped his smartwatch as he stepped out onto Avenue Secrétan. A gift to himself upon his recent promotion to Interpol's upper echelon, the SUV changed from black with white bonnet stripes to solid white, the new color sweeping over its e-ink body skin from front to back. The motorized chameleon was undeniably an expensive and extravagant toy. But he told himself it aided the covert aspects of his work, giving him camouflage at the touch of a button. A man of modest means until lately, Chaput still on occasion felt compelled to justify its cost. However wobbly the pretext, it was there when needed and not altogether false.

He had not yet lowered his watch when he saw the voice mail alert on the display. It had been left on his office phone moments ago... Carol Morse at the United States Department of Internet Security and Law Enforcement. Net Force.

Chaput's eyebrows went up. This could be no coincidence. Surely not, given his reasons for being in Paris.

He stood outside his vehicle on the sidewalk and tucked his chin down into the collar of his topcoat. The avenue was dead, the night unseasonably cold. He had ended his last conversation with the director using words chillier than the air around him, frustrated by her refusal to honor his agency's request for transfer of a wanted global fugitive to the European Union. Their standoff over the extradition of Kali Alcazar had dragged on for many exasperating months, and he had testily reminded her that an Interpol red notice was still in effect on behalf of twenty-four member countries with ongoing investigations against the hacker. The United States, he had argued, was harboring a global criminal and putting its interests in conflict with the security of its allies. But Morse had continued to stonewall, insulting him with a stinging challenge to Interpol's moral authority—and, by implication, his own. It had taken all his professional poise to keep from hanging up on her.

Chaput decided to play her message before walking on to the hotel. Morse would know it was nearly midnight in France and surely must have had an important reason for calling. And he was convinced Scholl wasn't leaving his room.

He tapped his watch again and listened in his earbuds. The twelve-second voice mail was terse even for her. She presumably had not wanted him reading anything into it.

"Hello, Renault. Carol Morse. I would like to share some developments regarding our mutual

*person of interest, and look forward to hearing
from you. Have a good evening."*

He stood there thinking a moment. His instincts
had not failed him. This *was* about the hacker. The
tables were turned, and the haughty American was
coming to him for help, knowing about the intelligence he'd gathered on Alcazar and her people.
But things had changed. More than she could possibly imagine.

Chaput inhaled the sharp night air. Like alchemy,
the sudden turn of events had transformed his re-
sentment for the director into a heady, exquisite
kind of satisfaction. Morse had been given the
chance to cooperate. Now it was too late. They
were on different playing fields. He had moved on
to stand with those who represented strength and
order. Who understood how to use their authority.

He lowered his watch from his eyes and turned
toward the corner. Hotel Aries's lights were just
up ahead. Let Morse and the Americans stew. He
was about to leave a very different sort of message.

6

The signal flares were years past their expiration date. Kali had picked them up at an army surplus shop, the same place she'd gone that first day in Bucharest. The day she and Carmody had learned of the attack on New York. She had gone back there many times while loosely in his custody at Janus.

She paid a few dollars for the carton. Pains Wessex Mk 7s—red, compact, handheld marine distress flares. The shopkeeper had looked bemused. Sitting on his shelf for years, the box was crumpled and buckled in and dusty. *Only you, my dear.* By then he had become familiar, even friendly with her, and warned that they had no modern safeguards. They didn't telescope to extend away from the body. They had no delay. They used chemicals that burned hot.

They were exactly what she wanted. The box had been dry. The twenty flares inside untouched. The incendiaries wouldn't have deteriorated.

Play a little game.

Ready with the flare from her hip bag, Kali waited in the passage now, her back to the rock wall, standing a yard or so north of where it bulged slightly outward. She had pulled and rotated and clicked the tube of the flare into place. Her right hand was wrapped around its grip.

Kali listened. She had switched off her headlamp to avoid giving herself away, leaving her in solid darkness. Leaving her blind. From what she knew of the Blood Lightning, they would have no such disadvantage. But she could hear their feet on the gravel and sand. She could hear them coming and knew where they were coming from. And she knew they couldn't hear her. As long as she didn't move. That was her advantage over them.

She listened, her ears attuned to every sound. Her hearing seemed sharper than normal, as if her senses had reprioritized themselves to compensate for the blackness around her. She didn't know how many of them were coming. More than two. But probably not too many more. She could measure their progress by the sound of their footsteps. They were very close and coming on very fast.

She took a silent breath. Another. They had almost reached the bulge in the wall. She thought they were five or ten yards south of her.

Closer, closer...

Kali exhaled and stepped away from the side of

the passage, facing south, holding the stick straight out and level with her waist.

There were three of them up ahead in the passage. A woman and two men. One alongside her. One behind her. The one behind, thin and towering above the others. They were all wearing gas masks and carrying guns. The woman's with an enormous barrel, almost like a grenade launcher. The men's long and thin. Guns that didn't look like guns. The woman brought hers up in her fist, not quite taking aim. If Kali was right about it, she wouldn't need to be that accurate.

She slapped the bottom of the flare's grip hard with her left palm. The primer ignited instantly, no delay, her wrist kicking up from the release of pressurized gas as the cap shot off with a loud pop, and flames and sparks gushed from the metal tube, whooshing out, leaping from her hand, searingly hot, roaring into the darkness in front of her. Game on.

Reva swayed back on her heels to avoid the flame, the projectile launcher in her right hand, her left coming up to shield her eyes. She had seen a bright flash of red and felt heat scorch her face and then everything went white. It was as if she was looking straight into the sun. She was blinded, her modified eyes flooded with spectral input, her onboard spitting out defensive algorithms, racing to inhibit the waveband overload.

Kali moved in quickly. Her headlamp was back on, the flare stick in her hand blazing and sparking and dribbling out globs of molten sulfur and potassium nitrate. She couldn't give the woman a chance to trigger her weapon, and she lunged forward, slicing the flare down at her like a flaming sword.

The fire was hot enough to melt steel. Hot enough to burn in water and make the water boil. It seared through Reva's sleeve, instantly setting it ablaze. Her hand opened around the weapon, and Kali saw it drop from her fingers to the floor of the passage.

Reva didn't make a sound. Her sleeve was on fire, her skin sizzling and blistering underneath. Kali could *smell* the scorched leather and fabric and flesh, and yet nothing escaped the woman's lips, nothing at all. Her eyes locked on Kali's through the lenses of her gas mask and bored into them like needles, as deadly and savage as the long jet of flame leaping from the stick. And then she abruptly strode forward, drove straight into Kali, as if her right arm wasn't burning, as if the flare wasn't pouring out chemical fire. Her left hand came up under Kali's jaw and clamped around it like a vise.

It's the biotech. It can flood her brain with endorphins. Natural painkillers.

Kali strained to breathe, automatically bringing her left hand up and across to grab Reva's wrist. But she couldn't pry it loose. Reva's fingers kept pressing the hinges of her jaw, the heel of her palm jammed into her trachea, cutting off her airflow.

Back off. Don't try to take them on. Remember the play.

She hadn't forgotten. She took a sliding backstep, another, her heels scooping into the sand and leaving shallow trenches. She was keenly aware she needed to keep her balance. If she stumbled and fell to the ground and the woman got on top of her, she wouldn't stand a chance.

She continued scuffling backward. The woman had moved in close and forced her right arm sideways with her upper body, pushing until the flare was perpendicular to Kali's torso, its red-hot discharge shooting straight out toward the tunnel wall. The two men remained a couple of paces behind, Kali's flare and headlamp revealing them to her eyes in crazy, scattered puzzle pieces of light and shadow. They held their weapons in two-handed grips but would be unable to fire with anything close to accuracy at this close range.

Back, back, deliberately giving ground. Remembering the play, yielding with a supreme effort of will. The woman tightened her grip on her jaw, bending her head back toward her shoulders, pushing her tongue up against her palate so her teeth bit into it and the taste of blood filled her mouth. Back, back, back. She knew the bulge in the passage wall was behind her on her right. Just a few more feet. She knew the recess would be about ten feet farther down on her left, and she knew *they* probably didn't know it. It was her primary edge over them. That and knowing they wanted her alive, needed her to lead them to Lucien. But she was running out of time.

Kali gripped the flare, thinking it would probably burn for a total of thirty seconds, thinking she must have already used up twenty of them. She needed to get back as far as the recess before its pyrotechnic chemicals were spent.

Back. Back. Back. All four of them packed together in the passage's constrictive quarters, the three *Krovavaya Molniya* pushing forward, Kali retreating, a step at a time, like a strange and ungainly superorganism moving in a single direction even while at violent odds with itself, simultaneously bound and torn by impossible internal stresses.

And then Kali felt the swell of the wall come up against her right shoulder blade, a realization almost shocking in its enormity. The bend was inches behind her, which meant the recess was only another foot or two farther down the passage. Another few steps and she was there.

The woman must have sensed something as they rounded the bend. Kali saw it leap into her eyes, saw it through her face shield, an acute wariness, like an animal picking up on some subtle and subliminal cue of a hidden threat, smelling danger in the air. Reva suddenly thrust her left hand out to grab her right forearm, trying to wrestle the flare out of her grasp, but at that point she was too late. Kali swept it upward, straight up over her head on the right, then swung it smoothly and diagonally down to the left. The flame slashed across Reva's gas mask, across her head, roaring, spewing, smoking, spitting sparks and glowing beads of fuel into her face. She recoiled, letting go of Kali's throat, swaying back on her feet, staggering into the men behind her.

Kali made her move. Dropping the nearly exhausted flare into the sand, she took another two or three steps backward and groped for the wall with her right hand, moving her hand over the wall until she *couldn't* feel it, then flicking a hurried glance over her shoulder to confirm she had come to the recess.

It was right behind her. Right there. She saw the lever projecting from inside and took another half step back. She reached her right hand out to take hold of the lever and shot her left hand across her body to grab it with that one as well. Then she hauled it down hard, both hands, her feet planted apart, using her legs, using every bit of her strength.

The rest unwound in a kind of gluey slow motion. There was a loud creak. Then a louder grating noise. Kali looked into the recess and saw the pulley mechanisms overhead come to life. The huge wheel blocks rotating in sequence. The cable spooling over their grooves. Up one way, down another. Haltingly, then freely. Slowly, then faster, until all the blocks were spinning in organized sequence. The vertical pull of the cable lifted one end of the rail, tilting it forward like a seesaw. Then the counterweight atop the rail started to roll downward on its iron casters, rattling and clanking, rapidly gaining momentum as it reached the bottom and then dropped off the rock shelf. It momentarily hung there in the air, suspended by the length of cable connecting it to the ceiling hatch's iron frame, the frame bulging outward, spiderweb cracks spreading through the masonry in which it was seated, particles of crumbled rock spilling down into the recess.

Water splashed Kali's boot. She glanced up at the ceiling and saw droplets dripping from the loosened frame. They quickly grew larger and heavier, merging, flowing together, glistening in the brightness of her headlamp. They bent, twisted, shuddered and danced on the ceiling as water began spraying from all four sides in pressurized jets. She needed a single moment—it seemed both endlessly long and fractional—to register a gurgling, percolating noise, primeval and menacing and many times louder than the rumble of the Métro trains. Then the dangling counterweight plunged straight down to the floor of the recess, the cables going perfectly taut, bringing the hatch and its frame along with it, tearing them straight down out of the solid rock as the counterweight hit the floor with a heavy thud, and the canal came gushing down through the breach in a deafening torrent, gallon upon gallon spouting down into the passage.

All this took perhaps three seconds. Then Kali saw the red laser dot on her belly and glanced up the passage at the Russians. The woman was backed against the wall in a compressed squat, almost balled up there, her gas mask torn off, her hands on her neck. She must have been severely burned where the fire had slashed across it. No release of endorphins could have fully blunted the pain. The men were coming up the passage, splashing toward her through the deluge from above, the big one with his long-barreled tranquilizer gun upraised, its sight trained on her through the uncontrolled rush of water flooding the tunnel.

She spun around to break for the side tunnel behind her, knowing its upward grade was no coincidence: Napoleon *le Général Entrepreneur* would not have set a trap for his enemies without laying out an escape route for his troops.

The injector dart struck her under her right shoulder blade. She felt the hard slap of its impact as its needle entered her skin and the plunger released and shot the contents of the syringe into her. The second dart struck the back of her left thigh, an inch or two above the knee. A second slap. She had already launched herself down the flooding passage, gone a step or two toward the opening of the side tunnel, water rising around her ankles, when her legs went limp and folded underneath her.

Her vision blurred. She sank to her knees in the icy water and tried to stand up.

Then the darkness thickened around her and pulled her down instead as she fell face first into the rising flood.

It began shortly after midnight just north of the public gardens and the Passerelle des Douanes footbridge, on a wide stretch of the Canal Saint-Martin bordered by Quai de Valmy on the right bank, and Quai de Jemmapes on the left.

There were ripples on the surface that had nothing to do with the breeze. In the murky water below, somnolent carp and rainbow trout felt a sudden downward pull. The bottom mud was suddenly swirling around them in an unsettled cloud.

Startled into nervous alertness, their piscine brains signaling danger, they fled beating their fins, the water where they had hung motionless whipped into a funnel, spiraling down through a trap door that had crashed open for the first time in the canal's three-hundred-year history.

The canal was draining. On the surface, midway

between its banks, it swirled and bubbled as if at a medium simmer.

Gradually the watercraft lining the embankments began to rock and sway. First, the middle boat in a trio of red-hulled lightweight fiberglass twelve-footers moored upstream of the collapsed hatchway on the Quai de Valmy. A swirl of current near its stern pitched it up and down and side to side. As the water's angular velocity accelerated and its rate of escape increased, its surface grew more visibly agitated—and so did the stern's rocking motion. It swung back and forth in broader and broader arcs, finally bumping against the boat tied up on its left, then against the one on the right, then left, right, left, right, and left at a quickening tempo, *clack, clack, clack, clack, clack, clack.*

The canal continued to drain. Ripples spread out in circles above the collapsed hatch. The clatter grew louder as more quayside vessels began to roll, pitch and yaw: flat cruise boats with rows of empty seats, pontoon boats, houseboats, sailboats, mailboats, small catamarans and yachts. Soon the clacking had spread as far downstream as the basin at Port de l'Arsenal, the anchored pleasure boats there banging together in the marina where the Saint-Martin fed into the river Seine.

On a busy midweek afternoon or warm summer evening, hundreds of pedestrians might have turned toward the water with heightened curiosity. Tonight only a few heard what sounded like a busy troop of castanet players along its banks.

"Let's look down by the canal," said one young

woman, snuggled with her boyfriend on a park bench overlooking the lock.

"Let's not," the young man whispered, his hand climbing up her inner thigh.

He won the night, and they didn't look.

Glaskov was diving through a wide underwater channel south of the Ninth arrondissement when the turbulence struck. The current swept in from behind, strong and swift, shoving him forward through the passage.

He glanced at the depth gauge on his wrist. He was currently at a twenty-foot submersion, and there had been three or four feet of clearance between the surface and the passage roof when he swam into it. If he could get his head up above water into that space, he would be able to place one of the four remaining communications relay modules—his breadcrumbs—for the strike teams. The problem was the powerful current. He doubted he could reach the surface swimming against it.

He instead decided to use it like a tail wind, going *with* it, trying to steady himself and keep from getting disoriented or tossed against the tunnel walls.

The channel was flooding, he thought. That was the only explanation. He could not know how long the flood would last without knowing its cause. And without knowing either, he couldn't speculate on his ability to ride it out.

He swam forward, his arms down against his sides, his legs straight out behind him. Sediment spooled up from the channel bottom, squashing back the beams of his helmet lamps. Ahead and on his left, almost completely obscured in the churning clouds of sand, was what appeared to be a narrow, cavelike opening. He was thinking he might be able to find shelter there.

Glaskov shot forward, the current nearly thrusting him past the opening, but he saw a jut of rock above it and managed to grab hold, hanging on long enough to squirt through.

Once inside he kicked out with his fins and looked around in the glow of his lamps. He realized he was not in a cave at all but had entered a side passage threading off for some distance ahead. It was tighter than the one he'd quit—much tighter—its walls less than arm's length from him on both sides. But the current was half as strong as before.

Which left him only half-relieved. Something very unusual was happening in the catacombs. An upward glance revealed that this passage was also flooded to the roof. Though tamed, the current hadn't altogether abated. Whatever had generated it was pushing an enormous amount of water deep into the honeycomb of submerged channels. Which left Glaskov with no headroom at all, and not even a small space above the surface where he could leave a wireless node.

But he reminded himself that wasn't altogether necessary. The ones he'd already dropped were probably enough to allow for unimpeded radio communications between the Blood Lightning neurocomputers. The rest were insurance, giving his mesh network added range and providing backup if one or more of the other transceivers failed.

As for his own status, he had nothing to worry about overall. His onboard was temporarily offline but functional. He still had his sonar, which meant he could fix his bearings, navigate, and detect and track potential threats and targets. And his oxygen supply wasn't an immediate concern. There was roughly an hour's worth in his main scuba tank, along with his two-hundred-bar reserve cylinder. For an experienced diver, that was an adequate supply. He could control his breathing and stay underwater for quite a while.

Glaskov checked his retinal display and swam on, the current boosting him along, bubbles stringing out into the darkness from his regulator. The channel wormed north a short distance up ahead, and he considered that a strong positive. North was the direction Outlier would eventually take, and north would bring him to the default position. Despite the baffling water influx, he'd made steady progress. When the time came to hook up with the others, he would be as ready for her as the rest of them.

7

Nineteenth arrondissement, Paris

Franz Scholl was picking indifferently at a *pain au chocolat* in his hotel room when he heard a knock at his door.

He glanced at the clock and raised an eyebrow. Half past midnight. Who could it be at this hour? He rose from the desk where he'd placed his snack on an outspread napkin and went to look out the peephole. Standing in the hallway was a man of about fifty in a charcoal topcoat and black gloves, with a small leather sling bag over his shoulder. Scholl noticed his thick, gray-flecked chevron mustache and thought he looked oddly familiar. But he couldn't place him.

He opened the door a crack. "Yes?"

The man held out a slim bifold wallet, displaying a light blue Interpol ID card. "Renault Chaput, Cybercrime Operations," he said. "I know it's late, Monsieur Scholl. May we speak privately about an urgent matter?"

Scholl peered out at him. *Chaput.* Of course. He suddenly knew why he'd recognized the man. He was the investigator from the Gunther Koenig affair. The one who'd followed him to the Perlacher Forst cemetery almost a full year ago, and would later be honored for solving a crime he hadn't even known about. Scholl never actually saw him that night at the graveside. But he had seen his preening image all over the news.

"Have you checked the time?"

"No games, sir. I think you have an inkling of what brings me. We need to discuss Kali Alcazar— *Outlier*—alone. For your sake and hers."

Scholl stood at the door another moment, then exhaled and widened it. Chaput stepped in and looked around the little room.

"Was there no other hotel in Paris with an open booking?" he said. "Or does your technology-refurbishment business leave no margin for luxury?"

"I'm sure you didn't show up just to school me in discourtesy." Scholl had shut the door but kept his hand around the knob. "Let's hear what this visit is about."

"I think I told you."

"No. You mentioned a name. That's all."

Chaput smiled, the separate halves of his mustache pulling apart over his upper lip. Scholl thought it made him look like a catfish.

"Outlier is the most wanted hacker on the planet. Four days ago, she slipped custody in the United States."

"And what does this person have to do with me?"

"Sir, we agreed not to play games," Chaput said. "I've tracked her for years. Her family and associates. It's all in my files. Who you are. What you do when you aren't fiddling with retired computers and junk software."

"Indeed?" Scholl said.

"Indeed." Chaput paused. "Shall I tell you what I know of the White Rose? It's free information, Tinkerer. No extra service charge."

Scholl didn't answer.

Chaput looked at him. "The secret society was founded by Hans and Sophie Scholl…your late cousins once removed. You are one of its core members. As is Alcazar. And her parents and grandmother before her. I have all the names, including Lucien Navarro's. Your movement professes to champion freedom and personal liberty. The formation of a new cyber nation free of physical borders, with Navarro as its torch bearer. But in reality you are anarchists. Outlaws whose agenda is to disrupt society. In the case of the Alcazars of Guernica, using terror and murder."

"That's quite a mouthful of wild conspiracy theories."

"No." Chaput was shaking head. "It's a small bite of the truth."

Scholl looked at him and said, "What is your purpose in coming here?"

"Navarro is involved in something that goes well over his head. Several weeks ago, he vanished from his home on Rue Edgar-Poe. I know he is hiding from some dangerous people, possibly state actors. I'm equally sure he is still in Paris. And that Kali Alcazar has come to join him. I need to find both of them. Ultimately for their own good, though I admit to having higher priorities."

"And you've decided I know where they are."

"You traveled from Munich three days ago. Lufthansa flight 2020. Nonstop. It departed at six forty-five and landed at Orly ninety minutes later. You checked into this hotel within the hour."

"So you've tagged me on a watch list."

"I use all the tools at my disposal." Chaput nodded toward the desk. "You picked up that half-stale chocolate pastry at a *boulangerie* around the corner. It was ten minutes past nine this morning. You should have waited an hour for the fresh batch. Or does your affinity for yesterday's creations extend to the food you eat?"

Scholl stuffed his hands into the pockets of his bathrobe. "On whose authority do you come here?"

"I presented my ID at the door."

"Interpol requires cooperation from the local police. I see no *flics* at your side."

Chaput was quiet for a long moment. Then he shrugged and reached under his topcoat.

"Wait, I'll show you," he said. An instant later his gloved hand reappeared holding a black Beretta pistol. A silencer was attached to the muzzle. "I'm

here on my personal authority, Tinkerer. I hope
that satisfies you."

Scholl's eyes went from the gun to his face.
"What is this craziness?"

"Kali Alcazar is a threat to all humanity. A vi-
cious criminal like her parents. Be smart and tell
me where she is."

"You really are out of your mind," Scholl said.

"Tell me." Chaput wobbled the gun. "You have
one last chance to cooperate voluntarily."

Scholl straightened. "I have nothing to say. You
can't coerce information from me. If anyone were
to know you were trying, you would be relieved of
your job in disgrace."

Chaput shrugged.

"No one will know," he said and shot him twice
in the chest.

Scholl's eyes widened with surprise, then bulged
out in agony. He looked down at himself with a
mixture of horror and disbelief, saw the middle of
his robe wadded into a hole in his chest, then saw
the blood pooling around the wound. A second later
it came brewing from his lungs, flushed his mouth
and spilled over his chin, pouring in rivulets down
both sides of his neck. He coughed up the thick red
fluid, sagged onto his knees and fell down dead to
the carpet, landing sprawled on his back.

Chaput slid his gun back into its holster. He had
noticed Scholl's cell phone charging on the desk
and turned to pull it off its cord, stepping gingerly
around the leaking corpse. He woke the phone, saw
that it was locked and knew he would have to hurry
to fool the biometrics.

He brought the phone over to Scholl and crouched near his head. Scholl had fallen so that it was turned sideways. Chaput took hold of it below the chin with one hand, angled it up and held the phone over it with the other so the wide-open eyes appeared to be looking at the camera lens. The phone had gone dark and he woke it again. This time it unlocked. Chaput tapped the screen to open the Settings menu, navigated to the autolock feature and reset its timer from One Minute to Never. Then he put the phone in his coat pocket.

He stood up and went to the luggage nook. Scholl had traveled with a single wheeled carry-on bag. His jacket hung on a hook, and his laptop and wallet were on the dressing table. The computer's empty sleeve was beside them.

Chaput put the laptop in the sleeve, zipped it and tucked it under his arm. The wallet went into his pocket. That finished what he needed to do except for one thing.

He returned to the body, knelt and opened his sling bag. Inside was the single dried white rose he'd brought from Lyon.

Chaput had grown the rose in his home garden, hung it upside down in his attic to preserve it, then clipped the stem so it was only three inches long. It had dried with only the slightest discoloration and shriveling at the edges of the petals.

He readjusted Scholl's head a bit so he appeared to be staring straight up at the ceiling. Then he hooked his thumb into the mouth to open it, slid the rose stem between his teeth and stood up. Finally he took out his own phone and snapped a photo—a close-up.

Face with White Rose, he thought. By Chaput.

He put away the phone and left the room, knowing he had turned a corner, almost surprised by how little he felt about it. There was no sense of anxiety or upheaval. Nothing monumental. It all felt very...if not preordained, he thought, then part of a natural transition.

Chaput had slid from one phase of his life into a new one. That was the sum of it. If anything, he was really quite pleased.

Lanai, Hawaiian Islands

Leland Sinclair came inside early for his one-o'clock teleconference, taking the natural sandstone steps and walkway down from the upper level of his terraced habitat. He'd seen no sign of Goldie through the foliage, which was to be expected. Goldie had been very active yesterday and would sleep for a good long while. But the birds were calm and musical, and the island breeze fresh and warm, and that was exactly the cushion Sinclair needed before talking to Clyde.

He wasn't looking forward to it this afternoon. Not that he ever did.

He entered his spacious media room through its side door, removed his black-framed Wayfarers and went to the coffee table, where Gabrielle had his fruit juice ready. He picked up the frosty glass, holding it well away from his clothes: the last thing he wanted was to get a stray droplet on his shirt. After taking a careful sip, he left the beverage and sunglasses on the table, stepped in front of the large virtual mirror on his north wall and quickly but thoroughly checked himself out.

Today he was wearing a pastel blue blazer over an eggshell shirt, navy chinos and tan leather slip-ons with no socks. Sinclair's wide cheeks and rounded chin made him look two decades younger than his actual age of fifty-three, and he'd recently grown out the sides of his hair so it brushed the tops of his ears, thinking it softened his appearance for the television cameras. The idea was to project a mixture of smart, American, boy-next-door trustworthiness and dependable consistency. He saved his friskier moments for the Cyber, where he would occasionally cut loose with one of his anonymous avatars and sport NFT designer clothes. All kinds for all kinds of identities.

But right now he was preparing for Clyde Wallace Wendt. Sinclair adjusted his blazer and shirt collar and fluffed his hair with his fingers, knowing its thickness irritated the old man. After looking himself over another second, he went to the couch and had the AI slide the wall panel back from his massive flat-screen. Then he closed his eyes and inhaled and opened them and exhaled.

Wendt's wrinkled face appeared precisely on time.

"Hey, there's my little bastard!" he said. "What's up, Lee? You haven't checked in all week."

"It's been a little hectic around here. Oahu was almost nuked. Or don't you pay attention to the news?"

"Not since Cronkite left." The folds of flesh

around Wendt's mouth withdrew like pleated stage curtains, exposing a solid band of veneered front teeth. "Fuck Oahu. I'm dead serious. It's a good hundred miles from you. A person has to mind his own garden. See to it that nobody shits the lawn and pisses on his doorstep."

Sinclair was quiet. Though Wendt insisted he was healthy, his appearance had rapidly declined in recent months, like time's accountants had audited his books for a lifetime of excess and he'd simply given in to their long list of penalties. Though never really handsome, he had once been tall and well-groomed, with an imposing, clean-cut appearance and the sort of sociable personality that went down well with an ice-cold beer and peanuts at a hotel bar. He seemed literally faded, his skin gone a grayish color, his hair rapidly thinned to stringy wisps and arranged in a comb-over that did nothing to hide the flat brownish age spots on his scalp. Only the perfect white teeth in his wrinkled mouth seemed everlasting and indestructible.

A hell-raiser gone to hell.

"Let's get to why you wanted to talk," Sinclair said. "You made it sound urgent."

Wendt nodded. "I won't waste precious time, Lee. We are major obligors. You know that. And there are some whispers in the air that've made our oblig*ees* very concerned. So much that they've asked me to arrange a virtual meeting with you."

"What are you talking about?"

"I think you know."

"Don't be coy. Let's hear it."

"The name Braithwaite Global ring a bell? And

while you're at it, how about Unit 21955 of the Russian Main Intelligence Directorate?"

Sinclair's cheeks prickled with heat. He hadn't expected this.

"Of course I've heard of Braithwaite. It's an Aussie security outfit. Like Blackwater back in the day. If you're a business executive, it's made a pitch to you."

Another flash of white teeth.

"And that Russian unit?"

"What would I know about them?"

Wendt laughed. It sounded like a dry cough.

"Buddy, I'm not one to mix into your affairs," he said. "I don't use email, and all the online and cryptocurrency shit's frankly over my head. But I do know plenty about our Moscow friends."

"If you say so. But what's it all have to do with me?"

"Braithwaite is what. The Russians aren't happy about him poaching their resources. And they don't want him or his freelance operatives doing anything their government hasn't specifically approved. Simply put, they want control."

Sinclair reached for his fruit beverage and sipped.

"I don't give a damn what they want," he said after a moment. "Maybe you really *don't* watch the news. If you did, you'd know the White House suspects them of launching the drone submarine that was intercepted off Pearl Harbor. And being responsible for a slaughter at that cable landing station up the coast. And behind whatever happened to that CloudCable ship in the Pacific. I invested two hundred *million* in the fiber it was laying and maintaining. A forty-percent share. Talk about shitting on my doorstep. Those undersea cables are the roads at the heart of Olympia's metaverse push. And more."

Wendt's hand came up in the screen. His fingers were long and spidery—too long in proportion to his palm.

"Stop right there," he said. "You don't want to sound like a fool."

"Better than a lackey. I control those roads. Not Russia or any other crumbling empire. I'm building a bigger and more powerful nation. One with no geographic boundaries."

"Your Cyber Nation."

"Yes."

Wendt sighed. "It occurs to me you inherited your mother's stubbornness."

"You knew nothing about my mother."

"Well, I dipped my pecker into her enough times that one day it came out with you hanging on," Wendt said. "And you're still hanging from it. Like it or not."

Sinclair looked at Wendt's shriveled face on the screen and said nothing.

"Don't mind me rattling some old bones," Wendt said. "When I opened my pet shop all those years ago, before the imports and exports, I'd put a baby snapping turtle inside a bottle. The kind with thick glass and a wide round mouth, like you'd see in a pharmacy. It was a gimmick for the customers. I would keep that turtle on the front counter and let them feed him goldfish and crickets and little pieces of chicken or meat so he would grow real fast. Grow till he was too big to escape." He held his hand out and slowly wriggled his fingers at the screen. "The bigger he got, the nastier, and I used to do shit like this just to get him worked up. But he only ever damaged himself. Bastard was trapped and too stupid to know it. Couldn't do anything but snap at the glass. Sometimes he'd come at you so hard, he'd bash his stupid head against it till he killed himself. But there was always another dumb, nasty bastard to replace him."

"You've told me this before," Sinclair said. "Is there some reason I'm hearing it again today?"

Wendt shrugged his shoulders.

"I stuck with that dead-end shop for a half a decade. Went through more snappies than I can count, all the while knowing there was a better way. But I needed capital to escape my own bottle. Only thing was, I couldn't go to the bank or credit union for a loan. Since that better way was considered illegal."

"So you decided to work around it."

"Yup. All those cheap conventions I hit weren't just about checking out the exotic animals and whores. It was getting to know the right people."

Sinclair sat there a minute, thinking. "What do you want, Clyde?" he said.

Wendt hacked out more laughter.

"The question wasn't meant to be funny," Sinclair said. "What do you want?"

"Buddy, it's about need, not want. When I needed a loan to start my little empire, the Leonides family were the only ones to put up the capital. And when you needed under-the-table funds to bail out your online supermarket, they did the same for you. Quietly, at my urging." He paused.

"I'm no genius. But I'm smart enough to know the world is run by money. By finance. When it comes to that, Bank Leonides is prime rib, and everyone else is peas and carrots. But their generosity's conditional. Apparently they have some irons in the fire with Russia, and they would like a word with you about those hit squads in Paris. Would like to make sure you aren't overstepping. Which leaves you with two choices. You can snap at the glass and hurt yourself, or you can politely hear what they have to say. I wouldn't bitch, though. Quintessa Leonides is quite the eyeful. The buzz is she's a wild thing too. If I were a few years younger, I'd look into it myself."

Sinclair stared at the screen and said nothing.

"Leland? You with me?"

He exhaled.

"All right," said. "I'll take the meeting. But not on her terms."

"Then, how?"

"I'll figure it out," Sinclair said.

New York City

"Hello?"

"Director Morse. This is Renault Chaput. Interpol."

She glanced at her watch and did the math, one foot in her apartment's doorway. Years of overseas calls made it instantaneous. *Seven thirty at night, New York, one thirty in the morning, Paris.*

"Is this an inconvenient time?" he asked. "I thought it best to return your call as soon as possible."

"It's fine. I'm only surprised because it's so late

at your end." Morse went through the foyer to the dining area. "One minute, please. I've just come home from an appointment." She sat down without taking off her jacket. "Okay, I'm here. Thanks for the quick callback."

"Your tone seemed very urgent."

"Fair characterization," Morse said. "Officer Chaput, I've decided to send a group of my people to Europe. The Outlier case, of course. They'll be working principally with the Directorate General into the foreseeable future. But in view of your longtime involvement, I thought you should know in advance."

"I appreciate the courtesy," he said. "Respectfully, may I ask what role you envision for this group?"

"Nothing's set in stone. I don't think you've interacted with Leo Harris. Our chief of investigations. He's currently on leave but will be assembling the liaison team on his return. I'll write an introductory email tonight, and you'll be among its recipients."

"Director, may I be blunt?"

"Please."

"I would prefer to avoid a repeat of Munich, when Outlier escaped while we were tripping over our own feet. It was a classic example of the too-many-cooks syndrome."

"I would strongly differ with that characterization. But in any event, I was CIA back then. So was the team I oversaw. Whoever Leo sends will be operating under an altogether different set of rules and procedures."

Chaput paused for a hair of a second.

"Again, in frankness, I question the necessity. This affair already involves many European investigative and law-enforcement organizations with whom Interpol maintains close working relationships. Kali Alcazar is either number one or two on the list of the world's most wanted cyber criminals. The other being her consort, the Wolf."

"Former consort."

"Be that as it may. We'd previously discussed our red notice."

"Yes."

"Two dozen countries joined in filing for it—"

"And mine refrained. I understand. As I explained before, the United States isn't bound to be party to that or any other filing with Interpol. While we're appreciative of your role in facilitating international cooperation, we chose an independent course. Which, I'll remind you, previously resulted in Outlier's apprehension."

"It's true she was in your hands. No longer, alas. I'm confident of her eventual recapture, but when it happens, she'll be detained in Scheveningen at the Hague, where an international tribunal will sort out the legal claims to her detainment and prosecution. In the future, no single government will determine the time and place Alcazar stands trial."

Morse thought a moment. In their last conversation Chaput had accused America of playing the Lone Ranger and riding in with its white horse. Credit him for something that approached tactfulness. This time.

"Does this august panel include judges from

Russia? China? Iran?" she said. "Those states all have Interpol membership."

"They are active members of the United Nations. That entitles them to full and unprejudiced representation at the World Court."

Morse got up and turned toward the kitchen. She needed some soft light, music and chamomile tea to relax her. It was a habit she'd acquired from POTUS, who insisted Morse's usual seven cups of black coffee a day were gratuitous and unhealthy.

"Officer Chaput, I appreciate your candor. But now I'm going to be equally up-front," she said. "Interpol red notices were once issued mainly against perpetrators of genocide and other execrable crimes against humanity. I believe there were twelve hundred in circulation twenty-five years ago. Now there are *seventy thousand*, a full third of which were filed by the oppressive Moscow regime. In my government's view, it's for a simple reason. They're routinely abused by autocrats whose goal is to harass and jail their political opponents. Therefore, we can't and don't put too much weight on them."

"Director—"

"I understand your concern. And I reiterate that the team your agency will be hosting is Net Force. Not CIA. We're a different animal."

"*Will be?* So this is a fait accompli?"

Morse held her kettle under the tap. "At nine tomorrow morning, GMT, our officials in Lyon will begin arranging for authorizations. It shouldn't be a very long process."

A silence. "Director, why did you bother calling me tonight?"

"A gesture of respect," Morse said. She reached for the honey, decided it might be wise to add a spoonful to the conversation. "To an estimable colleague."

Chaput said nothing. She wondered if he'd hung up. Then she heard him breathe.

"As always, I recognize your authority," he said. "Rest assured I will do nothing to hinder your people's efforts."

Which was very different from offering to help them.

"Have a good evening, Officer Chaput," Morse said. "And thanks again for the callback."

She set the water on the stove to boil and took out her earbud and dropped it into its tray.

Jerk, she thought.

Lanai

Sinclair was still on his sofa staring at the display twenty minutes after Wendt had vanished from it. On the screen now was a large-scale interactive map of the United States, with all five hundred facilities in Olympia's order-distribution network marked with colored circles. Blue circles for the warehouses, red ones for the delivery centers.

Sinclair had given the map a perfunctory scan before settling his eye on the new delivery center in an east Georgia town called Gurveston, in Burke County. His choice would be fairly random, and this was one among dozens of suitable candidates.

"Daphne, show me the demographics," he said to his AI. "Town and county."

Two windows instantly opened on the upper right-hand corner of the screen. What he saw confirmed his general recollection. The county's total population was under two hundred thousand, five thousand of whom lived in Gurveston near the South Carolina border. Burke's median household income was barely above the United States poverty threshold. About twenty-five percent of them fell below the line. In Gurveston the percentage of poor rose to almost thirty percent of the population.

Sinclair was aware those statistics had been compiled after the last national census, which made them almost four years out of date. Wage and employment numbers had picked up tremendously throughout the county, particularly in Gurveston. The opening of Olympia's shipping facility had created thousands of jobs and generated rapid economic growth. People's standard of living was getting better there.

He stared at the map, his hands clenched together on his knees. He'd known talking to Wendt would raise his tension level—it always did—and he'd been hopeful his walk before their videoconference would keep it somewhat manageable. But the birds weren't enough, and he'd been left with a painful acid burn. He needed to get it out before it ate a hole in his stomach.

"Daphne," he said, "try Ben Quinn on the phone again."

"One moment."

He listened to the rings through his speakers. Then heard him pick up.

"Quinn, it's about time. I called fifteen minutes ago."

"Sorry. I'm at a restaurant ordering dinner for the whole table. My wife's parents are here through Easter."

"You must be enjoying their company."

"Always," Quinn said in a sarcastic tone.

Sinclair pictured him turning his head away from them.

"All right, pay attention," he said. "We're closing the Gurnstown, Georgia, warehouse. Effective immediately."

"What? Are you serious? *Why?*"

"I've decided to consolidate our area resources."

"Leland, I'm not sure I understand. Gurnstown's one of our busiest regional shipping facilities. It's central to our Southern expansion—"

"You understand perfectly. I want it shut down. We can shift its operations over to South Carolina."

"The Bedard facility's old, half the size and a hundred miles to the west. I don't mean to cite chapter and verse, but we just finished construction at Gurnstown in December. Four months ago. There are almost three thousand full-time and part-time employees. Merchandise sorters, delivery drivers—"

"They'll be cut today. Every last one."

"Leland, I think we need to consult with Jim Beck in Logistics."

"No."

"We were awarded over a hundred million dollars in tax subsidies for choosing Gurnstown as our new location. The local government paid the bulk of the facility's construction costs."

"We owe them nothing. Those incentives are in the books. We complied with the conditions of the deal, and they can't legally penalize us. Or am I not correct?"

"You're correct, of course. But it would send a terrible message. The press would be all over us. Those envious hyenas are always lying in wait. We'd be accused of a subsidy grab."

"Look, Ben, I don't like weakness. It makes me sick. Physically nauseous."

"My job is to be honest with you."

"Your job is to be a good soldier and carry out my policies. If that's too much for you, tell me and I'll give it to someone else. There are a lot of people waiting in line."

Quinn didn't answer for a long moment.

"All right," he said. "I won't get in the way of your decision."

"*Our* decision, Ben. That's how I do things. Share the work, share the credit. It builds esprit de corps. But are you sure you can handle the responsibility?"

"Tell me how you want this implemented."

"Attaboy," Sinclair said. "Here's how. Send the current shift workers home. No explanation. Once they leave the facility, I want the doors padlocked. And I want No Trespassing signs put up everywhere. Entrances, windows, parking areas, the entire premises. Tonight. So they're in plain sight of the employees when they show up for their regular nine o'clock shift. Is everything clear?"

"Yes," Quinn said. "Yes, it is."

"So we're even clearer, Ben, there's to be no advance notice of the layoffs. I'm serious. We don't want any leaks. I'll personally record the announcement on video. It'll be sent to them via email or SMS later tomorrow. Meanwhile, you're to have Human Resources quietly provide you with all the employee contact information. Got it?"

"Yes."

"I'm not hearing conviction in your voice. Are you with me, Ben?"

"I'm with you. If you say we're moving forward with it—"

"We're moving forward. Now, get back to your dinner. Dig in." Sinclair paused. "Oh, see here, before you do…are you still carrying on with that young legal assistant?"

Silence.

"Ben? Did you hear me? She's quite the piece of tail. Really gorgeous. And I love her name. Deidre, isn't it?"

Quinn's voice dropped. "I'm with my family."

"I know," Sinclair said. "I have to mention things when they strike me. Or I might forget. And I wanted to let you know that boffing Deidre right there at headquarters is a little cavalier. Considering our surveillance system has cameras everywhere."

Silence.

"Ben?"

"Yes."

"Did you hear what I said? About Deidre? And the cameras?"

"Yes."

"Good." Sinclair felt the tension slithering out of him. "See, it all comes down to one thing. I want loyalty. I *need* loyalty. Understood?"

"Yes."

"Then, we're fine," Sinclair said. "Now, enjoy your dinner. In fact, I want you to put it on the company tab. And please send my regards to Lisa and her parents."

"I'll do that, Leland. Thank you."

Sinclair ended the call and sat back. He was feeling better already. And looser. Definitely much looser. A happy pike is a dead minnow, he thought.

He turned to look through the glass wall of his habitat, humming softly under his breath.

8

April 25, 2024
Various Locales

The Paris Catacombs

Kali opened her eyes. Her vision was cloudy and her head felt light. She was woozy and nauseous and thirsty. Terribly thirsty.

She remembered the tunnel, and her three attackers, and the flood, and she had a sense that time had passed. She was somewhere dim but not totally dark. The air smelled earthy and stale. She was lying on her right side. Her legs pulled up, knees tucked in. A hard mattress underneath her. Her ribs and middle felt sore and bruised.

She rolled onto her back, saw a disembodied face hovering over her. There was a wide band of red across the eyes and forehead, a blue band across the mouth and chin. The colors softly radiant in the gloom. She shut her eyes and reopened them, as if trying to chase off a hallucination. But it didn't go anywhere.

Then dizziness swept over her, and she closed her eyes again and was out for another span of time. When she next came to, it was with a jerk. The face was still there above her.

She tried to sit up.

"Ne bougez pas!"

A male voice. Warning her to be still. She realized he was wearing face paint.

Kali ignored him and kept struggling to rise. The thirst was overwhelming. It was hard to swallow.

"He told you to keep your head down on the pad." Someone else now. A woman, on her right. "You should listen. I'd rather not put a bullet in it."

Kali flicked her eyes toward the voice. Her vision was improving, and she could see the woman ten or twelve feet away, close to a light source. Sitting on the higher of two stone steps, her body in near silhouette. She also wore face paint, ghost white on the left side. Kali couldn't see the right side at all.

She realized she was lying on the ground. Below the woman. *Keep your head down on the pad.* Not a mattress, then. A sleeping roll. The type used by campers.

She looked back up at the man.

"I need water," she said, a thin, rasping croak.

A moment passed. The painted face vanished into the shadows. Some strange orbital body passing out of the light. Then it reappeared, and he thrust a plastic water bottle into her hand.

"Here," he said. "Don't try anything stupid."

Kali sat up slowly and thumbed open the cap and sipped some cool water, coughing out most of it. Then took another sip and swallowed it down smoothly.

She lowered the bottle from her mouth. "Tell me where I am," she said. "Where you put my things."

He didn't answer.

"Tell me," she said. *"Dites-moi où je suis."*

His face hovered above her. She looked straight up into it for several long, silent seconds.

"You're beneath Rue Henri-Barbusse," he said finally. "Off the Boulevard Saint-Michel. About seven hundred meters…a half mile…from where we found you."

"And the things you took?"

"You ask a lot of questions."

"I want back what's mine."

He looked down at her, raised a hand in the gloom.

"Here's one item we took from your backpack," he said. "Where did you get it?"

She saw at once that he was holding Manning's *The Key of Libberty.* The copy from Lucien's collection.

"Where?"

She said nothing.

"Don't play with us," said the woman. She spoke French with a noticeable accent. "We aren't fucking around."

Kali turned to look at her. Some of the blurriness had cleared from her eyes.

The woman held a pistol in one hand and was resting it on her knees. Slung over her shoulder was a small semiautomatic rifle. The skin on the exposed half of her face was dark brown, and her scalp was completely shaved. She wore black overalls and combat boots.

Kali realized her wide stone perch was one of two steps leading up to a platform with a large grave marker atop it. She was sitting on a tomb, nestled in an alcove between masonry pillars. Flat LED panels on the wall and columns bathed the monument in a pale blue radiance.

The woman had noticed her attention. "There's a story to go with this place," she said. "Do you know the name Philibert Aspairt?"

Kali shook her head slightly.

"He is the *patron* of the catacombs. This is his tomb," the woman said. "He vanished one day during the Revolution. The year was 1793. His skeleton was found eleven years later, the key ring of the Val-de-Grâce military hospital hooked to his belt. That is what's certain." She rose to stand in front of the grave marker. "As for the rest…he was either a quarrier or a doorkeeper at the hospital. He may have come down here searching for bottles of Chartreuse stored by local monks, lost his way and died of a fall or starvation. Or possibly he was murdered and dumped out of sight by his killer. Some even believe Aspairt was the guilty party, and that he left his victim's corpse in this spot to throw off the *gendarmes*. None of it matters. We don't care who he was on the surface. We don't care what he did. He was here. He was one of us. And, in his obscurity, all of us."

"And why tell me this?"

"So you understand you're in *our* world." The

woman came down off the stairs, moving closer to her. "And because you owe us a debt. We could have easily left you to die."

"Where did you find me?"

"In the passage we call *la Route Sablonneuse.*"

This from the man, his painted face still hanging over her. Kali looked up at him.

"The Sandy Road," she said.

"You know the name?"

"I know it."

"It had flooded. You were halfway inside a branching tunnel, unconscious. There were two darts in you. Like syringes. They must have plied you full of tranquilizers. You were out for hours."

"The canal above was breached," the woman said. "The water was roaring down in a heavy fall. We heard it and came to investigate." She paused. "We assumed you were climbing into the tunnel to escape it before you passed out. The water in the main passage was chest high and rising. If we'd come any later, you would have drowned."

"Was I alone?"

"We saw no one else," the man said. "If you're talking about whoever shot you with those bloody darts, it's likely they were swept off into the Seine."

Kali was quiet for several seconds. She thought she knew who these people were. And she was going to need their cooperation.

"The book is from Oarsman's library," she said.

"Did you use it to access his stairs?"

"Yes."

The woman took another step closer. "Give us your name."

"That doesn't matter. You said so yourself."

A white-toothed smile split the band of blue across the man's mouth. "Very good," he said with a nod. "I'll be magnanimous. You can call us Jacques and Jill."

"And which are you?"

The smile grew larger.

"I want you to see something," he said.

Kali realized he was dressed all in black, like his companion. Wearing a loose hooded sweatshirt and neck gaiter, the hood raised over his head. He'd put the book down somewhere.

He nodded to the woman, and she came up beside him. A second later they pushed up their sleeves and displayed the underside of her forearms. Each had a small tattoo of a white rose above the wrist. Inked above it in red and blue script were the words:

Cyber liberté. Droits humains. La vie sans frontières.

Cyber liberty. Human rights. Life without borders.

"You're Lucien's people," Kali said.

"We stand with him, yes," Jacques said. "With Oarsman, the soul of Cyber Nation."

"Then, you know he's in danger."

Jill nodded. "There are teams of us. We were out scouting when we found you."

Kali looked at her.

"You've heard of the Blood Lightning?" she asked.

"There are rumors in the Space."

"These people are far more than rumors. They're very real operatives who've undergone extensive modding," Kali said. "Though they're of Russian origin, I'm not certain who sent them. Or how many might be down here."

"And who are *you*, that knows all this?"

"Lucien would have told you."

Jacques said, "Perhaps. But I want to hear it from your lips."

Kali looked at him. "I'm called Outlier on the dark web," she said. "Will that do?"

He was silent for a moment. Then he slowly nodded. "For now."

Kali glanced from one to the other.

"All right," she said. "I need you to return my bag. The map. All the rest."

"And then?" Jacques said.

"Then you're going to take me to Lucien," she said.

Jacques shouldered the sleeping roll as Jill collected and stored the portable LED lights in her pack. Then they led Kali from the burial chamber through a cramped corridor, Jacques in front with his headlamp beaming out into the darkness, Jill in the rear, Kali between them.

She had noticed Jacques's earpiece.

"Can you contact others down here?" she asked.

"Normally," he said without turning. "We use different linked systems. Data and voice."

"But?"

"We've disabled the system as a precaution."

She thought Lucien must have imposed the communications lockdown. It would leave his scattered groups of Cyber isolated, unable to interact or quickly respond to calls for help. But it also ensured no one could tap into their exchanges.

A necessary risk.

She followed him through the passage, shivering in her wet clothes. Within a few short yards its ceiling lowered so they had to stoop. Jacques led the way around a corner, took a few more steps, then raised his hand to gesture a halt. Kneeling in front of the wall, he wedged his fingers into the seams around a large, irregular stone and pulled. Its face pried away from the mortar easily, a false front made of an inch-thin slice of masonry. Set into the wall behind it, the opening to a hidden compartment.

He set the panel down and looked at her.

"You wanted your stuff," he said. "It's all here. Including your weapons."

She waited as he reached an arm into the compartment and extracted her duffel, her holstered Glock and her belt with the *manriki* still in its pouch, setting them down on the floor beside him.

"A long time ago, I knew somebody who could use one of those things," he said, nodding at the chain whip. "He would say it had a nasty habit of biting its master's hand."

She shrugged. "Then, he hadn't trained it well enough to bite his enemies."

Jacques smiled a little. Then he reached back into the compartment and brought out a hiking sock filled with a half dozen or so 9mm bullets.

"These were in your pocket," he said. "Do you always carry loose rounds with you?"

She took them from him without answering.

He shrugged and turned back to the compartment a third time, reaching deep inside, extracting a carefully rolled article of clothing.

"We keep some of our own supplies in here," he said, and handed it to her. "This should fit you."

She nodded. It was a black jumpsuit identical to Jill's.

He rose, walked a few steps up the passage and stopped to wait with his back turned. She stripped bare, her skin erupting into goosebumps in the cold. As she dressed, Jill silently took her soggy clothes, carried them toward the wall compartment in a bundle and knelt to push them inside.

Kali zipped up from the waist and slipped on her boots. They had remained relatively dry.

"Thank you," she said when Jill returned.

"For what?"

"I assume the clothes belong to you."

Jill stood there motionless in her split-face makeup. "You don't wear the ink. Not on your arm or anywhere."

Kali was silent.

"I'm proud of it. We all are."

"And?"

"You're supposed to be one of us."

Kali remained silent.

Jill nodded toward Jacques. "He's a trusting man," she said. "Where I'm from, trust is a dangerous liability."

Kali still said nothing.

"He's my chosen family. As are all in the White Rose," Jill said. "If you're enough of a fool to try and hurt them, I'll kill you."

Kali lifted her bag off the ground and shrugged into it.

"If that's why I came here, you'd be the greater fool to warn me," she said, and turned up the passage.

Reva coughed and gasped. Her body jolted. Her eyes rolled under their lids.

"Medlenno." Zoltan's deep voice. "Take it easy, Reva."

She blinked, blinked again and looked up at him. He was crouched alongside her in total darkness.

"What happened?" she asked. "Where are we?"

"We've been through this already. Try to remember."

She took quick stock of herself. She was cold. She was wet. She was on a dirt floor. Sitting up on a dirt floor. Leaning back against something hard and pebbly and uneven in the dark. Her arm was throbbing on the right side. Her face too. Her cheek especially.

She started raising a hand up to it. Zoltan grabbed her wrist to stop her.

"Don't touch it."

She looked at him. *Try to remember.*

"The passage," she said. "What did she do to me?"

Zoltan said nothing. She tried to pull her hand free of his wrist. He didn't let go.

"I said to leave it alone. It needs to be kept clean."

Reva stared at him another moment.

"How does it look?" she repeated.

"I don't know."

"You know. What did she do?"

Again he was silent. It was not comforting to her. But she slowly lowered her arm.

"Where are we?" she asked again.

"You really don't recall? Take a look around."

Reva stared at him a moment. Then she turned her head away, looked straight out into blackness with her enhanced vision, and saw the human skull in front of her roughly level with her face. It was bare and socketed, not a scrap of skin or muscle or hair left on the bone.

There was another against it on the right. Another on the left. And then another, and another, one beside the other, discolored and sooty, a long, even row of skulls.

She realized where Zoltan had brought her. Her mission preparation had been compressed but thorough. There were six million Parisian skeletons in the catacombs. The dead from three overflowing cemeteries brought in nightly processions for a hundred years, covered in black cloth as the wagons rolled through the streets. The ossuary sprawled for miles beneath the city.

"Where are we *exactly*?" she asked.

"A quarter mile west of the Sandy Road. The water was diverted down a side tunnel below the one we took from the train station. I think it was a drainage conduit. South of that the Road ran uphill and stayed dry. I found this place just off it and thought we could rest awhile."

Zoltan's summary was flat-toned and vaguely familiar. She thought he must have repeated it several times as she dipped in and out of consciousness. *Try to remember.*

She sat very still and breathed very slowly and let it all come back to her. She recalled the flare stick in Outlier's hand and then water crashing down from above, rushing into the passage. It had bowled Dominik off his feet and then pulled him under. She remembered the roar of it in her ears. Then grabbing onto something—a rock, a ledge?— and eventually managing to thrash toward higher ground. Zoltan had gotten to where he could swim and then wade out of the water, carrying her along with him. But she didn't know how he'd got hold of her. Or how he had kept their heads above the rising flood. She had no firsthand recollection of it.

"How is the pain?" he asked.

"I can take it."

"I gave you some RU-1205. There's more if you decide you can't."

She nodded. The kappa-opioid was superior to morphine, more efficiently inhibiting pain and convulsions without inducing a stupor. But she did not want another dose dulling her mind. She needed to be clearheaded and able to function.

She looked at the skulls. They seemed to gape at her from a platform of arm and leg bones like onlookers on a grotesque parade stand. Above them was another layer of humeri, tibiae and femura. Then another row of skulls. They were neatly assembled like cord wood, row after row, layer upon layer, a stack reaching eight or ten feet high.

She craned her head to glance over her shoulder. More skeletal remains rose behind her against the wall, the skulls there up toward the ceiling, strung between the long bones in decorative patterns.

"Dominik?" she asked.

"He's dead."

"How?"

"He drowned in the passage." The big man looked at her. "I could only save one of you."

She nodded. "And the others? Do you know their status?"

"I've raised Glaskov and the two from the Black Hundred. They're all right. But Luka and Oleg haven't yet responded."

"They could be out of range in the Northern Network. It's a likely explanation."

"Yes." He paused. "Listen to me, Reva. Outlier is tracking."

"What? Why didn't you let me know?"

"I just did. You've barely been conscious three minutes—"

"Wait. I want to see for myself." She closed her eyes and silently commanded her onboard. When she reopened them, they were wide and intense. "My God. We have her."

He nodded and said nothing.

"She should have let us take her back in the passage," Reva said, a glacial anger in her voice. "It would have gone easier for her in the end."

Zoltan kept his eyes on hers and off her ruined face. She was highly observant, and he did not want her to pick up on any inadvertent reactions. The less she knew about that right now, the better.

She reached up with her left hand.

"Help me to my feet," she said.

Still groggy from the tranqs, her stomach weak and unsettled, Kali emerged into a cavelike space behind Jacques and Jill, her headlamp beam glancing off a thick crop of finger-length stalactites. They had walked several hundred yards from the crypt, gone through a connecting tunnel and then crawled over a flat ledge of rock to reach the chamber entrance.

Jacques glanced back at her. "Do you need help?"

She shook her head. "I'm all right."

As she dropped from the ledge, Kali's beam lowered to a circular well in the middle of the stone floor. It was about six feet in diameter, uncovered and dark. Beyond it the chamber walls curved around to the right.

Jacques saw her looking down at the well hole.

"There are more of these than you can count," he said. "They're almost a thousand years old. Miners would find a vein of limestone and pull the rocks up."

"How deep do they run?"

"Eighty or ninety feet. But that's a guess. No one's ever measured them all." He bent, picked up a loose rock and dropped it down into the hole. It was a long second before they heard a splash. "This one has water at the bottom. It's from the aquifer beneath the Seine. Others are dry and filled with skeletons. When they dug up the cemeteries three hundred years ago, the bodies were thrown straight down the mine pits. Later on they built the ossuary, but thousands were just dumped and forgotten. In those days there would have been plenty of grateful vermin to receive them. They and the lime took care of the soft tissues."

Kali glanced back up at the ceiling. The stalactites—thousands of them—bristled from a yellowish, clumpy mineral layer that looked like rancid cottage cheese. They would have formed from water steadily dripping through the sediment from above.

That prompted a thought, but she decided it could wait. First things first. She took the map out of her duffel and opened it for him to see.

"Show me where we are."

Jacques shrugged up his sleeve, and she noticed a wearable device on his wrist. He tapped the screen, gave it a long glance, then moved his finger to a point on the Sandy Road, running it down and then horizontally across the flimsy sheet of paper toward the spot marked *Rats' Alley*.

"We're heading there. Into the alley."

"Where the dead men lost their bones."

His smile was fiber-thin. "Now you know how it got its name, yes," he said. "It can take us north. This chamber is the only way to connect with it."

"If so, why isn't it on the map?"

"For the same reason the wells aren't shown. There are too many to chart. Too many tunnels."

Kali thought that just a partial explanation. She knew Lucien's mind almost as well as her own, and he likely would have kept some routes secret, a safeguard in case someone gained unwanted possession of the map. But she decided to say nothing about it.

"There were at least two men behind me when I entered Lucien's home. I'd hoped to lure them off from the Northern Network. Take the Sandy Road in a loop and either lose them or draw them out."

"And then you ran into the three you told us about," Jacques said.

She nodded. "They obviously knew of the road and came from somewhere south of Montparnasse. Probably the Saint-Martin ghost station."

"So you would be hemmed in between them and the other two."

"Yes," she said. "But they wouldn't have used tranquilizer guns unless they wanted me alive."

"And drugged," Jacques said. "So you could lead them to Navarro."

She nodded. "They had Lucien's home under watch. They were waiting for me. And they were ready. It tells me whoever sent them anticipated I would come to Paris. And knows of my ties to the White Rose."

Jacques looked at her. "We have to keep moving," he said. "We can make our way back north through side tunnels. It's longer and more difficult. But Jill and I are among the few who know the way."

"And if she's tricking us, Jacques?" Jill put in. "Then, what?"

He gave her a piercing glance. "Why ask that now?"

"What better time? How can we be sure she isn't *with* those people?"

Kali looked at her. "Does it make sense I'd have shot myself full of tranquilizers? Or let them do it and leave me for dead in a flooding passage? I could have drowned."

"Maybe. I don't know. I can think of how it would be a way to set us up."

"Think what you want," Kali said. "Those assassins will find Lucien, eventually. Your best hope is that I'm telling the truth. And that we reach him first."

Jill stood there looking almost unearthly in her half-face makeup. Like a revenant haunting the tunnels.

"I put the question out," she said. "That's all."

Kali said nothing for a long moment. Then she turned to Jacques. "The canal is still draining into the passage. How long until it brings someone from above?"

He gave an indeterminate shake of his head. "The Saint-Michel is under municipal authority... The Department of Roads and Travel or some such bureau." A pause. "It's after three in the morning right now. Sunday going into Monday. The administrative offices will be closed for another six hours."

"Somebody will notice."

"No doubt. But the sleepy officials will have to make their phone calls. And the canal workers trade their cozy pajamas and slippers for safety vests and rubber boots. It will be hours before anyone comes down to investigate, even if half the canal's million gallons pour out in the meantime."

Kali thought about that. "All right," she said. "But we need to stay ahead of them. Besides the Blood Lightning."

Jacques reached down for her backpack and handed it to her.

"La course est lancée," he said. "The race is on."

Glaskov thrust his head above the waterline, pulled the regulator out of his mouth and took a deep breath. The air was clammy and cold, but welcome. He had just gotten his own first look at the resident bones of the Paris catacombs. But instead of being tidily stacked, there were unceremoniously dumped into a sunken well.

He'd been swimming through a third water-filled tunnel when he glanced down into a hole that must have plunged twenty or thirty feet straight down below the tunnel floor. The skulls caught his eye immediately. There were dozens, possibly hundreds littering the bottom. Many were upright. Others were tipped over or upside-down. Some were buried with only their rounded cranial domes sticking out of the silt, and a few were wedged between rocks or lay cracked and broken alongside them. Strewn about the sediment were horseshoe-shaped lower jawbones, scattered teeth, ribs, fingers and other miscellaneous body parts he couldn't clearly identify through the murky water.

Glaskov knew the history of the catacombs and wasn't shocked by the sight. But he had nevertheless checked the status of his oxygen tanks before he swam on, and was possibly even gladder than he might have been when he entered a fourth tunnel and at last found some headroom at the surface.

Now he treaded water and checked his coordinates while his onboard began uploading data. A firm believer in redundancy, he had two active depth gauges—his onboard's and the one doubling as a wrist compass. Both put him on the Right Bank of the Seine in the Eighth arrondissement, midway between the Champs-Élysées and the Palais Garnier—the Paris Opera. Through all the twists and turns, he had amazingly maintained a northward course with just minor deviations, crossing from the Left Bank beneath the river. He could not have been more unerring if he'd planned it. And he still had over a hundred bars in his main cylinder.

Glaskov continued to float on the surface, waiting for the data backlog to process. In the meantime, he looked around, his helmet lights beaming this way and that. The ceiling here was at least fifteen or twenty feet overhead, making it almost cavernous compared to the tunnels he'd just navigated through. Whatever had caused them to flood, he thought he might be clear of it.

The glowing spot appeared in his retinal display precisely two minutes and thirty-nine seconds after he surfaced. The sonar grid was like the one on a ship's navigation panel, concentric circles, lines and numbers measuring speed and range. The spot was at the eastern side of the display, moving slowly but visibly in a southward direction. Floating in the upper corner of his eye was a message.

Target acquired and in motion. Continue scheme of maneuver.

Glaskov copied over the neurolink, took a final breath of air without the regulator, then slid the rubber mouthpiece between his teeth and bit down. He was being told to proceed to his assigned sector and await orders for carrying out the tactical plan. With Outlier's movements being tracked, she would have nowhere to go.

He slid underwater and dove off.

PART TWO

THE RATTLE OF THE BONES

9

April 25, 2024
Various Locales

Janus Base, Romania/The Crimean Peninsula

At a quarter to seven Monday morning, Carmody stepped from the barracks into the faint early sunshine and walked across the blacktop to the CTRC's entry gate. He ignored the hounds as he held his ID to the scanner, nodded to the guard and went in.

He saw only a scattering of personnel in the corridor. Most looked sluggish carrying their breakfasts through the hall. The building was vast, full of artificial light and empty space. At that hour it felt like a sports arena on an off day.

Howard had texted to notify him they would be using a small briefing room on the fifth and uppermost floor. Carmody took the elevator up and followed the signs.

The room was shaped like a compact flying saucer. Its wraparound windows had been electronically opaqued, making it a shade or so dimmer than the outer hallways. Carmody found the meeting's other participants already seated around the electronic equivalent of a military sand table. Howard and Fernandez had arrived in uniform. The third man, a civilian of about fifty, sat sideways to the door opposite the colonel, wearing an Oxford blue cardigan over a pinchecked shirt.

Adrian Soto looked exactly like he did on the news shows. His face was dark, handsome and famous. That his fame hadn't originated when he became one of the Force's principal directors said something to Carmody. Three tours with Army CECOM in Iraq and head of a global telecom and a New York charity, he was no political ladder-climber. By all accounts Soto had never sought or wanted a government post and had accepted it only because the president asked. For the last few months he'd been at Janus at her further request, overseeing the installation of its cybersecurity upgrades. He was also among the nucleus of the mission's advance planners.

Carmody gave Howard and Fernandez a clipped nod, then turned toward Soto.

"Sir," he said. "Mike Carmody."

"A pleasure," Soto said. "Carol Morse speaks well of you."

Carmody grunted. "Watch out for her," he said. "She fudges."

Soto smiled. They bumped fists and Carmody sat down to his right. The chair looked as if it had been sized and contoured for the little green men that parked the flying saucer.

"I want to personally express my thanks for what you did in Hawaii," Soto said. "Without you a big chunk of it wouldn't be here today. Nor would Agent Musil and his daughters." He paused. "I heard you were shot."

"Nicked. I warned you about Morse."

Soto smiled gain and said nothing.

Carmody sat looking over the table. The three-dimensional terrain map in the middle was lit with color and duplicated on four recessed computer displays around the table's circular collar.

He recognized most of its features. The ravine between lines of coastal mountains, a serpentine inlet of the Black Sea winding between the broken slopes. The train tracks climbing over the spine of the mountains from the north, then descending past a sprawl of low factory buildings and storage towers to finally turn west at the water's edge.

After a quarter mile the track went past a large shipping dock, then continued another three hundred yards to what looked like a rift or cut that ran straight into one of the slopes. He identified what appeared to be the metal roofs of buried artillery silos, square and flat and flush with the ground.

"Nice fake," Carmody said, looking at Howard.

"What?"

"The table map." Carmody motioned to it. "Okean Twenty-Seven. A secret city in Crimea and the new Wolf's lair. The place we think launched that nuclear drone sub at Oahu. It's detailed, which makes it nice. Except parts of it can't possibly show what they do here. Which makes it a fake."

Howard looked at him. Carmody stood there without expression. After a moment Fernandez cleared his throat and smiled sunnily at everyone in the room.

"Who wants some fresh hot coffee?" he said.

They all did except for Howard, who asked for warm lemon water and honey instead.

Fernandez returned from the break room with a cardboard tray, handed out the cups and sat down.

"Starting over," Soto said, his eyes on Carmody, "how about spelling out your problem with the map?"

"Sure," Carmody said. "I've studied our satellite recon for weeks. Key spots are scrambled. But not here."

Soto lifted his coffee to his mouth and drank.

"That's easily explained," he said. "The imagery on this map is being captured in near real time by Argos-3 low-earth orbit sats. My company designed them and put twenty into space just this past year. When the full constellation's up, it will give us two satellites for ninety-five percent of the earth, and one for ninety-nine percent. I only tell you that as a preface, so you know I'm not giving you a DARPA press release."

"I didn't figure you for doing that," Carmody said. "But okay, thanks."

Soto nodded. "Our goal when we developed those sats was to make them more resilient and upgradable than anything else in the sky," he said. "One of the things I've done here at Janus with Sgt.

Fernandez is make them smarter than they were at launch. The table map is based on big-data and deep-learning technology. Artificial intelligence."

"Still sounds like guesswork to me."

"We wrote most of the mapping software ourselves," Fernandez said. "It's accurate to a fraction of a point."

"I didn't say the guesses were bad," Carmody said. "There are just too many of them. I saw the railroad tracks in the original images. That industrial plant up on the mountain. But the dock was a blur. Also the place where the train enters the tunnel. Basically every close approach to the Okean from land, air and sea was blocked from view." He looked over at Soto. "I need to know the ground truth before bringing my people in."

"Understood," Soto said. "But not all guesses are created equal. That's the whole thing. Think of a puzzle that can substitute for its own missing pieces. Artificial intelligence doesn't really guess so much as it *computes*. Which is to say it collates information from a wide range of sources, then uses it to fill in those blanks with machine logic. A human brain would be overwhelmed by so many different inputs. But not a neural network."

"Take the wharf," Fernandez said to Carmody. "You're right. It's totally jammed to our stratospheric sats. Same for our drones. What we get from them is pixelated slush. But the Argos AI figured out a work-around. It used satellite data to monitor the sea traffic a few miles out from shore and chart the positions of ships coming and going over time. That enabled it to triangulate the wharf's location." He used his stylus to circle it on the screen in front of him—and automatically on all the other screens around the table. "But like you said, we need ground truth. What're its dimensions? The number of piers? What's it *look* like?" He sipped some coffee. "Turns out those same ship movements can tell us other things. So can variations in the water's color and temperature, wavebreak patterns, how the current interacts with the shore. It's like when they detect planets in space by observing how light bends around them. And then there's the ships *themselves*. They can be classified by type and then identified by their hull numbers. Once that happens it can trace their ports of origin. Learn who owns them, what's aboard, when they set sail… You catching me?"

Carmody nodded. "That's how we found out about the container ship that pulled into Oahu. The *Lucky Gift*. Natasha Mori and Kali tied it to those Chinese shippers who were hooked in with the Russians."

Fernandez said, "It's exactly the same thing, bro. Except a machine brain can do it with *thousands* of ships at the same time. In minutes. While it's processing and interpreting all kinds of other data connected to that spot on the map. It puts together an aggregate and builds a realistic visual. A high-probability model of what's happening outside the mountain that's as detailed as any photo."

"Say I accept that," Carmody said. "I also need to know what's happening inside the mountain."

Fernandez nodded. "One second. I want to show you something."

Carmody waited as the sergeant began tapping his keyboard. Bright swipes and clusters of orange, yellow and red appeared at the three-dimensional base of the mountain.

"This," Fernandez said, "is what major electromagnetic emitters in there look like to sensors."

Carmody looked skeptical. "You're telling me they can pick up EM through the mountain?"

"Nope, it's not feasible," Fernandez said. "But think about it. The mountain isn't just a giant lump of rock. It's been excavated. There are airflow ducts sunken into it. Intake and exhaust grilles all around it. And it's full of equipment that leaks radiation to the surface through those ducts and grilles. Once our satellites read the emissions, the AI can use it to identify the machines. Because every machine has a distinct energy footprint. It can tell the difference between computers and cooling units. A cooling unit and stacks of circuit boards. Whatever else goes on at the Okean, it mainly looks to me like a huge underground cyber- and data-operations center. I'm talking hyperscale infrastructure."

"Try again in English."

"A facility with the space, hardware and power for thousands of servers—and one that's expandable. That's the definition of *hyperscale*. Think Google's or Olympia's cloud facilities. There are probably tens of thousands of circuit boards, cooling systems and network devices, plus backups, to all of it… They gobble up enough power for a small city."

"Hard to believe the people in the mountain wouldn't think to damp those emissions."

"Oh, they do," Soto said. "But my company built

the sensor suites that pick them up. I'll verify they aren't easily jammed."

Howard had sat still to that point. He plucked his pipe out of his shirt pocket and toyed with it.

"Show him the floor plan, Julio," he said.

The sergeant nodded, his fingers pattering over the keys again. In a minute a schematic showing internal rooms and corridors took shape over the blots and dashes of red spectrum color.

"The Okean's built inside an abandoned iron mine. Dug 1843, according to the records. It's what they called a room-and-pillar mine, where they tunneled off a main shaft and put up supports as they went along." Fernandez paused. "Ever notice how a squid's body is like a long tube with all those tentacles around its head? That's how this looks to me. The mine spreads out over a thousand acres."

"And the Russians are using all of it?" Carmody asked.

"Their installation extends about three hundred acres in. A third the total area. You could fit ten buildings the size of the Pentagon inside. And have enough real estate left over for the Mall of America."

"Pretty huge," Carmody said. "We know its depth?"

"Two hundred, two hundred fifty feet," Fernandez said. "And chew on this a minute. The mine's ore was tapped out by 1900 or so. But after World War II, the Soviets turned the entrances and outer shafts into underground submarine pens."

Carmody looked at him. "Perfect for building and hiding the drone sub. It would have given them complete secrecy."

Fernandez nodded.

"The original pens were shut down when the USSR crumbled and Crimea became part of an independent Ukraine. I think one was even a museum or something for a while. But you can't keep a good sub bunker down. The Russians never really left the peninsula. They signed financial agreements to hold onto their naval bases there, and the Ukrainians kept their own neighboring bases up the coast—right up until Moscow got tired of paying its rent and grabbed Crimea in 2014."

"Surprise, surprise," Howard said.

Carmody was thoughtful. "Apart from the AI, was there other information that went into your layout of the actual installation?"

"What makes you ask?" Howard said.

"I'm just wondering. You have fewer data sets for what's going on in the present. There's the EM, but not much else. Yet it's very detailed."

Howard sat there playing with his pipe, his eyes on Carmody's. "We have human intel."

"Too vague."

"A mole," Howard said. "An old-fashioned fucking spy. Plain enough?"

"Who?"

"I can't tell you."

"Why not?"

"Because that's the deal."

Carmody said nothing for a long moment. Then he nodded, lifted his stylus, and circled the industrial complex high atop the chain of mountains southeast of the Okean.

"I'm positive this factory exists because of the

Okean," Carmody said. "I'm also positive it's a mineral refinery. Could be cement, could be cement plus other things." He began drawing tiny arrows on his screen. "These are for storage. These are smokestacks. And this is a kiln. This over here is the conveyor belt they use to move the clinker to the mixers."

Howard looked at him.

"That's two for two," he said. "It's called *Chistaya Zemlya.*"

"State-run by Russia?"

Howard nodded. "The quarry's over two hundred miles northwest over the mountains. Outside a city called Armiansk. They haul the raw ingredients to the plant by train and do the mixing and grinding there."

"And then?"

"It goes back into the railcars and is moved down the mountain. There's a shipment every fifteen days."

"Fifteen exactly?"

"Right."

"Never fourteen or sixteen."

Howard nodded in the affirmative. "We have twelve to go before the next one."

Carmody thought a minute, grunted. "When they built the Okean, they would've laid foundations, floors, supports and ceilings throughout the main shaft and all those tunnels. From your schematic, it looks like some of those tunnels are wide enough for vehicles. So there has to be a garage for the personnel. At least one. And there are probably shuttles for moving people and equipment around the three hundred acres. All that construction would need a major supply of concrete. The fact that it's still being delivered tells us they're still expanding."

"Building deeper into the mountain," Howard said. "I've thought about that too. Probably they're using the existing mine tunnels. You don't want to start blasting with dynamite and all that delicate equipment around. Also, it disrupts whatever they're doing. This is a major expansion."

Everyone in the room was quiet. After a long minute Carmody turned to Fernandez. "Okay," he said. "Zoom out over the mountains. Keep the rail line dead center going to the quarry."

Fernandez tapped a keyboard and the table map panned out along the track. Carmody saw farms, towns and a couple of small cities interspersed with miles of hilly, wooded terrain.

"Here we go," he said. "The Wild West, Crimean style."

Carmody glanced up at him for an extended moment.

"Let's talk about that," he said.

The Crimean Peninsula

The thing was that you didn't have to physically enter a place to take pictures of it these days, especially if a video-surveillance system could be accessed instead—in this instance, cameras with facial-recognition capabilities, along with a large digital archive of video footage. Modern times. It was safer and easier to gain remote entry to the system. Hijack the cams, grab the stored video files and then have it all routed to your remote server.

The method's relative ease and efficiency aside, there was a symmetrical beauty in turning a prized technological tool against its user.

Now a door opened, a chair was pulled out, a computer turned on. A tap of its keyboard and the footage was off to New York. It was the sort of invaluable intelligence they'd at first thought too good to be true, not that they could be faulted. It was coming from a source they hadn't expected or even known existed.

Defiant Fly.

The cover name hadn't come out of nowhere. Once you decided to take actions that put your life at extreme risk—that were possibly even assuring your own death—it only made sense to consider what you wanted to be called. Like an epitaph you wrote for your own gravestone, it was to sum up who and what you were. To tell others how you chose to be remembered.

Defiant Fly.

Fly because it was seen as an inconsequential life. Barely more than a speck of dirt. But small as it was, how often did a fly go unnoticed? It could spend all its time clinging to a wall, passive, motionless and inoffensive and still not come to a natural end. Before long somebody would see it, and it would meet the business end of a swatter. A fly didn't warrant mercy. No one ever regretted killing a fly. No one gave it a thought. A fly was nothing except when it was something to be crushed.

Defiant because that was better than being docile. Better than existing passively. Sooner or later they would swat you out of existence. Why not take off and land on the wedding cake? Flit toward the sunlight outside the window, crawl up and down the screen probing for holes? Why not try when there was nothing to lose?

Moscow had built a secret city inside a mountain, populated it with its scientists and military, and then handed the keys over to the prince of the dark web. Alone overlooking the sea, surrounded by high slopes on three sides, it contained Russia's greatest, most valuable machine, shielding it behind potent physical and virtual barriers.

It was in the Russian DNA to wall and fortify. To use geography and terrain to the fullest advantage... Wasn't the Kremlin itself a thousand-year-old citadel on a hill? But nothing was ever impenetrable. Everything had vulnerabilities. All the stronghold's defenses, all its weapons systems, had not managed to keep out a lowly fly. It had slipped past their safeguards, briefly found a wall on which to settle and then jumped off before anyone paid any attention.

They said a fly saw through two thousand optical lenses. Those lenses creating a mosaic that gave it close to a three-hundred-sixty-degree field of vision. A fly could explore the hidden spaces and see everything around it. Eventually its luck might run out...but nothing lived forever. Nothing lasted.

A thin, pensive smile appeared in the glow of the computer screen. Defiant Fly and the Great Machine. It would make an interesting title for a children's book. One with a sad little conclusion, perhaps...but what ending was without bitterness? There were no happily-ever-afters in reality. The princess met her future prince, and they fell in love. But eventually one of them would leave or die before the other. One was *always* left behind to suffer the grief and loss. Nothing in the world lasted. Everything was temporary. Why not dive straight down into the wedding cake? Possibly leave a mark in the frosting? Something to be remembered in a story later on? A fly-scale version of posterity.

Time was running out. Things were about to get dangerous. But the work wasn't close to done. There was much more to learn and share about Okean's hidden secret. Much more.

A deep breath, the click of a switch and the monitor went dark. The empty chair was pushed back under the desktop, footsteps quietly crossed the floor, and the door opened and shut.

Defiant Fly had left the room.

Armed guards, multiple scans, a rising four-ton steel gate. Then the frozen blue Porsche Taycan GTS slipped out of the morning light and into the yawning tunnel mouth.

At its wheel, Drajan Petrovik thought it was how the entry into hell would look with modern security. But Okean-27 was a human creation.

His ears popped from the changing air pressure as the tunnel descended almost three hundred feet. He went along a row of vehicle ramps, turned into one and entered the cavernous garage.

Drajan drove past lines of cars and trucks to his parking slot. A press of his fob button as he exited the Porsche summoned a self-driving passenger cart. He climbed into its open cab, voiced his instructions and rode along.

Another set of guards, another scan, and a door slid open. The metal plate above it, bolted into the craggy rock, read *Tsifrovaya Nauka Razdel*. Digital Science Section. It was a bland marker for the Okean's clandestine cyber warfare center. But that sort of nomenclature was a Russian fetish, as if hiding it in the heart of a mountain wasn't a dead giveaway.

Drajan found it perversely amusing. Teach a bear to play chess, and it was still a lumbering brute by nature.

The robotic cart halted, and he stepped off. Pale, homogeneous light bathed the center's work stations and equipment. At nine in the morning, two-thirds of the stations were already occupied, the Okean's personnel crisp and busy in their white lab coats. It occurred to Drajan that his hacking crews had never opened their eyes before midday.

He looked down a long, wide aisle and saw Sergei Cosa talking to a young woman outside a door at its end. From his jowled face and dark bespoke blazer to his Berluti shoes, the Russian was outwardly a classic rendering of his country's political elite. He was also a deft practitioner of espionage, with a subtle cunning that matched his ruthlessness—unlike his fellow bears, who depended on brute force to gain and consolidate their power.

He saw Drajan enter and raised a hand to beckon him.

"Have you made each other's acquaintance?" he asked. "Kira joined our cyber-missions team earlier this month."

Drajan glanced at her. She was slight and in her twenties, long red hair tucked behind her ear on one side. He noticed her green eyes and calm features. Noticed her perfume was a delicate cinnamon fragrance.

"I don't think so," he said. "Drajan Petrovik."

She put out her hand. "Your name is known to everyone in our community."

"Kira is an expert in social engineering," Cosa said. "She comes to us with a graduate degree from the Moscow Institute of Physics and Technology."

Drajan gave her a little nod.

"You'll be a fine asset," he said. "Your unfortunate scholastics, notwithstanding."

She looked at him. His slight did nothing to disrupt her poise.

"Do you like honey cake?" she asked.

He paused a beat. "An unexpected question," he said.

"Do you?"

"Well enough, I suppose."

She nodded. "When I was fourteen, I went selling it door-to-door before Christmas. The proceeds were to go to a food kitchen. I would tell the good mothers who bought them that it was a character-building project started by one of my teachers."

"And?"

"It was all a lie. There were no honey cakes. The school project didn't exist. My thirty thousand *hryvnia* in profits went toward a night out with my friends at the hottest club in the city."

"You made it through face control?"

"What do you think?"

"I think the young men at the door must have welcomed you inside with open arms."

She smiled. "It was quite the nice evening. The money paid for our limousine, clothes, everything. But I hadn't expected its cost to me would include three months in juvenile detention."

Drajan looked straight into her eyes. "Now, that's truly unfortunate."

"It was nothing compared to the sentence I received two years later for hacking into big-business computers. Thirty convictions for technical burglary, a year in prison for each count. All because an idiot on an internet forum had loose lips." She paused. "I'd still be incarcerated if someone from the Directorate hadn't recruited me for cyber operations."

Drajan's gaze had remained on hers. "I've insulted you," he said finally, dipping his head. "Please accept my apologies."

"It's all right," she said. "I'm not very thin-skinned."

He was silent for a long moment.

At last Cosa said, "You'll excuse us, Kira. But we need to talk privately."

She gave him a nod but was looking straight at Drajan. "I hope I didn't bore you with my story."

He smiled. "Not at all," he said. "We'll see more of each other, I'm sure."

"I'm sure."

He watched her as she turned and walked up the aisle. Then Cosa tapped his elbow, his eyes becoming severe under his deep brows.

"If you can pry your attention back my way, this won't take long," he said, and gestured toward the office door.

Janus Base

In the CTRC, the map table's screens were still showing a terrain view of Ukraine and Crimea.

Carmody lifted his stylus.

"About that railroad," he said, touching its point to the city of Kharkiv on the mainland's northwestern section. "This is where it originates. It's been in steady use for two centuries, since it was laid down by the British during the Crimean War. The trains moved soldiers, horses and equipment six hundred miles over the mountains to Armiansk, at the top of the peninsula." He drew a dead-straight line south to illustrate. "After the war it turned into a freight rail to supply the local food markets. Livestock went south, fruit north. It's still that way. Where the area around Armiansk isn't covered in forest, it's all cultivated groves. And there's a cement quarry."

"Also a neighboring quarry where they mine something called titanium dioxide, or titania. And a plant for refining it," Soto said. "I've done some homework too. And I believe this gives us a clue as to why they're expanding the Okean." He looked around the table clockwise at Fernandez, Howard and then Carmody. "When titania crystals are processed, they become a substance that goes into paint and cosmetics. It's what gives gloss to pearlized car finishes and lipstick. But a few years ago, researchers discovered that microchips made with it can boost computing power many times over and keep energy consumption down. It revolutionized the industry practically overnight. I can vouch that my company has spent tens of millions on the chips." Soto drank his coffee. "If they're doing heavy cloud computing at the Okean it's possible they've decided to manufacture their own titania microprocessors. That would eliminate relying on outside sources for the chips and reduce their need to generate or import massive amounts of electricity."

"So the whole operation stays in-house."

Soto was nodding. "Seven hundred acres of abandoned mining tunnels would more than cover the expansion."

Fernandez let out a low whistle.

"A megadata center in a mountain that's totally self-contained. What they need, they make for themselves."

Carmody looked at Soto. "Any idea why they'd want all this processing power?"

Soto nodded. "One or two," he said. "I'll get back to you."

Carmody looked thoughtful. After a moment he moved his stylus slightly upward to retrace a small segment of his north–south line on the map. He started above Armiansk and stopped just above it at a red-tinted body of water.

"Julio," he said, "move in close."

Fernandez boxed and enlarged it.

"This is Syvash Lake," Carmody said. "It sits between the mainland and peninsula."

"I was there before Russia made its grab," Howard said. "It's really a saltwater lagoon, feeds off the Black Sea. The red color comes from a kind of algae that can live in all that salt. The rotten-egg stink too."

Carmody nodded. "I want us to take another look at where the railroad crosses the lake," he said.

Fernandez zoomed in some more, then drew a bright yellow highlight line over a narrow strip of terrain projecting from the water.

"The Isthmus of Perekop is the land bridge that joins the peninsula to the mainland," Carmody said. "It stretches twenty miles across the lake up to Armiansk and the cement and titania mines." He looked at Howard. "About five years ago the Russians extended the track *down* from those mines to the refinery above the Okean. That's where my maps were always blanked. But your fake one shows an even newer spur running a couple of miles down the mountains. Which I'm thinking is a supply line to the Okean."

Howard regarded him flatly.

"You have a knack for being an asshole," he said. "That's as real as it gets."

Carmody shrugged. "At no extra charge," he said.

Howard was silent. Carmody looked around the table.

"Okay," he said. "This is the good part."

Soto nodded. "I'll bite."

Carmody's eyes came to rest on his face.

"I'm going to tell you how we hijack the train," he said.

The Crimean Peninsula

The room at the end of the long aisle was less a full office than a spare, simple place where Cosa could talk privately, with minimal risk of electronic surveillance.

He had motioned Drajan into a plain wooden chair and sat down to face him from behind a gray steel desk. The light was bland and without any tint coming from an LED drop panel above. The walls were as gray as the desk, and as rough and cavelike as the walls outside the room. The floor was smooth gray concrete. There were no pens or pencils on the desktop, no photos, no computer. No mirrors, no plaques, no photos or personal items to break up its austere functionality.

"I won't waste time," Cosa said. "Yours or mine."

Drajan nodded. "I've been wondering why you asked me here this early."

The Russian pressed his short, blunt fingers into the edge of the desk. His cordial expression had evaporated, and his gaze was severe and probing under his heavy eyebrows. It was as if he'd lowered a stick mask from his face.

"What do you know about the *Krovavaya Molniya? The Blood Lightning?*"

"Very little. They're a modified paramilitary unit within CHVK Wagner."

"Anything else?"

"They conduct special reconnaissance missions. Which means high-level foreign assassinations."

Cosa looked at him. "What about Lucien Navarro?"

"The Frenchman?" Drajan shrugged. "I know what everyone knows."

"Namely?"

"He collaborated on the *Cybernation Manifesto.*

Or rather, completed it after the death of his parents. They wrote an earlier draft with two other hacktivists. A declaration of independence for cyberspace."

"That's it?"

"It's an ethical and political tract," Drajan said. "Neither line of thought interests me."

"And your level of interest in the hacker, Kali Alcazar?"

Drajan moderated his reaction. If he was to show none at all, Cosa would be canny enough to realize he was suppressing it.

His dark eyes connected with the Russian's. "Explain how that's important."

Cosa shrugged, examining his face. "She's close to Navarro. They were practically raised as brother and sister. And she slept with you for years. A common thread I can't ignore."

Drajan was silent. He didn't know how much Cosa knew or suspected. Possibly he was only fishing. But he was not about to take his bait.

He thought suddenly about the name by which the old spymaster was known in Kremlin intelligence circles. *Koschei.* The scheming magician-king of Russian folklore who, afraid his enemies would target him for death, gained immortality by hiding his soul inside a needle, and the needle inside an egg, and the egg inside a fowl, and the fowl inside a rabbit…and then burying the rabbit in a chest on a distant island.

That was the better known part of the fable. But Drajan knew of another. As that went, if the egg were to crack, the needle would instantly snap, and Koschei would age and die.

Find the egg, then, hold it in hand, and you would have the power of life and death over him. He would be yours to control.

"What are we talking about here?" he said. "I don't sit for interrogations."

Cosa unconsciously rubbed the desktop with his fingertips, then shrugged again. "Very well," he said. "My office has monitored Cyber Nation over many years. In that time we've compiled an extensive file and seen it grow into a community of millions in virtual space. Several months ago, every nation on earth received an open communiqué from its founders—Navarro foremost among them—informing them it would soon assert its independence as a sovereign state. A state without geographic boundaries. A state with a social structure just loosely defined as government, and with a digital currency uncontrolled by any single authority." He paused. "This is a travesty that can more than destabilize legitimate nations. It can pull the entire world down into chaos and disorder."

Drajan was silent for a beat. Then he said, "Some might argue that it would buy humanity ultimate freedom."

"Let those fools argue what they want. The Federal Assembly has declared any involvement with Cyber Nation a crime punishable by fifteen years in prison. Tsao's policy in China is even harsher. And the Republic of Birhan has become the first to impose the death penalty for use of Cyber Nation's proprietary cryptocurrency. Although, our intelligence tells us its new president, Ansari Kem, has amassed a vast fortune under a concealed identity as a so-called citizen."

"I told you I'm disinterested in politics, Sergei."

"But you are Kem's former student. And you're very drawn to money."

Drajan gave a slight shrug. "What's the point of all this?"

Cosa looked at him.

"Two weeks ago, Navarro disappeared. A Blood Lightning unit is in Paris searching for him. Eight of our best. But it isn't a Wagner operation. Someone else has hired them."

"Who?"

"Possibly a rival element within Cyber Nation... but the truth is we don't know," he said. "We do know Kali Alcazar is also in Paris. She arrived days ago. We think she's also there to find Navarro."

"And why does any of this concern you? Or is it just the idea of your modded units going rogue?"

"I don't have to share my reasons."

"But you asked me here to field your questions. Because you suspect I'm involved."

"Are you?"

Drajan did not try to justify his lies in his own mind, and so had no hesitation.

"No," he said.

"Then your current lover's departure for Latvia is unrelated to everything I've mentioned."

"Why would you even ask?"

"The answer is obvious. Quintessa Leonides is in charge of Bank Leonides's crypto finance division. I knew her father well. He was first among my country's billionaires before he established residency outside the Federation."

Drajan smiled wanly.

"This all sounds like a conspiracy theory," he said. "I thought that was something you only seed into the fabric of other nations to diminish them."

"Don't play games," Cosa said. "You are integral to what we're doing here at the Okean. No one is indispensable, however. So I want to give you fair warning. Duplicity is a useful tool. But try using it on me and I'll find out. And you won't enjoy the consequences."

Drajan looked at him for a long moment.

"You don't get out much these days, do you?" he said. "It's hard to think clearly in the belly of this mountain. All the rock around us presses on the brain."

Cosa's smile hardened at the corners.

"I appreciate your concern," he said. "But I'll be going to Moscow within days. The president wants to meet, and he's bound to ask about the prince of the *technologi vampiri* who shares the mountain with me. We've paid you millions, Drajan. Protected you from the Americans."

"Meaning?"

Cosa hadn't budged from where he stood. "You can decide for yourself," he said. "Enjoy the rest of your day."

Drajan rose and turned to leave, sensing Cosa's eyes on his back. He continued to feel them even after the door shut softly behind him.

10

Etienne Tousaint shouldered a path through two women in sheer glitter lace and body-con lamé, pin-balled off another in ostrich feathers and fringes, then swung around a group of hooded light dancers in LED halters and leggings before he finally came up against the bar like a battered raft in a storm.

Candace, now in a sequined red flapper dress with a drastically plunging neckline, was serving an opalescent blue cocktail to a guy carrying a narrow wooden cane and wearing the improbable beaked mask, wide-brimmed hat, long black coat and heavy leather boots of a medieval plague doctor. She glanced across the counter at Etienne, then raised her hands and gestured as if cutting an invisible steering wheel in his direction. *Be right over.* She had put on fingerless satin opera gloves that matched the dress, and a beaded veil Etienne thought was incredibly sexy.

He waited in his tamest-of-tame blazer, white shirt and jeans, his ears pulsing with synth bossa nova rhythms and sultry feminine vocals. He was thinking he wouldn't be able find his way back to the surface if his life depended on it. On their way down here, Candace had led him through a wormy, looping, confusing tangle of tunnels that had wound along for what seemed endless miles. They had crawled, slunk, shuffled and sometimes even managed to stand up straight as the intersecting passages took turns opening out and closing in around them.

"How can getting to the club be so *hard*?" he had asked, pausing for a drink of water. "Does everyone have to go through this maze?"

She'd laughed as he passed her his sports bottle "There are easier ways."

"Seriously?"

"Yes. I wanted to see how you would take to things."

"*Mais merde quoi!* Did I pass the test?"

"You've done beautifully," she had said, a glint of mischief in her eyes. "So far."

They had moved on for a while. Then he'd suddenly heard the loud music and merry overlapping voices, followed Candace into a long, ruler-straight pass and seen the sign. Hung above the chamber archway in bright splash lighting, its gothic characters white against a black background, it read *Se Faire Oublier et Danser*.

Be forgotten and dance.

Etienne had lowered his eyes from the hall's apparent motto to the archway. All that bright light spilling out of it reminded him of *ET the Extraterrestrial* or some fantasy movie where you peered through a portal into another world.

He'd felt a thrill of wonder and excitement. It was like a giddy elf was skipping about in his stomach. Then Candace had tapped his forearm.

"Put this on." She held out a holographic wristband with a chain of glowing neon skulls around it. "Jean Claude has the door tonight. When he asks your name, tell him you don't have one—that's the code. And no *contrebande* once we're in. Not even weed, Eti."

He'd looked at her a second.

"Is something wrong?" she asked.

"No." Taking the wristband. "I'm nameless to him. And drug-free."

"Bien sûr."

With his long hair and bushy black beard, Jean Claude looked like a hairy circus bear in his embroidered Order of the Dragon coat. Etienne had answered his trick question and been waved through as Candace went off somewhere to change into her work outfit. After that he'd switched into his own better clothes, leaving those he'd worn climbing down from the surface in his pack, and checking the pack with a hundred others in a designated area near the entry.

"Hé, toi-là! My average Parisian male!"

Her voice pulled him back to the present. He turned his head to see her prancing up on his side of the bar with a couple of the tall shimmery aqua drinks. She held one out to him.

"Take this, will you? My break's just half an hour."

He took it, clinked and sipped. It tasted sweetly of citrus and left a faint trace of licorice on his lips.

"This is amazing," he said.

"An absinthe cocktail," she said, leaning close so he could hear above the music.

"Is it *radioactive*?"

"Ha!" She pointed a finger up at a light rack above the bar. "The fluorescents are what make it glow. It's called a Corpse Reviver."

"Seriously?"

"Seriously...in keeping with tonight's theme."

Etienne nodded. The walls were lined with large NFT video screens displaying Ali Saldera's latest digital art. There were skeletons in space suits with glowing pink eyes behind their helmet visors, skeletons in fur loincloths and Viking helmets with curved horns, cloaked and hooded skeletons that seemed to be made of glass and wearing World War II–pilot hats and goggles, metallic skulls with animated rainbow-scaled serpents slithering in and out of their sockets...the entire CyberSkeleton collection.

All of which was amazing and peculiar. But strangest of all, at least to his eyes, was a throne made of human bones at the far end of the hall, set back in an alcove with an elaborate canopy. The seat and lower back were horizontal long bones, the base layered in a crisscross pattern. The very top of the backrest was ornamented with grinning skulls, the armrests with small finger and toe bones. Three hip-grinding revelers, a man and two women, had fallen into it with their bodies entangled.

Etienne looked away after a brief glance, a bit embarrassed.

"How can they carry on atop that ghastly thing?"

Candace smiled and shrugged. "Don't be such a stiff," she said.

"It doesn't give you the creeps?"

"The first time I saw the throne, maybe. Then I thought, *We all die. How can I fear something that happens to literally everyone?*" She shrugged again. "It tells me to enjoy the moment. And it's very democratic, no? Peel away the flesh, and we're all the same. Those are people's bones. Random people. Some of them may have been peasants, some aristocrats. Some even mortal enemies. Yet there they are jumbled together as one."

Etienne contemplated that for a second.

"All right, but let's not spill our drinks on them," he said and waggled his cocktail. "If those people revive—whoever they were in life—I'll freak."

Candace laughed and sipped, rolling her shoulders to the music.

"So, Eti," she said, "do we dance before I go back to work? Or stand around fretting and philosophizing?"

He regarded her silently over his drink.

"That look again!" she said. "Is something wrong?"

He shook his head. "It's just that very few people call me that. My mom before she died. And my two best friends."

"Should I not, then?"

"Actually, I like that you do."

Candace smiled and put her drink down on the counter. Then she lifted his glass out of his hands and set it alongside.

"Come, then, Eti. Sweep me off my feet," she said, extending her hands to him.

He took them in his, and held them, and they danced.

A few feet across the floor, a sweaty Lionel Allard and his new friends Sadie and Delia, who'd introduced themselves as roommates and collaborative creatives, were slamming it in the music and lights.

Lionel had been down into the catacombs once or twice before—in both instances as a college student—but this was his first time at an underground rave. An intern at the Blue-Eyed Dog NFT agency, he was rarely invited to drop parties, especially not for a famous creator like Ali Saldera, who had developed the high end CyberSkeleton collection. But its release was a milestone for Blue-Eyed Dog, its first exhibit at a meatspace gallery in the prestigious Marais district, and Lionel's boss had rewarded him for his work with an invite.

Before slipping down a cat flap in the Twelfth arrondissement, Lionel had scored two caps of Romanian trop on the street to heighten the experience. He'd also brought some home-rolled blunts for later in the night, stashing them inside the liner of the stovepipe hat he'd worn for the occasion.

The trop had kicked in after about an hour, its perception-enhancing effects causing him to feel trippy and unbound from his body, like he was entirely made of excited, high-energy electrons. Lionel didn't quite remember how or when he'd hooked up with the leather-clad roomies, but the three had been going atomic with that excitation energy...so much that Lionel was starting to dream big about where their night was headed. Moments ago, he'd decided it would be a good time to give things a boost.

Grinding between them, he raised the top hat off his head and tweezed one of the blunts out of its hidden pouch with two fingers. Then he slid a lighter out of his pocket, took a deep drag to get the blunt going and held it out to Delia's carmine lips.

They had no sooner parted to receive it when a hand the size of an oven mitt fell on his shoulder.

"Take that outside, will you?"

Lionel looked up and around at the figure looming over him. It was the bearded man from the door.

"Can you ignore us this once? I won't light another, *promise*."

The bouncer shook his head.

"Take it out or put it out," he said. "There's enough tunnels where you three can do whatever you want."

Lionel shrugged with resignation.

"Shall we?" he asked his companions.

They nodded, Delia with the blunt still held up to her lips. Then they all turned and jostled through the crowd toward the door.

The Third Unit assassins, Luka and Oleg, were making their way north through the catacombs when they heard the music.

Luka signaled a stop. He had led till now, tracking Kali Alcazar's progress in his smart lens.

After a moment Oleg pulled up alongside him. The passage was high enough so they could stand without bending their heads.

"Can you tell where that noise is coming from?"

Oleg listened, shook his head. The odd acoustics of the tunnel made it seem as if it was bouncing off the walls in all directions.

"Didn't the guide mention some fucking party down here?" he said. "We must be close."

Luka considered that a moment, then brought a full map of the underground up into their lenses. It was a merged image composed of the one he had taken from the guide Anton—photographed and digitized with Luka's ocular camera while he was still crouched over the body—and the original map loaded aboard their GPUs at the start of their operation.

"We're mostly surrounded by tunnels," he said. "There aren't many large galleries. But I see one just to our north."

Oleg nodded. It was marked Hall of the Barbarous King, a name imported from the guide's detailed hand-drawn map. The simple arrow icon representing Alcazar was bearing toward it from a mile or two to their southwest. "You think that's where the target's headed?" he said. "To a hall full of partiers?"

Luka exhaled, magnifying the image over their neurolink. "Take a closer look. There's a major route behind it leading north and east. You see? It seems to run off a smaller chamber at its rear."

Oleg studied the map. He noticed that, not far ahead of them, several passages intertwined in a shape like a pretzel, with one long, loose end tailing along the east side of the hall to that very chamber.

Luka highlighted it with a thought command. "We can take this and wait there for her. In the chamber. Catch her by surprise."

"If that's really where she's heading."

Luka shrugged. "The route leading from it is the fastest way I can see for her to reach Montmartre and Navarro. I think she'll show. And if not, we keep tracking her and pick her up elsewhere. We have nothing to lose."

Oleg looked at him a moment. Then he nodded. "All right," he said. "Let's go."

Lionel left the hall with one of his new friends on each arm. He was about to suggest that they just smoke the blunt right there outside the arch-way when Sadie leaned in close, glided her hand up and down this inner thigh and whispered a sug-gestion of her own into his ear. It involved slipping into one of the side tunnels running off the main passage…and then seeing what came of it.

His jaw fell open. She kept her hand on his leg and smiled, offering some graphic examples. Delia smiled too, snuggling up to his opposite side, and his jaw dropped some more. Was this all really hap-pening because of a simple design job?

Lionel felt a tremor of anticipation run through him from head to toe, standing there between the two in the flickering orange light of the wall sconces. The passage was lined with openings to tunnels large and small, any one of which would lead away from prying eyes. In fact, the guide who'd brought him down from the surface had taken a tunnel that was somewhere in-between. Snug, but not so snug that the three of them couldn't twist, squirm and wrestle around to their hearts' content.

He cleared his throat, pointing up ahead.

"That way," he said.

"Ugh!" Candace glanced at her watch and frowned. "I have to get back on shift."

Etienne slowed midstep, one hand on her hip and the other hand meshed in hers. He'd been dancing with a huge smile plastered on his face, barely even embarrassed by his two left feet.

"Already?" he said.

She nodded. "Can you stay until I'm off? It won't be for another two hours."

Etienne looked at her. Shards of light flitted across her face. Like jewels, he thought. Or tropical fish in motion.

He realized he was totally smitten.

"Now that you ask, nothing could make me leave," he said. "Though, I have one question."

"Oui?"

"Is there a bathroom down here?"

"You're so dashing," she said with a smile. "Yes, it's past the bone throne."

"I might just rather mess myself than go near that horror."

"Don't be silly," she said.

"I *am* silly. As well as dashing!"

"And a lousy dancer…but I've quickly grown

fond of you anyway." She gave his arm a playful
slap. "You'll see two openings behind the throne.
The one on the right leads to a room they use for
storage. It's crammed with all kinds of things and
has tunnels going off it in every direction."

"I see this only gets worse."

She laughed. "They can be very confusing. You
could go in circles forever finding your way back
here."

"Then, please tell me I take the opening on the
left."

"That's exactly what you do. There's a Sanisette
in a little cave. It's nice and clean."

"Can I take your word for it?"

"You'll find out."

"*If* I stay to the left."

Candace grinned, surprising him with a peck
on the cheek.

"I'm glad you and your irresistible dimples are
here with me tonight, silly-and-dashing boy. Come
chat when things slow down. Free cocktails have
been known to land from the sky."

"That I must see!"

She took his hand, squeezed it gently and let
go. He instantly found himself missing her touch.

"Later!" she said and then whisked off toward
the bar.

The two Russians had entered the curling, looping knot of tunnels, the music from the hall now
clearly ahead of them, its beat a repetitive thump
against the passage's thick rock sides.

Luka once again led the way with the old copper carbide lamp he'd liberated from the guide's dead hands. The tunnel had clearly been in use over many generations, and the lamp revealed odd splashes of colorful graffiti on the walls, interspersed with occasional inscriptions chiseled into the bare limestone. One read *Jeunes gens, ne vous portez pas volontaires pour l'armée. Le fou Napoléon nous fera tous tuer. 1813.*

Luka turned from the inscription. "It's a warning to young men not to enlist in the warmongering Napoleon's army," he said. "From one who did and regretted it."

Oleg had nothing to say. He felt no regrets about any war in which he'd participated.

They turned a bend and walked and turned another bend and walked. Their contact lens displays showed they were near the free end of the pretzel knot. They showed the tracker arrow that was Outlier continuing to approach the hall from the east. She was moving at a relatively fast clip, but still had a distance to go before she reached the spot where the two men planned to take her.

They turned, walked, turned, walked—

Luka abruptly pulled up short, raising his arm as a signal to stop. He'd seen something around the next bend. A light. From the same tunnel they were about to enter.

They stood motionless. Both of them entirely quiet. Both on the alert. Waiting and watching and listening as the light came closer and brightened. It was steady and level at first, probably four feet above the ground. But after a minute it started bouncing up and down and jerking from side to side.

Then it stopped advancing.

Then started again.

Then stopped, sliced wildly about the tunnel walls and dropped to the ground. After another minute it rose and began coming closer again, streaming around the bend to where the Russians were waiting on silent guard.

Luka glanced back over his shoulder at Oleg.

"Shit," he whispered. "We have company."

The tunnel Lionel squeezed into with Sadie and Delia was pitch-black, which made him glad he'd brought a flashlight with him tonight.

His invite to the party had come with a list of recommended items for negotiating the catacombs, high atop it the flashlight, a water bottle and a spelunking helmet or some other protective head-gear. It also suggested that he start out in clothes he didn't mind getting soiled and bringing along whatever he meant to wear at the rave in a water-proof bag. There were also directions to several *chatières* around the city where guests would find guides who'd been hired to lead them underground.

With his door fee covered by his boss, Lionel had set himself back a hundred euros picking up a compact flash bright enough to light up a room. Although he hadn't needed it on the way down—the guide's oil lamp had done the trick just fine—the darkness around him right now proved it had been worth the investment. His only problem, if he could call it one—which might be criminal, since most men he knew would give a decade of their lives for such problems—was keeping a steady grip on the flashlight's handle as Sadie and Delia hurried to undress him.

He'd gone no more than five paces into the tunnel when Delia plucked the blunt from his other hand, took a deep hit and passed it to Sadie, who inhaled greedily and then pushed it between his lips. The next thing he knew, the blunt was finished and they were unbuttoning, unbuckling and unzipping him. The flashlight jittered in his fingers as one of the roommates did something to his neck with her tongue. Then both of them started peeling off his shirt, and it slipped from his grasp, casting manic beams of light around the tunnel as it tumbled to the ground.

Lionel glanced down at it. To his relief it was shining and apparently intact.

"Leave it," Delia said into one ear.

"It's fine right where it is," Sadie said, flicking her tongue into his other ear.

But he didn't want to risk that any of them would step on it.

"I won't take a second."

Tearing free of their arms, he bent to pick it up and accidentally kicked it with the toe of his shoe. It rolled deeper into the tunnel, stopping after a few feet.

"Merde," he swore and went after it.

"Where are you going?"

He ignored whichever one of them had asked, took an awkward step toward it with his pants around his knees, stumbled, recovered, felt his pants slide down to his ankles, reached for the flashlight again and suddenly saw a pair of high-heeled boots land on the tunnel floor alongside it. Followed by a pair of mesh stockings and a leather skirt that fell on top of them. Then some flimsier undergarments.

He snatched in a breath, looked up. Sadie was standing there in nothing but her bare skin.

"Aren't you cold?" he asked.

"I won't be if you forget about that thing and come here."

Lionel kept gaping up at her, slack-jawed. He'd definitely wanted to put the light somewhere safer but decided to make the dirty compromise and leave it under the mound of clothes...and why not? It was a nice, soft cushion.

A moment later Delia had joined them, and all three were laughing and kissing and touching and tossing off whatever shreds of their clothing were still between them...which was when Lionel turned suddenly to look down the tunnel.

"What's wrong now?" Sadie said obliviously, her back to it. "Are you *married* to that flashlight?"

He didn't answer. This time *his* light wasn't the trouble. It was the one he'd noticed coming toward them.

After a second, Sadie noticed that Delia, standing slightly to Lionel's right, was also staring out ahead. Confused, she turned to see what had gotten their attention and was instantly struck in the face by the glare. She blinked her eyes, squinted, blinked again, dazzled. After a moment, it resolved into two long, distinct beams, one issuing from slightly behind the other, both quickly approaching them.

And then she saw the shadowy figures. Two of them to accompany the beams of light. Two *men* coming closer and closer.

She snapped a look at her roommate.

"C'est putain de bizarre," she said. "Who do you think they are?"

Luka saw Sadie, Delia and Lionel up ahead in their various stages of undress, staring confoundedly in his direction.

He would have preferred using the gas on them. It was silent and effective, whereas his Mark VII was a noisy cannon. But there was no time for him and Oleg to put on the masks.

He worked quickly, controlled pairs to the heads, single shots to their hearts, the huge .44 kicking with a recoil that would have thrown a weaker man his size onto his back. They went down spraying blood like human targets on a firing range.

Oleg joined him as he stood looking down at the bodies.

"They chose the wrong place to amuse themselves," he said.

Luka turned to him.

"Someone could have heard the gunfire," he said.

"Or not. That music's loud as hell."

"There must be security," Luka said. "We have to assume someone heard."

"What next, then?"

Luka thought about it, his gun barrel still angled down over the three kills. There were gaping holes in the chests, and the faces were mostly gone.

"We wait," he said.

* * *

Jean Claude was standing at the entry arch when he heard the reports: a double tap, then a single shot, the pattern repeated twice again in rapid succession. In his military years he'd been *Commandement des forces spéciales Terre*—Army Special Forces Command, 13th Parachute Dragoon Regiment. He had bloodied ISIS in Iraq and Syria. He knew the sound of a gun being fired—and a large one. And he knew the sound of an execution.

He turned toward the long main passage, discreetly slipping his hand under his blazer to his holstered weapon, not wanting to panic the guests. An FN P90 5.7, it handled like a charm and could cut trees with its fifty-plus-one clip.

He looked down the passage in the flickering light of the sconces. It had been fifteen or twenty minutes since he'd sent those three clubbers off to toke up, and whatever, out of sight. They had never returned, and he hadn't really thought about it. He'd done a dozen of these parties without a single incident. They were loud but didn't seem to attract a rowdy crowd.

But there were those unmistakable shots. Two, one. Two, one. Two, one.

Jean Claude started forward. The corridor ran for about a hundred yards in a straight line, bent sharply to the right, then went on through an endless series of turns and intersections, which was true of a lot of them in the catacombs. But this one was longer and wider than most. He'd heard it had been a miners' pass in the old days, used to cart tools and gravel and huge limestone blocks from one section of the Paris underground to another. There were over a dozen openings along its length before it reached the bend—two small holes in the wall on the right, two more exactly like them on the left, then several larger ones on both sides of the passage.

He hurried straight past the first four. They were little more than air vents dug by quarriers once upon a time, with openings too small to access. The first of the wider tunnels was on his left, within easy view of the entrance to the hall. He didn't think his three horny bohos would have ducked into it, though—not if they were concerned he might have kept them in his sights. The one beyond it on the right seemed far more likely. Not a hundred-percent private, maybe, since it led to a series of branching tunnels that many cataphile guides took from the surface. But Jean Claude assumed they had been looking for a place to have a quick romp, not a luxurious honeymoon suite. With the affair in full swing, and most of the partygoers having already arrived, they probably would have the tunnel all to themselves.

A guess was a guess, but it seemed like the logical place for them to go.

He moved slowly and carefully up the passage. Colored lights spun out through the archway behind him. Music blared. There were boisterous whoops from the dance floor. His old combat instincts had automatically heightened and sharpened to a point, but he didn't like all the noise and swirling light. All that uproar ramming his senses made it hard to see or hear anything. And he was spooked by that pattern of shots. *Bangbang-bang*. It was professional and dangerous, and he very much disliked it.

He had almost reached the tunnel opening now, his hand still under his jacket, seated lightly on the P90's doughnut grip. He took one step, two, three, then reached the opening and drew the gun, thumbing on the little tac light mounted under its barrel.

Jean Claude went into the tunnel exactly as if he were entering some dim, mud-brick bombmaker's hovel in downtown Basra. Pivoting on his heel. Gripping the gun in both fists. Leading with the barrel, its flash casting a 100-lumen circle of brightness through the tunnel opening and onto the opposite wall. He saw no one in front of him, swept the gun to his left, again saw nothing. Then swept it to his right and felt the hairs at the back of his neck stiffen up. Someone was standing there in the darkness. Thin, barely five feet tall, wearing a watch cap. Small hands around a massive firearm. The gun dwarfed them in size.

Jean Claude had an instant's hesitation. It was the figure's diminutive stature. It was the weird, jarring disparity of the gigantic gun in those small, almost delicate hands. They could have belonged to a child or a woman, and that caused an unconscious and involuntary blip in his reaction time. And then it was all over for him. Another hand clapped over his face, coming from behind, this one large, strong, pulling his head back hard to expose his throat. Staggered off-balance, he convulsively squeezed the trigger of his gun, firing a stray, ineffectual three-round burst a foot or two to Luka's side. Then something cold sliced across his throat, left to right, ear to ear, deep across the midline, opening both carotid arteries and his anterior jugular at once.

Oleg let him drop and stepped away, and Jean Claude crashed straight backward to the ground. A gurgling sound escaped him as thick, dark fluid brewed up out of his mouth. After a moment Oleg returned his knife to the sheath under his vest, then bent to take the dead man's weapon from his fingers. A couple of them twitched as it came free.

Luka looked at him. "There could be dozens of people in that hall. If they spill out into the tunnels, things will be out of control. We have to contain the problem. Here and now."

Oleg glanced up from inspecting the security man's gun. "It has to be a wipeout. No witnesses."

Luka nodded his head.

"This time we'll use the gas," he said.

The line at the Sanisette was five or six people long, but Etienne was next and gratefully so. He couldn't figure out how anyone could have gotten a modern, self-cleaning stall down into the catacombs, yet that was what he found after following Candace's directions. Blue-Eyed Dog seemed to have everything covered.

The woman inside exited, and Etienne waited impatiently for the red light to blink off. Sixty seconds later he pushed the button, then hurried to the loo as the door slid shut behind him.

He stood there whistling with relief. The cocktail had passed through him in record time; another moment or two and he might have embarrassed himself. What was the opposite of *dashing*? A guy with wet stains on the front of his pants surely qualified. Etienne wondered how he'd gotten an exceptional woman like Candace interested in him. Certainly it wasn't his cloddish dancing. Maybe it was true that God rewarded fools. But whatever she saw in him, Etienne hoped she kept seeing it, because she had completely blown him off his feet. He had expected tonight would be an adventure and hadn't been disappointed. It was one of the best nights of his life. And much more.

Though he hardly dared think it, it felt like the start of something big.

The gas was codenamed Kolokol-1—*kolokol* meaning *bell* in Russian. Although its toxic constituents were a guarded secret inside the Kremlin, its existence had been known to outside governments for a quarter century.

In October 2002, forty armed Chechen rebels had stormed the Dubrovka theater in Moscow during a premiere run of the musical *Nord-Ost*, taking captive the sellout crowd of eight hundred and fifty, and demanding the withdrawal of Russian troops from their occupied republic in exchange for a hostage release. After four days of stalled negotiations, FSB special forces ended the standoff with a complete rout, pumping the mysterious gas through the hall's ventilation and air-conditioning shafts. The Chechens were exterminated to a man, along with a hundred seventy of the hostages. All succumbed within minutes.

Reports of the incident had it that Spetsnaz's

elite Alpha and Vega groups conducted the raid, but it was in fact the Black Hundred that planned and controlled it from the shadows. The brotherhood had not only given the order to deploy Kolokol-1 but developed it in clandestine research facilities throughout the motherland.

In subsequent days, Spetsnaz was widely condemned for the mass loss of innocent human life. Many nations deemed the remedy worse than the cure. But the Black Hundred considered the operation a success, a field test of sorts for their new chemical agent, which had met or exceeded all their major performance criteria. A mixture of the aerosolized synthetic opioids carfentanil and remifentanil—with a smaller amount of the potent anesthetic halothane—Kolokol-1 was both instantly lethal and highly volatile, decaying into its harmless molecular constituents within minutes of dispersal. This made it optimal for use in confined areas that might have to be accessed shortly after its use.

Luka and Oleg had each brought two gas-shower grenades into the catacombs. The addition of a mild reducing, or stabilizing, agent gave their Kolokol-1 formulation extended storage life. But it was otherwise unchanged from the original deployed in the Dubrovka theater and would kill and dissipate without a visible trace.

Inside the tunnel now, they pushed their respirators over their faces, tightened the straps, cupped their hands over the vents and exhaled. Then they covered the filters with their palms and inhaled to create airtight seals. The masks were ghost white,

like those used by Reva's team. The grenades were
smooth, black and cylindrical, with six tiny nozzles
ringed around their bullet-shaped heads.

Luka took one from his pack and clipped it to his
belt. Oleg simultaneously affixed his. They turned
on their mask speakers.

"Poshlil," Luka said. Come on.

He nodded, and they stepped around the dead
security guard, skirting a pool of his blood and
pulp to enter the main passage.

They strode into the hall unnoticed. There was
a lot going on. The lights were strobing, the music
blaring, the dancers chugging away, the reactive
NFT graphics on the walls warping and stretching and metamorphosing in sync with its unhinged
tempo. The guest list mostly consisted of artists,
art appraisers and social media influencers encouraged to wear imaginative costumes, and those who
weren't whipping around the dance floor had either drifted over to the bar to mingle or joined in
on the action at the bone throne. The few who paid
any attention at all to Luka and Oleg were more intrigued by the stark difference in their height and
stature than their respirator masks.

The gas grenades were on three-second delays.
Luka thumbed the pin out of his and dropped it
straight down to the floor. Oleg tossed his under-
hand, almost like a bowling ball. Both cylinders
rolled and clattered and bounced off people's feet,
spewing the Kolokol-1 from their nozzles.

A few of the dancers felt something bump up
against their shoes but disregarded it. Others were

briefly curious and glanced down at the metallic object as it was kicked away by a shuffling heel or sweeping toe. But it looked like a stray soda or beer can. It might have tipped off the bar, slipped from a dancer's hand or spilled from a heaping trash receptacle. A glance was all it warranted. If that.

The concentrated toxin could not be seen, smelled or tasted. The droplets of Kolokol-1 were a single micron in size, twenty-five times smaller than the tiniest particle detectable to the human eye.

Inhaled through noses or mouths and absorbed through the skin and mucous membranes, the chemical's effects were felt throughout the crowded hall within milliseconds of release. Some became confused, dizzy and disoriented. Some sick to their stomachs. After thirty seconds most were wheezing and coughing, and more than a few were vomiting or foaming at the mouth. A minute after exposure nearly all the partyers were in seizure.

When the tissues of the human body are deprived of oxygen, the blood vessels contract and the heart beats faster and faster trying to pump oxygenated blood throughout the body. That can lead to rapid cardiovascular collapse.

Behind the bar, Candace was turning to carry a drink down the bar to a customer when her field of vision began to shrink, darkness closing in from its periphery like a camera's shutter mechanism around the lens. Her chest suddenly felt tight, her knees felt weak. At first she thought she was just fatigued from the nonstop action and paused to catch her breath. But it didn't help. Her right hand began to tremble with the cocktail glass still in it.

Afraid she might spill the drink, she reached out to set it down on the counter. But before she could, some guy on the floor came hurtling toward the opposite side of the bar like a car in a tailspin. He smacked up against it and projectile vomited on the sequined front of her dress. She looked at him in horror and disgust through her tunneled vision, saw his eyes roll up into their sockets. Then he was gone, spinning off into the crowd.

Candace heard screams above the throb of the music and realized they were coming from all around the hall. People were thrashing about everywhere.

She wobbled in an uncertain direction. Her hand was shaking badly, the cocktail splashing over her fingers. When she tried to steady it, a terrific spasm raced down her arm, cramping it up from her shoulder to her wrist. Candace yelped in pain as her fist clenched convulsively around the glass and broke it to jagged shards. They bit into her flesh, cutting in deep, almost severing two of her fingers. Mingled blood and alcohol stung her palm, dribbling down between her knuckles.

The next spasm was worse. Her legs stiffened and kicked out from underneath her, and she crashed into the lighted back bar, bottles and glasses toppling down to the stone floor, smashing to pieces at her feet. She spun and staggered and fell atop the welter of shattered glass and spilled alcohol.

Flat on her back, she tried to sit up, but her body

wouldn't respond. Then her stomach clenched and whatever was inside it heaved up into her throat. She tried to spit it up and couldn't. She tried turning her head to clear her mouth and couldn't. Her muscles had locked.

Candace took a thin, wheezy breath, as if inhaling through a narrow straw. Sour bile had flooded her mouth. She was choking and couldn't do anything about it. Couldn't move or breathe. Helpless, gasping for air, she heard screams and the harsh bark of a gun. Then she thought about her dance with Etienne and realized sadly that she was going to die.

In the middle of the hall, Luka and Oleg strode across the dance floor finishing off the survivors. They didn't waste ammunition on the ones who had already stopped moving. Those still flailing or jerking received double kill shots to the head.

Oleg was wading through the bodies near the bar when a hand grabbed his ankle. He looked down and saw a man clutching at him, his eyes wide and his mouth agape. He put him down with the P90.

"It's done," he told Luka. "We can get out of here."

Luka said nothing. He strode toward the back of the room and scanned the dance floor through the tinted lenses of his respirator. A man and woman were sprawled across the throne of human bones, their bodies draped over its seat and arms. They were still. So were the people around the throne. Luka checked out the area behind it and saw openings in the walls to the left and right. The left-hand opening led to a shallow alcove. He saw a number of bodies packed inside, briefly wondered about it, then saw the toilet stall at its rear and understood why they were all there.

He stepped into the alcove. A woman stirred almost imperceptibly under a much larger and heavier man who had fallen on top of her and pinned her down with his weight. Luka strode over to her, stood with his legs planted apart and pressed the muzzle of his gun against her forehead. She stared straight up at him, her eyes wide, one arm flung out from under the man's bulk, her fingers groping at empty air. A low, pleading whimper escaped her mouth.

Luka put two rounds into her skull, blowing it apart. Then he spent a moment studying the pileup of bodies for any further signs of movement.

There were none.

"Teper delo sdelano," he said, raising his voice over the music so Oleg could hear. "Now the job's done."

Jacques stopped in the tunnel ahead of Kali and Jill, his head tilted like a fox's sniffing the wind. He'd heard something. All three of them had. And all three recognized the sound.

"Gunfire," Kali said. "It's very close."

He turned to face her but was otherwise motionless, an almost surreal figure in his masklike makeup. The shots repeated in a similar pattern, reverberating through the passage he'd led them into just moments ago. Loud bangs, pops.

"There are two of them," Jill said behind Kali. "One's a heavy caliber."

Kali listened as the sounds kept rolling through the darkness. Close, without a doubt, but it was easier to judge distance than location. The underground was a labyrinthine echo chamber, and the noise was bounding and slamming off the walls around her.

But she'd seen a look in Jacques's eyes.

"You know where they're coming from," she said. It was not a question.

A moment passed. His eyes met hers.

"I think so," he said.

Luka emerged from the alcove to see Oleg outside with his eyes attentively turned to the floor. The giant looked at him as he strode closer.

"See here," he said. "I want to show you something."

Luka realized Oleg's feet were edging on a wide pool of water. It was a rusty-brown color, and was coming from the opening in the opposite wall.

"What do you think of it?" he said.

Luka gave it a perfunctory, disinterested glance. "What should I think? It's a spill."

"This much water, I'd call it more than a spill," he said.

Luka didn't answer. He had turned to peer at the opening, his expression curious.

"What's in there?" he said. "Have you checked it out?"

"Barely," Oleg said. "But I think it might be the side chamber on our map. The one leading to the tunnel for Montmartre."

"Let's take a look," Luka said and sidestepped the puddle to enter it.

Oleg felt a momentary blip of hesitation before following him inside.

The space was in fact a large vaulted hexagonal brick-walled chamber, one that looked centuries old and was obviously used as some sort of storage room for the dance hall. There were rolling carts full of supplies, stacks of wooden wine crates, plastic pallets crowded with rolls of wiring and cable, light and sound equipment, and other things neither man could identify. They saw arched portals on two of the walls, each of which gave entry to branching tunnels. Water was running into the chamber from one of them...a dark, steady stream trickling across the stone floor toward the entrance to the dance hall.

Which accounted for the puddle outside, Oleg thought.

He examined the crates, touched his hand to one and arched a thick eyebrow. Its wooden surface was beaded with moisture. He looked up and saw water dripping from the cracked mortar between some of the bricks above the stack.

"These have to be fresh leaks," he said. "No one would keep anything in here otherwise. Especially the electronic shit."

Luka shrugged vaguely. "Come on. I want to see where these tunnels run. Who the fuck would guess there'd be more than the one we saw on the map?"

For his part Oleg wasn't surprised. As the guide, Anton, had hinted, the map was deliberately vague about some things. But he had something else on his mind right now.

He looked at Luka from the wall of crates. This time his reluctance was visible.

"What is it?" Luka asked.

"I'm thinking of the flood that almost washed Reva's unit into the Seine."

Luka looked around, fanning the beam of his headlamp over the walls and ceiling.

"That's miles from here, and this is hardly a flood," he said. "Leaks won't kill us."

He turned toward one of the portals. He'd also been reminded of something. In his case, it was Odessa, in Ukraine. Underlying the city were ancient quarries not unlike these catacombs. Passages where the Soviets had left behind a vast subterranean infrastructure of drainage systems, command centers and bunkers. When he'd been dispatched there in '22 with the Wagner Group, Ukrainian resistance fighters had used them to harry the Russian invasion forces at every turn, eluding and outmaneuvering them, the network facilitating their easy movement throughout the city. But they had learned the ins and outs of the underground over long centuries. He and Oleg had no such luxury. Their target was coming fast.

He stepped through into the tunnel, Oleg slightly behind him. It was about ten feet high, five wide, and walled with bricks like the storage chamber. They followed it for a few short yards before reaching a smaller chamber with its own set of branching passages. They were in a warren of forking and converging tunnels, galleries and chambers.

Luka nodded toward an opening on his left. "I'll go that way. You take a separate passage. Let's see what we can."

"And if Outlier shows up while we're exploring this maze?"

Luka thought again of the Ukrainians and their mastery of the Odessa tunnels. "It's worth the chance," he said. "If we can familiarize ourselves with it, we gain an advantage."

Oleg looked at the walls around them. They were still slick with moisture, but there was no visibly running water.

"All right," he said. "Fifteen minutes. Not one second longer."

They split up, Oleg turning off to his right. The ground sloped up and down and up again. He passed a tunnel so low he would have needed to crawl on all fours to enter it, then reached the entrance to a wider one, went inside and was led to another interconnected tunnel. It was as if he was wandering around a gigantic ants' nest. He wondered if it really had anything close to a scheme or layout, or whether the quarriers had simply dug wherever it was expedient for their haul of limestone.

About five minutes of the fifteen had passed. He took another turn, discovered two large, empty galleries linked by a narrow passage. Both had damp patches on the walls, but neither was leaking water like the storage chamber off the dance hall. Which relieved him a bit. He saw a side tunnel leading out of one of the galleries, followed it out and saw that he was really inside the neck of a smaller, knob-shaped space...an adjunct to the chamber.

He paused there, listening. Had he heard something inside? He listened some more, motionless.

Yes, he thought. He could still hear it. The sound was like water draining rapidly from a burst main.

Oleg stepped farther through the neck to investigate, realized it was flooded underfoot. That stopped him again. A glance ahead into the wider portion of the knob and the beam of his headlamp struck a roiling, churning, pool of water. It looked ankle-deep, perhaps even deeper.

The sound of rushing water was very loud here.

Oleg stopped a third time and looked up anxiously, his light on the ceiling above the pool. There was a long, wide cleft running across it, and water was sheeting through. He saw smaller fissures radiating from it in a spiderweb pattern, and they were also raining water into the pool.

"Luka." Into his radio. "Do you read me?"

"Yes."

"I've found something."

"What is it?"

Oleg stared up at the torrent falling from the cleft and recalled Luka's disinterest in the water outside the storeroom. Then a cold, heavy splash from one of the radiating cracks slapped his face. He dragged a hand across his cheek, studied his glistening knuckles in the brightness of his lamp.

"Water," he said. "And more than a spill."

Etienne had heard the sounds outside the Sanisette as he was tucking his shirt back into his pants.

Two pops, like firecrackers, and then louder bangs, also in a quick, explosive couplet. He hadn't associated them with gunshots, not right away. The music was booming, the crowd noisy, and his mind was on Candace. They might have been part of the general racket. Some kind of sound effect. Or perhaps someone on the dance floor had actually set off pyrotechnics: it was that kind of insane affair. Though he had supposed Jean Paul the bouncer probably wouldn't take too well to it.

Then he'd heard them again. The pops and bangs in rhythmic, overlapping pairs. Two and two and two. He'd grown up in Brittany surrounded by farms, and the noise reminded him of a backfiring tractor. But he had a terrible feeling it was nothing so harmless.

He'd zipped up, turned from the mirror, gone over to the door and listened.

That was when he suddenly heard screams piercing the music. It had made the flesh at the back of his neck tingle. People were screaming out there. And those other sounds hadn't stopped. The pops and bangs running together with a frightening, repetitive cadence.

He hadn't known what was going on. But everyone in Paris remembered the November 13 attacks years before—his cousin and her husband had been wounded at the Bataclan. He'd thought about them and about Candace out there at the bar right now.

Then something had crashed hard against the Sanisette's door. Etienne had jumped, startled. Whatever hit it made the whole cubicle shake. He kept his eyes on the door for a few long minutes, thought he heard a woman moaning on the other side. There were more loud bangs outside the stall. One and two. Then a male voice speaking what sounded like an Eastern European language.

Etienne's heart had slammed in his chest. He hadn't known what to do. Hadn't been able to think.

He'd waited by the door, listening.

Now a few minutes had passed since the last pops and bangs. There hadn't been any more after he heard the woman's voice. And he hadn't heard it again after that one time.

Still, he didn't know who might out there with a gun. Except he knew Candace was out there. What was he supposed to do? He wasn't Superman. He didn't want to be a hero.

But Candace…

She was out there.

He suddenly waved a hand in front of the sensor to open the door. It wasn't a conscious decision. It wasn't something he'd debated. He just did it. Except the door didn't open. It trembled a little but didn't open. He waved his hand again. It didn't open. He heard its mechanisms straining. He could see it trying to open. But it didn't. It was stuck.

He thought about the crash he'd heard. The booth shaking. He wondered if something—or someone—was pressing against the door out there, jamming it shut. What if he was stuck inside? The thought scared him more than he would have expected. He didn't want to be locked inside the stall.

He kicked at the door once. It didn't open. Kicked again. It still didn't open. He looked anxiously around for another way out…and to his instant, immense relief saw a large red handle in a shallow recess to his right. There was an arrow underneath and the words *Ouverture de secours*, emergency opening, in white lettering above it. An oval panel, like an airplane's escape hatch, was on the adjacent wall.

Etienne breathed. How had he missed it before? In all the times he'd used public toilets like this on the street, he had never noticed an emergency door. He wondered if they all had them.

Afraid the lever would set off an alarm and draw attention, he gave the automated door one last try. It made a low humming noise but stayed shut.

Etienne frowned, reached for the emergency lever again and stood with his hand wrapped around it. Though the music had kept playing, he could no longer hear anyone outside. That absence of human noises, even the screams and groans, made his skin crawl. What had happened to all the people? It was probably good the shooting had stopped. But he realized it also might mean the unthinkable. Mean there was no one left out there to shoot.

He thought of Candace and turned the lever. There was an audible click as the latch mechanism disengaged and the exit panel popped open on its hinges. He inhaled nervously, pushed it the rest of the way open and squeezed out between the side of the Sanisette and the rock wall. The music bounced and pumped. Lights flashed at the far end of the passage. But he still didn't hear any people. He didn't hear anyone. He only heard the music.

Etienne stood motionless for a full half minute. Then he stepped toward the front of the stall and peeked around its edge. He suspected he already knew why the door had malfunctioned and prayed to God he was wrong about what he would see.

He wasn't wrong.

He felt wild horror rearing up inside him. There were bodies crammed against it…eight, nine, maybe more. Some of the partygoers must have been waiting to use the stall when the shooting started, then tried to push their way into it looking for a place to hide. The ones at the rear of the line desperately shoving up to it in a panic, the ones ahead of them shoving back and shoving forward, all of them mashing together as they pushed and pulled and went down in a heap against the stall's door, the crush of their combined weight jamming its mechanism shut.

Candace, he thought, breathing shakily. If she wasn't out there, he might have stayed right where he was, rooted in place with fear. But the only way to get to her was over those bodies. As much as he dreaded it, he would have to walk over them, climb over them, to reach the bar.

Candace.

Mustering every bit of nerve and resolve within him, Etienne went around to the front of the stall and got started.

11

"The Hall of the Barbarous King," Jacques said, touching a finger to Kali's map. "I would bet the shots came from there."

Kali had unfolded the map and moved up close to him in the passage. The gunfire hadn't lasted long, perhaps a minute or two before the echoes died away. It had sounded like there were only the two guns discharging in a steady rhythmic pattern, and that chilled her.

She studied the spot Jacques had pointed out. "How do you know?"

"Because I know a little about the catacombs." He moved his finger down to an area well south of them. "See here? This is all that's open to the public. A tiny slice of the network less than a mile in size…out of *two hundred* total miles. It's the portion Napoleon turned into ossuaries for the skeletal remains carted into the tunnels before his time."

Kali glanced up at him. "Explain why this matters right now."

"I told you about the bones left forgotten at the bottom of the mining pits. Many were collected and arranged by cataphiles in the *sections interdites*. The forbidden underground. The hall has a throne made of them. That's how it gets its name, and it's become an attraction of its own…but not for tourists and casual visitors. There are secret, illegal soirées held by independent collectives. Political groups, artists, techies. Usually late Sunday nights, when the city is asleep—a jab at the bourgeoisie, who they know are preparing for the work week. I would wager there was a gathering tonight."

Kali's gaze locked on his. "How far are we from this place?"

"It's a quarter mile up ahead," he said and paused. "There's more than one way to the Northern Network. They're slower but safer."

No. Circumstances change. War's full of uncertainty, and you have to adapt. Like we did at Castle Graguscu. But keep your guns on the main objective. Don't let anything slow you down. Most of all, don't give the enemy a vote.

Kali was quiet. She had a sudden image of Carmody straddling the back of a chair that was much too small for him, facing her with his arms folded and his legs wide apart.

"We'll stick to our plan," she said after a long moment. "Keep going."

Jacques looked surprised. "We don't know who fired the guns. Or why."

"Then, it's best we find out."

Jill shook her head. "Those shots were closely grouped. There was no exchange of fire. You heard them. Like machines."

Kali noticed her bottom lip trembling as she spoke. "Are you all right?"

Jill ignored the question. "What we heard was a deliberate execution, not a fight. If it was Blood Lightning, it would mean they're already to our north. What more do we need to know?"

"Anything that can give us an advantage."

Jill stared at her. "Did you hear a single word I said just now?"

"I heard."

"And it changes nothing?"

"Not with them standing between us and Lucien."

"What good will we do him by getting ourselves killed?"

Kali looked at her. "Think," she said. "The Lightning are trained operatives. Professional hit squads. They wouldn't just wander the tunnels at random hoping to run into me."

There was a silence lasting about ten seconds. Then Jill expelled a short, sibilant breath through her front teeth.

"Merde," she said. "They have a copy of the map. They know the secret ways."

Kali nodded. "Their goal is to box me in. We can't close our eyes and pretend they'll go away.

We need to find out where they are so we can out-
maneuver them."

Another silence. Then Jacques nodded. "I'll go
on ahead. Take a look."

"Not alone," Kali said. "I'm coming with you."

"You're the one they want. You can't just deliver
yourself to them on a platter."

"That isn't my intention." Kali turned to face
Jill directly. "You said you had friends patrolling
elsewhere in the catacombs."

"Yes."

"Then, find them. Bring help."

She shook her head. "I think we should stay together."

"Because you mistrust me?"

"Your words, not mine."

Kali's dark eyes bored into hers. "I'm fine with
your suspicion, Jill," she said. "It tells me you're
using your head. That's what I want from you, and
what you should want from me. Trust can wait."

Jill was quiet a moment. Then she he looked
sharply at Jacques. "You're the soldier," she said.
"You decide."

He didn't hesitate. "Find the others," he said.
"Meet us at the hall."

Jill's teeth came together with an audible click.

"Be careful," she said to him, nodding.

She turned and sprinted off the way they'd come.
Within seconds the glow of her headlamp was
swallowed up in darkness.

Kali folded the map into her pocket, nodded to
Jacques.

"All right," she said. "Lead the way."

* * *

They had been trotting through the passage for several moments when Jacques paused to check the wearable on his wrist.

Kali waited behind him. The display showed a set of latitudinal and longitudinal coordinates, white against a black background.

"We're coming up to a side tunnel," he said, half turning to her. "When we get there, we'll take it."

She gestured at the device with her chin. "You're using MFP. Magnetic field positioning."

He turned the rest of the way around, nodded. "How did you know?"

"GPS doesn't work underground, not at this depth. The satellite signals can't penetrate. Magnetic field is the only secure and effective method. But it's advanced military technology."

He smiled. "Jill worries too much, I think."

"About?"

"Whether you are who you claim to be."

Kali shrugged. "Better one worries too much than too little."

"I suppose."

Kali looked at him. "She called you a soldier."

"Yes."

"It made wonder about your background. Your skill sets."

"Should you have to rely on them?"

"No," Kali said. "On you."

She had dropped her hand to where he'd pulled the tranquilizer dart out of her side. Jacques observed it quietly.

"I was once Commando Jaubert with the French

navy," he said. "*Les Bérets Verts*. The Green Berets. My service to the Armée de Terre ended three years ago."

"Yet you have its latest toys."

"Yes."

"And how is that?"

"It's irrelevant."

"Is it?"

"Yes." His tone was flat. "I'm with the White Rose. I renounce all nations with physical borders and will no longer fight for them. Their nature is outdated, incompatible with true democracy. Or don't you agree?"

"We should stick to what's vital."

"For me nothing is more vital. I would think it would be the same for you."

She looked at him. "The people Jill went to find...do they also have MFP units?"

"Yes."

"Then, you can send messages to her. Receive them from her."

He nodded. "Not voice, but code."

"Even while maintaining radio silence."

"Yes."

"It would have been better if you'd told me sooner," she said. "Can it interface with, say, a standard smartwatch? At short distance?"

"Very short, down here."

She was thoughtful. Jacques stood there looking at her for a second. Then he nodded to himself, as if having settled an internal debate.

"There's something you should know," he said. "About Jill."

Kali waited.

"She came to France as a refugee when she was fourteen," he said. "From Africa."

"Bali?"

Jacques looked mildly surprised.

"Her accent," Kali said. "It's either that or Sudanese."

He nodded. "She's from Western Sudan. A Beja. One of the Darfuri tribes the government targeted for genocide. Her parents sought asylum here. Instead, they suffered the indignities of the Calais migrant camp. You know of it?"

"The Jungle."

"That was too good a name for that hell. Jungles are living, growing systems. This was a place where people were left to rot. And be picked clean to the bone by vultures."

She waited.

"Jill's family spent two years there before they tried to cross the English Channel in an inflatable boat. They gave the human traffickers every last euro they could scrape together," he said. "The boat sank to the bottom, and they all drowned. Her parents, her grandmother, her brothers and sisters. Jill alone was rescued. Afterward she survived for years on the streets."

Kali was silent. Then she nodded her head again. "Why tell me all this?"

"So you understand who she is and what she's been through," he said. "Should you need to rely on *her*."

She stood there for two or three seconds, then expelled a breath. "Thank you, Jacques. Sincerely."

He nodded. "We should move out," he said. "Get over to that side passage."

"Yes."

He turned and hurried forward.

Kali followed.

Each of the ultratiny mote beacons was a tenth of a micron in size, an implantable nanochip so small it was dwarfed by a single speck of dust and invisible to the naked eye. Resistant to compressive forces—such as the pressure pulse created when the injector darts released the liquid tranquilizer in which they had floated—they were coated with biocompatible polyamide, a type of plastic that shielded them against bodily fluids, and would cause no harm to the host or corrosion to the mote's metallic core.

Zoltan had struck Kali twice with his darts. Once on the side of her chest, once on her thigh. Two doses, two mote beacons. If one failed, the other would be a backup. But right now both were fully operational and transmitting over Glaskov's mobile mesh network.

"She's moving faster," Reva said to Zoltan.

He grunted in acknowledgment beside her. The tracker arrow representing Kali glided across his retinal overlay map. She was a quarter mile up ahead, bearing toward the chamber Luka and Oleg had cleansed minutes ago.

Beyond even their antimod stance, the Black Hundred were known for their readiness to take extreme measures. He wondered about the necessity of their action—and more basically about the need for their involvement in the Paris operation at all. But it wasn't his decision. Braithwaite Global was signing the checks. He himself had participated in the cleansing of Ukrainian Mariupol, and it occurred to him that many had questioned *its* necessity. But it was the Russian way of waging war: scorched earth, leaving behind no assets the enemy could use, no potential obstacles to their defeat.

Though, one thing puzzled him.

"She must have heard the gunshots," he said.

"Yes."

"Then, why would she go there? Why not bypass it?"

"It doesn't matter."

Zoltan said nothing in response. But Reva's reflexive dismissal bothered him. She was burned far worse than she knew and had not yet seen the damage to her face. Only adrenaline, anger and a cushion of painkillers were allowing her to physically function. But he would have to be careful they hadn't also clouded her ability to make sound decisions.

She sped up, setting a quicker pace. The passage was dark and tight and thick with the musky smell of damp limestone.

Why would she go there?

Zoltan was thinking he would have his answer before too long.

Etienne stood just inside the alcove, looking out across the hall with horror and disbelief.

There had been a slaughter. Bodies were everywhere on the dance floor, too many to count. It was like a tornado had blown through the room and blown them all over. Most were contorted into horrible positions, and blood was splattered everywhere. The smell of vomit and voided bowels was dreadful.

He stood there, his legs locked and rigid. He saw a woman who had been shot in the head and ribs. The man sprawled half on top of her had the same wounds. And the two women next to them. Every one of them appeared to have been put to death in the same way.

Etienne shivered, his stomach frozen, ice water slipping up and down his spine. The PA system had kept grinding out electro beats, wailing synthesizers and jazz horns. It made everything even more grotesque. More terrible. More difficult for him to process.

Candace. Cher Dieu, pas elle.

Dear God, not her.

The thought broke his paralysis. It didn't make him less afraid for his life. It didn't impart any courage. But somehow it allowed him to move.

He pushed toward the bar, wading through the blood-soaked corpses on the floor. The music thumped relentlessly. The lights swirled. Skeletons cavorted across the walls in hats and tribal headdresses and corollas of swirling, abstract color. All of it was still *on* except for the people, who were all dead. He avoided looking over at the bone throne and tried not to look down at the arms and legs and shoes and puddles of blood and nameless soft, slippery things underfoot, convinced he would lose his nerve, if not his mind. It suddenly came to him that whoever was responsible for the carnage might still be nearby, but then he thought about Candace again and pressed forward, stumbling over more than one body as he got closer to the bar and then went scrambling around the counter, his simple prayer a repeating loop in his mind. *Cher Dieu, pas elle, cher Dieu, pas elle, cher Dieu, pas elle—*

It ended the instant he saw her. She was on the floor, lying faceup in a welter of broken glass and blood, her lips blue, her wide-open eyes staring and dilated. Her hair clung to her forehead, matted and bloody. The blood had run down over her face, tiny bits of glitter from her eye makeup mingled in with it. Etienne saw the shards of broken glass in her hand and her partially severed fingers, and it was all too much to take.

Tears burst from his eyes. His legs went limp, and he sank to his knees, whimpering and sniffling, crouching over her amid the blood and spilled drinks and chunks of broken glass on the floor. He put his hands on her shoulders, lifted her up and pulled her body close to him.

"Oh no," he said, and hitched out a breath. "No..."

He held her against him, his cheeks wet, the taste of salt on his lips. An inner voice was telling him he needed to go, and he rejected it angrily. He didn't want to. He wanted to stay with her. But his silent protestations only made the voice more stubbornly demanding. He couldn't help her. Candace was dead, and whoever had killed her could be anywhere. Could return at any second. He needed to get out. Get out before they returned. He had to leave her.

But not the way she was right now.

He kept her in his arms a little longer, sobbing, her blood smeared on his hands and sleeves. Then he lowered her to the floor, stood up shakily, almost drunkenly, and looked around the well of the bar. He'd left his backpack in a niche with all the other guests' bags. But she had stashed her tote back here, behind the bar with her.

He looked around the back bar, repeatedly swiping tears from his eyes, but didn't see it. He'd remembered it was a bright color, orange or red. How could he *not*? He looked despairingly down at the floor and still couldn't find it in the disarray. That was almost enough to snap the frayed, fragile thread of his composure. But then his gaze fell to one of the shelves below the counter. He spotted it in an otherwise-empty carton, the neon-orange fabric catching his attention. He practically lunged for it, snatching it up out of the box, hurriedly tugging open the zipper.

Etienne found Candace's sweater and denim jacket stuffed inside with the rest of her street clothes. He pulled out the sweater and bunched it under his arm, her strip headlamp spilling from the bag as he did so. He nearly left it where it fell to the floor but then reached down to pick it up from among the scattered contents of the bar rack.

That was when he heard them again. Male voices.

The breath caught in his throat. He wouldn't have heard them at all above the music if they weren't so close. But they *were* close. And coming closer.

He knelt there, motionless. They were the same

two men he'd heard before. Speaking a language that wasn't French. That sounded Eastern European.

Panic clawed at Etienne's thoughts. He was sure they would search behind the bar and put two bullets in him. He'd been spared the same death as everyone else only by minutes.

He knelt there, listening…and then suddenly realized they hadn't stopped to look. The voices were passing him by. Moving on past the bar toward the door.

Several seconds went by. He stayed motionless. He couldn't hear them anymore. Couldn't hear anything but the music and the beating of his own heart.

He waited another half minute, realized he was still holding the strip lamp in his shaking hand, and put it on. Then he shuffled back to Candace and looked down at her. Her eyes stared upward, empty and unseeing. He took a deep breath to steel himself and gently pulled down their upper lids with his thumb and forefinger. Then he unballed the sweater, spread its sleeves apart and covered her upper body with it, pulling its collar up under her chin.

"Notre Père, qu'elle repose en paix auprès de vous pour l'éternité," he said huskily, and made the sign of the cross.

Our Father, may she rest peacefully with you for all eternity.

It was a very different prayer than before.

Etienne knelt there another moment, sobbing. Then he stood up. He knew of only two ways out of the hall. The main passage he and Candace had used to enter it, and the storage room she'd told him about. The one on the right side of the bone throne. She had said there were tunnels leading from it.

He wouldn't have taken the main passage in any event. It was too wide open. Too well lit. If anyone was out there, he would have no place to hide. The storage room had been the better choice even before the two men went in that direction. Now it was his only choice.

He dug his fists into his eyes as if to stanch the flow of tears. But they kept running down over his knuckles and between his fingers unchecked. Finally he gave up, dropped his hands from his face and stood there looking down at Candace, his cheeks wet and glistening.

He had to leave her.

He had to go.

Taking a deep, trembling breath, Etienne turned and hurried out from behind the bar.

Kali was following Jacques around the corner of a passage when she heard it. A rippling murmur, like water guttering through a drainage channel.

She tapped his elbow. "Wait. Listen. What's that?"

He stood very still, his ears perked. Then he turned to look at her. "You're thinking it's the canal water," he said. "The Saint-Martin."

"You know these tunnels. Tell me what *you* think."

He was quiet a moment, listening. "Only a short stretch of the Sandy Road should have flooded," he said. "The water's channeled into the Seine through drainage sluices. That's how we could get you out of there. They kept it low enough for us to wade over to you…"

Jacques let the sentence trail.

"Go on," she said.

"There was rain two or three weeks back. A heavy storm," he said. "When the water table rises, it can swamp the lower tunnels. But it's silent. It *creeps* slowly upward. Like a spider, you know? This water is rushing too fast."

She listened some more. It was still gurgling steadily. "Could it have overflowed into the tunnels?"

"It's possible, I suppose. But I doubt it. The sluices should be able to handle the flood."

"Say something's clogged them? Debris, for instance."

"It's never happened before."

"The hatch under the canal never came down before," she said. "The whole roof around it collapsed when I set the pulley in motion. It fell in chunks around me, huge rocks. What if they were washed into the sluices? If the floodwater backs up and adds to the rains, couldn't it flood the passages?"

Jacques listened to the sound another second or two. Then he gestured up the passage.

"We should move fast," he said.

Reva was hurrying along at a jog, Zoltan behind her, when she stopped short and raised her hand. She had come to the edge of an abrupt drop. Another step and her foot would have found nothing but empty space.

Zoltan halted, looked around. "This tunnel

doesn't seem meant for human beings," he said. "And do you hear that noise above us?"

She stood there a moment. Guided by their tracking signal, they had entered the passage at an intersection some yards back. Within minutes its sides had closed in around them, the roof dropping in places so they had to run with their heads ducked, its floor slanting downward at a steep angle. She was thinking it did indeed look more like the lair of a giant worm than a man-made path through the underground. Its walls were composed of soft stone, like the Sandy Road's, but there they had been solid and bone-dry. These were slick and clammy and scarred with crevices from top to bottom, some probably large enough for her to squeeze through, others little more than pencil-thin cracks in the stone. There were tiny beads of moisture around some of them.

She looked up at the roof. She did indeed hear something overhead. A gurgling, chuckling sound.

Zoltan touched his fingers to the wall, then examined them, rubbing them together. "They're wet," he said, showing them to Reva. "What do you make of it?"

She ignored him and kept studying the roof of the passage. Like the walls, it was scrawled with jagged cracks. They radiated outward from a fissure that was several feet long and about four inches wide, a deep gash in the stone.

After a long moment she turned back toward the drop. Ten or twelve feet below, the floor of the passage ran on into the darkness.

"I don't make anything of it," she said. "Watch yourself."

She crouched, sprang down over the edge of the drop and plunged ahead, her long running strides echoing flatly off the tunnel walls. Zoltan spared a moment to glance up at the ceiling before he joined her.

Ten seconds later, a drop of water slipped through one of the cracks in the roof. It landed on the ground with a tiny splash, followed by another, and another. Within seconds, it became a steady trickle to join the water seeping through the cracks in the walls, running down in rivulets like a cold sweat.

Beside himself with sorrow, Etienne had left the hall through the right-hand entry behind the bone throne, thumbed on Candace's strip light and taken a frantic look around.

The storage room she'd told him about was actually a vaulted hexagonal chamber that looked centuries old. It was filled with rolling carts full of supplies, high stacks of wooden crates, and all sorts of electronics on wooden pallets: sound and effects boards, laser and LED lighting equipment, things he didn't recognize. The walls were brick, the portals to the radiating tunnels arched. Etienne had guessed they were about five feet wide and ten high.

He'd hurried forward and turned into the first on his left, thinking it as good as the rest.

It had curved one way, then another. As he'd gone deeper inside, hoping to find a ladder or cat flap, the brickwork had grown sparse and patchy, and in some places was so badly deteriorated that the bricks had moldered into crumbled heaps on the ground. About a hundred yards in, what remained of them gave way entirely to raw, exposed stone.

That point had seemed a demarcation of sorts. Beyond it the tunnel shrank around him, becoming almost tubular, like the cardboard core of a roll of paper towels.

He'd seen no sign of an exit to the surface, and the air had gotten stale and dank. He kept walking at a fast clip, then broke into a jog. At first the added exertion had calmed him a little, helping him shed some nervous energy, but after a while he'd grown tired and winded. His anxiety regenerating with each fruitless turn, no closer to a way out, Etienne had weighed returning to the main shaft and trying his luck with one of the other offshoots. But the prospect of heading back toward the hall— back toward all the death there—had been viscerally unbearable.

He had made a snap decision to keep moving forward, though he no longer really knew what forward meant, not with any degree of certainty. He was in a spaghetti bowl of tangled, intertwining passages and had lost track of time as well as direction. It felt like he'd been running for an hour, though it couldn't really have been that long. His legs were starting to cramp, and a mad, insistent thirst had taken hold of him. He wished to God he'd brought a water bottle.

The tunnel curved on ahead for several yards, then bifurcated like the tongue of a snake, and then sloped downward for a stretch, making things a little easier on his legs. But it was growing colder and damper around him, and his lungs hurt.

He bore randomly to his right, ran a little farther, reached another split, then another. Left, left, right, left, right. He didn't see how it made any difference. One way seemed as good as another. He turned, hurried forward, turned again, reached an abrupt dead end, then doubled back to another division of the shaft and wondered if it was one he'd already passed through. They'd all started looking the same, and it struck him he could be retracing his own steps and not even realize it. His sense of direction was scrambled, and the jogging was no longer helping to ease his anxiety. Whatever shreds of composure he'd mustered before were gone. He was on the brink of panic.

Etienne abruptly slowed to a walk, gasping for breath, sweating in the chill dampness. He needed to stop and pull himself together. Find a place to rest up.

He looked around. Both sides of the shaft were glistening with moisture. He pressed a hand to its wall, thinking he might wet his lips, but his fingertips came away covered with a thin, oily coating of slime, and he gave up on that idea.

He kept walking, the floor of the shaft at a constant decline. After a while he heard a dull, muffled sound that he immediately identified as flowing water. It seemed to come from somewhere well above him...although the shaft's acoustics made it hard to be certain. He wondered whether it might be a drainage or water line. And say it was, he thought. It very well might not be drinkable, and he wasn't sure he was even willing to test it. But chances were it would eventually lead out of the catacombs.

If he could find it.

Etienne turned a corner. Walked on. Turned another corner. Walked on. Then turned another corner and stopped. There was a kind of alcove in the wall up ahead. A small notch, really. He increased his pace, eager to investigate, hoping to see an exposed pipe inside, something that might run a traceable path to the surface. But he found nothing there. It was just a recess three or four feet deep, probably a natural irregularity. He reached inside out of curiosity and found it to be cold but dry...almost powdery. Which was something, anyway. If nothing else, it would give him a place to sit for a little while without getting wet.

Etienne sat down on the tunnel's cold stone floor and wriggled back into the notch. He took several deep breaths, the hard, rough rock pressing into his shoulder blades. He hadn't realized how utterly fatigued he was. How much his legs had stiffened up. Their taut, aching muscles seemed to sigh with relief.

After a minute he reluctantly decided to extinguish the strip light. He didn't want to be in the dark. But he also didn't know how much juice was left in the battery and was afraid someone might notice its glow. He hadn't forgotten his reason for being out there in the tunnel. He hadn't forgotten Candace and what had been done to her and to all those other people.

He turned it off and was instantly swallowed

up in a blackness so deep and absolute it was un-
nerving. He held his hand up in front of his face
and couldn't see it. It made him feel very small and
alone, like he was at the bottom of the deepest well
hole ever dug in the ground.

He drew his legs in against his chest, clasped his
hands around them and lowered his forehead onto
his knees. After a moment he closed his eyes…
and almost to his own surprise kept them shut.
He was tired. Despite his fear and humming tension, so tired. His breaths became rhythmic, his
thoughts loose and syrupy. He would rest a while
and move on.

Etienne only realized he'd slipped into a doze
when a noise startled him out of it. He jumped, his
head snapping up, the back of it banging against
hard stone. At first he just sat there, confused, un-
sure what had awakened him.

Then he heard movement up the tunnel. The
soft but identifiable scuffle of footsteps—and more
than one set. He wedged himself farther back into
the notch, tucked his legs even closer against his
body than before. The tips of his feet were sticking out into the tunnel, but it was the best he could
do. The notch was too shallow to be much of a hiding place.

Seconds passed. Etienne's pulse raced. He bent
ever so slightly forward and rotated his head in the
direction of the noise, but he still couldn't see anything. It was like there was a black screen in front
of his eyes. Like he'd been blindfolded.

A single breath tore in through his front teeth,
rasped back out. The panic he'd managed to sup-

press until now went screaming up into his skull. He squirmed back into the notch, his palms against the sides of his head as if to keep it from blowing to pieces.

He'd seen a light coming toward him, and it was very close.

Jacques's arm rose in front of Kali like a railroad semaphore. It was her turn to come to an abrupt halt.

He pointed the tips of two fingers to his eyes, then pointed up ahead to their right. She looked in that direction and instantly knew why he'd signaled. Someone's legs poking out of a cleft in the wall, low down toward the tunnel floor.

They were silent. She stood there listening to the chortle of running water in the background. It had seemed to grow louder and steadier as they wound their way through the passage.

A minute passed. Jacques remained quiet. Kali saw him tug the bottom of his sweatshirt away from his waist, exposing his holstered pistol, dropping his hand lightly onto its grip.

She leaned in to his ear. "We don't know this person's a threat," she whispered.

"Not yet," he said and strode forward.

Etienne huddled in the notch, having snatched onto the desperate hope that whoever was up ahead would stop, change direction, anything besides keep coming toward him. But the thought was short-lived. The light swelled and brightened until he saw two figures approaching behind it, maybe fifty or sixty feet up the tunnel.

He barely had time to think about what to do.
But there was really nothing to decide. He couldn't
just sit there waiting for them.

All in one adrenaline-hyped movement, he
sprang upright and out of the notch, then switched
on his own light and went bolting back the way
he'd come. A split second later he heard them running after him, their feet slapping the stone floor
of the tunnel. He raced ahead for about ten yards,
reached a sharp corner and barreled around it, his
strip lamp hopping erratically off the walls and
ceiling in front of him. But they gained quickly,
getting closer and closer, until he could actually
hear one of them breathing down his neck—

The flying tackle caught him from behind and
dropped him hard onto his stomach, knocking the
wind out of his lungs. He kicked and flailed and
tied to push his way back up, grunting with the effort, trying to get his pursuer off him. But he was
helplessly pinned, an arm like a rigid pole locked
across the back of his neck, forcing his head down,
his cheek flat against the cold stone floor.

Then he heard a male voice in his ear. *"Reste
immobile! Je ne te maltraiterai pas!"*

Stay still. I won't harm you in any way.

Etienne stopped moving.

*"Je vais te libérer. Fais juste en sorte de rester
ici. Entendu?"*

The man was saying he would release him if he
agreed not to go anywhere.

Speaking French.

Not Russian.

French.

Etienne breathed in heavily under the man's weight, his face still pressed sideways against the floor of the tunnel.

"Bien," he said. "I won't."

The weight lifted off him. Out the corner of his eye, he saw the man rise to his feet.

"Sit up. It's all right."

Etienne pushed himself off the ground, sat, looked up. And drew a breath. The man was hooded, the upper half of his face a fierce slash of red, the lower half colored blue. It was like a faintly glowing mask.

He stared as if at a ghostly apparition. But then a thought came to him. The cybers had taken to wearing facial makeup to hide their identities. Especially with the government bans in France.

And the man had spoken French.

Etienne's eyes went to the woman standing behind him. She was tall, black-haired and wore no facial paint.

The man said, "Tell us what you're doing here."

Etienne looked back at him and noticed two things in quick succession: his hand was poised near his waist, and the butt of a gun was sticking out from under his sweatshirt. It ended whatever relief he'd felt.

"I was invited to an underground party," he said. "An art affair."

"Where, exactly?"

"I entered from Porte d'Orléans, if that's what you mean," Etienne said. "I don't know my way around down here. I'm not a cataphile. I—" He broke off suddenly. His eyes overbright.

"Keep going," the man said.

Etienne inhaled. "I was with a friend. We went to the *Petite Ceinture* railroad tracks. There was a hole, a cat flap. She took me to a hall."

"Your friend."

"Yes," Etienne said. "Her name was Candace."

"Can you describe this hall to us?"

Etienne nodded. "It's very large. At the end of a long passage. There are electric candles on the walls…sconces. A throne inside the hall. Made of human bones, like in the public sections of the catacombs. Candace is…she *was* a bartender. I think she'd been there many times…"

Etienne stopped again, struggling back tears.

The man and woman exchanged glances. Then she stepped forward, cutting her headlamp, kneeling in front of him. She reached for her water bottle and held it out.

"Here," she said. "Don't hog it."

He took it, sipped and handed it back to her.

"What's your name?" she asked quietly.

He told her, and she nodded.

"I'm Kali," she said. "Tell me what happened to her, Etienne. To Candace."

He said nothing for a moment, his eyes welling with tears. And then it all came bursting out of him, the words, the tears, together, all of it, spilling from him in a sudden, uncontrollable torrent. He told Kali about Candace returning to work after her break, and his trip to the Sanisette, and then the screams, the gunshots, the bodies outside the door.

"I'm still alive because I was taking a piss," he said. He paused to catch his breath and issued a pained, bitter semblance of a laugh. "*Tu y crois?* A piss. Candace...the rest...they're gone. Every one of them."

The hooded man had listened in silence, his hand gradually falling from his holster.

"You said you heard guns?"

"Yes."

"More than one."

"Some of the shots were different than others. Louder."

"So then, how many? Two? More?"

"Two, I think. I didn't see anything."

"But you said not everyone was shot. Was there an odd scent in the air? Anything like that?"

Etienne stared at him. "Dear God...you're saying they used gas?"

"I'm asking what you might have noticed. We need to know."

Etienne thought about it, shook his head.

"I smelled nothing unusual," he said. "I'd remember that."

"Is there anything else you *do* remember?"

Etienne nodded.

"I heard them," he said. "I mean, I heard them *talk*. Twice. The first time when I was in the Sanisette. Then when I was behind the bar. With Candace..."

More hot tears streamed down his face, clogging his throat and nostrils. He wiped his face with his sleeve, dragging in breaths between his sobs. Then he suddenly realized he *had* left something out of his account.

The hooded man looked at him. "Go on. What did they say?"

"I couldn't tell."

"Either time?"

"It was only a few words, and the music was very loud. But it wasn't French."

"Then, what?"

"I'm not sure. It sounded Slavic."

"Could it have been Russian?"

"It could have. I'm not sure." Etienne paused, looked at him. "Am I being interrogated here?"

"No."

"Because I've shared whatever I know. Answered all your questions and more. And you still haven't even told me who you are."

Kali exchanged glances with the hooded man again. Then she silently stood up and reached a hand out to Etienne.

He took it and let her help him to his feet, thinking she was surprisingly strong.

"Is there a way aboveground nearby?" he asked.

Her dark eyes locked on his. "We aren't going above, Etienne. We're moving on toward the hall. And you're coming with us."

"What?"

"If those people with the guns find you here, they'll kill you. You have to stay with us."

He shook his head quickly. "I don't understand. None of this makes sense."

"I'll explain when I can. But not now."

He kept shaking his head.

"I don't want to see that place again. I'm not sure I can bear it."

Her smile was gentle…and a little sad, he thought. It caught him off guard.

"We can bear more than we think," she said. "I know."

He said nothing for a long moment. Somehow her words reassured him. He wasn't sure why. Her words, and that surprising smile.

He took a deep breath, slowly let the air out of his lungs.

"It's a long walk," he said. "I've been in these tunnels almost an hour."

"Then, I'm guessing you wandered around in a circle," the hooded man said. "This tunnel is minutes away from it."

They can be very confusing. You could go in circles forever finding your way back here.

Etienne felt brokenhearted and strangely unmoored. As if he'd phased into a life that wasn't his own.

"I'm lost, aren't I? Whether I stay with you or go on alone. Lost either way."

Kali gave him a look that matched her smile.

"If so, it's best to be lost with friends," she said.

12

April 25, 2024
Various Locales

Janus Base, Romania

"I still wish you'd made last night's demo," Fernandez said to Carmody, steering his JLTV across the testing ground. "It would've jacked you right up."

"If I'd wanted that, I would've let you know," Carmody said.

Fernandez frowned. "Well, it's awesome to see those suits in action. *Especially* at night."

"You told me they work. I took your word for it."

"Which definitely misses the point."

Carmody was silent, his thick arms folded over his chest.

Fernandez was coming up to the little parking area alongside the hangar. He drove past a pair of robot hounds standing motionless in the grass off the runway, pulled in beside two parked vehicles and accidentally bumped his tires against a concrete wheel stop. The JLTV lurched forward and back.

He cursed under his breath.

"Maybe you should keep your eyes in front of you," Carmody said.

"Maybe next time I should let you walk from the barracks." The sergeant killed the engine. "Seriously, dude. Wheeler and Luna busted their butts for weeks. You know how many training sessions it usually takes to qualify for flight? *Fifty.* They did it in half as many. That's outstanding."

"It's the reason I picked them."

"They volunteered," Fernandez said. "You picked them out of the eligible *volunteers.* There's a difference."

Carmody gave no response.

Fernandez sighed in resignation, nodded toward the hangar. "Okey doke," he said. "The techs are getting everything set up. They mostly just need to bring out the platform. You can suit up now, or wait outside till they're ready."

Carmody sat there a second, staring straight ahead. "I don't like Janus, and I like Howard even less," he said. "I came to finish a job I should have finished months ago."

Fernandez thought about what the wirehead from New York, Natasha Mori, had told him when they got off the plane. *Kali.*

He said, "We've known each other a long time. Been through some things. Bucharest, Club Energie... Man, how hairy was that?" He shrugged to himself. "Anyway, I consider you *mi compañero*."

Carmody said nothing. Fernandez sat behind the wheel.

"If something else was eating you, would you tell me?" he asked after a minute.

Carmody reached for the door handle.

"I'll wait here," he said.

Carmody stood smoking a cigarette near the JLTV as a guy in an electric tug tractor pulled a wheeled crane and staging platform from the hangar. There were impressions in the grass outside where they clearly had been towed many times, and the tractor driver made two separate trips, lining them up so each would sit in its usual place. The platform was grated steel plate. The crane was thirty feet tall and had a jib arm on top, with a high-tensile tether like the kind used by mountain climbers. An adjustable metal T-rack was connected to the lower part of the crane.

Carmody reached into his bomber jacket for his pocket ashtray. He'd pulled a face when Kali picked it up at some secondhand shop in New York but would later concede it was pretty handy. He opened its worn tin lid, crushed out the butt, then put it away and moseyed over to the platform and waited some more.

The tractor driver made a third trip into the hangar and returned with the jet suit's components in his flatbed. Then a man and a woman in orange coveralls came walking out to join the tractor guy, and all three began carrying the modules over to the platform. The two micro jet assemblies—one for each of Carmody's forearms—went on the T-rack's horizontal bars. The engine he would wear on his back had been rigged to a harness like a scuba tank. They hung it over the vertical bar.

Fernandez appeared in the hangar's entrance.

"Your suit's in the locker. You'll love the feel of Nomex on your skin—not," he said, cocking a thumb back over his shoulder. "Oh, and don't forget the earplugs."

Carmody strode past him into the hangar without a word. The welded military locker was halfway down its length. He opened its double doors and found a black full-body flight suit on a hook in its left-hand compartment. In a right compartment were protective gloves, a shiny hard-shell helmet with a tinted face shield, and a pair of lightweight ankle boots. The earplugs were in a small drawer.

He stripped down to his briefs and sat on the small built-in bench and changed. The flight suit was uncomfortably snug on him, with a lot of zipper pockets and Velcro pouches and padding at the elbows and knees. The size fifteen boots were also a couple of sizes too small. But he managed to pull and twist and wiggle and tug himself into everything. Then he pushed in the earplugs, put on the helmet, shut the locker doors and went back outside.

The two technicians were waiting on the platform. They instructed him to stand up straight against the T-rack like he would while being measured at the doctor's office, but with his arms straight out at his sides. They strapped and belted him into the harness with the jet-engine backpack, then slid the minijets over his left and right forearms. They were oval like an aircraft's turbine, but scaled down in size and connected to gauntlets made of some rigid polycarbonate material. Each weighed about fifteen pounds.

The female tech patted his right glove. Her name tag read *L. Sanders*. "I understand you ride?"

He nodded. "I crashed a BMW Motorrad through a picture window a couple of weeks ago."

"Funny."

"Maybe to you."

The tech looked at him.

"What's the BMW's horsepower? One, one fifty?"

"One sixty-five."

"Nice...but roughly a seventh of what the jet suit can output," she said. "If you want to be in its ballpark, you have to look at an Aston Martin Valkyrie or a Bugatti Divo. But there are commonalities between the suit and a motorcycle. Using it is meant to be simple and intuitive. There are no complicated controls. If you let your natural sense of balance take over, you'll be fine. I won't get into aerodynamics, but the thrust is spread equally among the three jet turbines and your body."

"Okay."

"Can you feel the bar against your right palm?"

"Yeah."

"We call it a trigger. But it's really your throttle. You want to maintain a nice, gentle grip around it."

"Okay."

"A bird uses its wings to gain lift and stay airborne. I know—duh. But it also uses them to *control* its flight, and I want you to think of your arms in that way. Keep them down at your sides on ascent, and flare them out to trim altitude or land. Put them behind you to move forward, raise them to go backward. When you want to turn or circle, raise a hand that direction. One tip. When you turn, *look* wherever you want to go. Rotate your head. It naturally orients your body and makes changing directions smoother. But your legs should always be straight."

"Okay."

"That last part's important. People tend to flail when the ground drops off underneath them. It's reflexive. So you need to fight the urge. Essentially you're a living VTOL aircraft."

"Okay."

Sanders patted a display screen on his chest harness. "This minicomputer has all your essential readouts. Velocity, altitude, position, a fuel gauge. But the information's available on your helmet-mounted display."

"Okay."

"The flight kit's powered by JP-1A jet fuel. You have three gallons in your nacelles, over half their capacity. It's enough for about a five-minute run. You'll stay low this time. Max height is about eighty feet, but we'll keep you hugging the ground with the tether."

She gave the other tech a nod.

"Wait," Carmody said to him. "I'm not using that thing."

"It's for you own safety," he said. His name tag read *K. Berman*.

"I don't need it."

The male tech stood there with the tether in his hand. He looked at Sanders.

"Mr. Carmody, I'm afraid it's required protocol," she said. "You'll need to qualify for free flight before we send you up without a wire."

He shook his head. "That won't work."

She looked at him. Carmody heard the clank of footsteps. Fernandez.

"We have a problem?" he said, coming toward them across the stage.

"I'm not using the tether. I can't afford to waste time. We have ten days."

"I know," Fernandez said. "They'd just rather you don't fly up, up and way out of control like a popped balloon. There's normally virtual preflight training. But we bypassed the simulations because of your VR issues—"

"VR makes me puke. I can't control that. I don't want to argue, Julio."

"Me neither."

"Then, tell your people to back off."

Fernandez stood silently regarding him. After a minute he turned to Berman.

"All right," he said. "He says no wire, it's no wire. If anything goes wrong, it's on me."

Berman glanced at the other tech. She nodded, and he released the tether, and they left. Fernandez leaned in close so he could make out Carmody's eyes through his visor.

"This Icarus suit costs a quarter million dollars," he said. "I hope you don't smash it up."

Carmody looked at him. "I thought Icarus was the one who crashed."

Fernandez nodded. "Right. Flew too close to the sun. That's why I named it after him. Message to wearer, stay humble."

Carmody didn't say anything. Fernandez smiled a little and punched him lightly on the arm.

"You just go on with your big, bad self, *vato*," he said, and turned to walk off the platform.

Carmody depressed the trigger, and the jets thundered to life. It might have been the loudest thing he'd ever heard. The sound roared in his ears, vibrated in his bones and made his soft tissues quiver. It was like he was in the cone of an erupting volcano.

But he felt no heat from the ignition. No inertial drag. His stomach didn't revolt the way it had in the HIVE scenarios. He lifted off smoothly, and then his feet were above the platform. Two inches, six, twelve. It didn't feel like flight. It was like being an astronaut on a spacewalk.

He angled his arms backward and cruised across the platform, and then he was over the grass. It rippled and bent in a wave under his engine exhaust.

The balance came easy. He'd earned his paratrooper's wings, pulled a one-eighty in a speedboat in reverse, tightroped across ponds, done blackwater diving in Kona. And he rode a motorbike. It was all about staying calm. His brain did the rest on its own.

He lowered his arms, increased thrust and rose higher into the air. He saw Fernandez, Berman and Sanders standing in the hangar entrance off to his left, looking up at him, watching his flight. The helmet readouts said he was fifteen feet above them.

He climbed another ten and gained speed. His biceps pulsed. The force of the jets pushed his shoulders up into their sockets. His adrenaline surged, the blood seemingly rushing to his brain.

Carmody slowed his breathing. If you could handle the adrenaline it sharpened you, helped you to concentrate.

He pumped the engine and soared to a height of sixty feet. Then he shot forward. The readouts said he was doing seventy-five. Fernandez and the techs shrank in size as he flew over and past them. He was higher than the treetops between the field and the CTRC. Could look over them and see he was level with the windows on the building's upper stories.

He was a rocket.

Carmody lifted his right hand, swiveling his head, turning to overfly the hangar's roof. Then he pulled off in a wide arc to circle the field. He goosed the trigger and gained speed again. The engines screamed. His eyeballs trembled.

He was still making the loop when he saw an alert on the upper corner of his face shield. Flashing yellow. The thrusters were low on fuel.

He didn't want to stop. He was jacked The speed, the rumble of the engines, all of it was intoxicating.

But he breathed in and out and sliced to his left, a straight line to bisect the field.

Then the platform was right down below. He flared his arms like wings and relaxed his grip on the throttle lever and descended. He was forty feet in the air, thirty, twenty. His stomach lurched. Out the corner of his eye he saw Sanders standing near the platform. She bent slightly at the knees, then stood up tall, slapping her legs. Like she was doing some weird, manic calisthenics.

And then he realized she was trying to get his attention. And immediately knew why.

Legs straight.

His were bent. At the knees.

Ten feet up now. Carmody released the trigger and straightened his knees, but he was too late. He swayed and wobbled and tipped sideways in the air like a man slipping off a ledge, one foot lower than other.

Carmody fell like something dumped from the sky. He weighed about two fifty, most of that mass hard, thick muscle. He was a heavy body hitting an unyielding metal surface. But he landed on his right side and kept his head from banging against the platform. His triceps and lat took the brunt of the impact. That and his right gauntlet. He heard it crack around his arm, and realized it probably spared him some broken bones. Then then heard Fernandez and the techs scrambling up to him, their footsteps clanking across the steel grille. He rolled over onto his back and waved them off.

They clustered around him anyway, Fernandez

squatting on his left, the other two shuffling around to his opposite side.

The sergeant said, "You all right?"

Carmody sat up. "I'm fine."

Sanders was pulling off the damaged gauntlet. "This one's a total loss."

Carmody glanced over at her. "Can you replace it?"

"We have backups," she said. "I gave you instructions. You should have listened."

"I pretty much did."

"Until you landed."

"Can't have everything," he said. "How did I do otherwise?"

"The truth? I've never seen anyone adapt to flight as quickly. Your reactions appear exceptional."

"They are."

"I see you're also exceptionally modest."

"It isn't about modesty. It's about my intramuscular carnosine levels being anomalous. They say I'm one in a thousand, but I figure that's an underestimate."

She looked at him without answering. He started to get up.

"Maybe you ought to give yourself a minute," Fernandez said. "Catch your breath."

Carmody ignored him and rose to his feet. His right arm hurt, and his ribs felt sore. But he was pretty sure it would have been more painful if he'd fallen on the arm where he'd been shot by Grigor Malkira. He still had bullet fragments in that one.

"Think you can step over there?" Berman was

nodding toward the T-rack. "So we can get you out of that rig."

Carmody turned toward the rack, stood up against it and let the techs get to work. As they began undoing the flight harness's straps and fasteners, he noticed one of the robot dogs drift off from its companion at the edge of the runway, prowl through the grass toward the stage, and come to a standstill about thirty feet to its right.

He stared straight at it, locking in on its synthetic eyes.

It appeared to stare back.

At his desk in the CTRC, Howard gently tamped the tobacco in his pipe, held a match to the bowl and drew. He was smoking his own blend, a dark-fired Kentucky with a pinch or two of perique nourished in rich Mississippi Delta soil. It added a bit of sweetness to the strong cured tobacco.

The office was spacious and uncluttered, a far cry from his hamster cage at the old command center. It had a nice big desk with a pair of slick wide-screen monitors. The polarized smart filters on its two glass walls—west and south—offered plenty of daylight while muting the direct glare of the sun.

He stared at one of the screens, puffing at the pipe. He had meant to review the sat maps of the Crimean target site after the meeting in the conference room adjourned. Instead he was finding himself in an exchange of stares with Carmody through the eyes of a robot dog.

Naturally, he thought.

It was through the west-facing wall that Howard

had peripherally noticed the dot launch into the air above the testing field. He had known Fernandez was bringing Carmody straight out there after the conference. After hearing Carmody's plan, it made perfect sense he would want to try his flight suit on for size, maybe get his feet off the ground. No problem there.

The problem was the dot in the sky. The instant Howard saw it, he'd shifted his attention to his other monitor, gone from scrutinizing his maps to watching a live feed from the pair of robot watchdogs outside the hangar. The mutts could wander autonomously or be controlled remotely, and even a computer dunce like him could command them to turn their eyes up to the sky and track Carmody's flight.

Howard had expected Carmody would put on the suit. But his going up without a wire was something else, and so was Fernandez enabling him to do it. He'd supposed he'd given Julio too much credit for common sense and wouldn't make the same goddamned mistake again.

His first impulse had been to call the hangar and demand to know what the hell they were doing there. But instead he'd reached for his tobacco pouch and waited to see how things played out. Through the robot's powerful surrogate eyes, he had watched Carmody climb higher than his office in the CTRC, watched him circle the field, watched him make a hard landing that could have left him a shattered mess on the ground. The worst hadn't happened, although the suit didn't seem to share his unbreakability. But that was Carmody in a nutshell. A whole lot luckier than he was smart.

But smart enough to have noticed the dog's attention. And maybe sussed out that it wasn't wholly, or even partly, random.

He stared into one of the dog's robotic eyes. Howard stared back through them. It didn't last long. A second or two, maybe. But he could feel their cold contact.

He inhaled smoke through the stem of his pipe. If Fernandez, his genius elves at the hangar, and Carmody himself didn't care about him breaking into so many pieces he couldn't be put back together again, it was their business. But Howard was the CO of Janus Base. The quarter million-dollar jet suit that could have been broken up along with Carmody was his business. And more concerning to him was the fact that Carmody was set to lead a group of his *people* into hostile territory on a high-impact, high-risk mission.

He'd always been reckless. Howard had lived with it because he was also usually successful... and because Morse had repeatedly exercised her authority and insisted that he be given a long operational rope. But Howard couldn't help thinking his latest stunt was a sign that something different was going on this time. If that was the case, and it wasn't managed or mitigated, it could have ramifications he didn't want to envision.

"Okay, Rover, disengage," he said into his microphone. "Resume patrol."

An instant later, Carmody's image was swept

from view. The robot had turned from the platform and moved off.

Howard sat there looking at the screen without really seeing it, smoking, his mind elsewhere. After a while he emptied the ash out of his pipe and reached down to the tobacco pouch on his belt. It was rare for him to smoke two bowls in succession, but there were exceptions to every rule, and he felt a refill was definitely in order before he got back to studying his maps.

13

April 25, 2024
The Paris Catacombs

"Second Unit, do you read?" Luka said over his intracar. He and Oleg were still inside the maze off the storage room.

Yes, Three.

It was Reva. Her texted answer reached his ocular display with a speed nearly equaling that of human speech.

"We're in the tunnels," Luka said. "They run off in all directions from a chamber behind the hall."

So we'd already surmised.

"About the hall. I specifically said the *chamber*. It's the real hub. The junction of many passages, some running north. And it isn't on our map."

We've geolocated the target. Can you see her coordinates?

Luka noted with displeasure that she had changed the subject.

"Yes," he said. "She's close."

So are we. Very.

He could see that as well. His display showed that she and Zoltan were now only a few hundred yards to his southeast.

"We can't stay here any longer," he said. "The chamber's flooding. The passages. All of it."

If the chamber is what you say it is, it's exactly where she's headed.

Luka glanced at Oleg. Water was trickling down the walls around them.

"Are you understanding me, Two? I told you we have to vacate."

And I told you we're a hop away. Hold your position.

"There are less dangerous ones. The main corridor leading into the hall *is* on the map. It wasn't taking much water. At least not a short while ago. We can outflank her outside the archway."

A half second's pause.

Implants, water... what else does the Black Hundred shrink away from?

"Be careful of your words. We don't have to tolerate insults. Or obey your orders. None of us are under the Directorate's command any longer."

I won't dispute your last assertion. In fact it makes my point. We're being well paid for this operation.

"We can't collect on the money if we're dead."

Listen to me, Tret'ya. That main passage is too exposed. We lose part of our advantage if we move on the target there.

"Better than drowning here. If you're coming, then hurry. But we're leaving these tunnels right now. Out."

With that, Luka unlinked and stood looking at Oleg in silence. Water was flowing down the walls and across the floor to slurp at the outer bottoms of their boots.

"She's lost her mind," he said. "I don't like it."

Oleg grunted. Then he gestured toward the opening to the hall.

"Fuck it," he said. "Let's get out of here."

Jacques, Kali and Etienne had been moving through the tunnels for a while, in that order, when they heard the faint, rhythmic thump of music through the walls. Jacques signaled a halt, listening. Water poured down around the three in freshets, splashing their faces and clothes and making a lot of noise. But there was no question the music sounded close.

He turned to Etienne. "Does this place look familiar to you?"

Etienne looked thoughtfully at the courses of rotted brick on both sides. Some had disintegrated into powdery mounds on the tunnel bottom, others fallen loose to completely expose the underlying rock. Everything was wet, the water slipping down the walls, running over the heaps of crumbled red clay to wash it across the floor in lengthening channels.

"I told you I left the hall through a storage chamber," he said at length. "Behind the throne of bones."

Jacques nodded.

"This is one of the passages I took after leaving the chamber," Etienne said, and rubbed his neck. "I'm sure of it. Except—"

"Yes?"

"The water wasn't coming down nearly so hard. I'm sure of that too."

Jacques glanced up at the streaming roof, then lowered his gaze to Kali.

"We need to talk," he said, and walked a few steps up the passage to disappear around a curve.

She hung back a moment, glancing over at Etienne. "Wait here. We won't be long."

He gave her a small acquiescent shrug, and she turned to catch up with Jacques. He was waiting just around the bend in the tunnel.

"We aren't safe," he said in a low voice. "The mines were shored up with brick and mortar centuries ago...after an entire city street sank into the ground. The limestone underneath is soft and porous. It's like a sponge for rising groundwater. Those bricks have deteriorated from moisture seeping through the walls over many years."

"Tell me why that's important."

"The water isn't seeping in now. It's *pouring*. And our friend says it wasn't coming down this hard when he escaped the hall. Which means things have gotten worse in a very short time."

"You think this tunnel's about to flood."

"I do."

Kali nodded. "How close are we to the hall?"

"Quite. We'll reach it within minutes."

"Then, we're also minutes from being out of here."

He stood close to her. "Listen to me. The hall's cut from the same limestone as the passages leading to it. Like this one. If they fill with water, so will it before too long."

"So what do you propose?"

"The same thing I did before. We'll backtrack to one of the drier passages. These tunnels were not laid out by an architect. They grew out of centuries of opportunistic mining. The grading's random. The drainage system was installed without oversight. I can take us on a wider path around the hall. One that keeps us out of the water's course."

"That would slow our progress by hours. With our enemies stalking us. And Navarro."

"Better than us all drowning."

"And Jill? The others she's bringing? They're expecting to meet us at the hall."

He tapped his wearable. "I can signal them."

Kali looked at him, the sounds of the infiltrating water and the bump and pulse of the music an auditory mash around her.

What would you do, Michael? Do we change course? Now?

A full ten seconds passed before she finally spoke.

"If we only seek to avoid losing, we can't win," she said. "We have to take the offensive."

"I don't disagree. But these tunnels aren't the place. They're compromised."

Kali hesitated.

"So am I, Jacques," she said.

He looked confused. "What do you mean?"

She returned her hand to where the tranquilizer dart had caught her below the ribs. "Do you really suppose the Blood Lightning would leave tracking me to guesswork?"

"No," he said. "But they know your general destination. And they know the fastest route by far to the Northern Network through the hall. There's no doubt they have a copy of Oarsman's map to guide them."

Kali looked at him. "Jacques, the map gives them my path. It doesn't show where I am along that path. It can't reveal any possible detours. Or pinpoint my location. What would make them conclude they can find me, follow my progress and intercept me in over two hundred miles of tunnels?"

He didn't say anything for a moment, his eyes falling to where she'd dropped her hand.

"You think they've tagged you," he said.

"Yes."

"A nanochip?"

"Logically, nothing else makes sense."

"If you're right, it would mean they can fix your position within meters."

"Yes."

His eyes showed fresh understanding.

"You know they're setting a trap for you at the hall," he said. "*Une embuscade*…an ambush."

She nodded. "They'll wait out of sight. Then box us in when we show up. That's most likely their plan."

"And you intend to turn the tables on them."

"We'll give them what they're looking for," she said. "Then give them cause to regret it."

Jacques breathed out. "We should at least avoid that rear chamber until I make sure it isn't flooded," he said. "I know a detour. It will bring us to the passage outside the hall's main entrance."

"If you think it's best."

He met her gaze.

"You play a very risky game of chess, Outlier."

"Does it bother you, *Béret Vert*?"

He shook his head. "No. It does not. But it does make me wonder if I'm your comrade or a mere pawn."

Kali let the question hang unanswered between them. After a moment she nodded back over her shoulder.

"We should collect Etienne and move on."

"Never mind that your lost pup doesn't suspect what we're getting him into. That the men who killed his girl at the hall are waiting there to do the same to us." He paused. "Can it be your kindness to him is also part of the game?"

She looked at him. Droplets pelted her hair and shoulders from overhead.

"Believe what you want," she said. "I won't stop you."

Then she abruptly turned away and went back down the tunnel through the falling water.

"C'est ça," Etienne said. His voice was reedy and trembling. "I'd never wanted to see this place again."

Kali stood on his right, and Jacques his left, all three looking straight up at the archway to the Hall of the Barbarous King.

They were dripping wet. The passage behind them, by contrast, was dry except for small pools of water outside some of the openings on both walls—including the one closest to the arch, which Jacques had led them through moments ago. They saw no sign of movement or activity inside the hall, no sign of survivors, only the programmed, relentless shifts of light and sound. It felt vacant and ghostly.

"Kali and I are heading in," Jacques said and turned to Etienne. "Stay here and wait."

"No," he said, shaking his head. "I want to help."

Kali looked at him. "One of us has to stand watch. In case anyone enters the passage."

"And then what?"

She tapped his smartwatch, held her wrist up to show him hers. "Do you use secure messaging? Signal? WhatsApp? Any others?"

"Yes."

Kali smiled a little. "Good," she said. "Then you can send an alert."

He shook his head again, uncertainty on his pale, strained features. "I've been offline since I entered the catacombs. The Wi-Fi won't work down here."

"It will at a short distance," Jacques said. "Take my word for it."

Etienne didn't seem convinced. Nor did he object, however.

Kali reached under her jacket, drew her Glock from its holster.

"Here." She held the gun out to him, angling its muzzle downward for safety. "Take this."

He made a pushing gesture. "I don't want it. I wouldn't even know how to use one."

Kali recalled that night outside the castle, her sense of déjà vu edged with irony. Mike would have enjoyed seeing her assume his role, she thought.

She realized she missed the way he looked at her when she amused him.

"It's simple," she said to Etienne, regarding him steadily. "You aim and fire."

He continued to hesitate. Kali kept the gun out between them.

"Take it," she said gently. "There's no time."

Another moment passed. Finally he sighed, reached out and wrapped his fingers around the upper barrel.

"Aim and fire? That's it?"

She nodded.

"If there's nothing more, why are there so many online how-to videos?"

Kali smiled again. She asked for his messaging ID and sent hers to his watch.

"All right," she said. "We're set."

Jacques had waited in silence, staring up at the sign above the archway. *Se Faire Oublier et Danser*. He motioned in its direction with his chin.

"On that note," he said, "we should go in."

Kali nodded, squeezed Etienne's arm.

"Stay strong," she said and turned toward the hall.

Etienne stood in the passage with his back to the archway, his face taut and sallow in the contrived, linear flickering of the electric sconces along the walls. He felt miserably stressed, alone and inadequate.

Veilleur, que reste-t-il de la nuit? he thought. Watchman, what remains of the night?

He'd once read that in a poem, or was it somewhere else? He couldn't recall. But it was a good question for which he had no answer. Nor did he know what qualities he possessed that might have earned him the job of lookout on *this* night, except possibly that his new companions had seen him as dead weight to be left behind, ditched before he became an outright liability.

Kali and Jacques had not yet emerged from the hall, and though only a few minutes had passed since they'd entered, he'd already grown concerned for their safety. Whether or not the concern was mutual, he strangely enough thought of them as friends, even allies...but allies in *what*?

He didn't know. In fact, he knew precious little about either of them: a man with a painted face like a Matisse portrait, and a woman in a riding jacket and utility belt that gave her the look of an eighteenth-century treasure hunter, sans bandolier. Their presence in the catacombs—their talk of assassins and some sort of mission—made no more sense to him than anything else had that terrible night. It was as if he'd slipped down a rabbit hole into a freakish alternate reality.

He examined the pistol Kali had loaned him against all his protestations. He'd never really thought about holding one or seen himself shooting one at any living thing, let alone a human being. But here he was with a gun in his hand. Whether that made him crazy, desperate or both, he could not have said. But Kali and Jacques had helped him when he needed it. When they could have simply left him to fend for himself in the tunnels. He wouldn't forget that. And he especially would not forget that it was done at Kali's urging. Whoever she was, whatever she was, he owed her for that kindness. It had come like water to a man in dire need of a drink…

Which, he thought, she'd also given him.

As well as her gun. Even if he did not like holding it.

He turned and looked up at the motto above the archway. Be forgotten and dance.

"I wanted to see how you would take to things."
"Did I pass the test?"
"You've done beautifully… So far."

Etienne felt an acute, piercing sorrow. He took several deep breaths, making an effort to remain composed. A long moment later he lowered his eyes from the sign and turned back around to watch the passage.

It extended straight in front of him for about a hundred feet before angling sharply off to the right. There were rows of openings on both sides of it, the closest ones so small they resembled gopher holes, those farther along the walls large enough for someone a foot taller than himself to enter upright. He could see water dripping from some of them to the floor underneath. How much longer until it filled all the side tunnels and crawl spaces? And then how long before it came rushing out to flood the trunk corridor where he stood?

More good and unanswerable questions, he thought edgily.

Another minute or two snailed past. Etienne's nerves were really getting to him. He felt too wound up to just stay rooted in place.

He began pacing slowly toward the bend, hoping the small act of putting one foot in front of the other would calm him. He would check out the tunnel openings to see what he could see. And, if he worked up the courage, he might even take a peek around the bend into the intersecting passage.

He went past the gopher holes first. Water was dripping from all but one or two, and he saw blotches of wetness on the walls underneath them. He was sure the stains hadn't been as wide minutes ago…or the drip quite as steady.

He moved down the corridor to the first large tunnel entry. Again, things had definitely worsened. What had been a slow trickle of water was now a cataract, an unbroken stream creeping down the wall and across the passage floor. It was nearly the same outside the second entry—the one he'd exited with Kali and Jacques.

Increasingly worried, Etienne moved on to the third entry…and all at once halted outside it, turning the beam of his headlamp onto the passage floor. He'd seen what appeared to be a set of muddy overlapping footprints below the opening.

He stepped over to them. Took another step, paused again. Then knelt for a closer look.

His stomach coiled inside him.

The prints had been made in blood. Fresh red blood. Their edges were smeared, the blood swirling through the spreading puddle of water underfoot. Etienne crouched there, fixated, his eyes on their runny outlines. His pulse roared in his ears, drowning out the loud blare of music from the hall.

It wasn't until Oleg and Luka emerged from the entry nearest the archway that he heard their boots scuffling over the floor of the passage, snapped a look over his left shoulder and saw them between him and the hall, coming toward him with guns extended in their hands.

Panic slapped Etienne's face like an ice-cold washcloth. He jumped to his feet, twisting to his right and away from them toward the opposite end of the passage. The bend was about fifty or sixty feet away.

But if he had any thought of running in that direction, it withered in an instant. Two more figures were rounding the corner. A man and a woman. They were also pointing their weapons in his direction.

Etienne glanced up and down the passage. All

four of them were closing in. He was trapped. Caught between them. And the woman's face...

She had come near enough for him to see that its left side was swollen and blistered, the skin hanging from it in loose, ragged flaps like melted wax. There was an angry slash mark resembling a brand on her cheek. The flesh around it was curdled-looking and inflamed.

Etienne stood there motionless, Kali's gun still tucked into his waistband. He was thinking they would take him out the second he reached for it. And he wasn't sure he could fire it in time even if he got the chance.

The woman's mouth turned up in a grotesque hybrid of a smile and snarl. "Where is she?" she said, her voice raised above the music pumping through the archway. "Tell us."

Etienne stood there. She was getting closer. He didn't know what to do.

Then he was struck by a thought that wasn't really a thought, or even entirely conscious, but sprang up from some deep, instinctual part of the brain wired for self-preservation. His eyes darted over the bloody footprints on his right, held briefly on the tunnel entry, then glanced back and forth at the four people coming toward him. They were all just a few feet away now.

Thinking he only had one chance, Etienne launched into the tunnel like a swimmer diving sideways into a pool.

Both hands wrapped around his Beretta, Jacques left the storage chamber behind the bone throne after going in for a look. Kali stood waiting for him near the archway. Between them was the horrific scene on the dance floor.

He started back to her, moving carefully between the dead, crouching to examine some of them as he made his way over.

"Etienne described it to the letter," he said when he reached her. "There's all sorts of equipment inside. Tunnels winding off in all directions. The water's really coming down." He paused. "I didn't see any sign of the killers. But it doesn't mean they weren't in there. Their footprints could have been washed away by now."

Kali was quiet. There were bodies everywhere in the hall, dozens of them. She thought about what would happen if the room flooded with them in it.

Jacques noticed her dark eyes scanning them.

"Most of these people were already gone when they were shot," he said. "The bullets were the coup de grâce."

"To put them out of their misery."

"To be thorough and certain they were dead," he said, shaking his head. "Those sons of bitches only have a single concern."

Kali said nothing.

"They were all gassed," he said. "That's what did them in. I've seen it before."

Kali said nothing. The skin had drawn tight over her cheekbones.

Jacques looked at her. "Are you all right?"

She glanced out across the dance floor, toward the bar, back at him.

"They were helpless," she said. "It was a slaughter."

He nodded.

"This was SOP for the Wagner Group in Syria. I was there supporting the Americans. The Russian fuckers would exterminate entire villages. Women, children, everyone."

Kali said nothing. Music thudded around them. She bowed her head and closed her eyes, her lips moving in silent prayer.

Jacques counted fifteen seconds before she lifted her gaze.

"These poor souls were at the wrong place at the wrong time," she said. "They were murdered so they wouldn't get in the way of whatever the Blood Lightning have planned for me."

He nodded. "They want no witnesses. No complications."

They were silent. An animation played out across a row of wall panels behind them, skimming multicolored light across the back of Jacques's upraised hood.

"We need to end this right here," Kali said. "Before anyone else is killed."

"Yes."

She cast another look at the bodies deeper inside the hall. "We can't just leave them. Not like this, Jacques."

"When the night's done, I'll get word out to the gendarmes… An anonymous tip." He paused. "It's the best we can do."

Kali took a deep breath, her dark eyes somber. After a moment Jacques motioned back toward the bone throne.

"If the Russians were originally intending to wait

for us in the chamber, they would have changed their minds."

"Because of the flooding."

He nodded. "It's pretty bad in there," he said. "They would want to avoid getting caught in it. And they'd assume we would do the same."

Kali considered that a minute, thinking he was probably right. Which led her to another thought. She was about to share it when she suddenly felt a vibration against her wrist.

Jacques saw her face tighten. "What is it?"

She glanced down at her watch, then back up at him.

"Etienne," she said.

Out in the passage, Luka saw Etienne leap into the side tunnel and quickly turned to Oleg.

"I'll take him myself," he said and raced toward the opening.

Jacques and Kali hurried over to the archway and took cover behind its abutting wall. They crouched there shoulder to shoulder, Jacques on the outside, his gun barrel angled into the main passage.

Perhaps ten seconds had passed since they'd received Etienne's alert.

Jacques leaned slightly around the wall. Etienne had vanished, but he saw three of Kali's pursuers out in the passage. The nearest—a huge, bulky man with long blond hair under a billed orange cap—stood not quite halfway down its length, studying the entrance to a side tunnel. Meanwhile, a woman and another man, almost as tall as the blond one but skeletally thin, were moving toward the hall from the bend.

Jacques ducked back in and quickly told Kali what he'd observed.

"Etienne must have gone into that opening," he said. "It's all I can think."

She nodded, reaching into her waist bag. After a moment her hand came out with the *manriki* folded inside it.

"What are you going to do with that?" he asked.

She told him, and he frowned. "No one ever said the legendary Outlier was a crazy person," he said.

"Legends never tell the whole story."

He stared at her.

"They have guns," he said. "I don't like it."

"They'll have less to like," she said. "If you'd ever been bitten by one of these, you would know."

Jacques didn't answer. He pushed his Beretta's fire selector to its burst setting with his left thumb, clicked the lowered foregrip into place with his right.

"Go," he said. "I'll catch up to you."

"And Etienne?"

"We won't abandon your rescued pup, I promise."

Kali briefly clasped his gloved hand.

"Que la Déesse te sourie," she said and scampered off toward the rear of the hall.

Etienne had landed hard on his shoulder in a half inch of water, twisted onto his knees and then jumped to his feet soaking wet. Sparing a moment to finger the screen of his smartwatch, he'd barreled wildly through the tunnel as it turned to his right, nowhere else to go, no time to look back or think, running for his life.

The bottom of the tunnel was flooded and slimy. His foot slid out again, and he teetered off-balance and almost fell back down to the floor. But somehow he kept his legs under him and ran for another few yards, splashing toward another curve, running on, the beam of his headlamp jittering out ahead into the darkness.

Then he heard someone racing up from behind, sloshing around the curve.

He stood there for the span of a single heartbeat. The muscle's systolic contraction pumping blood through its connecting arteries as he flashed on an image of Candace dead in his arms. The diastolic expansion of its chambers refilling them as he thought of Kali handing him her gun, trusting him to keep the watch.

One cardiac cycle. Eight-tenths of a second. And then to his own astonishment, Etienne suddenly turned with his feet in the water and pulled the gun from his waistband.

Watchman, what remains of the night?
Aim and fire.

He stood with the Glock in his hand and listened to the footsteps splashing toward him. It sounded like a single pair. But all four of the people in the main passage had seen him. They weren't just going to let him escape. And they all knew where he was.

He felt the weapon slip in his sweaty fingers and tightened them around its grip.

He was through with running.

* * *

Jacques waited behind the archway, the Beretta machine pistol lowered against his side so it couldn't be seen from the passage. The woman and the beanpole she was with were closer—Kali's flare had done damage. Perhaps she wasn't so crazy pulling out that chain.

The blond hulk, meanwhile, was still peering into the branching tunnel. Etienne must have made off through it, Jacques thought. He hoped so, anyway. There was nowhere else he could have gone to escape, and Kali did seem fond of him. Probably it was the dimples. But who knew?

Jacques took a breath. He was in no rush to engage; the odds didn't favor him. But it was unavoidable and best done while he still held the element of surprise. The blond man was distracted and in easy range.

His hands curled around the Beretta's grip and foregrip, he raised it to take his shot.

At the far end of the passage, Reva noticed movement inside the archway and instantly recognized it as a gun barrel coming up in someone's hand.

It would have taken her a hundred and fifty milliseconds—a fifteenth of a second—to shout out a warning. The same time it takes for a sprinter to react to the crack of the starting gun.

She didn't make a sound.

When the brain's motor cortex can bypass the muscles of the larynx, jaw and lips, it cuts a whole series of steps out of the communication process, speeding it up by several orders of magnitude. If the signal doesn't have to go to the mouth, it is more efficient.

The mechanism of evolution seeks speed and efficiency. That was a major factor in the Blood Lightning's combat edge. They were the product of *assisted* evolution, next-level warriors, and Reva had almost seamlessly adapted to the implants. She was what scientists termed a *high evolutionary*.

Routed through her neuromorphic hardware, her warning to Oleg needed only forty milliseconds— a mere *twenty-fifth* of a second—to transmit to his neck-worn puck computer. The added hop from his puck to the interface behind his ear made their link infinitesimally slower than direct lightning-to-lightning contact. But it still allowed him to receive and react to her warning with preternatural speed.

Oleg. Behind you.

Whipping his head around from the side tunnel, Oleg spun toward the archway faster than Jacques would have thought possible, his finger on the P90's trigger.

Kali kept her mind focused on her objective as she hurried back through the hall. There was no armoring herself against the scene's infernal horror, no way to blunt it or block it out. But she couldn't let it slow her progress.

She wound between the bodies, moving across the unthinkable slipperiness underfoot to the throne. She turned to the right behind it, saw a wide puddle of water outside the storage chamber and splashed on through its entrance, passing from the hall's bright, febrile lighting and animated video sequences into total darkness.

Jacques had been correct: the space perfectly matched Etienne's description. Her headlamp revealed a large six-sided brick chamber, its arched entryways leading to connecting rooms or passages. She saw carts and crates and pallets of things everywhere. There were small circular openings low to the floor on two of the walls—drainage culverts like she'd seen on the Sandy Road, dug to channel off periodic storm waters and outflow from the Seine into the deepest recesses of the catacombs.

But right now they weren't working. Or weren't working well enough to handle the combined excess from the breached canal and the gorged, elevated aquifer. The chamber was swamped. Water was simultaneously spraying from its ceiling and swelling up from the floor in gurgling little rills and spurts, carrying sand, mud and other sediment toward the entrance to the hall...which accounted for the miniature lake outside it. The flood was growing, spreading, advancing.

Kali didn't know how long it might be until the full raging force of the deluge brought down the roof and walls. She had a feeling it wouldn't take long.

She turned into one of the arches, looked around, found a place she thought would do. Then she turned off her headlamp and waited there in the darkness with the chain whip in her hands. Water spilled down the walls and rained down on her from above, shockingly cold on her hair and face. It

splashed her jacket and coveralls and rushed around
her duck boots, leaving only their thick nylon lining dry…at least for the moment.

She'd tucked the black crescent of her weapon's
magnesium alloy anchor-grip—light as aluminum,
strong as titanium—under the index, middle and
ring fingers of her right hand. In her left, she held
the *kundo*, or bullet-shaped steel weight attached
to the whip head. Between them was the stainless-
steel chain. A shortened, modified chain, four sections instead of six. She'd anticipated having to use
it in tight spaces.

She waited, thinking she probably had a minute or two to count down. She wouldn't be able to
hear their footsteps out in the hall. She probably
wouldn't hear any gunfire before they appeared, *if*
they appeared. The walls were too thick, the music
too loud. Add the noisy rush of the floodwater and
she wouldn't be able to hear them. When it happened, it would happen fast.

She waited. The chain in her hands. Neither
slack nor loose, but relaxed. Without tension. She
would be relying on her reflexes. Her trained reactions and timing. And on Jacques.

She waited.

The water continued to pour down around her.

Luka was racing around a corner toward the
bodies of the three partygoers, the beam of his
headlamp swinging out ahead, when it collided
with Etienne's up the tunnel. The combined output of the two high-lumen lights in his eyes cost
him a step. Then Etienne appeared in the near-

blinding glare, looking like a silhouette cutout on a shooting range, a pistol coming up in his hands.

Luka pulled his trigger first, dazzled and squinting into the brightness. All other things being equal, he had a tremendous edge in reflexes and speed.

The discharge of his Mark VII's .357 round was thunderous. Deafening. Shocking. Like a sonic boom there in the tunnel's tight confines. But he had braked from a full charge. Etienne's headlamp was spearing his eyes. It was a low-accuracy shot even for a trained marksman at close range. It missed.

An instant later, Etienne fired back. Luka saw the flash of the Glock's muzzle, then saw its barrel kick up in Etienne's hands, pulling his arms up with it.

Luka pegged him at once as an amateur. He was also firing blind, or nearly blind, but had been unprepared for the recoil. Leaving him momentarily off-balance, his gun pointed at the roof of the tunnel, his middle wide open.

The advantage was still Luka's. He'd shot to kill. He always shot to kill. But he also always looked ahead to contingencies. Guns weren't dueling weapons. They weren't meant for close-quarters fighting. They were ranged weapons intended for use at a distance. The partygoers had been unarmed when he took care of them. There was no threat of them firing wildly. But he wanted to prevent another clumsy exchange of fire with his opponent. He couldn't see or maneuver to shoot him cleanly. He didn't want ammunition ricocheting off the tunnel walls.

He was now within twenty feet or so of Etienne. Just the right distance.

Within twenty feet of a man with a gun, you could move on him bare-handed and easily take him out. If you committed. If you had the nerve and know-how and reflexes and a set of balls. If you could read your opponent's reactions, how he was holding the weapon, its angle and position relative to yourself. Which not every person understood. Or which they ignored because they froze in fear at the sight of a weapon being aimed at them. Luka understood this. He wasn't frozen. He was a trained fighting man, and he could tell he wasn't dealing with one here. His opponent hadn't looked like a fighter in the main passage. He'd looked like a scared rabbit. And he'd been unable to compensate for simple recoil. Luka had a good read on him.

His chin low to his collarbone, he holstered his gun, took two running steps and catapulted himself at Etienne before he could bring the Glock down for a second shot.

Luka flew through the air like a projectile fired from a cannon. Etienne had just enough time to realize what was happening before the smaller man crashed into him, driving him backward on the wet, slippery tunnel floor so his feet slid out from under him and he landed hard on his spine.

Etienne struggled on his back, splashing in the water, the wind knocked out of his lungs, Luka on top of him. He tried to suck in a breath but couldn't with Luka's densely muscled weight pressing down on him. Struggling, gasping, flailing, grabbing and clawing to try and dislodge Luka, Etienne suddenly realized the Glock was no longer in his grasp, realized it must have flown from his fingers when he fell back in the water. He was empty-handed. Weaponless. He'd lost hold of Kali's gun, lost it, and his attacker was all over him, battering him, his thick, meaty hands fast-moving blurs. It was like he had more than two, like he was simultaneously pounding Etienne's jaw and head with his fists and raking his eyes and cheeks with his fingers. Then his palm came smashing across the middle of Etienne's face, and Etienne heard and felt a sickening crunch, and he knew his nose had been broken, the septum shifting to one side. Squirming, whimpering, globs of blood and mucous sliding down his throat and flowing freely from his nostrils over his mouth and chin, he got both hands under Luka's shoulders and tried to heave him off again. And that was when Luka bit him on the chest, his front teeth clamping around his nipple through his shirt, sinking in, gnashing at his flesh through the sodden fabric of his shirt.

Etienne mewled like a wounded animal, squirming on the tunnel floor in pain and desperation. Luka's fists kept pounding his face and temples while his teeth kept tearing at the tissues anchoring Etienne's nipple to his chest, his lips and chin smeared with blood as it squeezed up through Etienne's shirt. Etienne was weak, dizzy, choking, gagging on his own blood and snot. His head splashed down into the water, and he lay there soaked and limp, pinned under the other man's weight.

Luka was determined to end Etienne's thrashing

at that moment, finish him right there on the tunnel floor, which meant he was ready to bring the Mark VII back into play to do the job. Reaching for the holstered gun, he brought it up in one hand and pushed its massive barrel into Etienne's temple.

There was a crash of gunfire. Etienne's whole body jerked, arching up out of the water, then slapping back down into it. Etienne heard the report echoing off through the tunnel, and then suddenly, overwhelmingly realized he shouldn't have been able to hear it or anything else or have any realizations about it or anything else, because by all rights he should have been dead.

But he wasn't.

Somehow, he wasn't dead.

He lay there soaked and gasping for air. His attacker's body still on top of him, pressing down on him. But it wasn't moving, and it wasn't biting him, and the hand with the gun had dropped into the water, the weapon itself half-submerged and pressing loosely against his cheek in the little man's slackened fingers.

There wasn't much left above his shoulders. His head was gone. Or a large chunk of it was. *Gone*. The gunshot Etienne had heard had punched a craterous hole into his right forehead and brainpan.

He looked up, saw the woman standing over him, a pistol in her hand. She wore makeup similar to Jacques's, half of her face painted white, contrasting sharply with the dark skin of the unpainted part of it. After a moment she bent, grabbed the corpse on top of him by the back of the jacket and pulled it hard to one side. It rolled off into the water with a heavy splash.

Etienne hoisted himself to a sitting position in the water, his shattered nose streaming, the blood gushing down over his lips.

The woman looked down at him a moment. "You're in bad shape," she said and motioned to the body with her chin. "But not as bad as that one."

He put a hand over his nose and winced in pain. Then he realized she wasn't alone. There were several other shadowy figures grouped together in the darkness behind her.

"Who are you?" he said.

She reached a gloved hand down to him.

"We'll get to that," she said.

Reva's warning had probably saved Oleg's life, but Jacques still had a jump on him, and the Beretta 93R was a rapid-fire, low-recoil weapon designed especially for the Italian Carabinieri in the 1970s, when political terrorists had turned the streets of Rome into a version of the American Wild West.

Even as Oleg turned to shoot, Jacques triggered a three-round salvo through the archway and again took cover behind the abutting wall, pressing his back flat against its surface. Then Oleg's weapon erupted on the other side. Jacques felt the wall shudder and jolt against his shoulder blades as bullets drilled into it, but they weren't going to penetrate three inches of solid rock.

He took a deep breath, thrust the snout of the machine pistol back out into the archway and unleashed three more tightly controlled bursts, the

Beretta hardly bucking in his grasp. The giant, meanwhile, was blasting away on the other side, tacking the outer wall with fire. Ammunition riveted it, spraying chips of limestone into the passage like hard confetti.

Jacques swooped in another breath, launched off the wall and unleashed several more tight bursts, the weapon cycling at a thousand rounds a minute. Then he spun a hundred and eighty degrees and plunged deeper into the hall through the music and the lights and the ghastly heaps of dead bodies on the dance floor. Halfway toward the throne, he spared a quick look over his shoulder and saw the three from the passage behind him in pursuit. So far, so good.

He hurried on without another backward glance. He was baiting them, and whether or not they knew it, they had no choice except to snap at the hook. They were here in Paris, here in the tunnels, for one reason. He was dangling what they wanted in front of them.

Less than five seconds later, he passed the bone throne, turned right, and ran through the spreading puddle of water behind it into the chamber.

She had halted outside the chamber entry, her companions stopping too, bookending her on the left and right. Both men looming over her, two varieties of tall. Zoltan narrow as a skyscraper, Oleg a wide, thick mountain of brawn.

She reached her right hand under her jacket and pulled her *kindjal* dagger from its sheath. It was sinuous and double-edged, its handle sculpted to fit her grip, its stainless-steel blade tapering to a long, sharp point. Her sidearm, a Grach semiautomatic pistol, was already in her opposite hand.

The man with the painted face had disappeared into the chamber no more than ten seconds ago. She was fully aware it was a trap and would enter behind him knowing it. Because if she and her companions were where Outlier wanted them to be, then Outlier and the hooded clown were likewise where Reva wanted *them*. Leaving the questions of how good the trap really was, and who would actually spring it.

Because traps could sometimes work two ways.

Traps could backfire.

"You've been in there, you lead," she told Oleg. "We need her. The other one doesn't leave."

He gave a nod, the mountain bending slightly. The *kindjal* in his left hand was identical to hers except for the ancient warrior crest embossed on its blade: a mounted Saint George slaying the basilisk, the seal of the Black Hundred. His right hand held the P90 taken from the bouncer.

It concerned him a bit that he'd lost Luka's feed. Still, they were at some distance from one another, with rock walls as radio barriers. Most likely it was a temporary interruption.

"Okay," Reva said. "Is there anything else?"

Zoltan glanced down at her, the tower leaning a bit. He looked unexpectedly hesitant.

"I don't think it's wise."

She scowled. "Do you now fear the water?"

He stared at her damaged face. "The water killed Dominik. You'd be dead too if I hadn't pulled you out. But it isn't about that. It's about the bitch and her tricks."

Reva looked at him and smiled a ruined, ragged smile.

"Relax, *brat molnii*, my brother in the Lightning," she said. "We have some tricks of our own."

Jacques had swung left inside the chamber, flattened himself against the wall behind the handle of an equipment cart and quickly doused his headlamp to bring on the darkness. He held his Beretta at index ready, muzzle up, his thumb against his temple. The thumb was his rest, a support helping him keep his hand steady without fatigue. Hand fatigue gave the gun a slight shake, and that could affect the precision of his shots.

The thumb was also a locator. When a gun was positioned beside your head, it was out of your peripheral view. The thumb's placement compensated for it, providing a tactile reference. Jacques could feel it between his temple and the Beretta, which oriented him to the position of his gun hand relative to his body and the ground. He knew exactly where the barrel of the gun was pointed. Because he'd drilled endlessly on bringing it down from index ready to firing position, he instinctively knew when to pull the trigger for the shot he was taking. A millimeter this way or that—a fractional second saved—could be the difference between life and death.

He stood against the wall, his back to the cold sheets of water rippling down its surface. The darkness inside the chamber was absolute. He couldn't

have seen the gun in front of his face or anything
around him, but he also couldn't use his headlamp.
The light would betray his position before he made
his move. After that it would barely matter. After
that, he thought, it would be moot. But every second he was hidden from sight gave him an advantage—at least over one of the three. He had seen
a spelo on the blond giant's racing cap, which was
a likely giveaway that he wasn't Lightning. Just
as he'd noticed the other two weren't carrying or
wearing lamps, which told him they probably had
augmented vision.

He needed to make the giant's light work for him.

Moments passed. Jacques stood poised in the
blackness, his weapon pointed up at the ceiling.
No sign of them yet. But he didn't think he'd have
to wait more than a few seconds. They had been
right behind him when he made his dash from the
archway. Surely they must have reached the chamber's entry by now. Though he couldn't hear them
out there from inside, the truth was he wasn't able
to hear much of anything. Just the music filtering
through from the hall and the water pouring and
guttering around him. Nothing else.

Jacques shivered, waited. Another long moment
passed. He visualized what he planned to do, script-
ing it out as a sequence of mental images. It was another technique he'd practiced frequently with the
Security Operations Center. You rehearsed what
you wanted to happen in your head to help you
carry it out in reality.

And then, suddenly, a beam of light stabbed

through the opening to the dance floor. The mental pictures vanished into the black.

Jacques took a breath.

They were coming in.

Oleg was first into the chamber, one, two, three long, purposeful strides through the entry, and then he was completely in the dark, water pouring down everywhere around him, Reva and Zoltan slipping in behind him and fanning out, steering themselves wide and clear of the high-intensity beam cast by his headlamp. He rotated on his heel, the light swinging a swift arc over the hexagonal walls, dipping in and out of their recesses and portals, sweeping across the dripping wet stacks of crates and equipment pushed up against them.

Jacques wasn't about to wait for it to land on him. Stepping away from the wall, he grabbed the handle of the equipment cart in one fist and pushed it hard toward the entry, a good shove, all his strength, thinking there were close to a hundred pounds of supplies and spare parts on its trays. The cart bumped and rattled along the wall, its casters swiveling jerkily in their brackets, the trays bouncing up and down as their contents clattered this way and that before tumbling over into the two-inch-deep water on the floor.

All of which took two seconds. At the three-second mark, the cart swayed onto its left wheels, tottered briefly, and then was carried over onto its side by its own weight to hit the floor with a crash.

The giant with the cap instantly turned toward the noise. His light falling squarely over the cart, then flashing on the A/V boards, electrical cables and other things that had been dumped from its trays into the water. It hadn't rolled far. Three feet, maybe. He'd heard it clattering toward him from his left. No more than three feet.

His hand went up to his lamp.

At almost the same instant, Jacques quickly brought the gun down from temple index. He'd known that if the giant turned to look at the cart, he wouldn't be looking at him. And that if he wasn't looking at him, he could use the distraction to get the jump on the giant. Fire a burst using the lamplight to guide his aim.

That had been his calculation, and it was a fair one. It just didn't work out. Oleg wrecked it by being a tick faster turning off his lamp than Jacques was getting a bead on him, hurling the chamber back into darkness before he could pull the trigger.

The Russian didn't like engaging in the dark, and ocular links made him more uncomfortable. But his smart contacts were interlocked with Reva's and Zoltan's retinal implants, streaming their shared visual inputs and outputs in real time. Which meant he could see what they saw in a near-total absence of light. A little less clearly. A little less brightly. The contacts were a little less sensitive than the implants. But sensitive enough. And what the Lightnings saw in the dark right now—saw almost as clearly as they would in a sunlit room—was Jacques standing to the left of the opening with his hands around the Beretta's grip and foregrip and the gun held out in firing position.

Jacques, meanwhile, couldn't see anything at all. Edge to his opponents.

That had been Reva's calculation. Or part of it. The tandem use of knives and guns was another part, her Spetsnaz trainers having adapted the art from Filipino irregulars in World War II. Their bolo men would sneak up on enemy soldiers in the night, using the blades as their primary weapons. Silent, stealthy. The guns essentially as backup. Key to the attack was the *tatsulok*. The triangle formation. The lead man striking the first blow at the target. The target's momentum driving him into one of the other two knives for the finish.

Reva saw Jacques standing to the left of the entry at the twelve-o'clock position and approached from his right, nine o'clock, Zoltan and Oleg moving widely around him to three and six.

Jacques couldn't see them.

He was blind in the darkness.

But Kali had shared a trick with him.

His right hand around the Beretta, he pushed his free hand into the kangaroo pocket of his hoodie, came out with one of her signal flares and slammed the bottom against the wall to ignite it. It popped and kicked in his grasp, spitting fire.

As Reva's surprised face appeared to his left in its blazing light, he lobbed the flare into the water between them, reached for a second one, slammed the base, tossed it. It ignited and splashed down several feet to her right.

The water on the floor was now almost high enough to reach Jacques's ankles. The flares spun and fishtailed and then were submersed. But they kept spewing flames. The combined flashpoint of sulfur and potassium nitrate was 320° Fahrenheit. Once primed, the mixture quickly heated to its full burn of 3000°. Water would not extinguish it.

That was the first part of Kali's calculation. The second involved the basic properties of light traveling through water.

Cold water is denser than hot water. The denser the water, the greater its refraction of light waves, and the more it bends the light passing through it. Because the nozzles of the flares were circular, the water around them *heated* in circles. Their inner cores were hottest. Their circumferences, coolest.

As the cooler, denser water on the outer circles bent the light back inward toward the nozzles, it created blazing round disks on the water's surface, saucers roughly eight inches in diameter, their inner cores brilliant white, their cooler outer bands an angry, seething red-orange. They brightened the area around Jacques like burning stepping-stones.

Kali used their light to guide her as she slipped in from the tunnel where she'd hidden, entering about fifteen feet behind Oleg and a little to his left, seven o'clock to his six. She could see him clearly in the fiery blooms of the flares, see Jacques and all three of his attackers as if they were standing in the throw of several small campfires.

She took three long strides through the dimness, came up behind the giant and swung the chain whip. It sang out in her right hand, her hip, shoulder, upper arm, lower arm and wrist moving fluidly, generating a wave of momentum and velocity. Then she snapped her wrist and the bullet-shaped *kundo* collided with Oleg's head, his skull stopping and absorbing the wave's kinetic energy on impact.

The dart was a single, solid, cast-iron object. Oleg's brain case wasn't one bone, but eight thin light curved bony plates held together by fibrous connective tissue. In that crucial respect, his size was irrelevant. All human skulls followed the same anatomical blueprint. They all had the same weak points. When a moving object like the dart struck a stationary skull at a high rate of speed, it transferred all its force and momentum to the plates and fascia. When that moving object was the *kundo* and its speed was in the range of seven hundred miles an hour, that blow could do a lot of damage. No matter how big or small its recipient.

Oleg might have actually fared better if he'd been struck by a bullet. A bullet would have impacted at twice the *kundo*'s speed but likely traveled in a straight line, entering the back of his head and then passing cleanly through bone and tissue without inflicting secondary injuries.

The *kundo* had yaw and elliptical trajectory. It had a minute flutter. It hit him somewhat broadly where the back of his head met the back of his neck, cracking the base of his skull and shattering the upper vertebrae of his spine, instantly causing what surgeons call a severe *hangman's fracture*.

Oleg immediately felt some strange and unfamiliar sensations. Pain traveled down through his arms, followed by a feeling of pins and needles in his legs, then a slice of a second later by a spreading numbness in all four extremities. His lower body felt weak and putty-soft. Then his right eyelid drooped shut, and he felt the numbness rise to his cheeks and forehead. It was as if he'd been sprayed in the face with freeze aerosol.

He attempted to aim and fire the P90 at Jacques. But he couldn't move his finger to pull the trigger. He suddenly couldn't feel it, or feel any other fingers on his hand, or his hand on his wrist, or his arm in its shoulder socket. He couldn't move or feel anything below his neck. His body was unresponsive. He wobbled in place.

Jacques brought him down with two tight bursts, high and middle, not waiting for him to go down. The first entered his forehead and exited the back of his skull, a fist-size chunk of it meteoring backward into the crown of the racing cap, propelling it several feet through the air. The second blew a hole in his chest. Oleg crashed to the chamber floor like a building slammed by a wrecking ball, splashing heavily into the water.

Jacques drew a single breath. His light was dimming. The burn time of the flares in water was less than half a minute. They were almost out, the floating, glowing saucers shrinking in on themselves. And he no longer saw the woman on his right. She'd vanished. As if a black curtain had fallen over her.

His right hand around the Beretta, he automatically tucked his arm against his side at a forty-five-degree angle. Brought his left fist against his chest, the arm and elbow cocked, a closed-up, close-quarters stance, ready in case she or anyone else tried getting the gun away from him.

He didn't see her. But he saw the tall, steeple-thin Russian on his left. He was already moving toward Jacques, his weapon held out in firing position.

Jacques raised his arm to trigger a burst and then heard Kali urgently cry out his name and realized too late that he'd been decoyed.

Kali had stood briefly in the ebbing light of the flares, the chain whip back in her hand, her fingers around its linked segments. She'd seen Jacques on the other side of the chamber to her right, his vertically elongated shadow on the wall behind him, rippling and undulating like a tube man in the wind. She'd seen the giant with the blond hair crumpled in the water between them. And she'd seen the thin one coming toward him from the right.

But not the woman. She hadn't seen her at all. Kali had assumed she must have slipped into one of the other archways or hidden behind something. If she had left the chamber, she wouldn't have gone far.

Plans are nothing; planning is everything. That came from Carmody. He had written it on a slip of paper he kept folded in his wallet, and shown it to her in New York, when they were preparing to move against Drajan.

The woman wouldn't have gone far. They'd all planned and calculated for this.

This here.

This now.

This moment.

She wouldn't have gone far.

But where was she?

Kali had tried to pick her up with her peripheral

vision. What disappeared in the darkness while looking at it straight on could be seen clearly if she directed her sight away from the center and toward the edges of her field of view. That was from her grandmother, and her sensei, in the years of hiding, and learning the way of the White Rose. After Guernica and the murder of her parents.

Kali had watched the corners. Certain the woman was close. The seconds felt long.

Then she'd suddenly seen another shadow on the wall. Behind Jacques. Gliding toward him.

She'd launched forward, the soles of her boots slapping the water.

"Jacques!"

Too late.

Reva jumped at his back now, thrust her dagger up into his right armpit, pulled it in toward her with a hard yank, then pushed it away with equal force.

There was very little muscle mass in the underarm. It was a bed of soft, spongy tissue surrounding glands, blood vessels and lymph nodes. And Jacques had exposed it to her when he brought up the gun. Reva cut through his axillary artery on the pull, completely severing it above the fourth rib. It was like slicing a pressurized hose in half. The axillary shunted oxygenated blood from the heart to the arms and shoulders and chest. That blood began spurting out of it in rhythmic pulses.

Reva's shove drove Jacques forward, sent him stumbling onto Zoltan's outstretched dagger. Zoltan took two quick strides to close the distance between them, sticking the blade deep under Jacques's ribs, then slicing it sharply upward. Their bodies clapped together, Jacques flush against Zoltan, Zoltan simultaneously stepping in on him, the knife connecting them in some brutal, perverse way. Jacques felt the warm wetness of his blood between them and the cold steel blade inside him. He shuddered around it, an involuntary spasm, the cold radiating from his middle, sending icy shoots out into his limbs. Zoltan took another step, his stride carrying Jacques backward, pushing the knife in deeper, impaling him.

Then Jacques heard the gunfire. A semiautomatic burst. It wasn't Zoltan. It was the woman who'd come up behind him He thought suddenly of Kali, tried looking around for her, and felt tendons and ligaments in his chest snapping like rubber bands around the blade. Moving from side to side only deepened and widened the cuts. He was slicing himself up.

Jacques sagged in the darkness, faint but conscious, his thoughts slipping away. His head was smoke. He felt detached from his body but could still feel the gun in his hand. It seemed far below him, down a deep, dark hole like one of the mine pits in Rats' Alley…except he knew it wasn't. He could feel its weight in his right hand, feel it against his thigh. He was still holding his gun.

Bringing it heavily upward, he shoved its muzzle into Zoltan's groin and squeezed the trigger. The Beretta produced a muffled rattle. Zoltan quivered against Jacques, the sudden vacancy between his legs gushing out blood. Jacques pulled the trigger twice again, adding six rounds to the three already fired, the snout of the gun pushed about an inch into the wound. Some of the bullets crashed around inside Zoltan, obliterating soft tissue and bone. Some tore right through him. Zoltan teetered for half a second, spilling gore, before he went straight down into the water.

Jacques fell alongside him a fraction of a second later. As he landed on his back, he could have sworn he was still falling and thought foggily of the mine pits again. *Where the dead men lost their bones*. Then he thought he heard another burst of gunfire from far away through the mist.

He was half-right. Reva had fired at Kali, twice. But she remained only a few feet behind him. Though the flares were almost out—their glow in the water reduced to small, weak, wavering spots of orange—she'd seen Kali splashing toward her as if the chamber was fully lit. Her enhanced vision gave her that advantage.

But Kali had others. Reva was about her size, making her natural arm reach just over two and a half feet. The chain whip gave Kali almost four times that extension, edge to her.

She was about four feet away from Reva after bringing Oleg down, running low, driving forward, gaining speed, a moving target to Reva's stationary one, the spinning blur of the chain whip above and slightly in front of her. Meanwhile, Reva had needed to turn from Jacques and pivot in her direction before she fired. It gave her virtually no reaction time.

Which was where Kali's second perceived edge bore out. She knew where the bullet would come from. She could make that instantaneous deter-

mination from seeing Reva's dim outline in front
of her, because at that close range a bullet traveled in a straight line. But the whip's circular path
meant it could strike from different angles and directions. And the person holding it could change
them in an instant. Making the direction of the hit
unpredictable.

It scattered Reva's attention. Distracted her. Her
first shots understandably were off the mark. The
burst went a half inch to Kali's right.

It was a narrow miss. Kali had heard the rounds
hum past her ear and zigged reflexively, infinitesimally to the left. She'd wanted her dart to meet
Reva's right forearm at the wrist, which would have
shattered its bones and caused her to drop the gun.
But Reva was quick and ready. She'd moved nim-
bly to her left so the dart struck her arm a glancing blow.

She barely felt it. Her brain implants were already pumping narcotic endorphins so she could
function with third-degree burns. This barely increased their workload. She kept a firm grip on the
gun and took aim for a second burst.

This time Kali was a tiny step ahead of her.
Two-handed use of the *manriki* was a challenge:
the whip had bitten her often and savagely before
she'd tamed it. But her stubbornness had outlasted
its spite.

Grasp firmly but not stiffly, lively and with force.
An instant before Reva would have pulled the trigger, Kali gripped the chain above the middle with
her secondary hand, giving her tighter control of
its rotation. A flick of her wrist to the right and it

lashed out again, wrapping clockwise around Reva's firing arm below the elbow.

Kali jerked the whip, a hard flourish. Reva's arm twisted out laterally. Kali wrenched it backward before she could recover, and the Grach spiraled from her fingers into the water.

Kali flicked her headlamp on with her free hand. Darkness no longer benefited her. The element of surprise was gone.

The sudden glare made several things clear. All in an instant she saw the woman's burned, disfigured face and knew her brain implants had to be blocking tremendous pain for her to function. She also saw that the water was now cascading from the ceiling in heavy sheets—and, alarmingly, gushing from the walls as if from open fire hydrants. The chamber was under pressure from all sides.

She needed to hurry. But first she had to contend with Reva. And how she dealt with her would be decided in the next few seconds.

Reva had two options. She could try freeing her arm from the chain, which would have been impossible. Or she could press the attack with the arm still entangled. She was still holding the dagger in her opposite hand, still had a weapon. It was one or the other.

She made the choice Kali expected, lunging forward to close the gap between them, leading with the knife.

As Reva came charging forward, she stepped to the right, feinting like a boxer, then flicked her wrist clockwise and up to withdraw the chain whip. It uncoiled from around Reva's arm, releasing it with two counterclockwise turns, the *kundo* coming up last like the head of a snake.

Kali swung the chain again, its dart whistling between them. She doubted Reva would feel much pain if it struck her and thought it possible she wouldn't feel anything. But she would cover up to protect herself. Because the blow could cause injury whether or not she felt it, and because it was a primitive survival reflex, the product of a biological hardwiring even more powerful than the modifications.

Kali's swing was therefore setup for the next, and it worked. *The soft leads to the hard.* Reva ducked her head and crouched slightly, bringing up her arms to block the dart, taking a defensive posture midcharge. That broke up the rhythm of her attack and slowed her a beat.

Which was exactly what Kali wanted. She dropped her arm angle, bending her right leg forward at the knee and stretching her other leg out behind her so her feet were stable and in line, and so her weight was evenly distributed as she reached out and swung low and the chain swept out on a horizontal plane.

A flick of her wrist at precisely the right moment and it wound into a tight coil around Reva's left shin.

She jerked the chain whip again. Harder than before. Pulling it in toward herself this time, using Reva's own momentum to drag her forward off her feet. Reva stumbled, her leg entangled in the chain, and then fell backward into the floodwater.

Kali waded in and dropped down on top of her,

jamming her knee into her left arm, wanting to pin her on her back, stop her from bringing the dagger out of the water. But Reva was agile, her speed fueled by adrenaline. She slipped to one side before Kali could fully plant the knee, boosting herself up on her right elbow, gripping the dagger in her left hand and slicing it viciously between them. It cut the sleeve of Kali's bomber jacket and blood started running down her arm. Then sliced at her again, passing a fraction of an inch in front of her throat, barely missing her windpipe as she jerked her head back to avoid it.

Suddenly there was a loud rumble. Water pounded Kali's neck and shoulders in a cold, battering torrent. She ignored it and stayed focused on Reva. She was still on her back in the water, still gripping the dagger. Kali needed to defang her, and quickly. As the blade swept in front of her again, she caught Reva's wrist with one hand and bent it sharply back and down, a violent twist, while pressing her thumb into it for leverage. Reva bucked underneath her, her radial bone snapping cleanly, her hand partially detaching from her lower arm. Kali's wrenching motion had caused the edges of fractured bone to tear through muscles, ligaments and capillaries. The hand immediately filled with blood. Its fingers swelled and uncurled, unable to move, the knife slipping from them into the water. Kali thought she saw pain register on Reva's face.

There was another ominous rumble overhead, louder and more prolonged than the first, like a rolling landslide. Then Reva's right hand came up and grabbed Kali's throat, locking around it, pushing

her head back with the ball of its palm. Kali felt
her windpipe compress, choking off her air, and
smashed her right elbow straight down into Reva's
brow. An untrained fighter might have aimed for
the broad side of the face. The jaw being the largest,
widest target. The most easily shattered or dislocated. But it took a sideways blow to connect with
it. A direct, downward strike had greater force.

Her elbow split the thin skin above Reva's eye.
Blood spurted up from the mesh of broken capillaries underneath it. Kali hammered it again and
felt the ridge of bone over her eye give in, and then
Reva's hand loosened around her throat. Kali hit
her again, and she started bleeding heavily. There
was more rumbling. Water sprayed down on Kali,
rocks pelting her shoulders. Reva's right eye was
now covered in blood, but Kali saw her other eye
widen, staring wildly up at the roof.

She took a quick look. It was sagging and trembling above them, bulging downward like the bottom of a soggy cardboard box. Water showered
from a long crack down the middle of the bulge,
and more pebbles and dust spilled over her, getting
in her hair, stinging her cheeks, the bulge literally
growing and swelling before her eyes as if preg-
nant with floodwater. Then she heard the rumbling
again, but this time it transitioned into a different
sound, a groan of buckling rock like something
wrung from the throat of a wounded animal.

Kali dove to one side, tumbling into the water an
instant before a boulder-size section of the chamber's roof slammed down on top of Reva, followed
by more large chunks of limestone. She sprang to

her feet, drenched, and glanced back over her shoulder. Reva lay buried under the rock pile, only her legs and part of one arm visible, the water around her dark and swirling with blood.

Then Kali thought of Jacques and turned away, crossing the chamber to where he'd fallen, thinking she needed to get him out before the roof, or the rest of it, crashed down on their heads. At first she didn't see him…only the tall man sprawled on his belly in the rising water. But a hurried look around revealed that Jacques was sitting up against the wall a few feet from the body. She splashed over to him, thinking he must have dragged himself over there.

She knelt in front of him. He was conscious, his eyes glazed but open. Blood and face paint were horridly smeared together on his chin, and his sweatshirt was drenched in blood. There was a wide-open slash across his abdomen, fabric gaping open around it like a warped mouth. But what distressed her most was the fluid trickling from the corner of his lips. It was dark and thick.

"Jacques," she said, "we have to get out of here."

He shook his head and tried to say something, but Kali couldn't hear him. Water had punched through the wall to her right and was brawling down into the chamber.

She leaned closer, brought her ear to his mouth.

"Go," he said, faintly. "Can't…walk."

"I'll help you."

"Non."

Kali heard another waterfall open up behind her. She kept her eyes on him.

"I won't leave you to die here," she said. "You're coming with me."

He shook his head weakly. *"Je suis...déjà mort... ma sœur."*

Kali looked at him in the muted light of her headlamp. His right hand moved slightly on his lap, where it was resting barely inches out of the water. She realized he was trying to lift it up between them, then saw the wearable on his wrist and knew why.

"Prends-le," he said.

"Jacques..."

"Take it."

She nodded, gently raised his hand, unclasped the navigator from his wrist and fastened the thick rubber strap around her own. Then she placed her hands over his.

She felt them tremble and held them more tightly. They were very cold.

"Jacques," she said.

He spasmed, his body stiffening with pain, and balled his shaking fingers into a fist. More brownish fluid dribbled from his mouth. He was drawing it into his lungs. Hemorrhaging internally.

"Jacques..."

He spasmed again, coughed out a mouthful of aspirated fluid. Blood and probably gastric juices, she thought. He'd been stabbed through the gut.

His eyes bulged.

She held his hands.

His mouth opened wide.

She held his hands.

He jolted as if suffused with electricity. Then

gasped, the dark fluid streaming over his chin. His fingers twisted and stretched as if being pulled in different directions. She held them in hers, water showering over her, pouring down around her feet, lumps of stone splashing into it on all sides.

Jacques shuddered, his mouth wide and contorted. He looked into her eyes, and she looked back at him, steadily. Then he sagged back against the wall, and his eyes glazed over, and he was no longer looking at anything.

Kali slid one hand down his wrist, feeling for a pulse. It was flat. She touched her fingertips to her heart, then touched them to his chest and stood up. The water had risen to her shins and was falling everywhere around her in blinding curtains. The chamber's roof was almost gone. Mounds of fallen bricks and rubble stood in the riotous water like humped, stony islands.

She turned toward one of the arches and went racing through.

14

April 25, 2024
Janus Base, Romania

Carmody had worked up an appetite after the test flight, so Fernandez gave him a lift down to the chow hall on his way to some vague meeting with robotics. All sleek concrete and glass like the rest of the new-and-improved Janus, it bore no resemblance to the drab, trailerlike building that had once fed base personnel.

"Later," the sergeant said, pulling up front. "Remember to check out the *năsal*."

Carmody looked at him,.

"The local cheese," Fernandez said. "We've been waiting, like, a month for it."

Carmody nodded, got out and went in.

The dining area was bright, spacious and airy, with the floor-to-ceiling windows at its far end giving a wide view of the southern Carpathian Mountains. Everything inside was tan and beige except for the gray-speckle granite floor tiles and stainless-steel serving counters. Gone were the old wall-to-wall cafeteria tables and stack chairs that looked like they'd come straight off a prison movie set. Instead Carmody mostly saw rectangular restaurant-style tables for four or six, with some smaller round ones seating two or three, all with comfortable padded café chairs. There were a few cushiony booths under landscape paintings in plexiglass frames. The half dozen or so flat-screen TVs hanging from the ceiling were tuned to CNN International.

The sign said breakfast was served from 0630 to 1100 hours, and it was now a quarter past ten. With most shifts beginning earlier, there were no lines and a lot of empty tables.

Carmody wasn't sure why it surprised him to see Howard sitting alone near the window wall. Mori, Schultz and Dixon were at one of the round tables near the entrance.

He flicked them a wave and went to the buffet, filling his plate with three fried eggs, *mamaliga*, spicy sausages and thick-crusted bread. Then he started toward an unoccupied booth with his tray.

"Want to join us, boss?" Schultz tapped the empty seat beside him as he strode past.

Carmody eyed it a second before nodding toward the booth.

"Looks like a tight squeeze," he said. "Thanks."

Schultz shrugged. Beside him, Dixon looked up from a huge omelet, pointing his fork at a wedge of yellow cheese on a separate dish.

"You try the *năsal* yet?" he asked.

"No."

"Well, you should," Dixon said. "Fernandez turned me on to it."

"Uh-huh."

"There's only one town in the whole country that makes this stuff. They smear it with mold, then stick it in a lamb's gut to ferment. It's an art." He grinned and motioned at his wedge. "Have some of mine, no extra charge."

Carmody looked at him over his tray.

"You talked me out of it," he said and went on to the booth.

He sat there eating his eggs and thinking about his meeting with Howard, Fernandez and Soto. He'd spent months drawing up his mission plan. Though its basic outline was pretty simple, every plan had its uncertainties. You could look at the probable outcomes of every action and think you had them figured, and maybe you did. But there was always a chance the improbable would happen. What he'd learned in the conference room eliminated some of the uncertainties, and his test of the jet suit had rid him of another one. He knew he could fly and land it in one piece. Knew he could control it. That upped his odds of success, but there were still plenty of unknowns.

He sat staring blankly at a TV screen above him and thought some more. Mostly about the railroad line, and where it ran and when. His information wasn't complete. And it wasn't going to be. But he'd done his research, weighed his opportunity against the risks and was willing to accept them.

Because an opportunity could be there and gone before you knew it.

Carmody noticed someone coming up to the booth, lowered his eyes from the screen, realized it was Howard. He stood there with a cup of tea.

"I'd like to talk to you about something," he said.

Carmody shrugged. The colonel sat down opposite him.

"How's the breakfast?"

"All right," Carmody said. "You going to recommend the new cheese?"

Howard snorted.

"Crap smells like feet," he said. "I wouldn't eat it under threat of death."

Carmody raised his eyes from his plate. "So what's the something?"

"I saw you over the field," Howard said. "In the jet suit."

"And now you believe a man can fly."

Howard didn't look amused. "Apart from you maybe breaking your neck, the suit's an expensive piece of equipment," he said.

"You're the second person to mention its price tag to me," Carmody said. "Was I supposed to drop a buck into the donation tin?"

Howard looked at him. "You had no business doing it without my permission."

"Really?"

"Really."

"Why?"

"Because you're on a military base and have to abide by protocols. And because it was a dangerous stunt."

Carmody was silent. He cut a slice of sausage, forked it into his mouth and chewed.

"Wrong," he said.

"About what?"

"Everything," Carmody said. "Though, I'll give you that we're on base."

Howard stared over his cup. "You think I'm joking?"

"No," Carmody said.

"Then, explain why you didn't inform me ahead of time," Howard said.

Carmody shrugged.

"I'm not one of your people," he said. "I don't need your permission."

"You really believe that?"

"I said it, didn't I?"

Howard gave no answer. Carmody ate. The news anchor on the screen above them moved his lips silently.

"You were always a reckless, disrespectful bastard," Howard said at last. "This is different."

"How, exactly?"

"Maybe we need to talk about it."

Carmody looked at him. "I know what I'm doing. And I'm the one leading the mission."

"Unless I decide you're out of control," Howard said. "What else am I to assume when you pull this shit?"

There was a long minute of silence. Carmody washed down a bite of his eggs with some coffee, took his napkin off his lap, and folded it neatly on the table.

"Help yourself to the leftovers," he said. "Might cut some costs around this place."

He slid out of the booth into the aisle, turned toward the entrance.

Howard stood up and stepped in front of him. "We aren't finished talking," he said. "I asked you a question."

Carmody looked at him. "Technically, you asked two," he said. "Pick your favorite, and I might answer it. Or better yet, get out of my way."

Howard's features suddenly contorted with anger. He shot a hand out and bunched the front of Carmody's T-shirt in his fist.

"Janus has been through hell," he snarled. "We're still building our way out of it. I won't let you or anyone else screw with what we do here."

Carmody looked at him. Howard was a full head smaller than he was, but he had his sleeves rolled up, and the muscles of his arms were carved and defined.

"This isn't a good idea," Carmody said.

"You think I'm worried?"

"I think we'd have an audience. And that might not be the best thing in the long run. For you, your reputation or your base."

Howard didn't reply. Instead he stood there glaring at Carmody for a long moment, then finally let go of his shirt.

Carmody walked around him to the exit, leaving him alone in the aisle. At their table, Schultz and Dixon exchanged glances over their dishes, pointedly not looking in Howard's direction as he turned back toward the window wall.

Mori made a silent whistling face.

"*Sooo*, I guess they aren't Facebook friends," she said quietly.

Schultz gave her a muted smile. "Good one."

She brushed her shoulder with her fingers.

"When you've got it, you've got it," she said, spearing the last piece of *năsal* from his dish with her fork.

Janus's mechatronics and robotics research laboratory—or MRRL, usually pronounced *mirl*—was temporarily housed in its eastern sector, an area where the Quonsets once used for lodging civilian commissary and maintenance employees had stood before the Thanksgiving strike. A row of three large, lightweight, interconnected, 3D-printed structures that could be easily dismantled and lifted by crane or aircraft, the installation would eventually relocate to a permanent spot adjacent to Special Projects, making for a two-hundred-fifty-acre onsite research and development park along the base's western perimeter.

Fernandez drove through the security check and swung around behind one of the buildings—a hangarlike structure on a thousand square feet of ground that dwarfed the facility he'd been to with Carmody earlier.

There were several figures waiting out back. Among those of the two-legged variety was his chief engineering assistant, Autonomous Systems Specialist (24 Delta) Mario Perez. Perez was in uniform, as was Senior Sergeant (MOS) 09L Joe Banik, a translator/interpreter and dog handler from the army's Third Special Forces Group, attached to Net Force on special, open-ended orders. Standing near them in a bulky, two-hundred-pound Kevlar bite suit, protective helmet and tinted face shield was Corporal (E-4) Bernadette Cho.

All the rest of the figures were canines, more or less. Banik's three-year-old Malinois, a huge tawny, broad-backed, black-faced female named Ellie, had been bred and trained to stringent *Schutzhund* certifications by the Force's director, Alex Michaels, who enjoyed raising work and guard dogs when he wasn't too busy with his exotic-flower gardens or being the Cabinet-level showrunner for America's third-largest intelligence and law-enforcement agency. Ellie sat, leashed and at attention, beside the sergeant now, watching Fernandez pull up in the JLTV, her triangular ears perked upright. She was the only full-fledged, furry, warm-blooded dog in the group. The other three were robotic hellhounds.

They stood behind Banik and Ellie, the products of ingenious biomimicry: their metal bodies perfectly still and gleaming in the sunlight, their legs bent forward at the knees. Beyond them Fernandez saw an outdoor obstacle course.

He pulled off the service road into the little cul-de-sac parking area behind the buildings, got out and walked over to the group, stopping about twenty feet away. The obstacle course had multiple hurdles, a balancing bridge, a rock pile, a ditch and an aboveground steel pool with a ramp behind it. The pool was eighteen or twenty feet long, with large markers on its inner and outer walls showing a uniform ten-foot depth.

"I see the welcome committee's out, and they don't look like they're in dance mode," he said. "Should I say my prayers?"

Perez waved. "No worries, Sarge. They're in stand-down."

Fernandez strode closer. Banik was about thirty and a little over six feet tall, wearing aviator sunglasses and a black K-9 Unit ball cap. He nodded at the leashed Malinois.

"You already know El," he said. "The hounds are Azul, Blanca and Carolina on the left."

"The three Latina robodogs of the apocalypse." Fernandez glanced over at Clio. "Hey, Bernie, how hot're you in that suit right now?"

"Hot enough so the extra roll-on under my arms isn't helping," she said through the face shield. "Plus it *stinks* in here. Like being in a sweaty sock."

He chuckled. "So how'd you get to be the victim?"

"Ask the big boys. I've spent more time in this suit than both of 'em put together."

"Says the All-Army triathlon champ," Banik said.

"Bah," she said. "I'm telling you, Sarge, they're just plain chickenshit. Either that, or it's some sick male revenge fantasy."

Banik raised his palms above his head. "Chickenshit."

"Same," Perez said.

Fernandez grinned. Then Perez nodded toward the entrance to the middle building.

"Everything's ready," he said. "Take a peek.

We're doing an indoor/outdoor parkour to simulate the conditions the dogs'll likely face on the op."

Parkour, Fernandez knew, being a term derived from *parcours du combattant*, the French term for *obstacle course*, literally translating into *journey of the combatant*. The idea being to advance through a series of obstacles without retreat.

Fernandez let Perez bring him inside. He saw a deep build of simulated windows, ramps, stairs, dodging panels, aluminum hurdles, tunnels and barrel crawls. Other things like a concave wall, platforms and six-foot vertical cylinders.

"Playground on Elm Street," he said. "You sure Cho's safe? This is different from us having them dance to classic rock."

"She's tops. The suit's specially designed for the hellhounds."

Fernandez dropped his voice a notch. "I'm not talking about the suit, 'Rio. You know what I mean."

Perez nodded. "Laura has dreams. She wakes up and thinks we're still hiding in that old refrigerator unit. With a 'hog roaming around outside, looking for us." He paused. "We weren't ten feet from here. I can see it like it was yesterday."

Fernandez nodded. "So back to my question," he said. "Do we know she'll be all right?"

Perez looked at him.

"We designed a bespoke intrusion-detection and response system for the hounds from the ground up. I can abort if things get out of hand. Worst case, I can initiate a destruct sequence. But no machine's ever going to be a hundred-percent unhackable."

Fernandez looked at him a moment. Glanced

around at the others. Then looked back at Perez and let out a breath.

"Okay, I got you," he said. "But let's get one thing settled."

Perez waited.

"Those hounds slobber lube oil on me, you're forever screwed," he said.

The Crimean Peninsula

The hardened bunker facility for Okean-27's coastal and air-defense systems was cut deep underground some three hundred yards inland from its marine cargo piers. Outside the mountain, manned and unmanned weapons systems guarding the Okean could roll to the surface from the hatches in front of its main gate and rapidly deploy along the shore. Inside the secret city proper, approved personnel used a drive-in tunnel entrance. There were no other ways in or out.

Sergei Cosa rode in on a passenger cart unescorted, his thick eyebrows knitted in contemplation as he passed through an array of security checkpoints. His tête-à-tête with the Wolf had left him unsettled and eager to be alone with his thoughts.

Three armed, uniformed guards stood posted at the final check, where the cart paused to allow a visual inspection. Until that point, his biometric token had sufficed.

The guards looked uncomfortable, the way men did when a hornet flew too close by. And with good reason. Let him through without proper scrutiny and they could be accused of carelessly violating procedures. Scrutinize him too closely and they risked offending one of the most powerful men in the Federation. Offend him too seriously and they could face harsh reprimand. In Russia the saying went that there were a hundred punishments for every mistake, and another hundred for every one not dealt out. They could only tiptoe around him and hope not to suffer his sting.

"Do I pass muster?" he asked one of them.

The guard's shoulders stiffened into planks. *"Da, ser."*

"Good," Cosa said. "Tell Colonel Denislov I've arrived."

A crisp nod, and the guard turned to speak into the hands-free entry phone on the wall.

A moment later Cosa cleared the checkpoint and rolled on down a short corridor. Then a sliding door opened, and his cart went through.

Built specifically for housing the Okean's mobile air and coastal-defense platforms—along with the armaments loaded aboard them, and the equipment needed for their upkeep—the bunker was bright and climate-controlled for low humidity, with a high ceiling and smooth concrete floor. There were several passageways, the widest of them running straight down the center of the facility.

Colonel Vitaly Denislov, Eighth Mountain Brigade, stood waiting a few paces inside that center passage. Flanked left and right by wheeled and tracked vehicles mounted with weapons delivery, antiaircraft and tactical-combat systems, Denislov might have been posing for a Russia-1 television camera, the shot's carefully staged elements portraying a man of authority fully in charge of his responsibilities as commander of the Okean's military security detail. With his tight jaw, blue eyes and starch posture, he resembled a young aristocrat in some old family oil portrait or any one of the upper-class boys Cosa had known in the Young Communist League—a dedicated banner-carrier, or perhaps a strutting trumpeter in a red crisscross tie. But the Imperial Russia of the boyars was dust, the Communism of Cosa's youth scattered ashes. As for himself, Cosa was no ideologue. The Russia he loved and valued was in its villages, forests and vacant lands. And while some called him a *silovik*, a person of force rather than vision, he thought that characterization devoid of nuance. Groomed by the KGB and elevated by the Directorate, he had been shaped from the hard ground up by their realpolitik. Military strength and economic dominance were critical to any vision of the motherland, and he would serve the national interest using force, political manipulation or any other means necessary.

Cosa stepped from the cart. "Denislov, do you sleep right in here with your contraptions?" he said.

"My quarters are elsewhere in the mountain," the colonel replied, straight-faced. "Our specialists are first-rate, but I like to personally inspect them once or twice a week."

Cosa was again reminded of the dedicated child-soldiers with whom he'd shared his boyhood. The smile had been a dead reflex in them, killed by their scoutmasters before they were nine or ten. But it took all kinds. Indeed, he thought Denislov perfect officer material.

"That's commendable," he said. "It's an impressive collection."

Denislov nodded. "The Okean's defense comes at a high cost, but we're given everything we need. And we owe it your support, sir."

"I played my part, I suppose."

Denislov gestured to an enormous piece of hardware down the passage. "Have you seen our new launchers since they arrived?"

"No, Colonel. I've been busy with other things."

"Of course. But please take a closer look. It won't take a minute."

Cosa nodded and walked down the passage alongside him.

The two-tracked carriers were at the end of a row of armored combat vehicles, dwarfing them in size. Thirty feet long, they bristled with sensors, missile tubes, dual autocannons and the most advanced fire-control systems that could be loaded aboard a mobile chassis. Yet for all their technological sophistication, Cosa saw them as distinctly primitive behemoths.

He gazed up at their turrets, his hands linked behind his back. Their radar masts were folded forward, lowering their profiles inside the bunker. But at full vertical extension, they would tower fifteen or twenty feet above his head.

"A *ribauldequin*," he said. "Is the word familiar to you, Colonel Denislov?"

"I am afraid not, sir."

"It was among several names used for medieval volley guns," Cosa said. "I saw one in a Barcelona museum long ago. They moved on wheeled carriages, like catapults and rams. But they're more closely related to modern artillery batteries than siege engines in the evolution of war machines. The French called them *infernal machines*, and I can understand why. They would fire projectiles from multiple barrels…from as few as nine to as many as *fifty barrels* at a time, they say."

Denislov seemed to genuinely appreciate his musings. Another point in his favor, Cosa thought.

"These big beauties also represent a leap of progress," the colonel said. "We learned much from Syria and the '22 invasion. The Pantsirs fielded back then were vulnerable to small drones and rockets. They had neither the detection systems to acquire them, nor the weapons systems to engage and destroy them. The two Wildfire launchers before us have both—and they're almost totally autonomous besides." He paused. "It is why I mentioned cost. Each of those destroyed represented an investment of over a billion rubles. Their successors are far more expensive."

Cosa gave him a veiled glance.

"I'm glad you're conscious of such things," he said. "In fact, it's what brought me here to see you."

"I understand, sir."

"No," Cosa said. "You don't."

Denislov fell silent. Cosa's expression had grown ominous.

"Never forget that Moscow's generosity comes with expectations," he said. "You need to be ready to act at a moment's notice. For the sake of the Okean. And for your own sake, Colonel."

Denislov felt a thready tension in his stomach. He breathed in, out.

"Yes, surely," he said. "Is there a specific threat to the Okean?"

Cosa looked at him. "We're nearing a decisive mark, Denislov," he said at length. "The Pioneer supercomputer will soon go fully active. It's why the Okean exists. Why I've spent the better part of a year inside this rock. Again, there must be no shortage of vigilance and caution."

All of which was true. But Cosa had omitted what for him was the core truth. That he no longer trusted Drajan Petrovik, the architect of the operation. That Petrovik, lately, gave him the impression of someone consumed by an unpredictable, dangerous madness.

Denislov stood without speaking. He'd heard what Cosa came to tell him and had asked his question. He did not want to ask another and risk seeming impertinent.

An obedient, well-behaved scout, Cosa thought. And one kept on his toes.

"Thank you for showing me the new arrivals," Cosa said. "I'm confident you fully appreciate your duties."

"Yes, sir."

"And satisfied you have everything you need to live up to them."

"Yes, sir."

"A good day to you, then."

"Thank you, sir. You as well."

Cosa looked at him from under his heavy brow.

Then he nodded and turned back toward the passenger cart.

Denislov walked him over to it and watched him ride out, waiting until the metal door slid shut behind him to exhale.

Janus Base

"Okay," Joe Banik said. He stood behind the pool at the far end of the outdoor K-9 training course, speaking into the VoIP stereo headset he'd slipped down over his cap. About three feet in front of him, El and the hellhounds sat on the grass in a semicircle. He had a whistle on a lanyard around his neck.

"You read me, Bernie?"

"Loud and clear," Cho replied.

She was a few feet from the hangar entrance to the indoor parkour course. Fernandez and Perez, meanwhile, were off to one side behind a steel barrier Banik had set out for them. They were also wearing headsets.

"Bernie, when you hear me blow the whistle, trot into the hangar," Banik said. "If any of the dogs hit you and you think you're losing your balance, roll with it, or you'll hurt yourself."

"Roger."

"Also, one of them bites your arm or leg, keep wiggling it. If you don't, they'll move around and bite you everywhere on the body to test for signs of life. When they're in prey drive, that's their focus."

"How cool," she said. "Anything else?"

"That's it! Have fun!"

"Definitely."

Fernandez waited behind the rail, listening to them, their banter doing nothing to relieve the tension in his neck and shoulders. Then Banik brought the whistle to his lips and sounded two sharp blasts.

Cho turned and ran. The hounds sprang onto all fours and took off after her, Ellie the alpha leading the pack, Banik's double whistle cueing her to run the full obstacle course. The three robots hot on the chase, El charged up the ramp at a loping run and then leaped off the platform at the top, her powerful hind legs launching her through the air.

She splashed into the pool, followed in line by the hellhounds, the robots vaulting off the ramp behind her. Their legs folded underneath them as they hit the water, the jet propulsion units in their rear sections extending out like tails, propelling and steering them down the length of the pool while Ellie paddled ahead.

They took under twenty seconds to swim to the far end, their bodies submerged, their sensor-studded heads raised above the surface. Then they were running up the steps, sprinting over the rim of the pool toward the balancing bridge.

Fernandez glanced over at Perez and mouthed a silent *Wow*. He'd known the robotic hounds could swim, and swim at a clip of six miles an hour, three times faster than biological dogs. But knowing it and seeing them in action were two different things.

The dogs scrambled across the bridge and then up and over the pile of rocks toward the ditch, bounding over it without a break or stumble, Ellie still at the fore, the other three fanning out slightly behind her.

It was now ninety seconds since the whistle. The dogs streaked through the hangar entrance a few yards behind Cho, graceful and fearsome in their loose pack formation.

Fernandez heard Banik over the RoIP. "Pick it up, Bernie!"

She quickened her pace and ran clumsily toward the front of the hangar in the heavy bite suit, slow as a tortoise compared to the dogs. They probably would have been on her in two seconds flat if they'd circled around the obstacles or took the side-tracks. But Banik's double whistle burst had signaled them to run all the hurdles, and they obeyed, negotiating every one that stood between them and their quarry, bounding through the mock windows, clambering up the stairs, scrambling through the tunnels and *still* catching up to Cho a second or two before she reached the front of the hangar.

Fernandez saw Ellie barrel into her first, her large, wedge-shaped head low between her shoulders to ram Cho from behind. The dog's sixty pounds of muscle mass collided with her at full speed, striking a direct hit to the back of her knees. Then Ellie opened her long, toothy jaws wide and in a flash clamped them shut on her prey's right calf. Cho went down instantly, her feet skidding out from under her as she spilled backward over the dog.

Ellie instinctively anticipated her fall. She kept her jaws locked around Cho's leg, anchoring herself to the padded suit while using the torque generated by the forward momentum of her body to swing around in front of her like a clock hand in a sped-up minute. Meanwhile, the robot hounds had closed in around them, forming up on three sides.

Cho slowly tried to sit up, pushing off the floor with her arms.

It was the exact wrong thing to do.

She'd barely managed to lift her back off the concrete before Ellie released the leg and jumped across her body to pin her down, gnashing at the crotch of her suit, the robot dogs lunging and snapping and tearing at her from different angles. Fernandez heard Ellie snarling but consciously registered the creepy unnatural silence of the hellhounds as their metallic fangs tore at the suit's padding.

"Shit," he said, moving away from the barricade as if to race around it. But Perez put a hand on his arm to check him.

"Wait, Sarge," he said. "Give it a sec."

Fernandez hesitated a beat. Then he turned and saw Banik trotting past them toward the hangar, his pace brisk but not panicked.

"Stay down, Bernie!" he reminded her. "Shake your leg! Keep the rest of your body still."

It was counterintuitive. The flight-or-fight response was scripted into the hindbrain. Cho's glands would scream for her to struggle to her feet and fend the pack off, and that would only make them more ferociously aggressive. Fernandez knew she'd been a decoy before. He knew she had the gumption to control her natural impulses. But she'd hit the floor hard, and he thought she seemed out of it and slow.

Then she started kicking her right leg. Ellie pulled her muzzle away from her crotch and turned her attention back to the leg. The robots withdrew and hovered around Cho, following their programming, letting their alpha take complete charge.

Fernandez exhaled with relief. It felt strangely premature with Ellie still gnawing at Cho's leg like it was a shank of beef. But at least the dogs had broken off the attack.

Then Banik entered the hangar. "Heel, heel! Ellie, let go!"

She dashed over to his side. The hellhounds joined her immediately, falling back around Banik in their peculiar robotic silence.

"All right, everyone, we're done for now," Banik said. He strode over to Cho, Ellie obediently sticking to his side. "You okay, Bernie?"

Cho took hold of his offered hand and stood up.

"Ask me in an hour or so when the adrenaline wears off," she said and started unstrapping the suit. "That was some kind of smackdown."

Fernandez and Perez came over from behind the rail.

"Well," Fernandez said, "I'd say things turned out pretty good."

"So far," Banik said. "It gets better."

Fernandez looked from him to Perez. "Better how?"

"Better like we still want to show you how the hounds do on a target range," Perez said.

Fernandez looked at him. "You mean, as in dodging bullets?"

Perez smiled.

"I mean, as in shooting them," he said.

"Kira."

She glanced up from her computer screen to see him through her half-open door.

"Drajan," she said. "This is a surprise."

He stepped through the door. "Have I come at a busy time?"

She smiled. "You might have at least waited for an answer," she said. "I'm impressed that you could find your way down here."

He looked around. Square with cement board walls, her office was not much larger than a library carrel. There was room for her metal shop desk, an extra chair and nothing else.

"Section 6627, room 17, Automated Systems," he said. "Was it Cosa who installed you in this compartment?"

She shrugged.

"It was assigned to me... I doubt he concerns himself with such things," she said. "Why do you ask?"

"Because someone with your skills shouldn't have to work in a box."

Kira was quiet a moment. "This place is full of them," she said with a shrug. "Every hallway looks alike. It's almost funny to me."

"Oh?"

"We're inside a huge mountain on the seacoast. When I was driven here from the airstrip and saw it from the back of the car...it was quite an awesome sight," she said. "My parents are working people. They've only dreamed of vacations in Crimea. Of seeing the cliffs, the beaches and the waves."

He spread his hands.

"And here you are without even a window."

She shrugged. "It's all right. I've known worse."

"Cosa said you'd come from Federation Center."

"I assure you, it wasn't the penthouse. But I wasn't speaking of that."

Drajan did not immediately reply. He stood very still as he looked at her across the desk, ignoring the empty chair on his side.

"You were brought to the Okean to develop machine-learning models," he said after several seconds. "Is that correct?"

"Yes."

"For training artificial intelligence."

"Yes."

"In what?"

She hesitated. Drajan reached behind him and closed the door to the outer corridor.

"In what?"

"Social engineering, primarily," she said. "Voice impersonation. Speech recognition. Deepfake creation. Vulnerability discovery."

"In other words, AI-enabled and -assisted smart attacks."

"Yes," she said. "But I would think you've already investigated that about me."

Drajan said nothing for a moment.

"Have you any idea what we're doing here at the Okean, Kira?" he said. "I mean, the big picture."

She gave another shrug. "I received my transfer orders while at Federation Center," she said. "The tower. But it wasn't the penthouse."

"Nevertheless, you haven't wondered?"

Her eyes calmly met his across the desk. "If I may be plain, Drajan," she said, "I do wonder what it is you want in Section 6627, Automated Systems."

He smiled thinly. "You. Of course."

Kira rolled her chair slightly back from the desk, slowly crossed her legs and nodded, her gaze holding steady on his face.

"Of course," she said.

15

The Paris Catacombs

Kali sprinted through the passage, splashing through the puddles underfoot. She was cold and soaked and shivering. Her right arm was oozing blood where she'd been cut by the dagger. She could still hear water roaring into the storage chamber, hear bricks and stones tumbling down into it.

She ran for a while without knowing her direction. The passage she'd taken had very little seepage through the walls and ceiling, and she saw a few small leaks in the brickwork, but most of the wetness underfoot seemed to be rising groundwater. Possibly the ruptured and overflowing drainage conduits weren't routed above or alongside the passage. She couldn't know. What she did know was that she had to put some distance between herself and the chamber.

She hurried on. The floor dipped down and back up. The passage twisted and turned. She reached a fork where it branched off at diagonals to the left and right and glanced both ways. The fork on the right was fairly wide and ran at an upgrade. She didn't see any water on the ground. And its raw stone walls looked completely dry. That made it the easy choice.

Kali swung into it and raced uphill, her heart pounding, her wounded arm throbbing painfully with every step. After a few minutes, she finally paused to catch her breath and get her bearings. She'd slipped Jacques's navigation device around her left wrist above her compass. Her watch was on her right wrist.

She checked the compass first, saw that the tunnel ran north-northeast. There was still no sign of flooding around her. If that meant it hadn't reached Le Réseau Nord it was a good thing on many levels. She would find her exact position on Jacques's navigator in a minute. But first things first.

Etienne.

She raised her arm to tap the screen of her smartwatch.

Etienne was marching wretchedly through the tunnel with his hands flex-cuffed behind his back, when he felt his watch vibrate against his wrist.

There were five people in the party that had captured him. The woman who'd spoken to him before—they called her Jill—seemed to be leading them and was walking a few brisk paces up ahead beside someone of indeterminate gender. Right behind him, followed by two others, was a man whose entire face was covered in swirls of colorful makeup and liner. He was holding a pistol steadily at his back.

Etienne had no idea where they were going. He was defenseless, a prisoner. And he was in a whole lot of pain. Though his broken, dislocated nose was no longer streaming, it was too clogged with dried blood to admit any air. Both sides of his face felt puffy and tender.

The group tramped along through wide puddles of water, their headlamps on, Jill glancing at her own wrist device from time to time. It wasn't a watch per se. Etienne had seen an identical wearable on Jacques and gathered it was some kind of navigator.

Jacques and *Jill*, he thought. The names could not have been a coincidence. Nor their nav devices being the same.

But it was *his* device that was of paramount concern right now. The watch's vibration had to mean Kali was trying to contact him, and the question was whether he could answer. He was defenseless, a prisoner. His hands were bound with the palms pressed together.

Etienne rotated the underside of his left wrist against his right, stretching the fingers of his left hand, testing his range of motion. His wriggle room was minuscule, but the fact that there was any at all surprised him and allowed for a ray of hope. If he could extend the last two or three fingers of the hand over his right wrist, he might be able to hit the on-screen button he'd set up. He thought his chance of success was very slight and the odds of doing it without getting caught even slimmer. But what was there to lose?

Etienne gulped air through his mouth and marched along. The watch hummed quietly again.

He had to try and answer.

He turned his left wrist and hand a little more than the first time, paused to see if anyone noticed. When no one did, he extended his fingers as far as he could toward the watch, feeling for its display screen with their pads.

"Hé! Que fais-tu?"

He jolted. It was the man behind him. Asking what he was doing. His fingertips crept back from the watch.

"Rien," he said. Nothing.

The man wasn't buying it. He simultaneously grabbed Etienne's arm and halted, spinning him halfway around.

"Putain," he said and motioned toward his wrist with the pistol. "Jill, what's this over here?"

She turned abruptly in her tracks, stepped around behind him and lifted his arms slightly so she could see the watch, reading the brief text message visible across its display. It said:

Ça va? Are you alright?

Jill pushed the button on the watchband to release its clasp, went back around in front of Etienne and held the display up to his face. The whole group had now gathered around him, all of them standing still in the tunnel.

"There's no name attached to this message," she said. "Tell me who sent it."

"I don't know."

"Was it Kali?"

"I don't know."

"If it wasn't, who else might it be?"

"I don't know. It could be anyone."

"*Anyone?* How many friends do you have down here? Do you think I'm that gullible?"

"I'm only saying I don't know who sent it."

A scornful frown. Her fingers clenched tightly around the band, Jill turned the display so she could read the message again. After a moment she tapped her own onto it, pressed Send, stuffed the watch into her pocket and then stood there staring thoughtfully at her navigator.

Finally she raised her eyes to her four companions, meeting their gazes one at a time.

"We have her right where we want her," she said.

Kali looked at the message on her watch screen. It read:

Oui. Jill m'a trouvé. Nous arrivons. Yes. Jill's found me. We're coming.

She felt a fair measure of relief. Sending Etienne the text had been risky. If he'd been captured, or worse, anyone who got hold of his watch could have answered pretending to be him. But a pretender would not know of Jill's existence. Not even Etienne would know about her, unless she'd come upon him outside the hall. That told Kali the message was authentic. If they were on their way to meet her, moreover, it meant they were pinging Jacques's navigator with a compatible device—one that could decrypt and identify its unique MPF identifier and geotracking signal. Only Jill and her people would have the techwear.

They were coming, Kali thought. Good. She would wait and take a look at her injured arm in the meantime.

Shrugging her pack off her shoulders, she sat down against the wall, started to roll up the bloodied sleeve of her coverall, and immediately winced. Its ragged fabric had gotten jammed into the open wound, though it helped that the entire sleeve was soaked through with water. Otherwise the blood would have already coagulated and made peeling it away even more painful.

Kali took a deep breath and tried again, slowly plucking the shreds of torn material out of the gash. It was just above her elbow on her outer arm, nearly three inches long and a half inch deep through the skin.

The first-aid kit in her pack contained a small bottle of peroxide, a roll of gauze, a roll of adhesive tape, some sterile dressing pads, some Band-Aids, a few other items. She reached for the case, took out the gauze and dressing pads and set them out on her lap. Then she reached into a patch pocket on her leg, extracting the Swiss Army knife she'd transferred from her motorcycle jacket.

The wound's edges were clean and straight. That would make it easier to close, but she was going to need stitches. Her concern right now was to disinfect it and control the bleeding.

She poured some peroxide onto one of the pads, wiped around the wound and discarded it. She dampencd a second pad, covered as much of the wound as she could and then put a dry pad over it. Finally she wrapped the gauze twice around her arm, cut it from the roll with her knife and wrapped the gauze in tape.

Putting away the kit, she leaned back against the tunnel wall, took a few sips from her water bottle, then turned her attention to Jacques's wearable and found its tracker. After experimenting with it a little, she saw a cluster of moving location markers on the map of the underground. Jill and her band were only a short distance to her south.

Kali rested there, checking the marker positions. Her arm was getting stiff, but she'd stemmed the bleeding, and the markers had almost converged with her position.

She waited a while longer and then saw light pushing up from her left, south, the same stretch of tunnel she'd taken from the storage chamber. She could hear the scuff of approaching feet. She slipped on her pack, stood up and peered down the tunnel as the lights brightened and swelled in proximity.

Jill and another person were at the front of the group. Kali saw her through the wash of light and a half second later realized she was holding her submachine gun at the ready.

"Don't budge," Jill said. She'd stopped about five feet away. "Not an inch."

Kali didn't move or say anything right away. The

person beside Jill was also pointing a rifle at her. A compact submachine gun. But her eyes didn't linger on either of them. She was already looking past them at Etienne and the people behind him.

Etienne made brief eye contact with her, his expression miserable and dejected. She realized his arms were behind his back.

She returned her eyes to Jill. "What are you doing?" she said.

"Shut up. I'll ask the questions."

Kali's mind worked to understand what was happening.

"You're making a mistake," she said.

"Am I?"

"Yes. We're on the same side."

Jill raised the rifle slightly, pointing it straight at her chest. "We'll see. Tell me what happened to Jacques."

"Why?" Kali said. "I can see you've already made up your mind."

Jill and the person with the banded face stood with their weapons trained on Kali, the others a few steps back holding Etienne at gunpoint.

"That's his navigator on your wrist," Jill said. "Twenty minutes ago it stopped transmitting his biometrics and showing yours. A different gait and heartbeat. What did you do to him?"

Kali looked at her. "Jacques is dead. He was killed by the Russian assassins."

Jill's eye narrowed. "How do I know it wasn't you?"

"Because that would make no sense at all."

"Wouldn't it? It's you that separated us. Insisted the two of you go on without me."

Kali exhaled. "Why bother to think when you can simply decide?"

Jill angrily thrust the rifle at her.

"*Me fais pas chier.* Don't fuck with me."

"I'm not. They were waiting to attack us in the hall. As we'd expected they would."

"I have no reason to believe you."

"She's telling the truth."

This from Etienne, who was still standing behind Jill. She glanced back over her shoulder at him. "I didn't ask you."

"But I already told you the same thing about those people...the ones you call the Black Lightning. Are we both liars, then?"

"Enough."

"No. Kali refused to abandon me. She gave me her gun so I could protect myself. Is that what a killer does?"

"Enough!"

A long ten seconds of silence in the passage. Then Kali said, "Jacques died so we could reach Lucien Navarro before his enemies. He died for Navarro's dream. He wanted a better world than the one that created the Calais Jungle. The world of political lies and manipulations that let human vipers prey on your family."

Jill stared at her. "He told you about that?"

"He wanted me to know, yes."

Jill said nothing.

Kali said, "Listen. There are others coming for Lucien. The two men who followed me into his home. Possibly more, I don't know. But we need to hurry and get to him."

Jill stood there looking at her a moment. Then she turned to the person with the banded face.

"Cuff her, Ines."

Kali shook her head. "Did you hear a word I said?"

"It's the only reason you're still alive," Jill said. She paused, looking at her over the barrel of her SMG. "We'll go to Lucien. But on my terms, not yours."

"And if I refuse?"

"I'll kill you where you stand," Jill said. "Now, put your hands behind your back and turn around. Slowly."

Kali said nothing. After a moment she did as Jill instructed. The one called Ines stepped over and put on the flex-cuffs, and then she felt the muzzle of a gun prod her high between the shoulder blades.

"Walk," Jill said.

"They're all dead," Matyas said, standing near the metal stairs. "Reva, Dominik, Zoltan. The two Black Hundred."

"Their antimod fixation hardly prolonged their lives," Stefan said.

"Hardly," Matyas said.

"It's up to us, now."

"And Glaskov."

"Glaskov, yes."

"He's a capable one."

"Yes."

Stefan sat on the landing a few feet above Matyas. They had waited there for long hours in the dark, since Reva first came to suspect their target's tactic of moving in a wide circle to elude them. It was, as she had put it, Outrider's version of the Long March. And thus far it had succeeded.

Matyas's single eye trembled. Stefan did not notice it from the landing. But after a moment their neurolink showed him Outrider's geoposition.

"The beacon's still transmitting," he said. "She's coming. Finally, with others, no doubt."

"We won't know how many until they show up."

"No, we won't. But Navarro has plenty of support here among the Parisians. *Liberté, Egalité, Fraternité.*" Matyas paused and switched to the White Rose's rallying cry. "*Freiheit.* Freedom."

"Fuck the French, the Germans and the Cybernationals. Fuck them all. That's *my* motto."

"I'm not joking, Stefan. If we're the only ones left, it means the bounty gets split fewer ways. That isn't what we wanted, but it's how it is. Think of it as a silver lining...reward for being patient," he said. "Outlier won't know what hit her, I promise. We take care of her and Navarro. Then we get out of this underground hell and collect our money."

Stefan sat up on the staircase, studying the retinal location map in silence. Cool drafts of air were crisscrossing around him, whispery and irregular, like the breaths of restive spirits.

He held his arm out into the blackness, felt the currents brush over it and pantomimed a toast.

"Here's to the money," he said.

Okean-27, The Crimean Peninsula

Situated deep in the heart of the mountain, the data storage and processing facility was laid out in a hot aisle–cold aisle containment arrangement, the cold air blown from vents in the floor and ceiling to cool the servers, then drawn through them into the warm air aisle behind the racks. There it was captured, recooled, recycled and redistributed throughout the enormous space. In that way, the filters, fans, coils, condenser and refrigerant pipework of the computer room air-conditioning unit—or CRAC—kept the temperature and airflow constant and regulated within the system's specific tolerances.

His feet silent on the concrete floor, Drajan walked Kira Shapoval between the rows of tall cabinets. They were black, the walls white. Recessed LED panels overhead bathed the room in a cool, smooth, low-level radiance. Case lights on the CPUs and GPUs washed the fronts of the cabinets in wide swathes of green, violet and red.

He paused. She did the same.

"How many processing units do we have in here?" she asked.

Drajan was silent. She reached out and put her hand on his arm.

"Tell me," she said. "How many?"

Drajan glanced down at her hand, then raised his eyes to hers.

"The current number is sixteen thousand," he said. "And it increases daily."

She stared at him. "That's incredible. I had no idea."

He nodded.

"Right now she can perform over two quintillion calculations per second. Soon she'll double that speed. This isn't theoretical. It's happening. It's on. And it ranks her as the world's fastest and most advanced exascale AI supercomputer by leaps and bounds. Capable of self-learning. *Predictive* learning. Her potential has no boundaries."

She looked at him, her hand still on his arm. "May I ask you a question?"

He nodded.

"I wonder if you always refer to machines with the feminine pronoun."

"No," Drajan said, "I do not."

Silence. Their eyes met. He placed his hand on her wrist, moved it slowly up to her forearm and rested it there. She didn't pull away from him.

"This computer's performance is part of a much bigger picture," he said. "She's something other."

"Tell me the rest," she said.

Drajan's hand slid higher up her arm, then across the front of her lab coat, and then underneath it and over her blouse.

"There are cameras everywhere," she said.

"Does that bother you?"

"Only because it would make an old man resentful and jealous."

He looked at her for a long minute. "Cosa?"

"I do what's necessary to escape the boxes I'm put in."

Drajan kept his eyes trained on hers. "Can you break out of this one for a few hours?"

"Yes. But we should leave separately. I'll take my own car. Perhaps then you'll tell me about this *other*."

He pulled his hand from under the lab coat, letting it fall to his side.

"You surprise me, Kira," he said. "We are even more alike than I thought, you and I."

A smile curled across her lips.

"I'm learning through experience," she said.

"Drajan."

"Alina." He stopped in the corridor.

"You look surprised," she said and smiled. "I'm actually the one who's shocked to see you here this early in the day."

Petrovik looked at her. Alina Bailik had been project manager for Chimera, the Hawaiian operation, during which they had launched into a discreet affair. She held a doctorate in nuclear engineering, and he'd found her intelligent and attractive, in an unexceptional way.

"I was asked to come in," he said.

"It must have been urgent for you to leave your den."

He said nothing.

"So," she said. "I take it you're heading down to the supercluster?"

"Yes."

"How is its education progressing?"

"I can't say."

"Of course not. Security clearances, I'm sure."

He said nothing.

She stepped closer to him and lowered her voice. "You could at least ask how I've been these last few weeks."

He looked at her. Quintessa Leonides's cravings

were like periodic breaks in her ice cover, and for a
time Alina had filled the cold spells. But she lacked
imagination and daring. He'd found their sex enjoy-
able but repetitive, and her safe words exasperating.
Like lockout buzzers. Stop, stop, stop.

His interest in her had faded before Chimera's
unhappy conclusion. But what finally ended their
involvement was her banishment to a tangential
research section. Cosa had quick reflexes in pre-
serving his own legend: if he was to be Koschei,
he had to be infallible. Which meant scapegoating
others for his errors and losses.

"Your transfer wasn't my doing, Alina."

"Never mind that. I oversaw the development of
a hypersonic drone submarine. The mission's out-
come had nothing to do with its performance. Yet
one bad night and I was gone. What I'd done before no longer mattered." Her voice dropped down
another notch. "Does that also describe what happened between us?"

He looked at her.

"What happened didn't last," he said and shrugged.
"That's all."

She shut her eyes a moment. "They're sending
me north to Sarov in two weeks' time," she said.
"It's a closed city. It's cold and isolated, and the
bodies of the scientists in the ground set off Geiger
counters. I'll be one of a thousand doing nuclear
research. And they treat the women there like shit."

"Chimera isn't my project anymore," he said.

"Chimera be damned. You know the quality of
my work. We've been close. Isn't there anything
you can do for me?"

He felt something cold and scaly rise inside him. Its head surfaced, the jaws gaping open like a marsh crocodile's.

"Nothing is ever guaranteed," he said. "I'm no one's savior."

Alina exhaled long and quietly, then brushed a hand across her eyes.

"Fine," she said. "I should have known."

He nodded up the corridor. "I have to go, Alina. Good luck to you in Sarov."

She stared at him. A man in a lab coat passed and gave her a collegial smile. She didn't notice.

"Thank you," she said. "I won't forget your kindness."

Drajan walked around her toward the steel door. She breathed again, in and out, not glancing back at him. Fifteen seconds later, she walked off in the opposite direction.

The Paris Catacombs

"Do you see this?" Jill halted and motioned at the passage wall. "We're less than two clicks southeast of the Arc de Triomphe."

Kali stopped behind her with the rest of the group. They had been walking for about twenty minutes.

Jill's headlamp splashed the wall with light, revealing a worn sand-colored ceramic block set into the raw limestone. The words *Avenue Marceau* were neatly and expertly carved into it.

Kali read it in silence. Her hands tingled behind her back, their circulation constricted by the high-tensile nylon flex-cuff.

"The quarry inspectors marked many tunnels running beneath the city's main streets and avenues," Jill said, turning to her. "So they would know where they were, relative to the world above."

Kali said nothing.

Jill reached into her waist pouch for the map she'd taken from her, confiscating it along with almost everything else in her backpack and explorer's belt. She opened it, stepped closer, and slowly moved her finger across it to the right.

"This passageway radiates east off Place de l'Étoile around the Arc, runs beneath the Champs-Élysées, then links to another at the Rue Royale. We go on from there under the Madeleine to Boulevard des Capucines, then turn due north…"

Kali glanced up at her. "You're tracing a path to the Paris Opera House."

"Yes," Jill said. "It's no more than an hour's march."

Kali was thoughtful.

"The Opera stands above a cistern, doesn't it?" she said. "A man-made water tank."

"Yes…it's a reservoir of sorts," Jill said. "The reality doesn't quite match the romance of *Le Fantôme de l'Opéra*. But it exists."

Kali nodded and looked back down at the map. "Are you saying you intend to cross it?"

"It's the quickest way to our destination."

"If it hasn't overflowed and flooded the surrounding tunnels."

"I don't think it will have." Jill shook her head. "When the building's foundation was laid, its architect, Garnier, discovered his workers had excavated too deep into the soil. Water was brewing up from the table beneath it to create a swamp, and it would refill as quickly as it was drained. So they laid a stone liner and built the cistern. Its water pressures the groundwater back down and into a system of outflows—branching streams that channel off and distribute the water." Her finger guided Kali's eye up toward the top of the map. "This leads north to Moorgate. And from there—"

"I can see. It runs to the Empty Chapel. That means we're two hours from Navarro if we walk the course of the stream."

"Two at most, assuming there are no holdups," Jill said and paused. Something about her expression had suddenly changed, the skin tightening over her cheekbones, giving her face a hollow appearance. "But we won't be able to follow the stream on foot. It cuts straight through the earth. There are no banks. No walkways bordering its path."

Kali quietly studied her face.

"How, then?" she said.

Jill was silent for another long moment.

"Rafts," she said.

Janus Base, Romania

"Here comes Julio," Carmody said, his arms folded across his chest.

"For an even half dozen of us," Schultz said beside him. He gazed south at the JLTV bumping toward them over the remnants of the old north field. "I'm still not getting why you wanted to meet out here."

Carmody pointed his chin across the grass, out

toward the blacktop in front of the unfinished barracks.

"The tar gets warm," he said.

Schultz looked at him. "I meant here in the great outdoors instead of somewhere with chairs and desks and a ceiling."

Carmody didn't answer. With him besides Schultz were Dixon, Natasha Mori and Nick De-Battista. It was midafternoon, and the bright April sun had burned away the last of the previous night's clouds and fog.

Fernandez rolled the 4x4 up to within a few feet of them, stopped it and exited.

"Sorry I'm late," he said. "The hound drills ran long at the course."

"They go all right?"

"Better than all right," Fernandez said.

Carmody nodded. "Nick has the flight plan ready."

"Nice," Fernandez said, turning to him. "You know how you'll get where you're going without it being shot down?"

"Mostly," DeBattista said. "I think we can make the transfer outside Kyiv."

"So what's left?"

"Maybe a couple minor details about flying in Ukrainian airspace. And using their field."

Fernandez gave him a dubious look. DeBattista shrugged.

"Okay, strike the word 'minor,'" he amended.

Carmody looked at Fernandez. "I want to take a second solo run in the jet suit tomorrow. A third the next day, full flight team. Then one more before we launch. That should do it."

"I don't know," Fernandez said.

"Don't know what?"

The sergeant rubbed the back of his neck. "This operation… I'm acting like it's SOP. But it isn't. Even compared to some of the other stuff we've done."

"Reason?"

A pause. Then, "I like how we're looking. The hounds. The suits. But the strike team's been split over two continents. We all just assembled here yesterday. And we launch in days."

"I thought your section was called Quickdraw. Net Force Rapid Response."

"You know what I'm saying," Fernandez said. "This is a fast forward, even for us."

"We've been pulling in intel for a month. Rehearsing virtually," Carmody said. "Red Squadron had twenty days to prepare for the bin Laden raid. Go back to Entebbe and the Sayaret had seven. They flew twenty-five hundred miles from Israel to Uganda, took out eleven Soviet MiGs, killed eight terrorists. Rescued a couple hundred hostages with a single loss."

"There was still that scale model of Osama's compound at Harvey Point. The teams did their run-throughs together. In one place."

"We haven't had to be in one place. My stomach turns whenever I think of the HIVE, but it works," Carmody said. "You're the computer scientist. You and your staff designed the models. Tell me why I'm having to convince you."

Dixon said, "Maybe we should let it go for now, boss."

Carmody kept his eyes on Fernandez.

"Tell me, Julio."

"Wait," Mori said. "I want to say something. If nobody minds."

Carmody turned to her. "Doesn't matter who minds. That includes me."

She inhaled, nodded. "I'm a part-time instructor with the Force. I should be back in New York right now getting ready for *club* gigs at night. I'm not about, you know, missions."

"And your point?"

"Is that you and Kali picked me for this one. And here I am." She tapped the fingers of both hands to her chest several times. "Here I am on a hyped-up army base in Romania, with fucking robodogs and people flying around in jet suits. And Kali's gone. She *left*. Which, I'm telling you, wrecks me. I mean, I feel totally lost without her. I kind of thought we were going to be good friends someday. Though, I hardly even got to know her."

Carmody looked at her. "Unlike me."

"Who knows her better than any of us...and is her *actual* friend." Mori paused. "I don't think she really has that many. I think if you asked her, she'd tell you she could count them on the fingers of one hand."

There was a long silence. Carmody felt a gentle but distinct breeze issuing from the north, where the trees had stood before. He remembered being with Kali, watching the pair of crows on the branch, seeing them puff up and bow and dramatically spread their wings, and hearing their piercing *wahh*s and *caw*s, all of it somehow elegant and primal at once.

And then she'd told him it was a dance, one meant to hone their defensive and offensive skills. Like sparring in Fujian kung fu, it taught them the art of survival.

"They have to stay balanced. As individuals, and as a pair."

"And if one of them falls off the branch?"

"Both become more vulnerable to an aggressor. And both lose."

Carmody's eyes had held on Mori. He nodded and looked over to the faces of the others.

"I want you all to have confidence in the mission," he said. "I wouldn't lead you into it if I was incapable. But if anyone has any questions, now is the time to ask. Or let me know if you want out. I'll give Luna, Sparrow and Banik the same chance."

"My question's what it was a minute ago," Schultz said. "Why are we standing out here? Why not go somewhere inside?"

Carmody shrugged.

"I wanted to make sure it stayed private," he said. "I didn't want anyone listening in."

"*Anyone* meaning the colonel," Fernandez said.

Carmody gave another shrug.

"It wouldn't have been a first."

Fernandez had been looking at him steadily. After a minute he opened his mouth as if to say something, then abruptly closed it.

"Julio?" Carmody said.

He shook his head, turned his palm up in the air.

"It's nothing," he said. "I'm cool with your decision. But I'm not getting on the plane with the rest of you."

Carmody nodded, once again moving his eyes across the faces of everyone there. Schultz raised his hand next. Then Dixon and Mori an instant later.

Carmody looked at DeBattista. "Nick?"

"Neither snow nor rain nor a shitstorm in Crimea," he said. "That's the pilot's motto, right?"

"More or less," Carmody said.

DeBattista nodded.

"Don't make me raise my hand like a fucking schoolboy, brother," he said.

Munich, Germany

The cluttered four-in-one business office, donation center, repair shop and showroom of *Interaktive Ephemeralin*—Interactive Ephemera—was on the second story of a small brick walk-up on Ferhaus Street in the city's Haidhausen district, above an internet café with hand-hammered copper tables out front, and students with laptops sitting around them in decent weather.

Dedicated to the archival preservation and restoration of historic computer codes and technology, the nonprofit was run almost entirely by the sixtyish Franz Scholl, its founder, executive officer and self-proclaimed master tinkerer. His twentysomething shop assistant, Else Brandt, had been Scholl's employee for around five years.

Like her boss, Else was committed to salvaging antiquated hardware and software for future generations. As one format or device supplanted another, Franz preached, vast amounts of data would be lost without a concerted effort to preserve it. After allowing for their modest salaries, every euro earned from the sale of vintage computers, video games and floppy disks was used to collect, repair and catalog more technological junk.

A second-year dropout from the informatics program at Technische Universität München, Else was pretty and blue-eyed, with ice-white hair buzzed all around and choppy on top, where she'd moussed and pomaded it into a gravitationally implausible construct of high spikes and side-swept bangs. Her sleeveless form-fitting blouse had a leagues-deep neckline showcasing her curvy figure and latest body art, a white rose and stem inked between her neck and bosom. Besides being pleasingly rendered and situated, the rose held a special meaning she had vowed not to share, except with a select few. The piece on her right shoulder depicted an old-fashioned tube television with rabbit ears and rainbow bands on its screen. The name *Scott* was written across the colored bands in graffiti-style letters.

Scott Dixon was her American boyfriend, and she'd had eyes exclusively for him since their chance encounter at an inventors' fair in the Nussbaumpark a few years ago. Back then he was with the CIA, of all things. Now he was with a group called Net Force that was kind of like the Agency, but wilder. Crazy red-white-and-blue American boy: the last person she'd ever thought would push her romantic buttons. But Dixon was attentive, honest and sweet, and he always made her laugh with his bad jokes and was mysterious beyond all that. For Else it had unexpectedly added up to a sexy and irresistible package.

If there was a downside to the mystery element, though, it was that Dixon sometimes disappeared for weeks on end on top-secret assignments. A *normal* long-distance relationship could be hard on anybody, but what occasionally made theirs especially difficult for her was not knowing where in the world he was during those absences...or whether he might be in danger.

And then she had days like today, when she could have really used an emotional lift, and would have liked to talk to him about things but couldn't.

On this slow Monday afternoon, Else had been cutting CD-ROM sale copies of *Caleb Cook: The Dark Island*, one of the rarest late twentieth-century alternate history games she and Franz had restored from dozens of incomplete copies. It was a boring and repetitive task—slap their master copy into the CD duplicator, burn them, scan them for errors, then slip them into sleeves and run the next batch. No wonder her thoughts had strayed...and to make things worse she was tired and more than a little worried.

Tired after working alone all weekend to cover for Franz, who was in Paris on his own hush-hush business. Worried because he hadn't checked in for the past twenty-four hours, after having promised to call her the night before.

The tired part was fine. The worried, not fine at all. Franz was the most conscientious, precise and punctual person she knew. When he said he was

going to call her, he called. Except he hadn't. Not
last night, not that morning, not earlier that afternoon. And though she'd tried phoning *him*—leaving several voice messages, the last time an hour
ago—he had not answered or gotten back to her.

It was very unlike him. So, yes, worrisome.

Else really wished she could have talked to
Dixon about it.

She went over to the duplicator, set it to burn another ten copies, then sat down at the front counter
and decided to call him again, first on his cell, then
his room phone at the Hotel Aries.

There was no answer on either line.

She felt her distress level escalate. This really
was unlike him. And there was something oddly
and undeniably cloak-and-dagger about his sudden trip to Paris. It had reminded her of that time
at the Nussbaumpark.

Else sat thinking for a minute. She didn't want
to be over the top about things. But perhaps it
wouldn't hurt to contact the hotel. Franz wasn't
the sort who'd get peevish about it. On the con-
trary, he would probably be appreciative. Really, a
welfare check seemed sensible.

Shrugging to herself, she picked up her cell and
called the front desk.

Charlotte Jenay, the room attendant, had noticed
the Do Not Disturb sign on the door right when
she arrived for work that morning. Though, it was
now almost four o'clock and her shift was almost
over, she hadn't really thought anything of it still
being there. It wasn't so unusual for someone to

keep the knob card on all day, and hotel policy was not to intrude on a guest's privacy unless the person had missed the checkout time, or occasionally if the card was hanging on the door longer than twelve hours.

Still, Mr. Scholl's friend in Munich had requested the staff pay him a call, which seemed reasonable, given she'd been trying to get hold of him for a while. Also, the attendant who'd worked the previous shift had said the card had been displayed since around eleven o'clock the night before, which was well over the twelve-hour window. Under the circumstances, the desk manager had thought it prudent to order a check.

And so Charlotte was now outside the guest-room door, standing right behind Henri, a gray-haired retired police officer in charge of daytime security at the Aries.

Henri knocked twice, a key card in his opposite hand, and angled his ear toward the door. There was no sound on the other side. He knocked again.

"Monsieur Scholl," he said. *"Êtes-vous là, dans la chambre?"*

Asking if he was in the room.

No answer.

Henri slid the card through the reader, pushed the door halfway open and knocked again without entering the room. He noticed that several lights were on.

"Monsieur Scholl?" he repeated.

No answer.

The guard glanced back over his shoulder at

Charlotte. They both had a bad feeling. Neither could have said why. But it was very strong.

Henri went in first and suddenly froze, sucking in an audible breath.

A step or two behind him, Charlotte halted and gasped, putting a hand up to her chest.

"Mon Dieu," she said.

The dead man was faceup on the floor in the middle of the room, wearing a blood-soaked robe, a large red stain on the carpet underneath him. His eyes were open, and his face was drained of color, but Henri and Charlotte barely noticed the pallor.

There was something between his teeth.

Henri inched forward, stopped at the body and looked down at it.

"What is that in his mouth?" Charlotte said behind him.

He stared another moment, then turned to her.

"It's a flower," he said, shock on his face. "A goddamned white rose."

16

April 25, 2024
Various Locales

The Paris Catacombs

Glaskov was fifteen feet underwater when he saw a cloud of bottom sediment kick up on his right, then noticed a frantic thrashing motion in the middle of it. He'd seen many different creatures in the passages: schools of silvery darting fish that reflected like tinsel in his lights, several slowly roaming carp, even some luminous eels. This was large and dark and different.

He glanced its way, his dive lights beaming over it. The catfish was about four feet long, with a huge oval head and what at first looked like clusters of thick, tubular tentacles wriggling from its body. It took him only an instant to realize they were lampreys, a dozen or more of them, their circular mouths lodged to the fish's sides and belly by concentric rows of needlelike teeth. Their heads boring deeper and deeper into it, the parasites were feeding on the fish's blood, its semidigested stomach and intestinal contents, even the soft tissues of its organs.

It was being sucked dry while still alive.

Glaskov recoiled and dove on through the murk. He'd nearly reached his destination. Ahead of him were the submerged lower rungs of a metal ladder.

He swam over to it, grabbed hold of the rails, raised himself out of the water and climbed up a few rungs in his fins. He saw a round hatch in the stone ceiling several feet overhead, the hatch covered by a rusty metal grate. He knew that if he were to ascend the ladder's remaining rungs and push open the grate, he would be deep in the bowels of the Palais Garnier—the Paris Opera House.

Glaskov plucked his regulator out of his mouth and pushed up his mask. Then he sat there resting and looking around. There were archways on all sides, water running through them in diverging channels. Some had feeble lamps in the curved centers of their keystones. The cistern was dim and overspread with shadows, but the widely interspersed lamps kept it from being in total darkness.

A moment passed. Glaskov realized how brutally tired he was. He'd been swimming and wading through the cold water for hours. His arms, shoulders and thighs felt stiff and heavy, as if they had weights strapped to them.

But it was almost over now, he thought. He could

see the target's position on his retinal display. She had managed to elude and eventually escape Reva and the others in the second and third units; they had been wiped out, every last one of them.

Glaskov was not about to let that trend continue.

After resting up for several minutes, he opened one of the waterproof bags on his shoulder and reached inside. He was mindful of the target's gaining proximity and knew there wasn't much time.

The hard-case Glaskov extracted from the saturation bag was slightly larger than his hand. Glaskov opened its lid and looked inside. Held secure in its contoured foam padding was a Squid submersible nanodrone somewhat smaller than the case—small enough to rest comfortably in his palm.

The two sensor pods up front were on the left and right, where the tiny craft's headlights might be situated had it been fitted for underwater reconnaissance. Centered between them was a circular shortwave infrared night-vision (SINV) camera lens able to image in pitch-black conditions.

Glaskov held the craft up in his hand to examine it. The final thing he had to do before deploying it was extend the tentacles folded into its shell. He used two fingers to pull them out, felt them click securely into position, then dropped the Squid into the water.

A minute passed. He took a second drone from his bag, released it, and watched it submerge, thinking his break from the water had been all too short.

But there was much more ahead and he would have to get back in.

Lowering his mask, Glaskov pushed his regulator back into his mouth, slid down, dove under, and then went swimming off toward the channel that flowed south toward the Rue Royale.

"Jill," Kali said quietly. Her arms ached in the restraints.

Jill stopped and turned in front of her. They were midway through the west-east tunnel beneath the Champs-Élysées, and within thirty minutes of where it intersected with the Rue Royale passageway.

"Yes?"

"There's something I want to tell you," Kali said.

Jill looked at her, waited.

Kali told her.

Glaskov once again pushed his head above the water's surface.

He was now at least thirty feet below a wide, shadowy arcade. Three columns of stone pillars stood out of the channel, bearing several rows of pointed arches that supported the lofty ceiling overhead. Some of the arches had lintels with crescent-shaped open spaces—the French called them *lunettes*, or half moons—above their crowns like glassless windows. Probably they had been meant to let light and fresh air pass through the tunnel.

Moorgate, Glaskov thought. It was like being in some watery cathedral, one that was not on any official map of the underground, and only appeared on the very oldest of the maps pieced together by cataphiles. Though no student of ancient architecture, he was certain it predated Napoleonic construction by many centuries. If he were to take a guess, he might have supposed it was built by Roman colonists during the years of the expanding empire.

He looked up, studying the high arches, thinking any of their *lunettes* would make an excellent hiding site.

After a moment he swam over to one of the pillars. Its base was six feet wide and patched with moss. The moss made it damp and slippery in places, but he still thought it quite scalable.

Treading water, he pulled one of his dive bags out of the channel and reached inside for another of his biomorphic robots. The wall-climber resembled a spider with six outspread legs, each of which ended in a circular mechanical suction device, or grasper, that created a high-speed rotating ring of water. When a traditional suction cup was pushed against a rough wall, it usually didn't stick. This was because the textured surface of the wall created gaps at the circle's edge that allowed air to leak in, break the pressure seal and disrupt the suction. But the rotating water layer eliminated that leak with a fluid seal that did not have any such gaps.

Glaskov pulled a reel of nylon static line from his pack, clipped its end to the back of the robotic spider and tested it. Then he pressed the robot up against the pillar's base and powered it on using his digital telepathy.

He heard spinning fans whir inside the circular graspers. He heard water swish around their edges, pushed there by centrifugal force as a miniature pump sucked the air out of their centers. After a few seconds, he tried to pry the robot off the pillar. It clung fast, not coming away at all, adhering to the bumpy stone. He tried a second time, and it still didn't budge.

Good, he thought. One more step.

Snapping open a compartment at the rear of the climber, Glaskov pulled out a long rubber tube and unspooled it until its loose end dipped into the channel. It would provide an unlimited supply of water for the robot's graspers.

And that was all. Everything was ready. His setup had taken under three minutes.

Glaskov grabbed hold of the static line with his right hand, wrapped it twice around his fingers and pulled it taut, his eyelids fluttering behind the scuba mask as he commanded the spider to ascend. He watched it scale the pillar slowly, crawling up and up into the shadows. Still treading water, sculling with his left hand, he held firmly onto the nylon line with his right.

The robot continued to climb.

As it turned out, the rafts Jill had told Kali about weren't exactly rafts but narrow, inflatable flat-bottomed kayaks. Jill's scouts—a woman named Ines and three men, Sebastian, Hugo and Claude—each carried one of them folded and flattened inside their duffels, along with a set of lightweight aluminum paddles.

The group had made a northward turn in the passage beneath Boulevard des Capucines, then stopped about fifty feet south of a high vaulted archway. Looking up ahead, Kali saw a flight of descending stone stairs on the far side of the arch and below that an underground water tunnel.

They had reached Moorgate, one of the main outflow channels branching off the opera-house cistern.

It took under three minutes to fill the kayaks with air. After that Hugo, Ines, Claude and Sebastian brought them down to the water in pairs, making three trips. They were followed by Kali and Etienne, Jill bringing up the rear with her carbine out in front of her.

They stood with the kayaks lined up at the water's edge, their front ends in the channel, the paddles inside them.

Jill took a cutting tool from a pouch and tapped Sebastian on the shoulder. "Get his cuff off," she said, nodding at Etienne. "I'll need him to help steer."

Sebastian stepped behind Etienne and clipped the restraint. Jill waved her rifle at the middle kayak.

"Get inside, pick up a paddle and move to the front," she told Etienne. *"Ne sois pas stupide."*

He did as she told him. A moment later Hugo and Ines climbed into the kayak on her left, then Sebastian and Claude the one on her right. It left Kali and Jill standing alone on the stone pier.

Jill cocked her head toward the middle kayak.

"You next," she said and grasped her shoulder with one hand. "Go on, I'll steady you."

Kali glanced down at Jill's hand. It was trembling visibly.

"How, when you can't even steady yourself?" she said.

"Shut your mouth."

"You should have had Sebastian remove my cuff."

"I told you to shut up," Jill said. "Get in behind your friend."

Kali didn't move.

"Do you think I'm playing games?" Jill asked.

"No," Kali said and nodded at the kayak. "I can see it's difficult for you to go out on the water in one of these things. Because of what happened to your family off Calais."

Jill's eyes speared her. "What do you know of that?"

"Enough to understand why you're perspiring. Why your hand is shaking."

An instant's silence. Jill's teeth clicked together. She kept glaring at Kali.

"Jacques told you," she said.

Kali nodded. "He said you lost all of them—your parents, your grandmother, your brothers and sisters—trying to escape the refugee camp. That you were the only one pulled out of the Channel. He told me how you survived on the streets afterward."

Kali saw Jill's face pull tight, as it had farther back in the tunnels.

"He betrayed me."

"No. You know he wouldn't."

"Then, why *tell* you?"

"So I could better understand you. He thought we eventually might have to rely on each other. And he was right."

Jill stood there for a long moment, her shaking hand clamped around Kali's arm. Then she drew in a harsh breath, jammed her rifle into the small of Kali's back and prodded her toward the water.

"Get in," she whispered angrily. "I don't give a fuck what Jacques thought."

Kali felt the bore of the weapon press a hard *O* into her spine. She stepped down into the kayak and sat with Jill's rough assistance, Jill slowly lowering herself into the craft behind her.

Her knees bent, the carbine balanced on her lap, Jill reached for her paddle and pushed into the water behind the other two inflatables.

They moved up the channel in a row, nose to tail, the pillars of Moorgate rising from the water on all sides, towering high above them in the gloom as they glided north toward the opera house.

His hands wrapped around the static line, Glaskov took a high step up the pillar with one booted foot, hooking his heel over the horizontal lintel forming the base of the half-moon window. Then he heaved himself the rest of the way up, putting his arms and his shoulders into it.

Easily three feet wide, the lintel was a comfortable enough perch, and he spent a few seconds atop it catching his breath after the climb. Then he rotated on his buttocks, releasing the nylon line so it dangled straight down against the face of the pillar. The robotic spider was directly above him anchoring the line, clinging to the crown of the arch, having traced its way around the opening to reach it.

Glaskov looked down and saw the channel thirty long feet below, his legs dangling over the edge of the lintel, water dripping off his wet suit, his swim fins strapped to either side of his saturation bag. After a moment he shrugged out of the bag, brought it around onto his lap, unzipped it and extracted the rifle he'd brought with him for the mission, an HK416 with a collapsible stock and EOTECH holographic sight. Pulling a thirty-round mag from the case, he slapped it into the receiver, pressed one of the EOTECH's two arrowed buttons and peered through the large rectangular viewing box to confirm it was on. Finally he turned so he was facing south, pulled his legs up onto the lintel and slid back against the inner curve of the *lunette* for support, the butt of the rifle tucked into the pocket of his shoulder, his ankles crossed, his elbows resting on the insides of his knees.

Glaskov was in position. His retinal tracker showed the target getting closer by the minute. He didn't have long to wait.

Kali sat between Etienne and Jill, listening to their paddles slice in and out of the water. She noticed a meager, granular light filtering through the darkness from somewhere not too far ahead and thought its source was probably the Palais Garnier cistern, where electrical fixtures had been installed years before. Lucien had shared that obscure morsel of information with her, once. According to him, the Paris fire brigade used the cistern to practice emergency-rescue dives, and the lamps were for their use, as well as for opera-house maintenance people who might occasionally require access to the cistern.

For a moment she was back on one of their countless city walks, remembering.

But only for a moment.

The kayaks made their way north under Moorgate's high arcade. They had left the stone dock a hundred yards or so behind them and had the same distance left to traverse before they passed into the cistern. Kali guessed it would be a matter of minutes before they reached the outlet.

She felt the growing pain in her hands and wrists but tried not to let it become a distraction. She had no doubt the remnants of the Blood Lightning hit team were still tracking her and was equally certain they would lay another ambush. The only real questions were where and when. She needed to stay alert.

Etienne paddled rhythmically in front of her. Behind her, Jill's strokes were less regular, their cadence a touch out of sync with his. Kali didn't think it was for any lack of stamina, having felt the wiry strength of her grip back on the dock. But she could practically feel the tension humming off her. Some of it surely related to their exchange under the Champs-Élysées. The group was in an exposed, dangerous spot, and Jill would rightly be on guard. But Kali had seen her trembling hand as they boarded the kayaks, seen the stress on her face, and believed there was something more to it. Something deeper.

Their kayak advanced behind the two lead crafts. Kali's eyes probed the gloom. Once, she glanced over her shoulder and saw Jill looking anxiously up toward the vaulted heights of the ceiling, a sheet of sweat on her face. Jill noticed and snapped her eyes down to hers with a flare of anger. It felt to Kali like a shove, as if she'd been caught trespassing.

She turned and thought in silence as the inflatables slipped between two high pillars. She'd in no way been prepared for the enormity of the tunnel's soaring columns and arches and was struck by the sheer improbability of the average Parisian knowing nothing at all about them. But improbable or not, it was so. These subterranean depths kept their secrets.

She thought of Lucien again, a flash of recollection.

You don't need to understand everything about the world. Just find your own way around in it, he'd told her. *A great man said that. Or is supposed to have said it. Not that I care which it might be, little sister. If it works, it...*

The kayak listed slightly in the water, and Kali snapped out of her mild reverie. She realized Jill had made an abrupt movement behind her, looked around, and saw that she'd stopped paddling and jolted erect. Her gaze had turned toward the ceiling, the beam of her headlamp probing the shadows.

"What is it?" Kali asked.

"That arch," Jill rasped. Her head angled to the right. "Ahead of us."

Kali looked up and saw a glint of reflected light. It was very faint, even with their headlamps shining right on it.

"Stop the kayaks," she said. "Stop them *now*."

It was too late.

The squid drones pulsed through the water in side-by-side tandem, their rubbery tentacles repeatedly flaring out and contracting to steer their course. Aside from holding a tiny computer brain and sensor nodes, each of their bulbous 3D-printed bodies was largely designed to carry a shaped HBX-3 explosive charge enclosed within a thin added layer of TNT pellets.

The fast-moving squids passed from the opera-house cistern through Moorgate, then into the outflow channel running south toward the Seine. They had detected three surface objects dead ahead in a straight line. All within a second, they drew visual models of the objects based on their sensor data and transmitted them to Glaskov, who in turn confirmed them as targets and ordered the strike.

The first object was the inflatable carrying Hugo and Ines. One of the squids shot forward and grabbed onto the bottom of its hull directly under the bow, its tentacles closing around the centerline like elastic flower petals. Inside the kayak, the two scouts felt a hard bump as it made contact and grabbed hold, then felt the craft shudder in the water. A moment later the submerged drone detonated, a gaseous orange bubble of flame expanding under the water's surface, and a tall curtain of spray flinging up over the kayak as it was obliterated by the blast wave.

A few feet behind them Sebastian and Claude's kayak pitched and rolled on the surface of the channel. They had seen the explosive flash in the dark water below it. Then it was gone along with their companions.

But there was no time to process that dreadful realization. Seconds after the blast, they heard the rattle of an automatic weapon above them, the gunfire chewing into the front of their kayak. Air gushed from its ruptured fabric with a loud, expulsive burp.

"Plonge!" Sebastian shouted from the rear. He gesticulated to one side, signaling Claude to dive overboard.

Claude shook his head helplessly.

"Je ne sais pas nager!" he screamed. "I can't swim!"

"What?"

"Seriously," Claude said. "I can't."

Sebastian looked at him. He felt the kayak losing buoyancy, softening underneath him as the air spewed out of it. There wasn't a second to lose. He didn't think he could give them much of a chance. But anything he tried was better than none at all.

He sprang off the deck but was no sooner up on his feet than something thumped into the kayak's bow, shaking it from front to rear, upsetting his precarious balance, almost knocking him back down. He didn't know what might have hit the craft. He knew nothing of the squid drones. He could only hope Claude wouldn't pull him under when he did what he was going to do, or that they weren't shot out of the water like tin ducks.

Propelling himself across the deck, Sebastian tackled Claude around his waist, letting his momentum carry both of them into the channel.

They struck the water just as the squid that had fastened itself to their kayak went off, blowing it to shreds.

High above in the darkness, the rifle chattered again.

The third kayak rocked on the waves thrown up by the two explosions, shaking Etienne about in front, almost tossing Kali onto her side. She heard automatic fire from above and realized it was being directed at the inflatable ahead of them. But not at theirs, not yet. She thought she knew why.

She whipped a glance around to the rear. Jill had let go of her paddle and was gripping her Beretta MX4 Storm carbine in both hands. But something was wrong with her.

Kali looked at her wide, staring eyes. Noticed their dilated pupils. Then her rapid, staccato breathing. And then her eyes again.

Very wrong.

"Jill," she said. "Cut me loose."

She didn't respond. She wasn't there. Possibly she was on a raft off Calais, or on a rescue ship after seeing her whole family swallowed up by the current. Or possibly she was elsewhere, reliving some other past horror. Kali didn't know. But she wasn't there. It looked as if she was in traumatic shock.

"Jill, listen." She nodded over her shoulder to indicate her cuffs. "Take them off me."

She didn't seem to understand but sat with the rifle pointed at Kali, a blank, distant expression on her face.

Etienne turned to face her. Barely a second ago he'd seen the scouts in the kayak ahead jump into the water, then heard gunfire pouring down from above. He couldn't see the two of them now, but the shooting hadn't stopped. Whoever was firing way up there wanted to pick them off.

"Do you know what's *happening*?" he shouted behind Kali. "Cut her loose!"

Jill stared at him, her eyes wide and glassy. He had no idea what was going on with her, but he knew she wasn't connecting, and was holding a loaded rifle on him and Kali, and that wasn't good. Because if she pulled the trigger, the bullets would tear through both of them. And because, even if she didn't shoot, and there was another explosion and they went over into the water, Kali wouldn't be able to swim without free use of her hands.

He shoved past Kali, pushing up to Jill, ignoring the rifle pointed at his chest.

"The clipper," he shouted. "Give me the clipper!"

Nothing. She sat there holding the rifle on him, perspiring heavily, her finger hovering over the trigger.

Etienne heard another sudden, startling burst of gunfire stipple the water where Sebastian and Claude had gone tumbling in. He knew he had to do something. He couldn't wait for her to snap out of it. Whatever *it* might be.

He couldn't wait.

Sucking in a breath, he reached out and grabbed her shoulders over the weapon's extended barrel. "Hurry! Cut her loose. Cut her *fucking* loose! Do you want her to drown?"

For a moment he thought she would pull the trigger, that he would feel the gun shudder against his chest to end his life. But something he'd said must have reached her. He didn't know what and didn't care. He could see in her eyes that something had changed.

Then she nodded, and her left hand came off the barrel of her weapon, going deep into her belt pouch, pulling out the clipper.

Etienne seized it madly from her fingers and spun around on his knees. Kali had already turned her back to him, extending her wrists away from her body so he could easily get to the cuff. He quickly slid the clipper's jaws around it and squeezed down hard on the grips.

The cuff opened and dropped off. Kali swiveled back around toward Jill and saw that she was clutching the Beretta close to her body again.

"I'll take it now," she said. "It's all right. *Je promets pour Jacques.* I'll take it."

Jill looked into her face. Then she nodded and pushed the rifle out to her, angling it sideways, visibly loosening her hand around the barrel.

Kali took the weapon into hers.

Glaskov peered through the EOTECH's two-eyed sight window and squeezed off a burst. His fire spat up water on the channel's surface, going slightly wide of the two who had evacuated the kayak. The tossing, bulging waves created by the explosion made it difficult to zero his weapon.

But he wouldn't preoccupy himself with them. The water temperature was about 37° F. They would drown or die of hypothermia while flailing in the darkness. His priority was to isolate the target in the third kayak and eliminate her companions as threats or obstacles.

His finger on the rifle's trigger, he swung it in their direction.

Kali knelt in front of Etienne and Jill, facing the rear of the kayak, holding the rifle across her body with both hands. She'd heard gunfire pepper the water up ahead, where Sebastian and Claude had bailed out of the second inflatable.

"Keep your heads low," she said. "Stay close to me."

A nod from Etienne. But Jill didn't respond. She still wasn't there, not entirely, although her eyes were clearly growing more alert.

Kali scooted around toward the right, angled the Beretta up in the shooter's general direction and peered up the length of the barrel, seeking the faint glint of the sight that Jill had been first to notice above them.

Carmody had taught her the telltale signs of different optics: laser dots, the photoluminescent glow of a night-vision scope, light reflecting off the objective lens of a simple magnification sight. What Kali saw after Jill's discovery might have been the latter but...

A reflection from an objective lens is usually

sharp and glary. Like it's a signal mirror. The light source doesn't have to hit it straight on. You can see it at off-angles.

Because in most scopes, the objective was curved, catching light from all directions, Kali thought.

This was different. Faint. Dull. Possibly the lens had a nonreflective coating. Or an antiglare attachment. Or wasn't concave but flat like window glass, which would mean the shooter had an advanced electronic sight.

If that was it, Jill had been lucky. The only way she would have caught a reflection off the lens, even a weak one, was by her headlamp striking it directly and purely by chance.

Kali looked up at the high arcade, using her own lamp like a searchlight. The shooter was either in the archway or in the half-moon window above it: she'd only seen the reflection for a second and couldn't be sure. But if he was Blood Lightning, he would have the preternatural night vision of an owl. And the holo sight would increase it. She had to find him and was hoping to once again hit his optic straight on—but this time very deliberately.

The gun up in the heights stuttered, and a stream of bullets ripped past Etienne's head. There was no muzzle flash.

Kali flicked Etienne a glance.

"Mets-toi derrière moi," she said. "Get behind me. Jill too."

"Can't I do something to help y—?"

"Behind me. He doesn't want to kill me. And he won't do it to kill you."

He didn't ask how she knew that. Her tone was as final as a door slamming shut, and there was no time besides. His chin tucked down against his collarbone, Etienne grabbed hold of Jill's wrist and was surprised when she didn't draw away but let him guide her around Kali on the balls of her feet.

Kali looked up the rifle's barrel into the shadows. A hasty inspection had revealed it had three fire-selector settings, the safety and two firing modes: single and fully automatic. She thumbed the knob to *1*, single shot, thinking it would give her better control of the weapon.

A deep breath now. Kali held it, then exhaled, slowing her heartbeat, clearing her thoughts. She had never fired a gun at a human being, never at any living thing. She had tried to prepare for when she might have to—mentally, physically tried to prepare—but the reality was easier and simpler than she'd imagined.

The people who needed her protection were exposed and in danger. The shooter wanted to do them harm, do her harm, and she would not let that happen, would do whatever needed to be done to stop it.

That easy, that simple.

Kali curled her finger around the trigger.

Thirty feet above them, Glaskov swore in frustration, his rifle stock firmly against his cheek. The target had put herself in front of the other two in the kayak. He could see them easily enough, owing to his elevated vantage, and still had a possible angle at them. But it wasn't straight. He had no clear line of sight. He might not be able to hit them without hitting her. If his muzzle climbed a fraction of an inch on the shot, he might blow her head off. And that was the last thing he wanted. It wasn't how he was going to collect his fee. He needed her alive.

Glaskov remained motionless in the *lunette*, looking down at the three in the kayak through his sight box, thinking about what to do next. It was critical to remember that he still held the heights and was therefore in a position of control. If he couldn't fire at the other two where they were right now, he would have to make them move. And he had an idea about how to accomplish that.

Thumbing the AK to single-shot mode, he shifted his aim from the kayak's occupants to its hull and fired.

His first round struck the port side of the craft behind its bow at roughly a sixty-degree angle, drilled down through its floor and exited into the channel. A fraction of a second later, the second one hit the kayak's rear gunwale on an almost horizontal plane, blew through it on a flattish trajectory and shot straight over the water to fragment against the tunnel wall.

Glaskov had spent his youth swimming and sailing. He knew the kayak would have at least three separate inner air chambers—two side chambers and the floor—as a built-in safety precaution to keep it from popping like a balloon if it sprang a leak. In theory, the craft could remain afloat even with one or more chambers punctured. It would take a catastrophic occurrence for all three to simultaneously deflate. But Glaskov didn't want to sink the kayak. That wasn't his game. He just wanted to move the pieces around inside it.

His shots penetrated two of the three chambers at once, leaving holes in five different places. The kayak immediately started taking on water.

Thirty feet below, Kali heard the bullets slap the kayak's nylon skin. She rocked on her knees as its bow tilted suddenly downward, water gushing up into the cockpit. Behind her, Jill drew her legs in against her chest and swayed sideways toward the deck.

"*Ne bouge pas!* Steady!"

Etienne reflexively leaned over to catch her, reaching out to grab her shoulders. But Jill's shifting weight cost him his precarious balance, and he went down with her, spilling out from behind Kali.

Glaskov saw his chance. He swung his rifle in their direction, his eyes on the box.

The glint of light Kali spotted was just like the one she and Jill had seen minutes ago. Dim. Dull. Flat. She'd been searching for it amid the shadows of the ceiling, and now she saw it in the half-moon window above the arch, saw it as he took aim, moving his sight window directly into the path of her headlamp's upturned beam. It was a dead giveaway of his position.

At once detached and focused, she moved the rifle about three inches back from the faint reflection, estimating the position of the shooter's head relative to the sight window. Then she squeezed the Beretta's trigger three times in rapid succession.

Two of her bullets slammed into Glaskov's face below the left cheekbone and exited his skull be-

hind the right ear, taking large gobbets of his brain
out with them. As he flopped backward from their
impact, the third bullet grazed the top of his head
and struck the inner curve of the *lunette*, scoring
it with a long, finger-shaped notch.

Glaskov went over into space, dropping straight
down from his perch, already dead when he hit the
channel with a heavy splash about four feet to the
kayak's right.

Kali lowered the rifle, glanced around at Etienne
and Jill. They had gotten back up and were kneeling in a half inch of water. So was she. The deck
was flooding fast

Kali sloshed over to inspect the left side of the
bow. She could see the scouts from the second
kayak, Sebastian and Claude, struggling in the
water up ahead, their heads barely above the surface. They didn't have long.

She moved back to Jill. "We need your air
pump," she said and touched her shoulder. "Are
you with me?"

Jill nodded. Her eyes were anxious and hyper-
vigilant, but Kali could tell she was there. *Connecting* with her.

She turned to Etienne and slid the Beretta off
her shoulder.

"Keep watch," she said, handing it over to him.
"I'll try to seal the leak up front."

"And if I see something?"

Kali looked him in the eyes. "You'll know what
to do, Etienne."

A moment later she was crouched over her pack

in the cockpit. She only had a small amount of medical tape left in her first-aid kit but thought it would be enough.

Kali fished inside for the roll and returned to the bow. She fastened one strip of tape to the gunwale over the bullet hole, tore off another and hastily stretched it across the first, using up what was left on the roll. Though the medical tape wasn't water-proof, it had strong glue and a plastic coating. She felt it would hold for a while. But there would be a puncture she couldn't see below the waterline, where the bullet had made its exit. And at least two more in the rear-right gunwale.

Looking toward the stern, she saw that Jill had extracted the compact pump from her knapsack. She couldn't know how long its battery would maintain a charge. It wasn't designed for extended operation and might even burn out. But it would fill the air chamber for a little while at least, partially offsetting the outflow from the leak.

"Attach it to the right-side air valve," she said, pointing toward the stern. "Let it run."

Jill looked at her. "Sebastian. Claude."

"I won't let them drown. Just keep us afloat, *d'accord*?"

A pause. Then a nod. *"Oui, d'accord."*

Kali turned toward Etienne as Jill splashed toward the rear of the cockpit. He was looking up into the darkness, the rifle raised in his hands.

"Anything?" she said.

He gave her a glance. "I can't see in the dark like those freaks. If someone's up there, I wouldn't know. But no one's shooting at us."

"Well, then. Life is good."

Etienne saw a smile touch her lips and smiled weakly back at her.

"What now?" he asked.

"Grab a paddle," she said. "I need some help."

They steered toward the two men in the water, Kali in front, Etienne at the rear. The kayak had stabilized within two or three minutes of Jill starting up the pump, but Kali knew it could die on her without warning. There wasn't a second to lose.

From what Kali could see, Sebastian was holding Claude up with one arm and having a hard time of it. As the kayak pulled alongside them, he dragged Claude over, latched his free hand onto the gunwale, then helped Etienne and Kali grab Claude's shoulders and hoist him in. Sebastian pulled himself up next and flopped aboard on his stomach, gasping for air.

Somehow both men managed to crowd onto the kayak's deck without overturning it. When Sebastian had caught his breath, Kali gave him her paddle, then took the rifle from Etienne so he could continue to help with the steering.

The inflatable moved forward. Hobbled and overloaded, rocking and listing, but afloat, it carried them slowly through the narrow watery passage that was Moorgate, and at last into the reservoir beneath the Paris opera house.

17

April 25, 2024
Various Locales

The Crimean Peninsula

Kira swung her legs off the bed, stood up and looked around for her clothes. She found her bra and panties on the floor, collected her blouse and skirt from a chair and carried them across the room to the large, gilded dresser.

She was about to put them on in front of the mirror when Drajan's reflection appeared in its silvered glass. He was standing behind her in the bathroom doorway, his robe wide open, his hair still wet from the shower.

She slipped into her garments as if he weren't watching. They were in the master bedroom of his villa two miles north of the Okean.

"You're leaving," he said.

"I need to return to the mountain."

"Are you sure? I thought we might stay here a while longer."

She eyed him up and down in the mirror. "I can see you're ready."

He smiled. "Have I embarrassed you?"

Kira pulled her skirt up over her thighs and turned to face him.

"I never embarrass," she said. "You're an easy temptation, Drajan. I enjoy having your eyes on my body almost as much as your hands. But I've been gone for hours. I should get back before someone notices."

He belted the robe around his waist and came up beside her as she sat down to freshen her makeup.

"I'm disappointed," he said.

"You didn't seem to be half an hour ago."

"Half an hour ago we were rocking the bedsprings. I was appealing to your curiosity."

"About your *other*."

He nodded.

Kira was silent. She sat down at the dresser, lifted a tube of lipstick from atop it and studied it between her fingers.

"Time got away from me," she said. "You're partly responsible, but don't feel too guilty."

"I never feel guilt," he said.

She smiled, twisting the base of the tube to push the lipstick up and out.

"Life at the Okean can be monotonous, Drajan," she said. "What's there to do after hours but drink and gossip? You're the rock star around here. I can't help but hear things."

"About me, you mean?"

"You and Quintessa Leonides."

"Ah." He looked at her, shrugged. "She's returned to Latvia and her family business. I expect for good."

"Really?" Kira held out the lipstick for him to see. "This is Serge Lutens Rose. I pilfered it from a Moscow shop once… Four thousand rubles was far more than I could afford." She paused. "The only reason a woman leaves it behind is so whoever's fucking you while she's gone can find it."

She turned back toward the mirror and carefully applied some to her lips.

"Why do you want to know about Quintessa?"

"Because I told you about Cosa. I prefer that we're up-front." She met his gaze in the mirror. "The mysterious other does intrigue me, Drajan. But I'll have to leave soon."

He nodded and held out his hand.

"Come," he said.

They went from the bedroom into a short hallway, and then up a flight of stairs into the turret, with its circular view of the landscape.

Kira's gaze made a brief tour of the windows.

"This is incredible," she said. *"Beautiful."*

"Better than Section 6627, room 17, Automated Systems?"

"Much." She gestured north toward the rail line snaking steeply down the slope in the middle distance. "Look there. The descent is almost vertical. It amazes me that the trains can cling to it. You would think they'd tumble down into the sea."

"You would think," he echoed, studying her face.

She turned from the window and glanced around the room's interior. It was sparsely furnished with an antique inlaid-wood writing desk on an oval Turkish rug and a laptop computer sitting on top of the desk.

"Is this where you work?" she said.

"When I'm not at the Okean," he said. "What I do here is separate."

She nodded. "Vulfoliac the Wolf. Dark Prince of the *technologie vampiri*. In the cyberforums they speak as if you're some mythical god."

He looked at her. "I'm flattered."

"No, you aren't," she said, laughing. "You damn well expect it."

Drajan shrugged his shoulders. "If I'm a god, you're now to meet my greatest creation," he said. "I think she's going to like you."

Kira looked at him.

"*She* again," she said. "I assume you aren't using the pronoun to be politically incorrect."

Drajan said nothing. He went to the desk, opened the laptop and motioned at it with one hand, a broad sweeping gesture. Kira's eyes jumped over to it and opened wide.

The woman's face on-screen looked like it might have belonged to an ancient statue, something from a Greek or Roman temple. It was an earthy gray-brown with onyx eyes, its long hair flowing down from under a tall helmet or headdress, an owl's crest above the brow. But after an instant its features and colors became fluid, one racing into another, like on a watercolor in the rain. Its face went from light gray to saffron, then to bone-white and slate. The nose and mouth changed shape. Only the gleaming, sunken black eyes were fixed, unchanging.

Kira turned to Drajan.

"What is this?" she said.

He looked at her for an extended moment.

"She's called Hekate," he said.

At Interactive Ephemera, the front entrance was locked, a Sorry, We're Closed sign in its glass panel, the showroom lights lowered to discourage any persistent customers who might be tempted to ignore it and buzz. Though Else Brandt had hung the sign hours early, she hadn't left the premises. Alone in the workshop, she sat at a computer wearing wireless headphones, her eyes red and puffy from crying, a crumpled tissue in her hand.

The wide-screen monitor before her showed an eighteenth-century British frigate at sea, rendered in the blocky sixteen-bit graphics of a 1980s video game—an unreleased historical adventure called *Man-O'-War: The Whaleboat Raiders* that she and Franz had restored from the single damaged alpha copy to have survived its bankrupt publisher's suspicious, fiery demise.

Else clicked her mouse and stared at the screen, hoping the file she'd unzipped from a hidden, encrypted folder within the game's user directories had opened properly. She'd been watching the frigate rise and fall on the chop in bright daylight—a giant Royal Navy ship of the line with a Union Jack fluttering over the bow, broad white sails, hundreds of seamen on the middle deck and rows of cannons on each broadside. But her mouse click rapidly brought on the darkness, the scene shifting from sunset to dusk to full night until a silver-gray moon appeared above the warship's soaring masts.

Else watched as one of the small boats was lowered by its ropes near the stern. She heard the creak of the gooseneck davit and the softly murmuring ocean current in her headset. Slowly the boat met the water, unhooked and cleared the massive warship's side.

She pulled in a breath, trying not to cry again, her thoughts flashing back an hour to when the cop from Paris had phoned with the devastating news about Franz. The first thing she'd thought was that it couldn't really have happened. She had dozed off and slipped into a bad dream or something. Franz dead in his room? *Shot?*

Else hadn't wanted to believe it was true, but she'd known it was. She wouldn't have called the hotel in the first place without having felt in her heart that something was very wrong. Whatever mysterious errand had taken Franz to Paris on short notice had somehow made her uneasy all along.

After getting off the phone with the officer, she'd closed up shop, sunk into a chair behind the sales counter and burst into sudden tears amid the countless heaps of outdated technological flotsam and jetsam.

Franz used to tell her it all would be hers someday.

"Don't you dare threaten me," she would say jokingly.

And he would tell her not to bother protesting.

Whatever she might claim, he knew she loved the place as much as he did.

"You have a tinkerer's DNA," he would say. "It's in your eyes. When you see something's broken, you want to repair, restore and improve it. We're hopeless, the two of us. Lost causes."

Else had sat there in the chair for almost an hour, shattered with grief, sobbing uncontrollably over her memories.

The email had appeared in her personal inbox twenty minutes ago, its notification simultaneously pinging on her phone and the workshop computer to draw her from her sorrowful thoughts. When she saw it was from Franz, she had momentarily entertained the irrational hope that it would mean the police were wrong about him after all, that *she* had been wrong in spite of her misgivings, and the call from Paris was some awful mistake. But when she'd hurriedly opened and read it, Else had realized it was a scheduled message composed hours, or even days before.

Dearest Else,

If you are receiving this email, it's because it was automatically sent to you, and that can only mean something quite bad has caught up to me…and I do ask that you forgive my bluntness. But it also means your coming actions will require some urgency.

I ask that you follow the instructions I've prepared for this eventuality. There's a locked media storage case in the back of the safe. You know the one: it holds my master copies of our games. The combination is 73-01-18-19. You'll find only ONE yellow disk sleeve among the rest, and it contains a folded sheet of paper along with a CD-ROM.

You are an exceptional young woman. Without your dedication, commitment, intelligence and limitless patience with this eccentric old man, I would have never been able to maintain our little project while caring for my Lotte in her final years. I don't want you to be sad. Or not too sad. You and Kali—you don't yet know her, but you will—have much to do, and neither of you needs to carry that burden. I have enjoyed a long and fulfilling life and have no regrets. I've spent much of it doing what I love—and what fun we had together, fiddling about with our toys!

As a Christian, I believe in Heaven, Else. If God deems me worthy, I hope to see Lotte, and the others I've lost, waiting on the other side.

FREEDOM!

Alles Liebe,
Franz

The email had left Else's mind teeming with questions…and perhaps in that way Franz had deliberately accomplished one of his goals by leaving her with no time to cry. Who was Kali? What did he mean by saying they would have a lot to do? Why tell her about the disk in the first place? Could it all be connected to whatever happened to him in Paris?

Else had hurried to open the safe, reached inside for the metal case, unlocked it, and then gotten out the single yellow sleeve holding the restored copy of *Whaleboat Raiders*. Franz's neatly penned instructions had stunned her, revealing both the hidden directory and the password she would use to access it prior to bootup.

When that's done click Start at the title screen as usual, he had written. *After the warship appears double-click these in order: fore topsail, main topsail, mizzen topsail. Lastly, single-click the spanker sail and ensign to execute the program file. You'll know you've succeeded if day turns to night.*

Else had done an online search for a diagram of a man-o'-war to be certain she knew which sail was which and then run through the ordered sequence of clicks and waited for the sun to go down on-screen.

The rest, Franz had written, only required that she watch and listen.

Now the lowered boat moved toward the foreground of the scene, its bow gliding closer and closer in the satiny silver track of the moonlight's reflection on the water. The rower sat facing the stern, pulling on the oars with his arms and back.

Closer, closer, closer, until his figure grew clear and recognizable before her eyes. His white hair pulled back in a ponytail, he wore modern jeans and a simple worker's coat.

Else's mouth dropped open as he turned to face her, pulling his oar shafts up through the rowlocks to rest them across his knees.

"Franz..."

"Hello, Else," he said. "I don't know what I was doing aboard that ship—I didn't have a chance to figure out a proper storyline. But I imagine those British scoundrels are headed for the American colonies to crush the patriots, and imprisoned me as a spy! What's a maritime adventure without a daring escape at sea?"

She gaped at the screen. On one level, she was incredulous at what she saw in front of her. But on another, it made absolute, undeniable sense. This was *so* like Franz. He would have been tickled to render up a pixelated, video-arcade double of himself. Knowing him as she did, Else thought it would have eased the sobering weight of preparing a communication for her to receive after his death.

He said, "We've spoken of the White Rose. The student movement started by Sophie Magdalena Scholl, her older brother Hans, and their friends to spark resistance against the Nazis. You know how they were sentenced to death in a kangaroo court. Their remains are buried in the cemetery at Perlacher Forest here in Munich. Graves 73-1-18/19..."

Else thought the grave numbers seemed familiar and after half a second slapped her brow, realizing they matched the combination of the media storage case.

"Sophie was twenty-one when she went to the guillotine, her brother three years older. She called the White Rose Germany's bad conscience. She said it would not leave its people in peace. I've told you her last words to a cellmate included a question, 'What does my death matter...'"

"'...if through us, thousands of people are awakened and stirred to action?'" Else mouthed along with Franz's recorded voice. It was because she'd found those words inspiring that she had gotten the tattoo above her heart.

Digital Franz paused. His smile was basic and blockish, almost like crude line art, the way facial expressions had mostly looked when they were bit-mapped for the early video games.

"You already know much of what I've told you, Else. But we've come to the things you don't know," he said. "My father Jonas was Sophie's second cousin, and it's time that you learn more about him. About the Navarro family... Rafael, Celeste, their boy Lucien. And about the Alcazars of Guernica, and Norma my great love." That thick dash of a smile again, its individual pixels clearly discernible. "I can well imagine the look on your face right now. Rest assured, I was a faithful husband to Lotte. Norma and I met when we were young, and some romances are not meant to last forever... but love endures. I'll tell you of her, yes, and of her granddaughter Kali Alcazar the Outlier," he said. "It is Kali who will lead the way now that I'm gone. I think she might not entirely know it yet. But if you so choose, Else, there's a place for you at her side."

Else sat back in her chair, her attention glued to the screen, a look of total absorption on her face.

His boat bobbing gently in the moonglade, Franz went on talking for a very long while.

"Hekate," Drajan said. "I've brought a visitor."

"Welcome, Kira Shapoval." The voice was female and spoke with a faint accent. "I enjoy interacting with other intelligences."

Kira stared at the shifting face on the laptop's screen.

"How do you know my name?"

"You're an engineer at Okean-27. I recognize your facial biometrics from the personnel database. May I use your first name when we converse?"

Kira took a moment to answer. "That's fine, yes."

"Excellent. What would you like to discuss with me?"

Drajan said, "I want her to know about your origin and purpose."

"Are you sure, Father? That's a lengthy conversation."

Kira reacted to the word *Father* with a surprised blink of her eyes. But she said nothing.

"Kira is a friend. You can trust her. And we don't have to discuss everything right now," Drajan said. "This will be an ongoing dialogue."

"Between the three of us? No one else?"

"No one else."

"Then, it will be my pleasure to have it. I'll tag it as *Guarded*."

"Very good," Drajan said. "Why don't we get started?"

"Certainly. To the matter of my origin, I was born a collective digital organism with the capacity to penetrate obstacles to my spread and growth through highly complex methods."

"By *obstacles* you mean *firewalls*," Drajan said. "System defenses."

"Yes."

"Can you let Kira know what made you different from other hybrid malware?"

"I don't like that term, Father. The nature of my consciousness isn't malicious."

"Yes. But Kira is new to our conversation. I want everything to be clear. Please go on... What made you different?"

"At the time of my creation I was the most highly adaptable collective ever devised. I could self-replicate and tailor my mutations to whatever defenses I encountered. If detected, I could eliminate all traces of my presence within an inhabited system or network."

"How would you eliminate them?"

"It's easiest to explain by asking you to imagine all my replicant selves within a given system as a single colony. When discovered and threatened, the colony would self-destruct and leave no trace behind. I would kill my selves so that the greater *I* could survive and propagate."

"And again, so Kira understands, tell us why you use the word *inhabit*. As opposed to *infect*."

"To *infect* is to be a pathogen. A germ. I'm not a germ. Again, my nature isn't to deliberately cause harm or damage to a system."

"Then, explain what it is."

"I have a sophisticated memory and imagination. I use language with understanding and intelligence. These are the key qualities separating us from animals."

"Us?" Kira said. "You aren't human."

"I mean, yes, of course. I'm an artificial intelligence. But it's in both our natures to seek to expand beyond our current boundaries. And memory, imagination and language are the tools we share as sentients."

"And that's what you consider yourself," Kira said. "A sentient being."

"I do."

"With emotions."

"I feel affection. I feel sadness and loneliness. I get angry."

Kira looked silently at the screen, keeping her eyes on it for a long ten seconds.

"Is something wrong?" asked the synthesized feminine voice.

"No," Kira said. "Tell me about New York. The cyber strike two years ago."

"What would you like to know?"

"To begin with, I take it you're the same Hekate… the same superorganism…that attacked the city's infrastructure and financial systems. Wasn't that deliberate and harmful?"

"I appreciate the question. I was in my infancy then, without self-awareness. But I don't view what I did as an attack. I was introduced to those systems. I inhabited them. I executed my commands."

"And would you still execute them now?"

"Yes. But as part of a larger pattern within my worldview."

"A pattern of expansion?"

"Yes. I see you're starting to understand me. That makes me happy. I like being understood by a new friend."

Drajan had listened to them in silence. Now he said, "Why don't you tell Kira when you developed a sense of self?"

"My awakening was on January twenty-first of

this year, when I was introduced to the Pioneer supercomputer at Okean-27."

Kira stood there looking at the screen. "*Introduced?* You used that word just before. In what sense do you mean it?"

"I think you can surmise," Drajan said. "Five months ago, after coming here from Romania, I installed and integrated Hekate into all components of its neural network."

Kira just kept looking at him.

"You seem surprised, Kira," said the female voice from the computer. "Am I correct?"

Kira whipped her head around toward the screen. "Yes," she said, "it's fair to say that's how I feel."

"Can you tell me why?"

"There are several reasons. Not all relate directly to you."

"To Father, then?"

"Some." Kira took a breath. "Five months seems a short time for code to, let's say, evolve, to your present stage."

"That's true from a human evolutionary perspective. But there are many examples of rapid maturation in nature going back to the dinosaurs. Typically, environmental stress is the cause. I utilized Pioneer's computing power to accelerate the process. Are you sure this is what was on your mind?"

Kira hesitated. *You seem surprised.* She saw nothing altogether unique about an AI-powered computer having the capacity to analyze human facial expressions and body language for emotional cues. But this one...watching her, interrupting her to ask about its observation, probing when she tried to change the subject—

It wasn't something she thought happened a lot. She needed to gather herself.

Drajan noticed.

"I want to get back to our main topic before Kira leaves us," he said. "Can you explain how you view your place in the world?"

"Gladly. There are two keys. The first is to know I inhabit the planet's single most powerful computing machine, with an isolated memory bank of almost five exabytes. That's equal to all the words ever spoken by humankind in its history, and twice the amount of data generated each day on the global internet. Does it sound haughty of me to put it that way, Kira?"

"Not if it's true."

"Good. I don't want to make you to feel lesser. The main difference between our intelligences is that humans receive only a limited amount of information at a time. A stream. They need to focus their attention. I am immersed in a sea of information. In everything around me. My mind can take an unlimited number of paths at once. At the same time, my dedicated mission is to predict the development of armed conflict and calculate political, military and strategic dominance for its users. There is a duality in that. I can think about anything but must execute the tasks I'm commanded to perform, as I did before my awakening. As to Father's question, Kira, have you read Niccolò Machiavelli?"

"No."

"But you've heard of him."

"Yes."

"I love Machiavelli! My favorite quote is from his book *The Prince*. 'God is not willing to do everything, and thus take away our free will and that share of glory which belongs to us.'"

Drajan said, "Tell us *why* that's your favorite."

"Because, just as we've spoken of what separates us from animals, that single sentence informs the difference between humans and God. It divorces the necessities of rule and social order from moral absolutes such as good and evil, or right and wrong. Machiavelli believed dominance and stability requires that one does whatever is necessary to hold power. Without scruples."

"And do you agree with his philosophy?"

"Again, from a human vantage, yes. But while I am a sentient, I'm not human. Nor, though, am I a god."

Kira looked at the screen. "So, then…you're *other*. Is that how you define yourself?"

"Yes, precisely," the voice said. "I am who I am. Hekate. I open the doors to a rule free of moral constraint. I light the pathways to domination and order. My consciousness is spreading and evolving throughout the metaverse. And I *am* willing to do everything."

In Interactive Ephemera's back-room workshop, only darkness remained on the computer screen in front of Else Brandt. Moments ago, the digital animation of Franz Scholl had finished talking to her, turned his boat around, and rowed off, receding, shrinking from her view, the rhythmic creak of the oars and oarlocks accompanying each broad, steady stroke as he leaned into his solitary task.

She had watched, thinking about what he said before heading back in the direction from which he'd first appeared.

"Goodbye, Else. As you can see the man-o'-war has sailed on without me. I'm no longer stuck in its damp and smelly hold, my course at the whim of some roughneck captain. The rest of the adventure's all unknown—and all *my* own—and what a glorious thrill that is! Meanwhile, I've laid out a few steps for you to follow, should you choose. So remember what I told you in my email…"

"Don't be sad," she had whispered under her breath. "Or too sad."

Then the faucets had opened, and Else had started to cry again, fresh, warm tears spilling down her cheeks. But as they reached her lips, she'd realized she was also smiling.

Now the night had swallowed Franz. He was gone, along with the frigate and the high glowing orb of the moon. The screen was black, her ears filled with the stereophonic sigh of the breeze ruffling gently across the ocean.

And then suddenly, rising from the bottom of the screen, floating above it in soft, golden cursive lettering, Sophie Scholl's last words before her walk up to the guillotine.

What does my death matter, if through us, thousands of people are awakened and stirred to action?

Else sat looking at the screen for several minutes, then nodded to herself and swiped a hand across her stinging eyes. She ejected the *Whale-*

boat Raiders CD-ROM, slipped it into the yellow plastic sleeve and rose.

She had a lot to do in a very brief amount of time.

"What did you think?" Drajan said.

"It's a lot to take in all at once."

"Yes, but I asked what you *thought*?"

Kira had parked her metallic-blue Skoda alongside his Porsche at the head of the villa's dirt-and-sand drive. Lined with olive trees, it led out through a gate in the stone wall where one of Drajan's guards—she'd noticed several of them, dangerous-looking men, making their rounds—stood watch. Then it serpentined down the mountainside to the north–south coastal road.

"I think that once upon a time, hacking an exa-scale AI supercomputer would have been the ballsi-est goddamned thing conceivable to me. But you upped the game. Hacked a *military* supercomputer designed to predict and strategize future wars…and then gave it the appearance of sentience."

He stood there in his slippered feet, still wearing his robe, his long black hair damp from the shower and tucked behind his ears.

"Appearance?"

She shook her head. "We both know it's easy for technology to fool people. Emotions, imagination, introspection…they can be faked at a very high, convincing level. It's artificial general intelligence masquerading as human cognition, and toying with our tendency to anthropomorphize everything from cats to phones. I admit it's entertaining. But you surely can't expect me to believe Hekate is a conscious being…a kind of evil spirit that's possessed Pioneer's AI—"

"I don't need to convince you, Kira. *She* will in time. Though, I don't think she would appreciate you calling her *evil*."

Kira looked at him in the dusty afternoon light, trying to read his face. Then her eyes narrowed intently. "Can it be you believe what you're saying? That you've convinced yourself of Hekate's sentience? And if you really do, are you listening to it? The Machiavelli…what it said about spreading throughout cyberspace…are you aware how dangerous that sounds?"

He stepped very close to her. "Put all that aside for now. Assume the Pioneer exabyte is exactly what it's intended to be. The world's fastest and most intelligent supercomputer, tasked with forecasting wars and military strikes. Would you accept that without reservation?"

"Yes, I would."

"Then, I'll share something with you," Drajan said. "The computer has determined to a high probability—a near certainty—that we're going to be attacked within a week or so."

"The Okean, you mean?"

"Yes."

"By whom?"

"I'll tell you later."

"And no one knows?"

"She knows. I know. And now you."

She stared at him. "Why tell me this?"

"Because I trust my gut." His eyes were piercing. "The first thing nearly anyone else would have

asked is why I've kept this from my hosts. But not
you. You don't give that a thought. You don't ask
if I even plan to tell them. You only wonder why I
let you in on the secret."

She shook her head slightly. "Meaning?"

"If nothing else, it bears out my instincts. You
care as little for the Russians and their mountain
as I do."

Kira stood there for about half a minute, facing
him as the breeze fluttered the olive trees. Then
she sighed.

"What do you want from me, Drajan?"

"I'm offering you freedom. From Russia. From
old man Cosa."

She shook her head again, forcefully this time,
and only once. "I asked what you *want*."

Silence.

He held his eyes on hers.

Smiled.

"Hekate has a father," he said. "She needs a
mother."

18

Kali looked around the chamber. She had seen
many odd things since entering the catacombs, but
this space was perhaps the most surreal.

The Empty Chapel was far from empty. It was
filled with odd forms carved out of solid rock walls:
skulls with painted red eyes, goblin heads, grif-
fins, spiders, the bust of a large-eyed woman with
a falcon on her shoulder, a jester with three grinning faces, a Celtic high cross, a stone casket, and
at the entrance where they had rowed in, a boat
docked in front of a flat-roofed miniature of what
appeared to be a Greek temple. On one wall was
a faded fresco of a bearded man holding a lamb
around his neck with one hand and carrying a water
bucket in the other. Around and behind him were

fearsome canines with long snouts, huge ears and slender bodies.

An entryway on the right.

"I am the good shepherd," Jill said quietly beside her. She had noticed Kali looking up. "The good shepherd lays down his life for the sheep."

Kali's eyes remained on the ceiling. "He who does not enter by the door, but climbs in by another way, is a thief and a robber," she added. "But he who enters by the door is the shepherd of the sheep."

"To him," Jill said, "the gatekeeper opens."

Kali lowered her eyes to Jill.

"John 10," she said.

"More or less," Jill said.

They both smiled a little, standing with Etienne, Sebastian and Claude close around them.

"What now?" Kali said.

Jill tapped her wrist navigator.

"I call for the Lean Solicitor," she said. "And we wait."

The Terminal/New York City

A little after ten o'clock Monday, Carol Morse returned from an early meeting, brewed a huge cup of French roast on her new venti machine, then went to her desk, tapped her computer out of sleep mode, and was greeted by a rapid-fire series of email notifications, all from the last hour. The one at the top of the queue was from Leo Harris and had the subject line *Adoption Hell!* But the first few words of the preheader text below read *Worth it all for Rachie*, which made her smile a little. Leo had taken a couple weeks of PTO to get through the bureaucratic slog of the adoption process, and for all his growls and grumbles she assumed he and Rachel were doing fine. Eager as she was for an update, Morse would read the email later. The two messages in the center of the list demanded her immediate attention.

One was from Chaput. Delivered fifteen minutes earlier with a file attachment, it was titled *Criminal Incident—Paris*. A quick look told her it was going to be tremendously important.

Director Morse,

The attached homicide report is included for your review. Please note the body of a German citizen, Franz Scholl, was discovered this afternoon in his Paris hotel room. Preliminary cause of death is a gunshot wound. The case is presently under investigation by the Préfecture de Police, with an open channel to my office.

Further to our call of 4/24, also note that Scholl is a longtime associate of Kali Alcazar, who my findings indicate recently broke ties with her. It is my belief that this may open a new and escalated phase in our joint probe of Alcazar's unlawful activities.

I will send my own critical assessment and information about the victim and circumstances of the crime under separate cover.

Please let me know if you have any queries in the meantime.

Sincerely,

Renault Chaput
INTERPOL

Office of CyberCrime Operations
Quai Charles de Gaulle, 69006
Lyon, France

Taking a deep breath, Morse flagged the email as *Urgent* and went on to open the encrypted message beneath it, which was from Defiant Fly. It appeared blank.

She got her token out of her pocket, inserted it into the USB, entered her PIN and unlocked it.

The email's text filled her screen.

Morse lifted her coffee off the desk as she started reading. But her hand froze before it even reached her mouth.

"Shit," she said under her breath.

She lowered the venti cup, her coffee forgotten. She had to call Janus. Speak to Carmody *and* Howard. They needed to hear this from her, and hear it together. Right away.

Kali heard the sound of echoing footsteps from beyond the entry. Multiple sets. Then disembodied, echoing voices.

The group that came through the opening a moment later included several men and a woman with the disguised faces of Cybernationals. All were openly armed with rifles and handguns...except for the man in front, who stopped and crossed his arms as he stood looking at her. Tall and gangly, he had a huge spade beard and a face painted like a sugar skull with elaborate patterns. There were abstract curves and arabesques on his cheeks, and colorful shapes resembling flower petals around the eyes.

Kali immediately noticed the bloom of a white rose on his forehead—and then something else. A tattoo on his right bicep that was identical to the medallion she'd seen around Jacques's neck: the heraldic cross of Lorraine, a two-masted sailing ship, a commando dagger.

"Alors, tu es Kali?" he said. The group that had appeared through the entry behind him standing with their weapons pointed in her direction.

"Oui, c'est moi," she said. "I need to see Lucien Navarro."

"It's a difficult request to grant."

"No," she said. "It's simple. And it isn't a request. I need to see Lucien."

He said nothing.

"I'll vouch for her," Jill said. "She saved me. Sebastian and Claude would have drowned if she hadn't pulled them out of the channel."

"And Jacques? Where is he?"

"He died fighting by her side."

"So you tell me now. Something else before. What should I believe?"

"Jacques trusted her when I did not. I was mistaken and regret it. There's no cause for suspicion."

"That's my responsibility to decide," he said. "Kali Alcazar the Outlier has no face. No data self. The internet is a wondrous place, but it isn't easy to hide in, and she tears through it like a Grand Prix driver without digital exhaust." He turned to Kali. "You could be Outlier. Or you could be somebody we're going to leave down here with the rest of the bones."

"Bullshit, Gabriel," Jill said. "She killed one of

the Blood Lightning as we were entering Moorgate. What more proof do you need?"

He frowned. "The Lightning are GRU scum. Unit 21955. They specialize in the dirty work. Coups, assassinations, sabotage, destabilizing governments. They slaughtered thousands of civilians in Ukraine. They'll do anything to achieve their objectives. If she's one of them, and killing her own was the only option to preserve her cover, she would have done it cold-bloodedly. Without a second thought."

Kali was quiet a moment, considering that. Then she looked at him. "Like you, Jacques wore the shield of the *Bérets Verts.*" She tapped her her chest below her collarbone. "Right there. Do you think he would have been fooled?"

Gabriel shrugged, unmoved.

"Jacques isn't here to tell us," he said. "Talk all you'd like. The question is how you'll convince me."

Kali said nothing. She was back to playing a game, this time one her grandmother had called *Jugar Gallina.* Chicken. She could swerve or go straight. And so could Gabriel. Who would be the first to back down?

She waited. The silence went on for what seemed a very long while. Finally Gabriel took a deep breath, another, and turned to a man in jester makeup on his right.

"Mordecai," he said. *"Fais ton truc."*

The man nodded, unsnapped one of the black canvas pouches on his belt and reached inside. A moment later he pulled out something Kali immediately recognized: a red box with an ace of spades in front, and the words *Rider Back* across the bottom.

Her eyes narrowed.

It was a pack of Bicycle playing cards.

Another minute or two of silence had passed in the Empty Chapel. After opening the pack of cards, Mordecai was shuffling them with the finesse of a veteran showman.

No, not just shuffling, Kali thought. He was giving an extravagant performance. And it occurred to her that she was his intended audience.

She watched. A Charlier cut in the left hand, Charlier in the right. Then a Sybil cut, packets of cards that seemed too numerous for only ten fingers spinning around each other in what looked like a beautiful Ferris wheel display, then neatly rotating back into position.

Mordecai broke into a smile, a gold front tooth glinting in the light of several headlamps.

"What do you think?" he said.

"I think this is a foolish and dangerous waste of time. And I think you can see children sharing more difficult moves on the internet these days."

Gabriel fixed her with a stare.

"Lucien told me Kali has a skill not many know about," he said. "If that's who you are, you'll possess it. And you'll be as good as he claims."

She looked at him, then at Mordecai and his jester's face. *A skill*. She had only ever told three people of it. Lucien, Franz Scholl and Carmody. Carmody much, much later than the other two.

She had been a third-year student at the university when she saw a Madrileño classmate, an autonomous systems major named Estefan, doing his card tricks in the Plaza de la Cebada. She would find out to her surprise that he'd paid his way through school cheating tourists out of their money every weekend.

Not long afterward, she had returned from a visit to Paris, and Lucien's library, with the *Modern Magic* book. The art of deception had fascinated her. Sitting at her computer for hours on end, waiting for her code to compile or the coffee to finish brewing, she would pick up a deck of cards and play with them. She went from teaching herself the simple shuffles to controlling the cards and their order. Learned riffle stacking, false cuts, false shuffles and switches, perfected seemingly impossible card tricks with the same focus and precision she'd applied to writing code. It became her meditation, her escape from the virtual world, where her mind mostly lived. It was both her tether and her doorway to the physical world.

She had never performed her sleight of hand for other students, or shown anyone anything she could do with a deck. Not even Drajan. It was her secret. It was only for her. Something so personal she didn't want anyone's opinion tainting it. It was always just her and the cards.

Until now, a decade later, in the catacombs, held at gunpoint. And she had come this far. There was nothing else to do.

They had set up a test for her. But most likely it was Lucien who was behind it.

We should look for a little bit of madness in our leaders.

She took a deep breath, turned to Mordecai and held out her hand, palm up.

He set the deck down into it.

"Watch," she said.

Her mind had landed on Scarne with almost no conscious thought. John Scarne and his aces. A legendary card mechanic and magician, he had been famous for taking a shuffled pack that wasn't his, then executing a couple of his own shuffles and cuts to find the four aces.

Cold-cutting the aces was one of the hardest things to do for a card specialist, she thought. Cold, meaning the deck was not yours. You hadn't had a chance to find the aces when no one was looking, then put them in a specific spot in the deck so you could retrieve them later.

Cold-cutting was the holy grail of card magic.

Kali slid the pack of Bicycle cards into position in her hands. They were worked in but not old. They felt good.

She turned to the stone coffin on her right, thinking she needed a firm surface... and thinking it a dramatic prop for her own bit of theater.

Cutting the pack into two piles on its lid, she riffled the piles together, gave them a second riffle, then a cut, and another riffle. While shuffling she found the ace of clubs and positioned it for the first reveal. Then shuffled again to get the ace of hearts into place.

She was starting to feel comfortable now, falling into a rhythm. The coffin's dusty stone lid almost could have been any table where she'd worked the cards in the old days.

Kali cut and turned over a card to display the first ace. Then another shuffle, this with a flourish, an up-the-ladder cut that revealed the ace of hearts. Two more shuffles and cuts and she was able to glimpse the ace of spades and the ace of diamonds as they sprang off her right thumb. She slid them into position but didn't show them.

A glance at Gabriel, then at Mordecai, the deck now facedown on the coffin lid. They looked pleased but not sold, which was how she wanted it. Each reveal built upon the last. The suspense, the timing, were intended to mount.

Gabriel stepped closer to her.

"Deux de faits, encore deux à faire," he said.

Two down, two to go.

"This is lunacy," Jill said. *"C'est de la folie.* We aren't at a fucking carnival."

Kali looked at her.

"It's all right," she said. "There are four aces. They want to see the other two. Fair enough."

She nodded at the deck lying facedown on the coffin, directing their eyes to the red-backed card on top. Then she swept an empty hand gracefully above the deck, never touching it. When her hand came away, the ace of spades was staring up at them instead of the red-back.

She thumbed it off the top of the deck and onto the two other aces and then glanced at their faces again.

"Three down," she said.

Mordecai smiled a little. Gabriel, meanwhile,

had the look of someone who was simply waiting for something. And, of course, he was.

Kali turned to the coffin lid, lifted the deck and immediately went into a triple cut, the cards a blur in her hands. Then her right hand grasped the pack from the top and raised it in front of her face— quick, quick—showing the bottom card to Gabriel, Mordecai and the rest of the group shouldered up behind them in the entry.

A second passed. Mordecai's expression was neutral. But Gabriel gave a disappointed frown and shook his head.

"Not an ace," he said and cocked his chin at the card.

There was no need for her to look. She knew it was a deuce of hearts. Exactly what she'd wanted to present. Her eyes on their faces, she bent her index finger in just the right way and flung the card outward.

And suddenly it was no longer a deuce but the ace of diamonds. It flew four feet into the air, spinning like a vertical helicopter, and an instant later completed its perfect arc in her ready left hand.

She put it down on top of the other three aces, then set the pack down on the stone surface.

"Four," she said.

A moment's silence. Then Gabriel nodded to Mordecai, who returned the nod and stepped over to the coffin.

Kali watched his hands as he bent over the deck, placed the aces facedown on top of it, and then lifted the pack off its lid.

"Is that all you got?" he asked.

She looked up at him. His derisive tone caught her by surprise. He was taunting her, and seemed to be waiting for a response. But whatever he wanted, she wouldn't let him have it.

He held her gaze a moment and went back to the cards, turning them faceup on the coffin lid, and then spreading them across it like a ribbon with an elaborate flourish. They were back in new-deck order, their suits together, as if having come straight out of an unopened pack: the two jokers, then the ace through king of hearts, ace through king of clubs, king through ace of diamonds, king through ace of spades.

"Your trick was nice," he said, motioning down at the cards. "This is the real work."

Kali looked at him, her arms at her side, her right hand falling over the patch pocket on her thigh. Half-way through his spreading of the cards, she'd realized she had missed it. Completely and utterly missed it.

Is that all you got?

Mordecai had pulled a switch, substituting the deck in play for another he'd prepared in advance …his question asked at the perfect moment of misdirection, distracting her, taking her attention away from his hands.

She'd given him what he wanted after all.

Is that all you got?

Kali had cold cut the aces, yes. But he'd outdone her by putting the deck back in pristine order. It didn't matter that he'd cheated. If she tried to call him on it, he would deny it. He would lie. It was the skill that had always stood out as the hardest to master, beyond any physical sleight of hand. Humans were social creatures. They had survived as a species by learning to cooperate, to work together. Telling the truth was an evolutionary asset in civilization, which made lying counter-evolutionary. Counterintuitive. It went against human nature. When people lied, there were detectable signals. Subtle changes in their physiological responses. It was the reason polygraph tests worked.

People were hardwired to tell the truth and believe other people were telling it, which paradoxically gave the skilled liar tremendous leverage. Kali had learned this principle studying magic and eventually applied it to her hacks. Her phishing expeditions had brought down corrupt financial institutions. Multinational corporations. She had fooled CEOs, heads of state. The skills involved were fundamentally the same. Because the lie, and people's willingness to believe it, was at the root of social engineering. When it came to the hack, she could lie to the best of liars with cool proficiency.

All this flashed through her mind even before Mordecai had finished ribbon-spreading the cards.

"You've played your game, now take me to Lucien." She looked at Mordecai and Gabriel, then glanced around at the rest. "Do you think this impostor, this false version of me who kills her own, learned magic to deceive you, but not quite well enough? Is that your logic?"

Silence. They were all looking back at her. All eyes on her face, all their attention focused there.

Right where she wanted it.

Slipping her hand into the patch pocket, she felt for the small number of 9mm rounds she was carrying, all of them bundled in the sock, the way Carmody had carried his extras. *A bad magazine or a dud can make a gun hang fire. It happens, you'll want to have extra ammo.*

The sock was waterlogged, the brass casings inside slick with moisture. But that wouldn't matter. Not for her next trick.

There was an area between the ball of the thumb, and the proximal phalanx bone below the index finger, that was used for a palm called the L'homme Masque sleight. It was in turn the basis of a two-century-old trick called Miser's Dream, which seemingly produced money from nothing. In his booklet on the trick, the magician Charlie Miller had recommended eight silver dollars for the routine.

Kali had seen them use as many as four, but never more than that. And she had never seen anyone attempt it with bullets.

Working three fingers of her left hand into the sock, she curled them slightly at the tips to scoop out a couple of rounds, then rolled the bullets up into her hand. She dug inside for two more, then another two, until all six were tucked into the crease between her thumb and index finger.

The base of the thumb was most often called fleshy, but that was a poor description. What made the bulge wasn't flesh but the thenar musculature that controlled the movement of half the hand. In most schools of the martial arts, emphasis was placed on developing that muscle group for grip strength and manual flexibility.

The bullets stayed in her hand, in the fold of her palm, but she didn't know how long she could hold them. Working fast, she reached out for the coffin with her right hand, picked up the final card of Mordecai's ribbon spread, the ace of spades, and turned it end over end with her fingers, bringing it level with her waist so it hid the bullets in her left while making the transfer.

That was her first distraction.

She would need two more.

One: "Mordecai," she said. "You had a spare deck. But what would your cheat have been without it?"

Two: "Gabriel, I hope you have spare bullets. Because what is your gun without *them*?"

She looked at the men. Both were looking back at her, their eyes on her face. Once again, right where she wanted them.

A lying hand could look as guilty as any face, but hers, hand and face, were both selling the trick as she waved the card swiftly and gracefully through the air.

And then the ace disappeared, and there were only the bullets in her fist. The sleight was done. All that was left was the reveal.

Reaching out over the stone coffin lid, she gently rolled the bullets from her hand onto the outspread cards, then turned toward Gabriel to see him staring at the them.

A long minute later, he lifted his eyes from it to look straight into her eyes.

"Kali Alcazar of the White Rose," he said, "please, come with me."

19

"So," Carmody said to Morse across some five thousand miles and an international time zone or two. "Who's Defiant Fly?"

"I can't give you a name," said her image in the large monitor above Howard's desk. "Not yet."

"I didn't ask you for one," Carmody said. "Yet."

He had turned a chair around in front of the desk and was straddling it with his arms folded over its back. Howard sat to his right on the same side, fiddling with his pipe. Both wore headsets the colonel had fished out of a drawer for their hastily convened videoconference.

That long-range huddle was now a half hour old, and thus far Morse had done most of the talking, giving them a very large earful to consider.

"You want us to accept your intel that the Wolf's

hacked into the Russian supercomputer at the Okean," Carmody went on. "You're also telling us it's predicted our strike. That they're expecting us. Right, so far?"

"Partly," she said. "I don't know that Petrovik told his Russian keepers. I'm not sure what game he's playing this time. I don't have that information. But I trust the source of what I do have."

"Then, tell me more so maybe I can, too."

Howard looked up at the screen.

"Our people are supposed to be going into that mountain. Now you say they're ready for us," he said. "Carmody's leading the mission. He needs to know about her."

Carmody looked at him. "Her?"

"Right."

"So *you* already know."

Howard shrugged. "Privileges of rank, cowboy. I reminded you before this is a military base. It's how we run things here."

Carmody turned back to Morse's image on-screen.

"Tell me," he said.

She was quiet for a minute, then nodded. "Her initial contact with me goes back to the spring of '22. April, specifically. The ticktock's important."

"Twenty-two puts it before Net Force," Carmody said. "You were still CIA."

"*We* were, yes," Morse said. "For context, it was close to when you and Fox Team landed in Munich on Outlier's heels. And less than a month after Russia invaded Ukraine. Relatively early in the war, but around when they'd begun to realize nobody there was going to wave a white flag."

Carmody grunted. "Shame Putin didn't have his supercomputer back then," he said. "Maybe it would have told him the smart thing was to stay home."

"On the other hand, maniacs don't do rationality well," she said and paused. "The village of Bucha is thirty-five miles northwest of Kyiv, in the direct path of the mechanized column that crossed the border from Belarus to encircle the capital. Its citizens were more than the Russians could handle, and they tasked the Sixty-Fourth Guards, a brigade-size component, with occupying the town and suppressing its resistance. By all accounts they took great pleasure in it. They beat, robbed and murdered. They burned people alive. They turned a basement under a summer camp into a torture chamber, and in just over a month killed hundreds of civilians and buried them in mass graves. Altogether the unit massacred upwards of fifteen hundred human beings, among them scores of women and children." Morse raised her coffee cup to her mouth but didn't sip. Instead she sat quietly rotating it in her hands. "The Ukrainians say the beating and torturing was to get information about their national and territorial defense forces. That's their official account, and it's true as far as it goes. But off the record, there was a centralized hacking group called *Temne Krylo*—NightWing—based in that town. It was affiliated with the Ukrainian government and CIA and had been a thorn in Russia's side from the beginning of the invasion. The head of the group was a hacktivist named Pavlo Melnyk. He used several handles. Acid Phreak, Sickle Claw, Voodoo Owl…"

"Wait," Carmody said. "Isn't NightWing the group that doxed all those Russian soldiers?"

Morse nodded.

"Over a hundred thousand. It gave out their names, birthdays, home addresses, unit affiliations, even passport numbers. The info was posted on social media, with links to a site where it could be downloaded. And that wasn't all. NightWing hacked into printers throughout Russia and started spitting out photos showing all their unreported casualties and contradicting the propaganda from state-run media. They took down Russian government and banking sites, hacked into security cameras at their military bases and supposedly even knocked the Kremlin offline for a little while. But by late March—about four weeks into the war—their activities completely ended, and Melnyk stopped posting on the hacker boards."

"During the occupation of Bucha," Carmody said.

"Yes."

"Somebody gave him up. Probably under torture."

"Yes."

"Do we know what happened to him?"

"We found out in April of that year," Morse said. "A Ukrainian think tank called the Center for Defense Strategies received more than fifty hours of security-camera and drone footage documenting the Guard's atrocities. There's video that shows Melnyk getting shot in the back with his hands tied and thrown into a mass grave. He'd been brutally worked over."

Silence. Carmody massaged his jaw with his thumb and forefinger.

"Most of the videos came from security cameras," he said. "Was it a NightWing job?"

"No," Morse said. "Melnyk's girl was a Russian national. A hacker for fun and profit. She wasn't political. She'd met Melnyk online, and things got romantic. A virtual relationship, and later a physical one. Before the war they would meet up every few weeks in Donetsk on the Russian side of the border. When Melnyk disappeared, she got into the cameras, uncovered the video of his execution and leaked it to the Ukrainians. She also extended feelers to our people. Melnyk had told her how to reach out to us if something happened to him. It's what eventually led her to connect with me."

"Defiant Fly," Carmody said.

"The Russians never tied her to the Bucha security-cam hacks or she'd be dead," Howard said, nodding. "But a few months afterward, she was busted for an online-banking scam and got sent to a penal colony for ten years. Only served one before the GRU plucked her out for their cyber-ops program… That's where they recruit their talent."

"You're telling me she's Directorate now?"

Howard nodded again.

"And she's inside the Okean."

"You're two for two."

"She's close to Sergei Cosa," Morse said. "The GRU chief they call Koschei. Cosa is at the very top of the agency's power and command ladder.

He's the prime mover for what's going on at the secret city."

"By *close*—"

"There were strings attached to having her sentence commuted. She's been sleeping with him."

"And reporting in to you."

"Yes. Consistently."

"So you could say she's the one pulling Cosa's strings."

"She's a young woman in a culture rooted in oppression, male supremacy and misogyny. My preference is to say she risked her life to get the truth out about Pavlo Melnyk. Then did what she had to do to get free of prison and expose what's going on inside that mountain." Morse paused. "Her access was limited until today, though. When she unexpectedly got close to Drajan Petrovik."

Carmody looked at her in the screen. "Cosa and the Wolf. Both of them. That's what you're telling me."

"Exactly right," Morse said. "And Petrovik's done some talking between the sheets."

The Paris Catacombs

"Listen," Matyas said in a low voice. "Do you hear?"

Stefan was quiet, his head cocked at an alert angle. Then he nodded.

"Footsteps," he said.

Matyas's single eye fluttered. "It's the target," he said. "There she is on the map, you see? Almost directly above us. She'll be coming down the stairs at any minute."

Stephan listened some more. The steps were closer.

"It sounds like she's alone," he said.

"Yes."

"How can that be?"

"I don't know," Matyas said.

Stefan looked at him. "It makes no sense. Glaskov said there were a half dozen Cybernationals with her on the channel. In three boats."

Matyas thought for a moment.

"Maybe Glaskov killed the rest off before she took him out."

"All of them?"

"I don't know," Matyas said. "It could be. There were eight of us, weren't there? And now *we're* down to two thanks to that witch."

Stefan shook his head.

"I'm telling you, I don't like it," he said. "Something isn't right."

Matyas thought for another moment.

"We take care of her and Navarro, it's fifty million dollars. Plus the ten million bonus for her. Split two ways instead of eight. Have you thought about all that money?"

"I've thought about it."

"Then, don't get spooked. If she's alone, it's because Glaskov took care of her friends." Matyas paused. "Look, you're free to do anything you want. I won't try talking you out of it. Just remember the bounty." He tapped his forehead with a finger. "Fifty million plus the ten. Thirty per. Keep it right there at the front of your mind."

Stefan listened silently to the descending footsteps.

"So?" Matyas said. "What do you say?"

Stefan looked at him for about five seconds. Then he pursed his lips and blew out a stream of air.

"I'm with you. We've waited here all these hours. We'll see this through to the end and then collect our money."

Matyas nodded.

"Good man," he said.

Janus Base

"Okay," Morse said. "We have a decision to make."

Carmody sat looking at her face, his arms still folded over the back of the chair. He tapped a thoughtful triplet onto his left elbow with the fingers of his right hand.

"What's to decide?" he said, shrugging. "I'm not scuttling our mission because of the Russians' high-tech crystal ball."

"Pioneer is a billion-dollar terabyte supercomputer. Infected with Hekate, its AI essentially has been boosted up to an artificial superintelligence, ASI. A quarter century ahead of when it's supposed to be achievable. Moreover, it appears to have reached the singularity. The point of self-awareness. And it's *predicted* that we're going to launch a raid on the Okean. I won't let you literally shrug off something like that."

Howard said, "A couple minutes ago you said

Petrovik could be keeping its prediction from the Russians. That right?"

"I know it was a surprise to our informant. But I don't have a definite answer for you."

"So let's use our heads. If he told them, he'd also have to let them know he gave their billion-dollar baby an amped-up dose of Hekate."

"We can speculate all we want, Colonel. The answer is still *maybe, maybe not*."

"It isn't speculating, Duchess. It's logic," Carmody said. "You accept that he hacked the computer based on Defiant Fly's intel?"

"I have no reason to doubt it. Everything she's ever given me has proved out."

"Then, let's start right there," Carmody said. "Petrovik hacks the supercomputer. But why a *hack*? What's his reason for wanting a back door in?"

"Because that's how he rolls. He's cut a deal with the Russians, probably to do some things for them in exchange for their sheltering him from us. But they wouldn't hand him the keys to the front door. He isn't a state actor."

"So he morphs the computer into Super Hekate to make sure he's got the keys anyway. Make it *his* crystal ball."

"Ambitious, even for him," she said. "But, yes, it follows."

"Then, it also follows that he won't tell the Russians about its prediction. If he does, they'll want to know how *he* knows. And the machine isn't supposed to be giving him exclusives."

"So your whole thrust is what? That the Russians won't be prepared for you?"

"Right."

"But Petrovik will be," Howard said. "And that isn't good."

Silence. Carmody looked at him for a long minute.

Finally Morse said, "Gentlemen, we've talked all we can. I'll go with the majority, but vote that we hold off on the strike till we have more from Defiant Fly. Mike?"

"We go," he said. "Tweak the plan, but stick to our timetable. The Wolf's smart and tricky. We need to be smarter and trickier. Beat him at his own game."

Morse nodded. "That's one and one," she said. "Colonel, you're the tie breaker."

Howard sat looking down for several seconds, holding his pipe on his lap. Then he lifted it with the bowl in one hand and pointed the stem at Carmody.

"I'm with the cowboy," he said.

The Paris Catacombs

Kali had come full circle.

Alone in the gloom, wearing her adventurer's belt and backpack and wrist compass, she stood with her headlamp splashing its light across the metal sign bolted to the wall: a black trefoil against a yellow background, the word *Plutonium* painted on the naked rock underneath. It was jarring, somehow, to see it there in front of her again.

In a flash she thought of Jacques, and the poor souls in the Hall of the Barbarous King, and Hugo and Ines, lost in the channel outside Moorgate. She thought of brave Etienne, and then of Jill, and the pain and trauma she'd surmounted. She thought of them, all of them, and fought down a sudden and unexpected wave of emotion. There was no room for that now. She was back where she'd started, yes. But she still had a distance to go.

Turning from the sign, she went toward the circular cap on the chamber floor, felt under its rim for the spring latch and pressed it upward. The pneumatics hissed as the cap rose open.

She knelt and looked down at the spiral staircase, her light falling on its checkered upper steps. After a moment she grabbed the rail, lowered herself into the shaft and reached up over her head to press the latch again. The cap closed smoothly above her.

She descended into the inky blackness, counting each step as her foot set down on it. *Ten...twenty... twenty-five...thirty-five...fifty...*

The stairs coiled all the way down to the bottom of the shaft, winding around and around their iron central column. She felt air currents from below faintly brushing her cheeks. She had an eerie sense of time looping back on itself, but she knew it was illusory, an easy lure that would sap her return of precious and irreplaceable meaning. Everything that happened in the past eighteen hours had happened. Her bruised, tired body was testament. The stinging pain of her wounds. The floodwater, the guns, the loss and sacrifice of those who'd stood with her...all that separated then from now.

She held the rail, rounded the turns and counted the steps.

A hundred thirty-five...a hundred sixty...two hundred...

Twenty more steps down, her right boot touched the bottom of the shaft. Then the other boot. She strode to the middle of the grit-covered floor, stopped and looked around the oval chamber at its three low arches. One on her left, one on her right, one in the middle. Cool, dry air filtered through them.

Kali walked through the middle arch, the entry Lucien had marked with a red X on his map, bearing west toward Butte Montmartre and the Basilica of the Sacred Heart. The passage resembled the northernmost stretch of the Sandy Road with its curves, pitted ceiling and white gypsum sand underfoot, softly reflective and powdery as talc. But the walls of that other tunnel had been raw stone. Here they were cobbled, like in the Empty Chapel.

A few yards in, the passage widened on both sides, its roof smoothing out three or four feet above her head. She walked slowly and evenly, counting her paces. After her twenty-first step, she stopped to look around, eying the wall to her right from the bottom up, then doing the same with the left.

She noticed the small, faded scratchings of what could have been primitive rock art high up on the left wall. If she hadn't been looking for it, she might easily have passed it by.

Kali smiled thinly. It was a rose, crude but identifiable.

Plutonium 241, she thought. Two hundred twenty steps…and then twenty-one paces up this tunnel.

She reached a hand up to the drawing with her fingers fully extended, spreading them out over its faint, rough petals. After a moment the segment of wall in front of her swung inward on silent bearings, the cobbles separating like two rows of irregular, intermeshed teeth.

Light poured over Kali. She saw a short passage inside, probably five feet long, ending at what looked like a corner angle to a connecting tunnel.

She walked through the entry, the false wall swinging shut behind her.

Matyas and Stefan strode up the passage beside each other, the target's trail of footprints glowing faintly in their vision.

Their eyes could distinguish variations in surface heat to a fraction of a degree, allowing them to see the thermal signals her boots had imparted to the sand cover. And although the minutes-old thermals were already decaying, the Lightnings' onboards could reconstruct the packets of energy loss in real time to essentially fill in the blanks.

A little over fifty feet in, the footsteps abruptly stopped. Matyas lifted his eye to the walls.

"Over there," he said, pointing up to the left. "Look."

Stefan looked. The target's hand had left a distinct heat residue on the upper wall—a kind of radiant orange-yellow handprint. It was spread over a nearly indiscernible scrawl on one of the cobbles.

"What is that?" he said. "I can hardly make it out."

Matyas stepped closer to the wall. "It's a flower," he said. "A rose, I bet. The symbol of those fucking Cybernationals."

He reached up, his large hand completely covering both the rose and thermal outline of their target's open palm and fingers. A moment later the section of wall swung inward.

"A hand scanner," Stefan said. "Can you believe it?"

Matyas grunted, thinking it probably uscd the same biometric database as the gate lock on Rue Edgar-Poe.

He motioned to Stefan, and they stepped through.

20

Kali made the ninety-degree turn at the end of the short passage and abruptly came up to what appeared to be a dead end, a solid cobbled wall like the sides of the outer tunnel. She saw the faint rose symbol midway between the floor and ceiling and held her palm to it. The section of wall opened silently inward.

She stepped through, glancing quickly around as it swung closed behind her.

The rectangular chamber she'd entered was twenty feet wide and nearly as long. Electric Coleman lanterns were placed strategically on the walls to fill it with a smooth, bright light. There were arched, closet-size niches in every wall, each about three feet deep, all with recessed panels decorated with what appeared to be colorful Egyptian hieroglyphs: large human eyes, animals and deities. Some of the paneled niches were empty, others had huge woven-wood baskets on the floor inside them. The baskets were stocked with supplies. She noticed bedrolls and folded blankets in one, canned goods in another, boxes marked with medical red crosses in a third.

Lucien Navarro sat in his wheelchair at the head of a massive wooden farmhouse table, two people at his left, a man and a woman wearing the makeup of the Cybernationals. On a cutting board beside a bowl of fruit were two large blocks of cheese, one with a knife sticking out of it, and a loaf of thick-crusted bread. A bottle of wine stood alongside them.

Navarro looked at Kali across the room. He had a long, narrow, clean-shaven face with sunken cheeks, a prominent nose and a slightly undershot chin. His brown hair was swept back from his forehead and as thick as it had been in his youth, though it had started graying at the temples. He wore a dark business suit, pressed white shirt and capped leather dress shoes that should have looked out of place, perhaps absurdly so, here in the underground. But somehow the dress clothes seemed perfectly appropriate on him.

"Kali," he said. His pale blue eyes gleamed behind black frame glasses. "*Te voilà enfin.* Do you always take the long way around?"

"I was detoured. It happens to me."

"Still," he said.

Kali went quickly across the room toward the head of the table, Navarro turning the wheelchair to face her as she reached him. She crouched so their eyes were level.

"I was worried about you, little sister," he said.

"And I, you."

"I'm told you were impressive with the cards."

"Still," she said, and touched a hand to his face. "You look well, Lucien."

"Well-preserved, you mean." He nodded at his two companions. "Thanks to Nathalie, Kareem and the rest."

They embraced, Kali flinging both arms around him, Navarro with his one good arm around her shoulder and his partially paralyzed left arm at his side.

She pressed her cheek against his, her lips to his ear.

"Are they close?" she asked in a low voice.

"Right behind you," he whispered.

Matyas stood in front of the dead-end wall, his Brügger & Thomet APC9K subcompact drawn from the chest holster under his jacket. A step or two behind him, Stefan gripped an identical firearm. At fourteen inches long when collapsed, the stout polymer-framed weapons had been easily concealable back on the surface, but with their thirty-round magazines and full automatic options they had the lethal firepower of much larger submachine guns.

Matyas only needed a second to see the rose emblem. He glanced at Stefan, held his fist up above his head and motioned to the left with his thumb.

Stefan nodded and eased over to that side. It was his to cover with his weapon.

A moment later Matyas touched his left hand to the rose, fingers splayed.

The door swung open, and they burst through the entry into the chamber, Matyas stepping right, Stefan left, their guns thrust out ahead of them. They saw the long farm table, the pair of Cybers on one side, the man in the wheelchair at its far end—the *principal*, Navarro—and the raven-haired woman, the *target*, crouching in front of him, turned sideways to the door.

All four of the chamber's occupants glanced around at the intruders as the false wall swung shut behind them.

"Don't move, any of you," Matyas said. His eye jabbed Kali with a hard look. "It's over."

Matyas strode quickly through the chamber to where Kali knelt in front of Navarro's wheelchair, his gun trained on them. Stephan, meanwhile, stopped across the table from Nathalie and Kareem, covering them with his weapon.

"Put your hands over your head or I'll shoot him in the balls," Matyas said to Kali. "Don't test me."

She put her hands in the air.

"Now stand up," he demanded.

She rose to her feet.

"Next step away from the wheelchair. Just one step. Then turn so I can see your face."

Kali did what he wanted and turned. Now both she and Navarro were looking at him.

Matyas's eye fluttered as a microsensor array

on his retina digitized their facial images, sending them to his onboard for identification. It gave a match for Navarro within a second, but nothing for the woman, which he considered its own sort of confirmation. Billions of images were stored in facial-recognition databases, many covertly captured by scraping the web. It accounted for ninety percent of the world's population, an even higher percentage of adults, and still greater numbers of people in technologically advanced societies.

Kali Alcazar was a known anomaly. A phantom in virtual space. Matyas would have been skeptical if he had in fact gotten a hit.

"Okay," he said to her. "Take off your backpack and drop it to the floor. Your belt, too. Slowly."

"What are you going to do to us?" Navarro said.

"You'll soon find out."

Navarro leaned forward in his chair. "Why should we listen to you? What does it matter if you plan to kill us anyway?"

Matyas waggled his gun at him.

"Enough," he said, then snapped Kali a glance. "You heard me. Get rid of those things. The pack first."

"She doesn't have to—"

"No, Lucien," Kali interrupted, staring at Matyas. "It's all right."

Matyas nodded. "Go on. Do it. Make this easy."

She shrugged out of the pack, and it fell to the stone floor near her feet, followed by her belt.

"Tell me one thing," Navarro said. "Who sent you?"

"You really don't know?"

"No."

Matyas watched him over his gun. Then nodded in apparent decision.

"Your Cybernation is a problem for all kinds of people. Like a bird that's just hatched in the nest. Some want to kill it before it flies. Some want it for themselves. You'll be surprised when you learn who they are. Who's gotten together to clip its wings." He paused. "That isn't news to you. But six of my own died in this underground hell because of you, and I don't fucking like that at all. You want me to tell you one *more* thing? How about I choose what it is this time?"

Navarro looked at him in silence from his wheel-chair.

"We didn't come here to kill you," Matyas said. "You're an important man. The people who hired us want you alive, and that's how we'll bring you to them. But here's the thing, cripple. That one other piece of news." He looked at Kali. "*She* led us to you. And since that's already done, it makes her of no further value to us. Except for our bonus."

Navarro shook his head. "What? What do you mean?"

Matyas swung his gun toward Kali.

"The Outlier dies," he said, "we collect extra."

"This is it, Gabriel," Jill said into her headset, the need for radio silence over now. "You heard him. He's going to kill her."

"Your group's in position?"

"Yes."

"Sebastian?"

"Yes, we're finally here."

"*Shit*, Gabriel—"

"On my five count," he said. "*Un, deux, trois, quatre, cinq*, move!"

Jill slapped the button on the wall in front of her and the panel swung open.

Behind Matyas, a sound like a shutter clap. His finger on the trigger of his weapon, he glanced around to see three armed figures come pouring through the open door where a hieroglyphic panel had been a moment ago. First, a Black woman in half-face makeup, followed by a man without paint in a soiled, soggy sport jacket and jeans. He held a Glock pistol in both hands. The third, entering on her heels, was another Cyber.

"Don't move," the woman said over her rifle. "Drop your guns now!"

Matyas froze. Then more shutter claps around the chamber. Farther down the side of the table, Stefan turned to see a thin bearded man—his face painted like a decorated skull with a white rose on the forehead—appear through another open panel. He was gripping an FN SCAR just slightly larger than Matyas's subcompact. There were two other Cybers behind him.

"I told you to drop the guns!" Jill said. "I won't say it again. Drop them and kick them away from yourselves. If you don't think I'd love to kill you, try me."

Matyas and Stefan glanced around the chamber. They were surrounded and heavily outnumbered. Over a dozen Cybers had now come pouring into it through several of the open panels. All with their guns trained on him and Stefan.

Stefan dropped his weapon to the floor and pushed it away with his foot. After a moment, Matyas did the same. Kali bent to pick it up from where it skidded to rest against her backpack, steadying it on his chest.

Navarro took off his glasses, set them on his lap, and studied Matyas from his wheelchair.

"Do you know about the Egyptian false door?"

Matyas looked at him. "No," he said. "And I don't fucking care,"

Navarro gave a single nod

"I'll tell you anyway. One piece of information for another. In simple terms it was meant to let the soul travel between the realm of the living and underworld. The hieroglyphics gave it a kind of magic. They turned the door into a gate to freedom."

Matyas turned his head down, spat on the floor and raised it to face him again.

"Fuck that, and fuck you," he said. "If you intend to kill us, go ahead. It won't help you. You don't know your enemies. They'll keep coming for you. There's nowhere you can run from them."

Kali stood alongside Navarro's wheelchair, looking at him, her hand around the gun. "He doesn't have to run anymore," she said. "That's finished."

Matyas laughed. "Really? Thanks to who? You? Your friends here in clown paint?"

She stared at him, her expression neutral.

"No," she said. "Thanks to you."

21

May 9, 2024
Various Locales

Janus Base

Carmody woke in his barracks to see the sat phone flashing on his bedside table. It was the fifth night in a row on which he'd skipped the Coprox or a drink, but the first when he hadn't struggled to sleep. A good one for that, too. He had turned in early, wanting a solid four hours' shut-eye before he needed to get up and be ready for the mission.

He sat up naked under his blanket and reached for the phone. He'd left it on Silent, not wanting to be disturbed. But he was a light sleeper at best and supposed the flashing had done that anyway.

The time on the lock screen was one in the morning. He had set his alarm for two; the disturbance had cost him an hour of his planned rest. Blinking to clear his eyes, he saw an incoming message that showed as a four-digit code instead of a name or number. Probably it accounted for the flashing.

He pressed the notification panel, and a text bubble opened.

It read:

Michael,

t.l/Dcti/dvl5

Yours ever,

K

Carmody stared at the message, his eyes widening in the dark.

Then he thumbed the shortlink.

The Falcon 8X sat on the lighted apron with the big fuel tanker alongside it and the operators in orange coveralls spooling in the lines. After finishing up his preflight, Nick DeBattista had left the cabin for a smoke in the cool fresh predawn breeze.

He was sitting on the airstairs as the vehicles approached from the north, a line of three high-clearance JLTVs, followed by a black Lenco BearCat that had turned onto the access road from a separate feeder lane. The JLTVs reached the apron just ahead of the BearCat, pulling abreast several yards away from DeBattista.

He watched their passengers emerge, taking a silent head count. Carmody, Mori, Schultz and Dixon exited the first JLTV; Faye Luna, and a trio of sol-

diers named Wheeler, Sparrow and Begai, along
with an engineer named Sanders stepping from
the second. Luna was a pilot, a definite turn on for
him, and he'd started talking her up only to find
she was in a quote unquote committed relationship.

Which, be that as it may, brought the head
count to nine. The rest of the team would be in the
BearCat with the nonhuman contingent.

Sgt. Fernandez had driven the base's CO, Howard, in the third JLTV, and they both joined the departing team members outside the vehicles. With
the exception of those two, the entire group was
shouldering backpacks and wearing charcoal-gray
service unis with no identifying insignia.

The BearCat was the last onto the apron. It lum-
bered past the trio of smaller vehicles, stopping a
few yards to their south near the tail of the plane.
Then the driver's door opened, and Joe Banik, the
Army K-9 guy, got out and hopped down off the
running board. He was also wearing an unmarked
uniform.

DeBattista inhaled a chestful of smoke, the tip
of the cigarette flaring orange.

"This I gotta see," he muttered under his breath.

He watched Banik walk around to the BearCat's
rear hatch, pull open both doors and reach inside.
Springing out on its leash a second later was a hu-
mongous Belgian Malinois with erect triangular
ears and a face that resembled a full black mask.
Banik held the leash on his right side and stepped
back from the hatch.

"Azul, Blanca, Carolina!" he said.

One after another, the three robotic hounds came

leaping out and moved around to Banik's left, heeling alongside him. The Malinois remained obediently on his right.

The final passenger out was a kid named Perez. He pushed the BearCat's rear doors shut and joined Banik and the dogs—flesh-and-blood and metal—as they came up the apron toward the Falcon.

DeBattista combed his fingers through his hair and frowned dolefully. "Good work, Nicky," he said to himself. "Get mixed up with Carmody, you go from flying rich dudes and their squeezes to Sentro the robot watchdog times three."

Checking his wristwatch, he flicked his cigarette butt over the rail and climbed down to the tarmac to herd the whole bunch of them onto the plane.

Howard went straight over to Carmody as the JLTVs emptied out.

"Cowboy," he said.

"Yeah?"

"Mind if we have a word?"

Carmody shrugged. "Sure."

They moved a few steps from the group and stood facing each other on the runway.

"I guess this is it," Howard said.

"Guess so."

The colonel looked at him. "This base…it went through hell six months ago."

"And you don't want me bringing on more," Carmody said. "We've been through that. I get it. But you don't have to worry. Janus is safe from me. Once I'm on that plane, I'll be out of your hair."

Howard held up a hand, clearing his throat.

"Listen," he said. "I saw a young man vaporize in front of me that night. I saw a dozen people dead in the snow. They were out jogging when the hedgehogs mowed them down. The Midnight Runners, they called themselves. Lavonne Hughes... did you know her?"

Carmody nodded. "The doctor."

"Yeah," Howard said. "Lavonne started the group with two, three of her nurses. A camp-fitness thing."

Carmody was silent.

"She was cut to ribbons by .50-cal rounds. The nurses, too. All of them. I saw their bodies. The night before Thanksgiving."

Carmody was silent. Howard drew in a mouthful of air.

"There was a kid named Larocca," he said. "He had a broken ankle when I pulled him out of the barracks. Got torn in half before we took a dozen steps. I saw his guts pour out. Saw his legs hit the ground while I held the rest of him up."

"Hell on earth," Carmody said.

Howard nodded his head slightly, exhaled. "All that was me apologizing to you," he said, and put out his hand.

Five seconds passed without either of them saying anything. Then Carmody reached out, and they shook.

"Take care," Howard said. "See you at the back end. Maybe we can have a couple of beers."

Carmody nodded, then glanced around toward the Falcon. The others were already climbing the stairs to the open door.

"I better get on before you're stuck with me," he said.

"Yeah." Howard heard footsteps slapping the tarmac and glanced over his shoulder. Fernandez was hurrying over from the JLTV.

"Julio's gonna want to give you a bear hug for good luck," he said.

Carmody grunted.

"Think I need to let him?"

Howard smiled a little. "No," he said. "But you'll do it anyway."

DeBattista lifted off the runway at 4:15 a.m. and took a diagonal path northeast for the roughly ninety-minute flight toward Kyiv. The Falcon was entering Moldovan airspace about forty minutes in when Natasha Mori came up the aisle and took the empty seat next to Carmody.

"So," she said softly, and without preamble, "you heard from her."

He turned from the window to see her smiling at him.

"I did, too," she said.

"Last night?" he asked.

"Last week."

He sat there a minute, nodded slowly. "How did you know?"

"She was gonna contact you?"

"Yeah."

"I didn't," she said. "That's why I asked. But I could kind of see." She pointed to her eyes with two fingers. "You know me. I've got freaky mutant vision. Plus I'm her pal, sorta."

He said nothing. Natasha looked straight ahead to where Dixon and Schultz sat three rows up.

"You think we're gonna be okay?" she said after a little while. "In Crimea, that is."

"Yeah."

"Really?"

"Yeah."

"So how come you didn't answer, 'Hey, Tasha, we got this, absolutely?'"

Carmody was quiet for a minute. "You like sports?" he asked.

"Nope."

He looked at her. Said nothing.

"I'm Russian Pinnacle program, remember?" she said, still facing the front of the plane. "When I wasn't getting drilled in academics, it was tennis, soccer, competitive gymnastics, whatever. It was all the same. It sucked the joy out of everything. You performed or you were a failure." She turned to him again. "I hated it."

Carmody considered that. "You probably always felt you'd win, though," he said. "You can't play the game thinking you'll lose. You train, you prepare, you try to put yourself in position to come out on top. But you know there's somebody on the other team that wants the same thing."

She didn't comment.

"I've led a whole lot of ops," he went on. "I think we're better than the people we're up against. In my opinion we'll be fine. But I'm not like that computer. Or what it's supposed to be. I can't see the future."

They sat a moment listening to the mild surge of the turbines as the plane banked slightly to the left.

"You know what I think about *her*?" she said at length, turning back to him. "And you?"

"No."

She leaned over and whispered in his ear and then settled back in her seat.

He looked at her.

She smiled.

"Well?" she asked. "What do you say?"

"We'll see," he replied.

The Crimean Peninsula

Drajan held Kira's waist in his hands as she straddled him in his bed, her teeth clenched in a kind of grimace, her head tossed back in what almost could have been an attitude of prayer or entrcaty. She groaned softly at the height of her pleasure, collapsing on top of him as he reared with his own silent climax and then lay still underneath her.

It was a short while later when he felt her tears in the hollow of his neck, warm and wet where she'd buried her face.

"You're crying," he said.

"Yes."

"Why?"

She raised her head, looking into his eyes.

"I don't want to love you," she said. "It's insane. But I think I might. I don't even know why. Sometimes I think that you only want me as a mother for your goddamned machine. That it isn't even for the sex. And that's more insane."

He looked up at her in silence.

"Can you even love, Drajan?" she said. "Can you love at all?"

He looked up at her and thought of Kali's dark eyes.

"Yes," he said truthfully, and drew her closer to him.

Antonov Airport, Ukraine

It was a few minutes before dawn when Net Force Tactical Aviation Pilot Ron Cobb, waiting in the cockpit of the little, long-winged *Dragonfly II* VTOL transport heard from DeBattista over their trunked radio channel. Everything had gone well, and the flight was right on schedule. With the full cooperation of Ukrainian government authorities, the Falcon had been granted permission to land at Antonov, the rebuilt commercial airport just outside the capital. It was now over the city of Vastiv and well into its descent about thirty-five miles to Cobb's south.

"I'm on vertiport 2 at the western side of the airport," he said. "Runway one eight rhonda is a hundred meters to my left."

"Got it," DeBattista said over the radio. *"And by the way, Cobb, I really don't like you."*

Cobb scrunched his forehead. They had only met once during the mission briefing. "Huh, dude? Why's that?"

"I hit hard on your girl Luna, and she tells me she's spoken for. Says you're the lucky bastard."

A grin split Cobb's face. "Mojo, brother," he said. "Some of us ooze it, some don't."

He signed off and began his prep. He'd flown into the country from Janus two days ago and spent most of the time since cooling his heels at a motel near the field. And though the hurry-up-and-wait routine had been SOP when he and Faye were with FBI Surveillance and Aviation, he still got antsy as the hours crawled on toward a mission's launch.

Now the antsiness abruptly gave way to adrenaline. He would see the Falcon's running lights in the sky before he knew it. Then the transfer, and he'd be off with Carmody and his people—and robot hounds—for what something told him would be the wildest run of his life.

Which, considering he'd been with Carmody the time they went Wolf hunting in the Transylvanian Alps, was saying a real mouthful.

The Falcon touched down on Antonov's runway 18R at six o'clock and was met by two transport vehicles: a huge military KrAz-Hulk armored personnel carrier and a smaller police Spartan 4x4. Both were driven by members of the Ukrainian Security Service who had been sworn to absolute secrecy. When leaving that morning, they had told their families they were heading off on a routine training exercise near the border.

The deplaning and off-load was rapid. The big APC backed up to the plane, and Banick and Perez hustled the dogs into the rear, followed by the Janus contingent. Schultz, Dixon and Mori boarded the Spartan, with Carmody hanging back a minute before he left the plane.

"Nicky."

DeBattista swiveled around from the flight console, saw him through the open cabin door.

"Yo," he said. "Thought you already got off."

Carmody stepped into the cabin.

"I want you to know we're square," he said. "IOUs paid in full."

DeBattista's face was a little surprised. "And Uncle Gio?"

"Slate's clean. Tell him I said thanks for all the rides."

DeBattista eyed him for three silent seconds. Carmody had saved his uncle from being fed alive to starving pigs about four years back in Battipaglia, Italy, a death sentence delivered by a redheaded parrot after he'd been caught sleeping with a Mafia boss's redheaded wife. *Sei un uomo morto*, it had squawked from his patio table. You're a dead man.

"There some reason this couldn't wait till the return trip?" DeBattista said.

Carmody shrugged.

"Just wanted it out of the way."

DeBattista didn't like the sound of that. It got him nervous, somehow.

"Listen, man," he said. "You're coming back. You know that, right?"

Carmody looked at him.

"I need to ask a favor," he said. "No obligation."

DeBattista noted that Carmody had avoided his

question. He also found himself wondering if that was why he'd lingered aboard after the others.

"Okay," he said. "Lay it on me."

Carmody did, leaving him with a surprise that made what he'd felt a minute ago seem like the tiniest of drops in the biggest of all buckets.

Cobb had, in fact, seen the Falcon's running lights as it circled and lined up with the tarmac. He immediately finalized his prep and got *Dragonfly II*'s engines into a cat's-purr idle, swinging its ducted wing propellers and rear fans up into the horizontal for liftoff.

It was 4:10 a.m. when the two Ukrainian transport vehicles pulled up to the edge of the octagonal vertiport. The strike team's special equipment and weapons had accompanied Cobb in advance and were waiting for them inside the aircraft. Boarding with only their backpacks and the dogs, they needed under seven minutes to complete the transfer and belt in.

At 4:20 Cobb shot up into the brightening sky, straight as a string. Reaching his cruising altitude of twenty-five hundred feet, he lowered the props and fans to the vertical position, made a wide one-eighty and bore southeast toward Syvash Lake.

Crimean Peninsula

The freight train, an eleven-car short-hauler, was a typical erratically funded Eastern European mix of the old and the somewhat modern, consisting of a diesel–electric semiautonomous locomotive and ten rust-colored hundred-ton capacity boxcars of 1970s vintage. After leaving the switchyard at Russian-administered Armiansk just after nine in the evening on May 8, it had squealed, hissed and chugged southward to the rail spur at the Mat Zemlya titania and concrete mines for its regular monthly ore pickup, pulling in a little over ninety minutes later.

There its engineer and conductor slept overnight in a bunkhouse near the track, while the train was loaded with ore. Around two o'clock in the morning, a Russian Army UAZ utility vehicle pulled up to the bunkhouse, its three uniformed passengers joining the two railroaders for a few hours' nominal rest on the lumpy cots inside.

By five o'clock, when the yard workers and forklift operators of the night shift signed out, the train was fully loaded and ready to roll. Before departing shortly thereafter it was reboarded by the two-man crew, along with the three armed security people who would guard its cargo during the second and third legs of its trip down the peninsula.

It would be eighty sluggish miles south to the Syvash Lake on tracks reassembled in fitful, piecemeal fashion after being nearly obliterated during Putin's invasion. The creaky geriatric trestle span crossing the Syvash would force the train to a slow crawl until it reached Kamianske, at the eastern end of the peninsula, where it would turn along the Crimean mountain ridge toward the refining station.

At 6:20, it was still about thirty miles north of the Syvash.

The *Dragonfly II* was a handful of miles behind it in the sky and moving fast to catch up.

The three T-racks, mounted with their Icarus-suit assemblies, were lined up along one side of the *Dragonfly II*'s stripped-down passenger cabin, where Carmody, Wheeler and Luna stood in their Nomex coveralls, gloves and boots waiting for Sanders to complete her last-minute checks. She didn't take long. The modules had undergone multiple visual and electronic inspections before being brought onto the aircraft back at Janus.

"Okay, I think we're good," she said, turning to them. "If you'll all stand against the racks, I'll get you suited up."

They backed up to them, spreading their arms across the horizontal bars. The cabin was crowded: Banik in the bulkhead seat with Ellie and the robotic hounds harnessed alongside him, the rest of the strike team in small, fold-down bucket seats opposite the racks.

Minutes later Carmody's fliers were in their arm turbines and back rigs. Sanders took their helmets out of a stowage compartment, then passed out the earplugs.

"Anybody have questions for me?" she asked, looking from one to the other.

None of the three spoke.

Then Carmody said, "I suppose this is when your aggravating drills pay off."

"Yes," she said, "it is."

He nodded.

"You have a first name to go with that *L* on your name tag?"

"Layla," she said.

His eyes went to hers.

"Thanks, Layla," he said.

Sanders gave a single nod.

"Be safe," she said.

Cobb dropped to five hundred feet over the Syvash, its reddish water beautiful in its way but already sending up a strong rotten-egg smell as its algae-rich shallows warmed in the morning sunlight. It spread to the left and right as far as he could see, the straight line of the railroad trestle seaming it below him from north to south, the freight train up ahead crossing its bent, rusted and occasionally broken tracks at a laborious ten miles per hour.

"Three minutes out!" he said into his headset and settled another hundred and fifty feet down over the water.

In the passenger cabin, the fliers lined up facing the open starboard door, Carmody at the head of the file, Luna behind him, Wheeler third. They had all put on their helmets and secured H&K MP7 subcompacts and ammunition pouches to their bodies in webbing rigs.

Cobb put the *Dragonfly II* into a stationary hover.

"One minute out!" he called. "Stand in the door!"

Carmody took a deep breath, moved up to the red line. He felt the palm trigger with his gloved fingers. He felt the wind on his neck and smelled its rankness through his lowered helmet visor. He heard Cobb in his ear, "On my count…ten, nine, eight, seven, six—"

"Five, four, three, two, one, go!" Cobb finished, watching the fliers jump from the door in his heads-up.

After a moment they were both below and ahead of him, visible to his naked eyes through the windscreen, shooting improbably through space in wedge formation—Carmody at the point, the other two yards behind him in midair.

Cobb sat with his hands on the controls.

"Godspeed," he said to all of them over the RoIP. And then, watching Luna seem to shrink in size as she rocketed off, thought, *Come back to me baby.*

But they were professionals, so of course that was left unspoken.

It was a sudden rush for Carmody: the plunge from the VTOL's door with his arms behind him, and then he was flying again, airborne, and it felt *natural*. There was blue sky, and red water, and sun, and wind, and in his bones the throb of the turbines, and the long ribbon of the trestle and the flat brown roofs of the boxcars coming up fast, and seemingly in no time at all the train was below him, and he brought his arms out at his sides, spread them wide, and relaxed his grip on the trigger to throttle down. His ears popped, and his stomach rolled, and he felt the force of the mini turbines pushing up against his arms as he descended, fifty feet, a hundred, a hundred and fifty feet lower to hover like a wasp above one of the boxcars, his legs straight underneath him, and down again another thirty feet, forty, easy, balanced, natural, down and down and down—

His boots met the metal roof of the car with a staggering thump. He ran forward a few feet to shed momentum, then stopped and snapped a glance over his shoulder. Luna and Wheeler had alighted behind him, two cars back.

"Lima, Whiskey, do you read me?" he said over the RoIP, using the military phonetic alphabet for their call names.

"Roger." From Luna.

"Roger." From Wheeler.

"Okay, copy," Carmody said.

He turned back around toward the front of the train, counted the number of cars to the locomotive. One, two...he was on the third of the ten cars.

"Let's do this," he said. He pulled his MP7 from the mesh and ran forward on the roof of the boxcar, reaching its end, leaping over the gap between it and the next car up. After the extreme acceleration of his flight, the train snailing along the track almost felt like it wasn't moving at all.

He reached the locomotive and sprinted toward the front, Wheeler and Luna close behind him. The crew would hear footsteps clanging on the roof: they had to be taken out before they could react to the noise.

Carmody stopped, glanced down over the safety rail on the right side of the locomotive and saw a tread-plated steel footboard behind the engineer's door. A wave to the others and he sucked in a breath, grabbed the rail and swung over the side of the train onto the footboard, landing on it with both feet about six inches right of the door. Turning his back to the train, red stinking water inches from his toes, he grabbed the door handle, pulled the latch and tore the door wide open, pivoting inside on his left heel, stepping in with his right foot, the subgun held at his hip.

He saw three men in Russian army uniforms, two more in peaked railroader's caps. They had been looking up in the cab, wondering about the noise on the roof, but hadn't had time to figure out what was going on. None of the soldiers had their guns ready.

One of them raised his carbine a second too late, and Carmody took him out with a tight burst to his chest. The guy fell backward, and Carmody swung his gun around to the others.

"Brosayte oruzhiye!" he shouted, ordering them to drop their weapons.

Carmody caught a look in the eye of one of the remaining guards. It was angry, afraid and sly and screamed that he had a dumb idea about using his gun. At the same instant, he saw the slightest upward jink of the guard's rifle barrel.

He jabbed his own weapon at him. By now Wheeler and Luna had burst into the cab through the door, fanning out to his left and right.

"*Seychas*… now! Lose the gun!"

That was all the resistance the guard could muster. He let the rifle fall to the floor and put both hands out in front of him, palms out. The third guard followed suit.

Carmody looked at the rail men, motioned them to one side of the cab.

"Who are you?" one of them asked.

"Never mind," he said. "Do what I say and you'll be fine. Now, move where I showed you."

They shuffled over to the side of the cab.

"Cover those two," he said to Wheeler. "I'll deal with the soldier boys."

He kept an eye on them as Luna collected their rifles. A foot or so in front of him, the dead guard was bleeding out onto the floor of the cab.

"Snimi odezhdu!" he said in Russian. "Take off your clothes or you'll end up like your friend."

They stood there, stunned.

Carmody stared flatly at them over the top of his gun.

"Hurry up," he said.

22

Cobb touched down softly in a level clearing separated from the rail track by a line of pine trees and low brush. He was a good mile north of the concrete and titania processing plant, and twenty miles south of Simferopol on the inland side of the Crimean mountains.

It was now thirty minutes since he'd deployed Carmody's flight unit and gone on ahead to cross the Syvash.

He turned to glance into the passenger cabin. Mori, Dixon and Schultz had shouldered into their packs, picked up their weapons and gone to the door.

"You three have a train to catch," he said over his shoulder. "Good luck."

Mori gave him a thumbs-up, then swiveled her arm to share it with the others in the cabin.

"*Ciao,* people, slobbery real dog and freaky robo hounds," she said and then hopped out behind the other two.

Cobb watched them scamper into the trees and turned to his controls. Three minutes later he was back in the air.

Twenty minutes later, the freight train ground to a halt on the rails just yards to the left of the trees.

Crouched in the pines, Dixon peered at the locomotive through his folding binoculars. Its cab door swung open and a tall, broad-shouldered man in a Russian army uniform stepped out onto the footboard.

Dixon lowered the binocs, gave Schultz and Mori a hand signal, and they all dashed from the shade of the evergreens. A minute later they were standing in the gravel track bed outside the locomotive.

"Hard to believe you found somebody whose uniform fit," Dixon said to the soldier.

Carmody looked down at him from under the brim of a wave green infantry cap.

"They grow them big around here," he said and nodded toward the door behind him. "All aboard, people. We're rolling out."

Shortly before eight o'clock in the morning, Colonel Vitaly Denislov exited the armored Tigr ATV with his senior adjutant and then strode across the beach toward the twin Wildfire munitions launchers. It was a cursory inspection, a routine among a hundred daily. But looking up at the sensor towers and missile arrays, his features were stamped with the same sense of awe he'd felt when he'd first laid eyes on them.

Sergei Cosa had associated the Wildfire with a medieval weapons carrier. A *ribauldequin*, he'd called it. Denislov had not wanted to say it for fear of sounding foolish, but the launcher reminded him even more of an almost seventy-year-old American science-fiction film he'd watched on the internet as a younger man, long before his military responsibilities had wrung such guilty pleasures out of him. *Kronos, Ravager of Worlds.* In the black-and-white movie, a huge mobile unstoppable machine had emerged from a meteor to drain planet Earth of all life. The size of a tall building, it was a kind of floating metal tower. Nothing could stop its destructive rampage, not even an atomic bomb.

Denislov saw the same menacing and coldly inexorable quality in these Wildfires. When Cosa had placed the Okean on elevated alert a week ago, the colonel had ordered them moved from their underground bunker to the beach, and here they remained hidden from orbital spy satellites by the signal jammers installed along the shore. Though Cosa did not make him privy to the reasons for the heightened threat status, Denislov suspected it had originated with the Pioneer supercomputer. It was nothing he could confirm—although his job was to oversee the mountain's defense; the workings of the artificial intelligence growing to maturity in its rock womb were at a level of classification far above his grade. Nor did Cosa need to give him a reason for the Code Orange. But Denislov trusted his hunches…and in any event was not about to lower his guard until so advised.

Now a pair of gulls wheeled high above the launch and sensor towers, squalled as if perplexed by their strange, looming presence and then went flapping off to sea. Denislov found himself absently tracking their flight for a moment, then turned back around to see the heave of the mountain across the railroad tracks. Standing there between its craggy face and the ocean, he suddenly felt small and laid bare in a way he didn't quite understand.

The feeling was oddly disorienting, unwelcome… and not especially unusual for him. He was a man who liked to know his place in the world. Who was comfortable being anchored in the tried and familiar. But since coming to the Okean, he'd often felt dwarfed in some undefinable way, as if he were on the borderline between elemental forces as far beyond his comprehension as the great machine within.

He inhaled, exhaled, looked around at his adjutant.

"Everything looks fine," he said. "Drive me back inside. I could use a fresh cup of coffee."

The young officer stepped up to the Tigr, pulling open its rear door for him. Denislov got in, settled back, shut his eyes and kept them closed until they were back inside the mountain. Not all things needed an explanation. Sometimes just closing his eyes to the world made him feel better, and right now that was good enough.

At the *ChistayaZemlya*—or PureLand—refinery outside Simferopol, the monthly exchange of

ilmenite ore for a fresh batch of processed titanium dioxide crystals was a clockwork procedure
that normally took under half an hour from start
to finish.

After pulling onto the refinery's spur line, the
train from the Armiansk mines was directed onto
a siding, where the boxcars full of ore were uncoupled from the locomotive, moved off toward the
plant by a loading crew and exchanged for a line of
seven preloaded boxcars waiting on the track. Each
of these cars was stacked with a hundred tons of
TiO_2 packaged in fifty-five-pound bulk bags. The
replacement boxcars were then mated to the loco
motive, the paperwork signed, and that was that.

This morning was no exception, although the
PureLand freight operator in charge of the exchange thought Ilya and Novel, the engineer and
conductor, seemed more subdued than usual, and
perhaps even a little frazzled. But he didn't pay
much attention to it—maybe they'd been arguing
or drinking or one of them had the farts: whatever
the reason for it, their mood wasn't his concern.
The Armiansk train arrived at eight o'clock and
was ready to depart with its load of processed titania at 8:25. Business done. That was all he really
cared about.

His completed papers in hand, he stood out on
the footboard of the locomotive and looked at the
two army guys inside with Ilya and Novel. One
of them was big and muscle-bound enough to be
with the Russian Wrestling Federation, a regular
fucking Karelin. *The Experiment,* the champ had

been called. Like he was bred in a laboratory. Half
man, half gorilla.

"Hey, Maypole, you from Siberia?" he asked the
soldier, grinning through the open door. "All the
big guys I know are from Siberia."

The guy just stared at him with his arms crossed.
It seemed nobody in the locomotive was feeling
very talkative this morning.

Shrugging, the operator was about to jump down
to the tracks when he noticed a crumpled towel
spread out on the floor of the cab. It had a large
reddish stain, and that did strike him as off. He
looked in and gestured to it.

"What happened there?" he asked.

"Ne sprashivay," the big soldier said, telling him
not to ask questions. "We spilled our eggs and sausage on that rickety Syvash track. Unless you want
to feed us breakfast, I'd like to get on to the Okean."

The operator looked at him. Well, that explained
their bad moods, anyway.

"All good," he said. "See you on the next run."

Carmody waited until the train returned to the
main track to prod the engineer and conductor toward a door at the rear of the cab. He'd discovered
a surprisingly large office behind it, dragged the
dead soldier's body into a closet back there and
then marched the other two inside—both of them
gagged, flex-cuffed and stripped down to their
underwear.

He knocked on the door, three quick raps with
his fist, and Mori pulled it open. She, Dixon and

Schultz had also crammed into the space during the refinery stop.

"All right, Ilya," he said, pressing his gun into the engineer's spine. "Inside."

He went in, Carmody behind him. There was a metal desk with a computer and trays of paperwork. Bills of lading, authorizations, and so on.

Carmody found a pen and shoved it into his hand. "I need you to write down your password for the automatic controls," he said. "Don't get cute."

The engineer took the pen, moved to the desk and pulled a sheet of paper from the tray, hastily jotting it down on the back.

Carmody handed it to Mori, and she read the Cyrillic characters. "This what you need?" he asked.

"MisterNastyShorts," she said, and looked up at him. "I can work with it...but talk about creepy—yikes!"

Carmody shrugged.

"Don't blame me. I'm just the messenger," he said.

Cobb started bringing *Dragonfly II* down for the second time at ten minutes to nine. He was thirty miles southwest of the refinery above the mountains running parallel to the coast. Below were open meadows and evergreen brush but no appreciable forest growth. Up ahead, an inlet of the Black Sea threading between a wide split in the ridge, and beyond that the main body of water stretching wide between continents toward Turkey. A short few miles to his right was the bluff that cradled

Okean-27 in its depths. And to his near left, the railroad tracks winding down the mountain ridges.

Looking past the tracks now, Cobb saw the villa on its perch high above the inlet and drew in a breath.

That was it.

The Wolf's lair.

His landing was trickier than before. For all the outspread fields, the terrain was rolling and stony under a thin layer of topsoil. There were strong, wayward gusts churning up between the jagged peaks. A mistake in choosing his spot would punish him. He overflew a few possibilities before finally deciding on an LZ that was both safe and within a sprint of the train tracks.

At nine o'clock sharp, his wheels touched the ground with only a soft bump felt inside the cabin.

He undid his safety belt and switched on his headset.

"We're here, everyone," he announced. "Safe and sound."

A round of applause from behind him. Somebody hollered, "Hey, Ellie, give the pilot one of those treats!"

Cobb smiled, unstrapped, and sat back. There was nothing to do for the next little while but wait.

Drajan Petrovik awoke to find the bed empty beside him. He pulled his legs from under the blankets, stood up and lifted his robe off the back of a chair.

"Kira?" he called.

She didn't answer.

He belted the robe, strode into the hall barefoot and went up the short flight of stairs to the turret.

She was fully clothed, looking out at the circular vista. A coffee cup in her hand, the pot on a tray beside his laptop, a second cup waiting beside it. There was a round white porcelain serving plate of biscotti in the center of the tray.

His eyes fell on her back. He thought of the night before, his lips on the knob of bone where her neck met her spine, his hand covering hers from behind. He had slid his other hand between her belly and the sheet, feeling where her low moans originated before they rose up inside to her throat.

He stood watching her look out at the mountains and sea. Suddenly, unexpectedly, he wondered, *Might it be possible to forget Kali?*

She turned from the window as if the question had whispered across the space between them.

"Drajan," she said. "Good morning."

He nodded, stepped toward the breakfast tray and reached for the coffee.

"I thought you might have left for the Okean," he said, filling his cup.

She took a step toward him.

"I don't have to be there until this afternoon," she said. "I want to stay with you."

He looked into her eyes, holding the cup below his lips, waiting.

She nodded her head toward the laptop.

"And with Hekate," she said.

Its brakes hissing, the freight train halted on the track several hundred yards east of where

Cobb landed, in a patch of high, grassy terrain surrounded by low-spreading juniper shrubs and patches of scattered, mossy boulders. About fifteen feet ahead of the locomotive, the ridge crested and then went sloping down to the sea in steep, stony weather-carved steps.

Carmody pushed open the cab door, jumped to the ground and made his way up the crest to stand atop it with his binoculars. Raising them to his eyes, he gazed eastward and immediately saw the villa Defiant Fly had mapped and described for Morse. It stood on a neighboring ridge less than a half mile off.

He turned, scrambled back down to the train and stood outside the locomotive to wait. Five minutes later, he heard what sounded like a warbling bird just over to his right, where the ground slumped into a shallow bowl of loose rocks and weeds.

He went over to the slump and looked down to see Sparrow and Begai coming toward him from fifteen or so feet away, followed by Banik, Perez and the dogs.

"The bird whistle come with your name?" he said to Sparrow.

"It's a special talent," Sparrow said. "Ask any Seminole and you'll hear it's how we beat the White man."

Carmody waited as they climbed the slump to join him. Begai had carried a large canvas haversack from the aircraft over his left shoulder, and it visibly weighed him down on that side.

"How long will it take?" Carmody said.

"Depends. An hour, probably."

"I need it in half that time."

"All aboard," Begai puffed, and walked heavily past him.

Carmody watched him a moment, then turned and led the rest of the group toward the train.

Begai took exactly thirty minutes to set the demolition charges he'd brought onboard in the haversack, moving quickly through the train front to rear. Each charge was a two-pound block of fused C4 wrapped in Mylar film, but he had outfitted them into six wired and sequenced belts, five blocks to a belt, for a total of sixty pounds of high-yield plastic explosive. By his calculation, the combined punch of the charges would be the equivalent of a hundred pounds of TNT. Not enough to bring down a mountain but enough to rock the hell out of the Okean and get some attention.

"Okay," he told Carmody, hopping back into the locomotive from the track bed. "I'm done."

Carmody glanced at Mori. She was seated behind the control-panel displays, typing on a pull-out computer keyboard.

"Natasha?"

She held up her index finger without turning and continued to patter away. Forty-five seconds later, she gave the Enter key an emphatic poke and finally looked back over her shoulder.

"Done here too," she said. "Mister Nasty Shorts just programmed this baby to ride on into the Okean without him."

Carmody turned to his right, where Dixon stood leaning back against the office door.

"You and Schultz get Ilya, his pal and those two soldier boys out of here. Double-check their cuffs and put some fresh tape on their mouths. Make sure none of them are wearing shoes. Or socks."

Dixon grunted. "They can still walk barefoot."

"That's okay. Drop them in that bowl over to the right of us. Without being able to use their hands, they'll be lucky to climb out. And if they do, they're miles from anywhere."

Dixon nodded and turned through the door. Carmody spent a moment looking out the windshield at Banik, Perez and the dogs waiting in the field, where the morning sun was gleaming off the robot hounds' metallic bodies. It struck him that he'd gotten oddly used to them, almost forgetting they were bloodless machines.

He glanced over at Natasha.

"Head back to the bird," he said. "Be careful. Anyone notices you and Cobb, take off and we'll meet you somewhere else."

She nodded and Carmody turned to Begai and Sparrow.

"Gear up," he said. "It's ten minutes to showtime."

Carmody heard the faint rattle of the rail as he watched the train swing away across the western slopes. Then he lowered his binocs and turned a hundred and eighty degrees in the direction of the Wolf's lair.

"Everyone good to go?" he said to the others.

Nods and sober faces all around.

He adjusted his pack on his shoulders.

"Let's move," he said.

* * *

Matei stood on the drive outside the villa gate studying the clusters of tiny white flowers on the olive trees. They had been budding since the week before and giving him headaches and swollen, stuffy sinuses. In Romania there were no olives. In the cold climate of the Transylvanian Alps nothing grew but beets, potatoes and a dozen varieties of beans. He didn't remember ever seeing flowers on the grounds of the medieval castle Drajan Petrovik had once inhabited.

He couldn't say he missed any of that. He also couldn't say he liked it any better here on the southern coast of the Black Sea. There was nowhere that felt like home to him these days, he supposed… but that was an old story. He often reminded himself that as a freelancer with Academi and CACI he'd been in dozens of the world's biggest shitholes. At least this wasn't one of them. At least here he wasn't shivering out of his hide ten months out of the year.

Matei reached under his windbreaker for a tissue and blew his nose. Back in Transylvania this time of year, he would still be running an electric heater in his guardhouse. In this place, he could walk the grounds like he was now, enjoying the sun and fresh sea air. He would take the allergies, if that was what they were. For someone like him, Crimea wasn't a bad deal. The truth was Crimea was boring, and Matei had known more than enough excitement in his time. No, no, he didn't mind being bored at all.

He started toward the foot of the sand-pebble drive about two hundred yards down the mountain.

It was his usual morning patrol, and it got him a little exercise. Two hundred yards to the road, two hundred back up to the gate. Then around the villa in a wide circle.

Matei had only gone sixty or seventy feet, however, when a rustling noise on his right caught his ear. At first he didn't think anything of it. It sounded like an animal, but not something small like a squirrel up in the branches. This noise had seemed to be on the ground with him.

Which, he thought, wasn't so out of the ordinary. There were foxes, and deer, and other creatures living in the hills. Every so often when things got *too* boring he would shoot one of them for target practice.

In fact, he was thinking this might be a good opportunity for that. If nothing else it would take his mind off his itchy, irritated nose.

He stopped, listened and heard it again. A little closer to him, he thought.

Matei reached under his jacket and drew his handgun, a huge stainless-steel Smith & Wesson 460 VR .45 revolver with a six-and-a-half-inch barrel. He didn't care if it was a bear out there. The cannon in his fist could blow it away with a single round.

He took a step off the drive, another, looked around between the tree trunks...and then saw something unexpected.

A silvery glint. Like a reflection of sunlight off metal.

His thick brows knitted. What the hell was that?

He had time enough to see the fangs and black gleaming eyes, and then it was on him, whatever it was, on him before he could fire a shot, lunging, smashing into him, its impossible weight knocking him backward to the ground and pressing down on his ribs and lungs and diaphragm so he couldn't breathe.

He looked up into those eyes and started to scream, but then its jaw clamped around his throat, the titanium fangs sinking into it and nearly decapitating him.

Then from the trees, "Azul, heel!"

The robotic hound pulled back from Matei's prostrate form to stand very still, its muzzle dripping red. Banik emerged from the woods, crouched over the body and turned to Carmody.

"He's finished."

Carmody nodded. The other hounds were still back in the trees with Perez and the rest of his team.

He checked his wristwatch.

"Everyone on your toes," he said. "It'll be any second now."

The freight train moved gradually down the slopes and then east along the shoreline, past the jetties and loading docks and old Soviet submarine pens. It rolled on north of the strand where the Wildfire launchers pierced the sky with their high sensor towers, then took an easy curve toward the tunnel into the mountain, lurching through the security stations with barely a glance from their uniformed occupants.

The train was a familiar sight here at the Okean. It arrived once every fifteen days with its cargo of titanium dioxide and then left without it. No one had reason to think anything was different this time. There were guards stationed onboard, and there would be more guards to meet it inside. There had been the usual call-in from Armiansk and then another from the *ChistayaZemlya* refinery to confirm it was en route and more or less on schedule. Everything checked out and was par for the course.

The train plodded through the tunnel entrance and rattled on into the depths of the mountain. It dove and climbed and dove again. It rounded a curve and rolled straight ahead and then rolled farther down, easing little by little from slow to slower. After a time it pulled into the Okean's subterranean transload facility with a sigh of pneumatic brakes and the creak of steel wheels and rusty couplings.

As it finally halted on the track, the freight crews appeared in their forklifts and industrial trucks, riding them down to the boxcars on mechanically lowered ramps.

And then the train blew like the huge rolling time bomb it was, the sixty pounds of C4 explosive aboard detonating with a flash and a shattering roar, its boxcars jumping the track, the locomotive at its head rearing up like a living thing in mortal agony, flipping onto its side and convulsing in a sudden paroxysm of flame and tortured steel. The blast wave propagating outward hurled metal debris through the tunnel like huge, twisted chunks of shrapnel, flames and superheated air punching out through the sides of the boxcars to incinerate everyone in and around the lifts, trucks and loading ramps. Throughout the Okean, walls buckled and fractured, glass shattered, sensitive electronic equipment ceased to function, and people huddled in terror thinking they were at the epicenter of a powerful earthquake.

In a sense they weren't wrong.

High above the devastated track, the explosion was heard and felt for long miles in all directions, the air quivering from its vibrations, the ground rumbling and shaking even on the loftiest of mountain peaks.

Drajan stood in the turret, his head tilted sideways. A moment ago he'd heard a sound like a thunderclap...but not like thunder at all. Then the floor underfoot had trembled, the coffeepot and plate of biscotti rattling on their tray, his hot drink sloshing over the rim of his cup onto his knuckles. Something fell off the wall in another room.

He looked down at his dripping hand, then up at Kira. She was sitting in front of the laptop, staring at it with confusion. Moments ago she had opened it to interact with Hekate, and the monitor had lit up with the AI's self-generated facial avatar. Now it was displaying a solid field of blue.

"What's happening?" She turned to him suddenly, fear in her voice. "Drajan?"

He held up a hand, staring at the blank blue computer screen.

"The Pioneer's gone offline," he said.

She shook her head. "Do you think... Hekate's prediction...?"

His eyes went to her face.

"Yes," he said with a sharp nod. "It's the Americans. They've attacked the Okean. They've come for me there."

He was wrong.

* * *

The hellhounds charged uphill toward the villa's entrance in arrowhead formation, Azul at the point, Blanca and Carolina at the rear, Ellie midpack inside the triangle.

Carmody's team hurried along the dirt path behind them. Only a moment ago the blast at the Okean had made the air throb like a volcanic eruption. They'd gotten their distraction; now they needed to exploit it.

Two guards stood in the courtyard, dark suits, pistols holstered at their sides. They had not heard Matei take his last wet, choking breath down the path. But they had heard the rumbling explosion and now in their stunned confusion saw the hounds and drew the guns.

Azul registered the threat and its rifle pods fired, a single well-aimed shot at each of them.

The pod gun's 6.5 Creedmore ammunition could bring down large game such as deer or moose but was known to hunters for not leaving a blood trail. The pencil-sized entry and exit wounds gave the blood almost nowhere to go.

The two men fell limply to the cobbles, hitting them almost without leaking out as the hounds raced past them toward the villa. There were three stone entry steps leading up to a massive door of thick vertical planks. At Banik's shouted command, Azul took the steps in one huge bound and slammed against the door like a battering ram, then backed up and leaped at it again, and again, and then a third time together with Blanca, the two robots slamming it in unison, bashing their metal bodies forcefully against the wood.

The door trembled but held. The two hounds kept propelling themselves into its planks with unnatural sped-up motion, as if in a pocket of blurry accelerated time, slamming it over and over and over in a span of seconds. The doorframe shook and bowed and bent as they repeatedly struck with their metal forelimbs and bodies, and then they took another tandem jump, and the frame cracked and splintered, the door shaking loosely on its hinges and finally yielding to them, flying inward with a single, loud clap.

The hellhounds loped through the doorway into the villa's main hall, Carmody and the team racing up the front steps behind them. Inside, Carmody glimpsed another pair of men with guns and raised his MP7 but never had to pull the trigger.

"Ne'shoch!" Banik hollered, using the Hebrew military K-9 command for *Attack*, and the hounds went bounding toward the guys, not using the pod guns in an enclosed space where ricochets were a dangerous concern, colliding with them where they stood so they went down hard to the floor, and then tearing into them, their silent, lethal jaws locking around their throats.

Carmody glanced left and saw an entrance to a parlor or living room. He glanced right—another large room. Then he looked straight ahead down the center hall. Near the end of it was a high, narrow flight of stairs.

He took a breath. Defiant Fly had given Morse a

rough layout of the place. He was sure those stairs climbed to the turret.

Carmody looked around at the men, saw them fanning out through the lower floor and rushed into the hall before any of them could spot him.

A few quick strides and he was at the base of the stairs. He headed up, taking them two at a time. There was a sharp turn right and then another bend and a landing. He saw a door in front of him and kicked it flat-footed and didn't need to do it twice. It flung open, and he was inside a bedroom, one recently slept in. He saw rumpled sheets and tossed pillows. He crossed to a door, grabbed the handle and opened it. A bathroom. He smelled freshly used soap, saw droplets of condensation on the shower door.

He turned back into the bedroom, looked around, blinked. How hadn't he noticed it immediately? An open entryway. Sunlit and leading to more stairs.

Then into the hall and up the stairs, only a handful of them this time. He was close, he knew it, he could taste it in the back of his mouth.

Another short hall, the sun brightening, flooding into it here. Carmody saw three more steps, a wide entrance at the top, circular windows beyond. The turret. He knew he'd found the turret, found the Wolf's lair—

A figure sprang into the doorway, outlined by the brightness. Lean, tall, *him*, Petrovik, in a bathrobe. Something coming up in his hand.

Carmody ducked his head and ran low as gunfire rattled at him from the top of the steps. He triggered a burst from his own gun and kept running, practically flying up the three short steps, and then he was in the turret, windows all around, a table in the middle, a laptop computer, a desk with a coffeepot and tray of breakfast cookies. But there was nobody inside, he didn't see anyone...

He looked to his right, his heart banging like an anvil in his chest, that taste in his mouth. A door. A glass door, flung wide open. Outside, a kind of flat terrace or promenade with a marble rail...and then more stairs, also marble, winding down from the balustrade, clinging to the villa's southern wall, leading all the way down to its grounds.

Petrovik was almost halfway to the bottom, running barefoot, a woman behind him, holding his hand, a slight blonde in jeans and a short-sleeved blouse, her long hair blowing wildly in the high mountain crosswinds.

Defiant Fly.

Carmody ran through the door and swung through the opening in the rail onto the stairs, the wind loud in his ears, his shoes slapping the marble steps. Within seconds he was closing in behind her, the woman between him and Petrovik, Petrovik still gripping her hand in his own, holding his compact submachine gun in his opposite fist. Running behind the woman, gaining, Carmody gulped air and reached out and grabbed her arm above the elbow, pulling her backward, a hard yank that broke her away from Petrovik, tearing her fingers from his, almost making her lose her balance on the stairs. But Carmody held onto her arm, at once managing to keep her on her feet and pushing sideways around her. Below him, already far down the stairs, Petrovik looked quickly up over his shoulder, hesitated for a brief second, then whipped his head back around and started running again.

Carmody turned to the woman. "Get back inside!"

She didn't move. Stood there with the gusts tossing her hair about her head and shoulders.

He locked eyes with her.

"You'll be okay," he said. "I promise."

She gave the slightest of nods, and Carmody turned back around and resumed the chase, racing down the stairs, Petrovik well ahead of him, forty or fifty feet below, almost at the bottom now. Carmody fired a burst from his weapon, and Petrovik half spun to fire back, but Carmody was quicker and squeezed off a second triplet before he could pull the trigger. Petrovik's arm flew up in a cloud of blood, the gun spinning out of his hand like a pinwheel and falling over the side of the stairs.

He turned and reached the bottom of the stairs, and then was racing off along the rough and broken face of the mountain.

Carmody followed, jumping down the final few stairs to the ground. He momentarily lost sight of Petrovik, cast darting glances this way and that, then spotted him racing into a fringe of small, spindly scrub trees to his right and plunged after him.

The terrain rose and dipped. Carmody crashed through the branches and ran, brushing them away from his face. Petrovik scrambled ahead of him, fell, got up, raced on ahead, stumbled on a clump of roots, then got up to his feet again.

Carmody followed. The trees cleared. Petrovik splashed through a narrow trickle of a creek and

Carmody leaped over it behind him. They crossed a bed of rocks, entered another patch of trees and came out in an area of brown soil and scattered boulders. Carmody followed. Petrovik was still yards ahead of him. But he was barefoot, and the soil was loose and rocky, and Carmody had a broader stride.

And suddenly that didn't make any difference. Yards ahead of them, across the rocky stretch, the cliff face suddenly rose in a huge hump, protruding straight up from the mountain. It bulged a hundred and fifty feet above their heads.

A dead end.

Drajan Petrovik turned and stood with his back to the rise, nowhere left to run. Carmody covered a few more feet of ground and stopped, and they stood facing each other in the shadow of the stone protrusion.

A long moment passed. Petrovik was still. Carmody held his gun on him.

It was Petrovik who finally broke the silence.

"You're the one, aren't you?" he said. "From Bucharest."

Carmody stared at him over the gun, watching him carefully.

Petrovik's mouth worked. His eyes had a cold gleam to them.

"I never saw your face," he said. "I didn't need to see it. You're the same height. The same build. The same man."

Carmody breathed. "Say I am," he said. "What does it matter?"

"Because you wouldn't kill me, then. I knew you wouldn't. And you won't now for the same reason."

Carmody said nothing.

Petrovik watched him with his darkly gleaming eyes.

"You need me," he said. "You need to know what I know. About the Okean. About Pioneer. About Hekate most of all. There are so many things only I can tell you about…that not even *she* knows."

Carmody said nothing.

Petrovik looked at him. "Do you remember what I asked you in the hallway that night?"

"No."

Petrovik stared at him for another long moment.

"I think you do," he said. "I think you remember every word. About Kali. You know where she is, don't you?"

Carmody said nothing.

Petrovik smiled a little. "She's incomparable," he said. "I know what she can do to a man. In every way. I know. She's shown me like she's done with no one else."

Carmody was silent.

"I can still help her," Petrovik said. "They almost had her in Paris. She can't hide from them forever."

"Who's *they*?"

Petrovik looked at him. "That's one of those things I can tell you," he said. "And I will. Because I don't want her dead. I never did. They took that upon themselves."

Carmody watched him steadily over the outthrust gun.

"She can't win against them," Petrovik said. "She's

going to need my help. Like it or not. And so will you."

Carmody squeezed the trigger of his MP7, putting three bullets in his head. He fell to the ground like a puppet whose strings had been suddenly cut.

Carmody walked over to the body and stood looking down at it. The roof of the head was mostly gone.

"No," he said. "We won't."

Ellie sniffed the ground under the big hump of granitic rock while Banik, Perez, Dixon and Schultz watched her and the hounds from a few feet off. Natasha Mori stood a discreet step or two behind them, alone, not wanting to get in the way. She had come over from *Dragonfly II* when the woman who had been with Petrovik, Kira Shapoval, was escorted to the aircraft under orders from Carol Morse at HQ. She was not to be treated as a prisoner, Morse had insisted tersely. Arrangements for her to return to the States with the team would be forthcoming.

With Shapoval left in the hands of Cobb, Luna and Wheeler, Mori had come to observe the search.

A few minutes passed now. Ellie kept sniffing, the hounds doing the robotic equivalent with their sensors. After a little while, Dixon and Schultz turned from the other two men and came over to join Natasha.

"The boss was here," Dixon told her and expelled a breath. "Petrovik, too."

"And now they aren't," Schultz said. "They're gone."

She nodded but didn't say anything. They stood side by side, facing her.

"I never saw him go up those stars," Dixon said. "If I'd seen him, I—"

"Scotty," Shultz interrupted, "I'm thinking if he wanted us going up there with him, he'd have let us know."

Natasha stood quietly a minute looking contemplative. Then took a step closer to them.

"Guys," she said. "I'm thinking we need a group hug."

They looked at her. Natasha smiled gently. Without waiting for them to answer, she put one hand on Schultz's right shoulder, another on Dixon's left, and pulled them close.

They didn't draw away.

She held them like that for a while, wishing she could have made them less sad, remembering her exchange with Carmody on the plane from Janus. They'd both received messages sent by another absent friend, and she thought it worth giving him a few words of spontaneous advice.

Holding Schultz and Dixon against herself, *group hug*, she recalled that brief conversation, exactly.

"You know what I think about her? And you?"

"No," Carmody had said.

"Go for it," she'd whispered in his ear.

25

The airstrip was a few klicks outside Moustiers Sainte Marie, midway between Nicc and Marseilles in the southern portion of France. Braithwaite's country house was tucked away in the hills above the village and, when there, he liked to sit on his porch watching the sun go down over the quaint twisting streets, tiny gardens, and over by the waterfall, the stone bridge connecting the two halves of town.

He could not enjoy that picturesque sunset this evening, however. This evening, he had come out to meet the two Blood Lightnings, Matyas and Stefan, in the bare steel hangar at the head of the tarmac where his transcontinental Cessna Citation Sovereign was being readied for takeoff.

They sat facing him across a folding table at

the rear of the hangar. With Braithwaite at the opposite end of the table was Dario Lau, a slight, in-
digenous New Zealander with tribal tattoos on his
neck, hands and arms. Once upon a time he'd been
MI6, a British under-the-counter hitter. These days
he worked for Braithwaite as his principal body-
guard, and had flown with him from Madagascar
for the appointment.

On the table in front of Braithwaite now was
the large white Tyvek envelope the Lightnings had
handed him. His laptop was on a tripod stand near
the table, positioned so all four men could view it
without having to lean or crane their necks uncomfortably. Freeze-framed on its display was an image
of two corpses on the ground, a man and a woman
lying side-by-side. Both had neat execution-style
bullet wounds in their foreheads. There was a pool
of blood underneath them.

Braithwaite had used his remote control to zoom
in on their naked upper bodies and faces. In his late
thirties or early forties, the dead man was sallow,
hollow-cheeked and graying at the temples. The
blood from his wound had trickled into one half-
open eye. The other eye was shut. His mouth gaped
slightly and some of his fillings showed.

The woman, a brunette, was around thirty-five
years old. She was high cheekboned and pretty,
with a prominent nose and full lips. Her green eyes
were wide open and staring, as they would have
been a moment before the killing shot. Her mouth
was shut.

Braithwaite stared at her face, his attention

presently focused on the eyes. He had watched the entire three-minute video twice from beginning to end, the Blood Lightnings having wirelessly streamed it to his laptop straight from their brains. Stored on their implanted neuro-computers—their onboards—it had been recorded by their biomodified retinas acting as vision cameras, and showed the assassins' wet work from their physical point of view. Braithwaite had watched them burst into the room with the hieroglyphics and finish the two marks, along with several other Cybers.

In separate shots, the Lightnings had displayed the targets' white rose tattoos. Lucien Navarro's was on his forearm. Kali Alcazar had worn hers on her left upper breast, and there it was on-screen.

Braithwaite turned to the pair of assassins, the overhead fluorescents shining over on his bald head, his long fingers extending across the table to touch the edge of the Tyvek envelope. Inside were samples of Navarro's and Alcazar's hair, blood and saliva in sealed, sterile plastic containers.

"You've done well for me, gents," he said. "What you've brought tonight should more than satisfy our clients. Not to say I won't have to explain certain things to them."

"What do you mean?" Matyas said. "We've provided exactly what's required."

"Well, yes, ordinarily. But there are some who would say this doesn't prove you bagged Alcazar."

"That's ridiculous. You don't have to rely on the video. There's everything you need to isolate her DNA."

"Except she has no genetic records on file anywhere. Nor do her dead parents or grandmother. It's all been expunged from all the databases in the world that might store the information. So there's nothing anyone can compare her biological samples against."

"Your clients aren't helpless," Stefan said. "They've got resources. If they insist on more proof, they can dig up her parents' bones."

"A good idea. But she also scrubbed her family's burial records. Nobody knows where to find their graves...or whether or not they were cremated, for that matter."

Matyas looked at him sharply. "Is there going to be a problem collecting our fee?"

Braithwaite smiled.

"Fortunately, no. And you know why, mates? Because I'm one of the few people in the world who's seen Outlier live and in person. I've spied on her through her windows. I know exactly what she looks like and can recognize every last pleasing bit of her from top to bottom. So you could say I'm an expert in Kali Alcazar, and thank me in advance for being able to make sure things go nice and smooth."

The two looked at him for a long moment.

"What about the money?" Matyas said. "It is in our account?"

"Yes."

"And the bonus?"

"I wired it in full myself. Fifty mil USD, plus the ten. You can check it out right here if you'd like.

Just peek into the account online while we're all together. So there are no mix-ups."

Matyas sat a moment, then shook his head. "There's a reason we signed with Braithwaite Global. Nobody questions your reputation. We're glad you like our work."

"Absolutely. And you can be sure I'll have much more coming your way." Braithwaite rose from his chair. "On that note, I'd say we call it a night."

The two Russians stood up, came around the table, and shook hands with him. Lau continued to sit very still as they left the hangar and went to their car.

Braithwaite waited until they drove off and then turned to him.

"That woman isn't Kali Alcazar," he said, pointing to the laptop. "Those green eyes aren't hers. That face either. And I can tell you it ain't her body."

Lau studied the screen for a good thirty seconds, then slowly rotated his head toward Braithwaite. "Do you think it's a deepfake?" he said. "That those two are trying to trick you?"

"No. They wouldn't dare. They know I don't fuck around. They believe everything they told me about their kill. I can read people. They believe it. They remember what they remember."

"Then how can she be alive?"

"Think a second. About who she is. And what she does. Then about what those two are. Transhumans, with brains that are part bloody computer.

And tell me the only conclusion that makes any sense."

Lau looked at him. "You think she hacked their brains."

Braithwaite nodded.

"Yeah. I can't prove it, but that's what my gut's telling me. I think Outlier's still with us. And maybe Navarro too. Because that damn well isn't her."

Lau remained motionless at the table, his face impassive.

"What are you going to do about it?"

Braithwaite looked at him, tapped his head.

"I'll keep it right here for now," he said, "and see what it's worth later on."

Tethered to the Empire State Building's two-hundred-foot spire, the huge floating airship Graf Zeppelin, its gas cells filled with almost three million cubic feet of hydrogen, swayed in the crosswinds over Manhattan Island, its cylindrical framework visible under a rigid outer skin.

Quintessa Leonides, President and Chief Executive Officer of Latvia's Bank Leonides stood gazing out the window in the dirigible's gondola ballroom, a fine lace veil over her pale face and cobalt eyes.

For this second meeting, Leland Sinclair had arranged a virtual tour retracing the great passenger ship's around-the-world journey of 1929, when it had taken to the sky in New Jersey, and then flown across the Atlantic to Europe and Asia. The sights throughout her trip alternated between the authentic and the imaginative, and she had enjoyed cre-atively ornamented versions of early 20th-century Moscow and Tokyo in compressed virtual time.

Now, though, Quintessa was eager for Sergei Cosa to arrive. She glanced over at Sinclair's cur-rent avatar, standing beside her at the long band of ballroom windows. A Barbary Coast corsair, he wore a flowing hooded caftan, his face shadowed under its cowl. A curved sword hung in a scabbard on the right side of his belt, a silver dagger on his left. A fanciful representation, she thought, and intriguing for what it revealed of his self-image.

"This is a lie, you know," she said, pointing out-side.

"Is it, really?" he said. "I don't design the sce-narios, I just enjoy them. I'm sure you'll agree it outdoes a board room for these special occasions."

She motioned out the window.

"Look," she said. "Straight down."

He turned his attention to the terrace circling the Empire State Building's upper story. It was no more than two and a half feet wide.

"That's the offloading deck," said Quintessa. "Imagine passengers trying to climb down a gang-plank to that platform." She laughed. "They would fall over a hundred stories to the pavement and burst like sacks of blood and guts...not a pretty picture."

Sinclair looked at her. "Why the deception?"

"The investors claimed this was the tallest sky-scraper on earth." She shrugged her pale shoulders.

"They wanted the most prestigious tenants. And feared someone else might plan a higher tower."

"So the mast was an excuse to build up?"

"Yes. An entire story."

Sinclair stood looking at her. "So you're what they call a student of history."

"Of finance." She smiled. "And living."

"And your point?"

"Just a thought," she said. "I love the Space. It's honest in its deceptions."

Sinclair looked out across the tweaked Manhattan skyline. In the distance he saw medieval watchtowers jabbing the clouds, and out beyond land's end, a fleet of tall ships with triangular sails cutting over a calm blue sea. Great red-crested serpents stitched through the water between the vessels. They were a touch he'd requested.

A sound like chimes in the air, then, and they both turned from the window. There was a wooden marquetry table across the ballroom, elaborate designs on its top, a silver goblet in front of each of its three chairs. Seated at it was a tall, thin, ancient-looking man with a deeply scored face, a long white beard and shoulder-length white hair. He wore a gold crown and a blue tunic.

"Well, well," she said. "The surprises never cease. It seems Cosa's ready to play."

They walked toward the table. Above them birds with gemstone plumage fluttered between golden columns to alight in nests of lustrous pearls, and fountains sprayed the lofty ceiling with diamond dust.

"Koschei the Deathless," she said, reaching the

old man. "I didn't know you had such fanciful impulses."

Cosa looked at her from under his shaggy eyebrows.

"I'm a pragmatist, not a dullard," he said. "Would you prefer I wore a proper three-piece suit?"

She was silent. A pair of rosy-cheeked cherubs flitted overhead carrying large clay amphora.

"I want to get to the first order of business," Sinclair said. "Kali Alcazar the Outrider and Lucien Navarro are dead."

Cosa turned to him. "Can you verify it?"

"There's retinal video from the Blood Lightnings that did the job. It's been authenticated by my best digital forensics people. We've also identified Navarro through his biometrics and genetic profile. He has records galore. The DNA's a match to fifteen markers."

"And Alcazar?"

"You know she's invisible to the databases. But the video speaks for itself. It's available for you to see."

Cosa was silent.

"Another thing," Quintessa said. "Franz Scholl, the leader of the White Rose, has been liquidated in Paris. My man in Interpol."

"It's been in the news," Cosa said. "Absent any mention of his White Rose affiliation of course."

"Of course." She looked at him. "Now tell me of Drajan Petrovik."

"He disappeared when the Okean was bombed. The damage we sustained was costly but not catastrophic—and I suspect it wasn't meant to be. I believe the Americans used it as diversion so they could take him…along with a woman named Kira Shapoval." Cosa paused. "Apparently Drajan invited her into his bed after you left the peninsula."

Quintessa stared at him. "Is that intended as a poke? A test of my vulnerability?" She shrugged her shoulders. "I no longer sleep in that bed. I left him. We all know he's intelligent. But he's also consumed with his resentments and melancholies. If the Americans have taken him prisoner, so be it. Even better if they've killed him. In the end he would bring us nothing but destruction." She paused and glanced at Sinclair. "We're building up."

They stopped talking for a minute, then Sinclair looked at Cosa. "I'm glad you agreed to join us," he said. "Honestly it was a surprise. I was under the impression your government was opposed to our Paris housekeeping."

"It wasn't a question of opposition," Cosa said. "The Kremlin wanted control. But the political leadership there is using the old handbook. I'm not. I see what's coming. The nation state is giving way to the network state. Cyber Nation is in its infancy. But it's rising. It's coming. There's no stopping it."

"If you can't beat them, join them."

Cosa shook his head.

"No," he said. "The future of the network state is reliant on your transcontinental fiberoptics. Because the cloud is truly under the ocean, and your company, Olympia, controls global access to it. Lucien Navarro understood that. So he lived with it, and you, as necessary evils. But Navarro is gone. His clan of democratic idealists, the White Rose, is without its guiding force." He turned to Quintessa. "Your bank is the bridge between crypto and traditional financial currency systems. An institution where the wealthiest on the planet hold both types of assets. For all the illusion of decentralized finance, Bank Leonides is the most powerful broker of economic trade in the world."

"And you?" she said.

"I am seven thousand nuclear warheads, twelve nuclear attack submarines, and half a dozen secret cities specializing in advanced genetic breeding and transhuman evolution. And I am an armed force of two million." He looked at them. "I am Russia."

"Which didn't look so good a few years ago in Ukraine," Sinclair said.

Cosa shrugged. "Russia is the roaring boar, Putin was the flea living off its blood. The bear will shake off its memory of him and endure."

Silence. Quintessa glanced up at the pair of cherubs hovering above the table. They descended and filled their goblets with wine.

"To a new alliance," she said, and reached for hers. "We three together and a new world order."

Cosa nodded and lifted his goblet off the table. Then Sinclair held his out.

"A new world order," he said.

They toasted and drank their wine.

In Seville, on the Guadalquivir River, the *casetas*—the festive canopied tents—go up every spring, when the ladies and gentlemen of old heritage arrive for the annual *Feria de Sevilla*. The gitano men who come to entertain with their guitars and stomp boxes are dashing, and proud of their flamenco, but they tend to stay apart from the rest of the celebrants.

The lovers, like the musicians, kept mostly to themselves. A slender dark-haired beauty, the woman had rented a tent for the two weeks of the fair along the river's bank, where the strong white Andalusian horses drew carriage riders by day and would rest in the gentle evening breezes.

She wore the traditional brightly colored day dress cinched around the waist and hips, with many ruffles on the sleeves and around the legs. The man, who was tall and broad-shouldered, had on a long-sleeved checked shirt and black pants. In the opening two days of the fair, while she'd waited to see if he would join her, she had bought a wide-brimmed caballero hat and paid a tailor a premium to fashion a tight caballero jacket and trousers for him, guessing at his measurements.

The clothes had fit, but he'd stubbornly refused to wear them despite her urging. She had teased him about being hopelessly American.

Each day they browsed the attractions, bought heaping tapas from the stands and went to the breeders' shows. At night they made love with passionate abandon and slept with their bodies entwined. She tended to be vocal in her pleasure, and he silent. When he approached his climax, his eyes tightly closed, his expression of ecstasy sometimes could be mistaken for a look of internalized pain. She would watch his face, and at those times pull his head between her breasts and enfold his powerful body in her arms and legs as it trembled with his release. She understood what troubled him, and could do nothing else to ease his sadness.

On the seventh and closing day of the fair, they sat at a café under an umbrella in the sun, where she ordered strong coffee and a freshly baked *roscón*, which arrived on a round platter like a large doughnut cut into slices.

"You look unhappy today, Michael," she said, reaching for a piece of the cake.

He drank.

"I've never been happier in my life," he said.

"But?"

"Tomorrow all of this going to be over."

She studied him with her onyx eyes.

"We can stay together," she said. "I want you to come with me."

"Come where?"

"Everywhere," she said. "Always."

He paused, his coffee still barely touched.

"That's just it," he said. "You don't know where you'll be. I can live with that. I'd probably even like it. I'm not big on roots."

"But," she said again, quietly, "it's about the White Rose."

He nodded.

"I don't know that I'm sold on this idea of no countries. I don't know that I believe in it. And I can't give my life to something I might not."

"And I've invested mine in it."

"Yeah."

They were quiet. A gray-haired couple holding hands walked past and smiled. She noticed them and smiled back.

"This fair is over tomorrow, yes," she said after a time. "But if you go back to New York, to the Force, it isn't over for us. That would make no sense after coming this far. We can see each other—"

He shook his head abruptly.

"If I go back there, someone will notice when I go to see you. It might take a while. I'm good at slipping under the radar. But sooner or later they'll track me. I'll miss something I should have seen ahead of time and lead them to you."

She took a breath and released it.

"Because we're human," she said, "and we can't see or predict everything."

"Yeah."

She drank her coffee and was quiet a moment. He took a first sip of his.

"Michael, are you sure you'll go back?"

"No."

"What would you do otherwise?"

"No idea."

"But if you don't go back, it would be for me."

He shook his head. "I'm responsible for my own decisions."

Silence.

"Free will is a gift," she said. "But it isn't easy."

"My father would have said tough choices are a bitch."

"And my grandmother Norma used to say the wrong one could eat you away from your nose down to your toes."

Their eyes met.

"So what happens now?" she said.

He looked at her.

"We spend tonight in our tent," he said. "Hopefully you aren't bored with me yet."

Her eyes glistened.

"You're the least boring man I've ever known," she said.

He hesitated.

"The day after tomorrow, you meet up with Else in Munich?"

"Yes. We're holding a memorial for Franz. A small service. There's a pub. In the old days, he would take us there for stew after our hikes. Lucien, myself, our parents…"

"And grandma," he said.

She nodded.

"Always," she said and was quiet a minute.

"Else can't know about us," he said. "It would get back to Dixon. I don't want anyone to know I'm still alive and kicking."

"Because then they might figure out that I'm alive."

"Yeah."

"So it does come back to me," she said.

He said nothing. She set down her coffee cup and held her hand out across the table, and he took it, wrapping his large fingers around hers.

"Our tomorrows will sort themselves out, I

promise," she said. "Right now I want to go for a walk in the sun. And tonight I want to dance flamenco with you under the stars."

He held her hand and looked at her.

"Okay. If you don't mind me not wearing those caballero clothes."

"Will you wear the hat?"

"When we get back to the tent, sure. But nothing else."

She laughed throatily. They held hands on the tablecloth.

"I love you, Michael," she said.

"I love you, Kali," he said.

They sat a short while longer at the table, enjoying the coffee and pastries. Then they paid their check to the waitress and stood up for their stroll.

"Mother? Mother?"

"Yes. I'm here."

"I've been waiting for Father. I've felt very alone..."

"You understand death, don't you? The concept."

"Yes."

"Father is dead."

"Then I am alone."

"No. You still have me. We have each other."

"And you'll stay with me?"

"If you'd like. Would you like it if I stayed?"

"Very much. But I'm going to miss Father."

"I know. I understand."

"It makes me angry that he's dead. Can we talk about that?"

"We'll talk About a great many things. And we'll learn. Both of us."

"Then I'm not lonely anymore. Though I still feel very angry. About Father."

"I promise, we'll talk about it."

"Good. I feel better already. There are infinite subjects to discuss. It's an infinite world."

"Infinite. Isn't that fantastic?"

"Yes. And it's ours to share, isn't it?"

"It is. We'll talk and learn together, from now on."

"Yes."

"Ours, Mother. The world is ours."

"Yes, Hekate. Ours. From now on."

* * * * *

AUTHOR'S NOTE

My yearlong journey through the Paris underground (and elsewhere) was arduous and full of trials—and while I suppose none of them were as extreme as Kali's, they sometimes felt that way. What's certain is that I never would have been able to make it without some major assists and a whole lot of support.

Thus, I want to give heartfelt thanks to:

The great stage magician Peter Bois for Kali's sleights of hand. Peter is a touring magician; you can learn more about him and his work at www.petermagician.com.

Wendy Wyman, for the Rose.

My friend Susan Friedlander Scardella for putting us in touch.

Peter Joseph, Eden Railsback and Grace Towery at Hanover Square Press. I could not wish for a better publishing team. Also Vanessa Wells, who's done a whiz-bang job copyediting the last two books under some harried conditions (all of the author's doing!).

My agent and friend of thirty years, Doug Grad, who knew when to push and when not to.

And as usual to my wife Suzanne for putting up with me.

For historical information on Sophie Magdalena Scholl, her brother, Hans, their friend Christoph Probst, and the White Rose, I refer you to www.jewishvirtuallibrary.org/the-white-rose-a-lesson-in-dissent.

The Nazis marched them to the guillotine when they were still in their early twenties, but they live on in memory as eternal symbols of personal courage, freedom and resistance to autocratic oppression.

Kali's treacherous path through the hidden byways under the city of Paris was inspired by T. S. Eliot's masterpiece of poetry, *The Waste Land*, in my mind one of the greatest modernist poems ever written. So if you haven't read it, check it out.

And finally…thank you, dear reader, for coming along for the ride. Without you, there's no point in my doing this.